KT-420-660

Kathryn Ross was born in Zambia, where her parents happened to live at that time. Educated in Ireland and England, she now lives in a village near Blackpool, Lancashire. Kathryn is a professional beauty therapist, but writing is her first love. As a child she wrote adventure stories, and at thirteen was editor of her school magazine. Happily, ten writing years later, DESIGNED WITH LOVE was accepted by Mills & Boon. A romantic Sagittarian, she loves travelling to exotic locations.

'I'm still weighing all the possibilities up—I assure you. Trophy wife versus convenient mistress?' Damon shrugged. 'Or should I just take custody of Mario and walk away...? The choices are endless.'

'You wouldn't get custody of Mario,' Abbie told him heatedly. 'And I wouldn't marry you if you were the last man left on the planet and lived in a gold-plated palace.' She angled her head up proudly.

Damon laughed at that. 'Oh, but we both know that you would.'

'You always did have an inflated opinion of yourself.'

'I know how Ms Abigail Newland's gold-digging mind works.'

'You know nothing about me. I would rather die than go along with the idea.'

THE ITALIAN'S UNWILLING WIFE

BY
KATHRYN ROSS

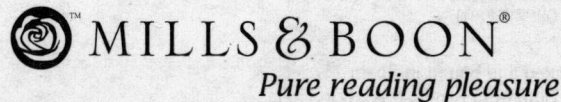

MILLS & BOON™
Pure reading pleasure

All the characters in this book have no existence outside the imagination of the author, and have no relation whatsoever to anyone bearing the same name or names. They are not even distantly inspired by any individual known or unknown to the author, and all the incidents are pure invention.

First published in Great Britain 2008
Harlequin Mills & Boon Limited,
Eton House, 18-24 Paradise Road, Richmond, Surrey TW9 1SR

© Kathryn Ross 2008

ISBN: 978 0 263 86455 7

Set in Times Roman 10¼ on 12 pt
01-0808-52801

Printed and bound in Spain
by Litografia Rosés, S.A., Barcelona

PROLOGUE

REVENGE was an ugly word. Damon Cyrenci preferred to think of his actions in more clinical terms. He had seen a business opportunity and had taken it.

The fact that he'd had his eye on the Newland Company for a while, and that this takeover gave him a greater sense of personal satisfaction than any other, was irrelevant. What was important was that John Newland's days of trampling his opponents into dust were almost at an end.

As his chauffeured limousine travelled along the Strip, Damon watched the sun setting in a pink glow over the Las Vegas skyline. This was the city where his father had lost everything. It was also the city where Damon had made the mistake of allowing a woman to get under his skin. It seemed fitting that it should be the place where he would put everything right, get back what he wanted.

They passed the MGM Grand, Caesar's Palace, New York New York and, as the pink of the sky turned to the darkness of night, the desert lit up with fiercely glittering light.

The limousine pulled up outside the impressive façade of the Newland building, and Damon allowed himself to savour the moment. His target was almost achieved. In a few moments he would meet John Newland face to face, and have him exactly where he wanted him.

For a second his thoughts drifted back to the last time they had met. How different that meeting had been.

Two and a half years ago it was John who had held the balance of power. He had faced Damon across a boardroom table and had calmly refused his request for a stay of execution on his father's business.

One week—that was all Damon had needed in order to release valuable assets that were in his name and save everything. But Newland had been coldly adamant. 'I am not a charity, Cyrenci; I'm in the business of making money. Your father must honour his commitments immediately and hand over the title deeds to all of his properties. However…' He'd paused for a moment's reflection. 'Your family home in Sicily is listed as one of the company's assets. I might allow you to keep that—on one condition.'

'And what's that?' Damon had asked coolly.

'You walk away from my daughter and never see her again.'

Damon could remember his incredulity and the hot fury in his stomach as he had looked across at the man. Somehow he had remained calm and impassive. 'I am not going to do that.'

And that was when John Newland had laughed at him. 'Abbie really fooled you, didn't she? Let me enlighten you, Cyrenci. My daughter has been brought up with a certain standard of living. She enjoys a luxurious lifestyle—a lifestyle you can't match now the family business has gone. I assure you, she won't be interested in you now.'

'That's a risk I'll take,' Damon had told him smoothly.

'Your choice.' John Newland had shrugged. 'But you lose all ways round. Abbie only dated you in the first place as a favour to me. I needed you out of my hair, and she was the perfect distraction. You think your weekend away together in Palm Springs was a wild impulse?'

John had asked the question scornfully and had shaken his head. 'It was planned—all set up by me. Abbie knew I needed some time to finish my business with your father, and she was happy to help me—but then, just as long as the money is flowing, Abbie will be there. Believe me, she won't hang around you now the game is over and your money is gone.'

The chauffeur opened up the passenger door for Damon, letting in the intense heat of the desert night, a heat almost as intense as the anger he had felt back then. It hadn't been hard to discover that for once John Newland was telling the truth. Abbie had known what her father had been up to, and had in fact assisted him.

Just like her father, she was nothing but a cold-blooded, money-grabbing trickster.

Snapping out of his reverie, Damon stepped out of the limousine.

It had been a lesson hard learnt. But Damon had picked himself up and with strong determination he had seen to it that their fortunes had been reversed.

Briskly he walked up the red-carpeted steps into the cool of the air-conditioned foyer. The entrance to the Newland hotel and casino was palatial; gold-leafed ceilings and stained-glass windows gave it the air of a cathedral, and only the rolling sound of nearby slot machines revealed the truth.

With just a cursory nod to the hotel staff, he headed for the lifts. He knew his way to the boardroom and he strode with confidence towards the door he wanted. This was the moment he had been waiting for.

John Newland was sitting alone at the far end of the long polished table. The lighting in the room was dimmed, his face in shadow. Behind him the picture windows gave a panoramic view of Vegas, glittering like a mirror-ball in the night. But Damon wasn't interested in the view.

'I believe you are expecting me.' He closed the door quietly behind him.

There was silence.

Damon advanced until he could see his nemesis clearly: grey-haired, thickset with glittering hooded eyes. The last time they had met, the man's features had been alight with triumphant disdain. Today, however, his expression was carefully schooled, but Damon could see the signs of strain in the pallor of his skin and the tight way he held his mouth.

It was hard to believe that this was Abigail's father. For a second a picture of her drifted into Damon's mind.

He remembered the day he had met her. She had been swimming here in the hotel pool, and he had watched as she'd pulled herself out. Water had dripped in silver beads over her toned skin. He remembered the sensational curves of her body in the scanty bikini, the perfection of her features, the wide blue eyes, the softness of her lips.

How he had wanted her.

The sudden memory of how badly he had wanted her made heat rise inside him.

'You're early, Cyrenci. The board isn't due to meet for another half an hour.'

John Newland's terse words focussed Damon's thoughts back to where they should be. He would have time to concentrate on Abbie later.

'We both know that the board meeting is just a formality, Newland.' Damon put his briefcase down on the table and opened it. 'You are on your way out.'

John Newland blanched. 'Look—Damon—we've had our differences in the past. But I hope we can put all that behind us and perhaps come to some mutually acceptable deal.' The brusque tone was gone now, replaced by pure desperation. 'I've spoken to a few members of the board—'

'It's over,' Damon said coolly. 'I think you would be advised to just accept that.'

'But you could help me if you wanted to.'

Was the man serious? Damon looked at him with incredulity. 'Why would I do that? To quote something you said to me years ago, John: I'm a businessman, not a charity.'

'I have a few bargaining chips left.' The man shrugged.

'Such as?' Damon was barely listening. He was taking papers out of his case and his eyes were running down a list of the company's assets—assets that now belonged to him. He knew John Newland held no aces, because they were all right here in his hand.

'Well—I recall you once wanted my daughter…'

The words trailed away as Damon fixed him with a cool, penetrating stare. He could hardly believe what he was hearing.

'In fact, you wanted her so badly you were willing to give up your family home for her,' John reminded him tentatively.

'We all make mistakes.' Damon's voice was icy.

'She had her twenty-first birthday last week, and I assure you she is even more beautiful now than she was,' John Newland continued swiftly. 'And her mother was Lady Annabel Redford, you know. Abbie has some influential connections in England that could open doors to a businessman like you.'

'I'm not interested.'

'I think you should be. And if I were to have a word with her…'

'Still at Daddy's bidding, is she?' Damon remarked scathingly.

'I have influence.'

'You have nothing.' Damon put his list of the company assets down on the table in front of the man.

'That's her, isn't it—the property that's marked a few lines underneath my old family home in Sicily?' Damon pointed to a line almost at the bottom of the page. 'Redford Stables, St Lucia.'

John Newland made no reply, just stared down at the list.

'Do you think Abbie will be happy to assist you, John, when she finds out her luxurious lifestyle and her home are lost as part of the company's assets?'

Still the man made no reply, but he started to drum his fingers with agitation against the table.

'No, I didn't think so. As we both know, Abbie's loyalty is to the highest bidder. So I don't believe you or indeed your daughter are in any position to negotiate,' Damon continued smoothly. 'But rest assured I will be looking over my new property with close attention to detail. In fact, I'm heading out to St Lucia tomorrow. Have you any message you would like me to pass on to your daughter?'

There was a moment's considered silence before John looked up. 'No, but I have one for your son—tell him his granddad says hello.'

John Newland watched the shock hit Damon Cyrenci and felt a gleam of satisfaction.

CHAPTER ONE

IT WAS hurricane season in St Lucia and the warnings had gone out. 'Michael' was a category three, but was gathering pace at sea and heading for shore. The weathermen were predicating a direct hit sometime within the next twenty-four hours.

But for now the sun was setting in a perfect blaze of glory over the lush rainforests, and not a breath of air rustled the tall palms that encircled the stables.

Abbie, however, was not taken in by the deceptive calm. She had experienced the full force of a hurricane the previous year; it had taken the roof off her house and almost decimated the stables. It had taken a long time to put everything right, and financially she was still reeling from the disaster. She couldn't afford another direct hit.

So she had spent the afternoon trying to prepare. She had nailed down everything she could, and long after most of her hired help had gone home for the day she was still moving heavy equipment into the storerooms.

'Abbie, your father has been on the phone for you again,' Jess called across to her as she came out of the house. 'He's left another message on the answer machine.'

'OK, thanks.' Abbie brushed her blonde hair distractedly back from her face. She had nothing to say to her father, and she wasn't interested in his messages, but she couldn't help but wonder why he had started ringing her again.

Putting the last of her work tools away, she headed up to the veranda. Mario was in Jess's arms, and as he saw his mother walk towards them his eyes lit with excitement and he held out his arms to her.

With a smile, Abbie reached to take her baby. He snuggled in against her and she kissed him, breathing in the clean scent of his skin. Mario was twenty-one months now, and adorable. He was the one thing in Abbie's life that made everything worthwhile.

'Do you want to get off now, Jess? You've got a date tonight, haven't you?' she asked as she cuddled the child.

'Yes. If you are sure you can manage, that would be a great help.'

'Absolutely. You go and have a good time.'

For a moment Abbie stood and watched as the young woman strolled towards her four-wheel drive. At eighteen, Jess was the youngest member of her staff, and also the hardest working. Not only was she a qualified child-minder and a superb horse-woman but she helped out a lot around the stables. Sometimes Abbie wondered how she would manage without her.

She waved to Jess as she reversed and pulled away down the long driveway.

Darkness was closing in now. The stables were on a lonely track leading down to a deserted cove. Her nearest neighbours were miles away, and very few cars passed this way. Usually Abbie didn't mind being on her own; she enjoyed the solitude. But for once as Jess's car disappeared she was acutely conscious of her isolation.

It was probably the approaching storm that was making her feel so on edge, she told herself as she went back into the house. Plus all these phone calls from her father.

As she stepped inside, her eyes were immediately drawn towards the phone, where a flashing light proclaimed there were now ten messages.

Whatever her father wanted, she wasn't interested. She would put Mario to bed and delete the calls later, she told herself as she headed for the stairs.

The child went down into his cot easily. Abbie set the musical mobile playing above his head and watched over him until he fell asleep. Then, leaving the night light on, she crept from the nursery to her bedroom across the corridor to shower and change.

Abbie had just put on her silk dressing-gown and was about to go back downstairs to make herself a drink when the phone in her room rang again, and the answer machine clicked on.

'*Abbie, where the hell are you?*' Her father's irate tones seemed to fill the house. '*Have you received any of my messages? This is important.*'

It was strange how just hearing his voice made her nervous. She supposed it was all those years of conditioning—of being afraid to ignore his commands.

Wrapping her dressing gown more closely around her body, she reminded herself fiercely that her father no longer had a hold over her—he couldn't hurt her any more.

'*Do you hear me, Abigail?*'

He probably wanted to summon her back to Vegas to host one of his parties. She shuddered at the thought. She'd escaped from that life over two years ago—she would have thought he'd got the message by now. His bullying blackmail tactics no longer worked. She wasn't going back.

She was on her way across her bedroom to switch off the machine when she heard him mention a name—a name that made her freeze and the world start to zone out as darkness threatened to engulf her. *Damon Cyrenci.*

For so long she had tried to block that name out of her mind, pretend he had never existed. And the only way she had been able to do that was by filling her every waking hour and making herself so bone-tired that personal thoughts were a luxury. But, even so, sometimes in the silence of the night he would come to her as she slept and she would see his darkly handsome face again. Would imagine his hands touching her, his lips crushing against hers, and she would wake with tears on her cheeks.

'I've lost everything, Abigail—everything—to Damon Cyrenci, and that includes the stables because they are part of the company's assets.'

Through the turmoil of her thoughts, Abbie tried to concentrate on what her father was saying. The stables were hers, weren't they?

'And he's on his way out there now to look over his property.'

The words hit her like a hurricane at force five. Damon was on his way here! Her heart raced—her body felt weak. Damon—the love of her life, the father of her child, the one man she had given herself to completely. The memories that went along with all those facts twisted inside her like a serpent intent on squeezing her very soul. And along with the memories there was a fierce longing—a longing that had never really gone away, a longing that she had just learnt to live with.

She sat down on the bed behind her; it was either sit down or fall down. *Damon was coming here.* It was all she could focus on.

What would he look like now, what would he say to her? Would he still be angry with her? What would he say when he discovered he had a child?

Had he forgiven her? The wrench of yearning that idea brought with it was immense.

As the phone connection died, she buried her head in her hands.

She remembered the day she had first met Damon. She remembered that the blistering heat of the midday sun had come nowhere near matching the heat he had stirred within her. She remembered shading her eyes to look up at him as she'd climbed out of the pool. He was tall—well over six-foot-four and he had been wearing a lightweight suit that had sat perfectly on his athletic build.

'You must be Abbie Newland?' he had said quietly, and the attractive accent had added fuel to a fire that had quietly and instantly started to blaze inside her.

He was ten years older than Abbie, Sicilian, with thick dark hair and searing, intense dark eyes, and to say he was good-looking would be an understatement of vast proportions. He was quite simply gorgeous.

'I'm Damon Cyrenci. Your father said I would find you here.'

The disappointment inside Abbie was almost as intense as her attraction for him. Because this was the man her father had ordered her to date. The command had infuriated her, but she wasn't at liberty to refuse; her plan had been to snub him, then just walk away. Then she could honestly tell her father that he hadn't invited her out. But, as soon as her eyes met with the handsome Sicilian, her body didn't want to comply with that idea at all.

'Do you want to join me for a drink?' He nodded over towards a bar that was cocooned in the tropical shade of the gardens.

'Maybe just for ten minutes,' she found herself saying. 'I haven't got much time.'

'Why, what else have you got to do?' The question had been asked with a glint of humour, and it had been apparent right from the outset that he had judged her as little more than a social butterfly.

She didn't really blame him. To the outside world, that was probably exactly how her life appeared, but the remark still smarted. She wanted to tell him that appearances could be deceptive, that she was in fact trapped within her gilded cage, forced to dance attendance on a father whose every whim was her command. But of course she didn't—he wouldn't have been interested and anyway, if word got back to her father that she had said anything, the consequences would have been dire.

So somehow she just forced herself to shrug. 'Let's see. I'm the rich, spoilt daughter of a millionaire—what else could I be doing this afternoon?' She slanted him a sardonic look. 'Apart from lying in the sun, shopping and visiting the beauty salon, you mean?'

He smiled, unapologetic. 'Must be a tough life.'

'It is. But someone has to do it.' Although she tried to sound flippant, something of her annoyance or distress must have shown in her eyes, because suddenly his tone softened.

'Shall we start again?' he asked, and held out his hand. 'I'm Damon Cyrenci, and I'm in town to negotiate the sale of a chain of restaurants owned by my father.'

She looked at the hand he held out, and she hesitated a moment before taking it. What exactly was her father up to? she had wondered. What harm would following his orders do?

Then her eyes met with Damon Cyrenci's and she told herself that, no matter what her father was up to, this man was more than capable of looking out for himself.

'Abigail Newland.' The net was cast as she placed her hand in his. She liked the touch of his skin against hers, liked the feeling in the pit of her stomach when he smiled.

She remembered having dinner with him that night. She remembered him kissing her, a searing, intensely passionate kiss that had made her long for so much more.

She had dated him for five short weeks, but with each meeting her feelings for him had intensified. Her hands curled into tight fists just thinking about the way he'd made her feel. But because of the situation she had always forced herself to pull back.

Damon hadn't been used to a woman pulling away from him, and somehow it had made him all the more determined to pursue her.

Yes, the net had been cast—but she had been the one caught in its fine weave, because somewhere along the way in those few short weeks she had fallen in love with Damon Cyrenci.

The phone rang again, interrupting Abbie's thoughts, and she listened as once more the answer machine cut in.

'Abbie, please pick up the phone.'

Abbie just sat numbly, listening. She hadn't spoken to her father since her mother's death just over two years ago. And, no matter what was at stake, she still couldn't speak to him now.

'This is about revenge, Abigail—and you are next on Cyrenci's list. He knows what you did—knows you were perfectly complicit in his father's destruction.' Her father's voice was abrasive. *'But luckily I'm still thinking for both of us. I told him about Mario. He was shocked and angry, I could see it in his face. But the child gives us a bargaining chip—it means he doesn't hold all of the aces.'*

Abbie felt sick inside. She hated her father—hated the sordid, horrible way he even thought.

The line went dead again. Abbie didn't know how long she just sat there after that. Her father stopped phoning, but the silence of the house seemed to swirl around her with his words.

Then she heard the distant sound of a car engine.

He's on his way out there now to look over his property...

Certainly, whoever was in that car was heading for this house—there was nowhere else out here.

CHAPTER TWO

THE shrill ring of the doorbell cut through her. And for a few moments she was immobilised.

Was Damon really outside her door? There had been moments when she had dreamed of this, dreamed that he'd come to her when he found out about his child, and that he would forgive her.

But they were just dreams. She was sensible enough to realise that the reality was encapsulated in her father's phone messages.

Damon wasn't going to forgive her—she'd known that at their last meeting, when he had angrily confronted her about what she had done, and she had tried desperately to explain her actions. He hadn't wanted to listen; all he'd been able to think about was the fact that she had assisted in his father's downfall. Even when she had falteringly tried to tell him that she was as much a victim as his father he had cut across her contemptuously.

'You must consider me really naïve if you think I'm going to fall for any more of your lies. I know what you are. I have evidence to support exactly what a lying, conniving, deceitful—'

'Damon, please!' She had broken across him tremulously.

'Please believe me, I never wanted any of this to happen. The time I spent with you was special to me, and I—'

'Give the acting a rest, Abbie.' The scorn in his voice had cut through her like a sword. 'At least the one good thing about this whole sorry mess is the fact that, as far as I was concerned, our time together was all about sex—I felt nothing for you, other than the pleasure of taking your body. Nothing at all.'

There had been a harsh coldness in his words and in his eyes that she had never seen before. It was as if a mask had been ripped away at that moment and she had seen the true Damon for the first time. It had shocked her to the core, and it had hurt. God help her, it still hurt!

But it also made her very sure that if it was Damon outside he wasn't here for any sentimental reasons, and he certainly wouldn't be interested in the fact that she'd had his child.

The shrill ring of the doorbell sliced through the night again, and Abbie tried to focus on what she should do. There were a few heartbeats of silence whilst whoever it was gave her a moment to come to the door. When she didn't, he put his finger on the bell again and held it there.

It had to be Damon! If there was one thing she should have remembered about him, it was his determination to get what he wanted.

He was going to wake Mario up! Her son was a deep sleeper, but he had his limits.

Suddenly anger surged to Abbie's rescue. She wasn't going to hide up here, feeling guilty about the past, because the truth was that it hadn't been her fault. She had been forced to do what she did. And nobody had a right to roll up here and make such a racket at this time of night.

Drawing her dressing gown closely around her slender figure, she marched downstairs, and, taking a deep breath, she threw open the door.

Damon Cyrenci was standing on her porch, leaning against the door jamb with his finger on the bell. Even though she had been expecting to see him it was still a shock.

He stepped back as the door opened, and silence reigned.

For a second his eyes swept over her with audacious scrutiny, taking in everything about her from her bare feet to the wild tumble of blonde curls around her shoulders.

And the strange thing was that for a moment Abbie was transported back to their first meeting, when he had looked at her in exactly the same way. She felt a tug of sexual attraction rising from somewhere very deep inside her. His appearance had hardly altered. The business suit he wore emphasised his fabulously well-honed physique, and the dark thickness of his hair was unchanged. Maybe there were a few silver strands at the temples, but they just made him appear all the more distinguished.

As her eyes held with the dark, searing intensity of his, her heart lurched crazily. He was the same drop-dead-gorgeous man who had stolen her heart away—except that man had only ever been an illusion, she reminded herself fiercely. Despite the heat of the passion they had once shared, she had never meant anything to him. Behind the façade the real Damon had just been a seducer—a predator who'd enjoyed the thrill of the chase and nothing more.

Falling in love with him had been a mistake, and she had learnt her lesson.

The memory helped her to pull herself together and focus her senses.

'Hello, Abigail. It's been a long time.'

His voice was coolly sardonic, and yet the attractive accent still managed to lash against the fragility of her defences.

'What are you doing here, Damon?' Somehow she managed to sound calm and controlled.

'Is that all you can say after all this time?' Again there was the same mocking tone to his question. 'How about "nice to see you, Damon—why don't you come in?"'

The strange thing was that one part of her—the wild, illogical part—wanted to say those words, but his manner forbade it. Something in the cool tone and the glint of his eye told her very clearly that although he was here on her doorstep nothing had changed from their last meeting, and his opinion of her was as low as you could get.

'I haven't got time for games, Damon,' she grated unevenly.

'Really? Strange how you had plenty of time for games in the past.'

Her father's words reverberated through her consciousness. *This is about revenge, Abigail—and you are next on Cyrenci's list.* She swallowed hard and slanted her chin up. 'Obviously this isn't an impromptu social call, so just say whatever it is you've come to say, Damon, and then go. You'll forgive me if I don't invite you in.'

'No—I don't think I will forgive you, Abbie.'

Although he said the words matter-of-factly, there was an undercurrent that struck her and hurt—and that in turn made her angry. Why should he still have the power to hurt her like that? She tightened her hold on the door. 'Well, you are not coming in.'

He shook his head. 'I really don't think you are being very friendly, and I'm sure given the circumstances you can do better than that—in fact, your father assured me that you could.'

What had her father been saying to him? 'I don't know what's been going on between you and my father. I believe you now control the Newland empire—well…' she shrugged '…I don't care. It has nothing to do with me.'

'That's where you are wrong, Abbie. This has everything to do with you.'

The chill certainty in his voice flayed her.

'I just want you to go now.' To Abbie's distress, her voice faltered slightly.

'I'm not going anywhere.'

'Well, you are certainly not coming inside my house.' She started to try and close the door but she didn't move quickly enough, and he put his foot in the way, effectively stopping her.

'Let me spell things out for you a little more clearly.' His voice was suddenly very serious. 'We have unfinished business, and I'm coming in whether you like it or not.'

'Damon, it's late and you're scaring me.'

'Good.' He sounded cold and unyielding.

'I'll have to ring the police if you don't go now,' she threatened shakily.

'By all means, you do that.' For a second his eyes narrowed. 'At least that way we can speed things up.'

'Speed what things up?'

'The legal side of things.' He watched impassively as the colour drained from her face. 'As you have so rightly pointed out, I'm in control of the Newland assets now. And according to company records no rent has been paid on this place for—oh, quite some time.'

'That's because the place belongs to me!' she hissed furiously.

Damon shook his head. 'No, it belongs to me,' he corrected her quietly. 'And I'm here to take stock of my belongings.'

'Well, then, you'd better contact me through my solicitor.'

Damon smiled at that. 'Oh, don't worry, I will be doing that. Because I also want access to my son.'

The words dropped into the silence like a bombshell, and Abbie's limbs suddenly felt as if they didn't belong to her.

'So are we going to do things the easy way or the hard way?' he enquired silkily. 'It's up to you.'

She couldn't answer him. Her hands dropped from the door, and as she momentarily lost her hold on the situation he took his opportunity and walked past her into the house.

His eyes swept over the lounge area, taking in the brown leather sofas, the polished wood floors and the huge stone fireplace. The place was very stylish, but it wasn't what he had been expecting. The furniture, when you looked closely, was old, and everything had a slight air of faded opulence. But Damon wasn't interested in décor; he was searching for telltale signs of something that interested him far more. He found what he was looking for as his eyes lighted on a box of toys by the far end of the sofa, and a discarded teddy bear on a chair. At the sight of those toys his insides knotted with a fierce anger.

'So, where is he?'

As he rounded towards her again, Abbie sensed a seething fury that made her truly afraid. She could hardly think straight for a moment, never mind answer him.

'Where is my son, Abbie? You may as well tell me now, because I will find him even if I have to go through every room in this house—or every house on this island.'

The determination in those words stunned her, but they also brought an inner answering strength welling up inside her. 'You keep away from him, Damon. He is not a belonging listed under the company assets. He is a little person in his own right, and I won't have you marching in here upsetting him.'

'And what about his right to have a father—or doesn't that count in your twisted logic?'

The question smote Abbie's heart. It was something she had asked herself time and time again—something that had kept her awake long into the lonely nights when she had discovered she was pregnant. Yes, she wanted Mario to have a father—a loving father who would put his needs first. But

Damon had left before she'd realised she was pregnant, and she hadn't known where he had gone. She'd tried to track him down, but to no avail. She had consoled herself with the fact that he wouldn't have been interested in his child anyway. Damon didn't go in for commitment, he led a playboy lifestyle. He'd told her that when they'd first met.

But the strange thing was that when he'd held her in his arms she had imagined that his feelings for her were different, that what they had shared had meant something. But of course she had been fooling herself. That had been quite clear when he'd walked away from her.

The memory hurt so much that she wanted to tell Damon that the little boy upstairs was not his, and that he had a father in his life—a wonderful, loving father, a man who also loved her. She opened her mouth but the words refused to come.

When it came right down to it, she couldn't lie about something as important as that.

'Of course having a father counts,' she said shakily instead.

'Right—which, of course, is why you came to me and told me you were pregnant?' Damon's tone was scathing.

'And if I had would you have wanted to stay around and play happy families? I don't think so. We had had a few weeks together of wild sex—it meant nothing.' Even as she said the words, the memories that flared inside her made her hot, made her voice tremble with suppressed feeling. 'You said as much yourself—you said…' She shook her head and pulled herself together before the tears could gather in her voice. 'Anyway, all that is in the past and irrelevant. The truth is that I didn't find out I was pregnant until after you'd gone. I didn't know how to get in touch with you. You hadn't left your address or contact numbers. I didn't know where you were.'

'You are good at making excuses.' Damon shook his head. 'No, Abbie, you didn't tell me because your father held the purse strings and you thought I had nothing. That was a more important consideration for you at the time.'

'That's not true!'

'Like hell it's not. You forget, Abbie, that I know you exactly for what you are.' Damon's eyes raked contemptuously over her, but as they did so he couldn't help noticing the sensational curves of her figure beneath the silk of the dressing gown. How come her beauty could still blow his mind? he wondered hazily. How come when he looked at her now after all this time he could still remember exactly how she had felt when he touched her—how she had tasted, how she had moved beneath him?

Back then she had been firm and pert and he had wanted her like crazy—but he could excuse that because he hadn't known the truth about her then.

How come he could feel the same stirrings now?

'We're wasting time,' he grated, furious with himself for being sidetracked even momentarily like this. 'And I've already wasted enough of that.'

To Abbie's horror Damon started to head towards the stairs with a look of determination.

'You can't go up there.' She hurried to stand in his path, tried to grab hold of his arm, but he brushed her away as if she were an annoying fly and swept past her.

'Damon, you have no right!' Her voice caught on a sob as she raced after him, but he didn't break his stride.

'Actually, as the child's father, I think you will find I have lots of rights.'

The words brought a strange kind of helplessness washing over Abbie. It was the same feeling she used to get when dealing with her father. It was the knowledge that someone more powerful than you could dictate your life, and there wasn't anything you could do about it, because if you didn't comply the consequences would be more than you could bear.

She watched as he pushed doors open along the landing into deserted bedrooms.

'Stop it!' The anguished whisper made him halt in his tracks to look back at her.

'Don't bother to try and turn on the false tears, Abbie, because it's not going to work,' he told her acerbically. 'I don't care how you feel—in fact I couldn't give that—' he clicked his fingers softly '—for your emotions.'

'I know,' she said softly. 'I've always known that.'

Something about the way she said those words caught at him, and for a brief second he felt a tug of some long-forgotten emotion as he looked into the blue depths of her eyes. He remembered the first night that they had made love. He remembered the vulnerable way she had looked up at him as she'd allowed him to unfasten the buttons of her dress, almost as if she'd been afraid to trust her emotions to him.

The memory infuriated him. Abbie Newland was an actress—there had been nothing remotely vulnerable about her. She had been playing the part her father had set for her, and she had done it very well, and had enjoyed a little fun along the way.

His dark eyes hardened at the memory. 'Well, at least we understand each other.'

'Yes, at least there's that,' she whispered numbly. 'But you should also understand that my child is more important to me than anything and if you upset him in any way I will make you pay for it.'

She tried to draw herself up as she said the words. It was probably a bit like facing down a lion without any real weapons, but she wanted him to know that she would fight to the death if necessary for her child.

'Just because I don't care about your feelings doesn't mean I don't care about him.'

The answer should have reassured her slightly, but it just stung at raw nerves. Still she held his gaze with determination. 'He's in the room at the far end of the corridor,' she said quietly. 'Let me go into the room first, just in case he's awake. You are a stranger to him. I don't want you scaring him.'

Damon considered her words for a second, and then stepped back to allow her to lead the way.

Her whole body felt as if it were shivering with reaction as she walked past him. She guessed she was in shock.

Why did Damon want to see his son? She couldn't believe it was out of any paternal interest. Those sentiments didn't fit with the man she knew him to be. Maybe this was just curiosity. Maybe he would take one look at his child, make a token pretence of being interested, before getting back into his car to get on with the real things in life that mattered to him, such as revenge and money and power... And, of course, womanizing.

Yes, that was probably what would happen, she told herself as she opened the door to Mario's room.

She was relieved to see that the child was still sleeping. He was lying on his back, his face turned sideways against the pillow. He looked the perfect picture of peaceful innocence, his cherub mouth slightly parted, his long dark lashes resting against the satin-smooth skin.

She glanced back at Damon. 'You can come in, but only for five minutes.'

'I think your days of being in charge of this situation are over, Abbie,' he said quietly as he stepped past her.

The words hit Abbie like a punch to the solar plexus. But the feeling was nothing compared to the reaction she felt, witnessing the powerful intensity on Damon's features as he looked down at his sleeping child.

She felt her heart racing against her chest as the realization hit her that this was about far more than just idle curiosity, and to try and dismiss what was happening in such a way would be to vastly underestimate the situation.

For a long moment Damon just looked at his son. Then abruptly he turned and left the room.

For a second Abbie couldn't move. Her mind was reeling with confusion—she couldn't get a handle on this situation at all. What were Damon's intentions? Why was he really here? Hastily Abbie followed him back out onto the landing.

He was already at the other end of the corridor. 'So, now you've seen him,' she said breathlessly. 'Where do we go from here?'

He made no reply; he didn't even look around at her, just headed down the stairs. The front door was still lying wide open, and he marched through it without closing it behind him.

'Damon, where do we go from here?' she asked again, a note of desperation in her voice. She needed to make some sense of tonight, needed to understand what Damon was thinking—and she couldn't let him walk away without giving her some clue as to what was to happen next.

'Damon?' She followed him downstairs and out onto the porch. 'Damon, *please*!'

His footsteps slowed and then he looked around. 'That's better.' There was a gleam in his eyes as he looked over at her. 'If you keep that tone in your voice, we just might get somewhere.'

The cold churning in the pit of her stomach intensified.

'I agree that we need to talk rationally about this situation.'

He made no reply, and she thought he was going to climb into his car and drive away, but then to her surprise he went to the back of the vehicle and took out a small bag.

With the flick of a switch the car was locked again, and then he was heading back towards her with resolute strides.

Although there was a part of her that was glad he wasn't just going to drive away, leaving her wondering what was going to happen next, she didn't like the look of this latest development at all. Her heart thumped nervously against her ribs. 'Where do you think you are going with that bag?'

'I'm bringing it inside my house,' he said curtly. 'And then I'm going to have a drink and get into bed, because it has been a very long day and I'm tired.'

'You can't stay here!'

'Why not?'

'Because...I don't want you here.'

He stepped past her and into the house. 'Tough.'

The door slammed closed behind him.

CHAPTER THREE

FOR one horrible moment she thought he was going to turn the key in the lock, leaving her stranded outside in the dark in her dressing gown. But to her relief the door opened easily as she turned the handle.

With a mixture of trepidation and fury, she glanced around. His bag was at the base of the stairs and she could hear him opening and closing cupboard doors in the kitchen.

She followed the sounds and watched from the doorway as he found a bottle of vodka and poured himself a drink. 'What are you playing at?'

'I think I just told you.' He lifted the glass in a mocking salute.

With difficulty she reined in her temper. This situation was not going to be resolved by losing her cool.

'Damon, you can't stay here. It's not appropriate.'

He laughed at that. 'As if you'd know anything about appropriate behaviour! I have to say, all those years mixing with the aristocracy at those English boarding schools weren't wasted, were they? You've certainly learnt the art of pretending to be genteel.'

With difficulty she ignored the insult. 'This isn't solving anything. Why don't you go and check into a hotel for tonight and then come back tomorrow? We can talk properly when we have both calmed down and are thinking rationally.'

'I am calm.' He took a sip of his drink and regarded her levelly over the rim of the crystal glass. 'And I'm thinking very rationally. It's one in the morning, there's a storm coming in, and I have no intention of going to a hotel now—especially as I own a perfectly good house here.'

'Damon this is ridiculous!' Her voice rose in panic. 'You are not being at all reasonable.'

One dark eyebrow rose. 'Really? I think given the circumstances I'm being extremely reasonable. Let's look at the facts, shall we? You don't actually own this property. In fact, you are heavily in debt and behind with rent—'

'I am no such thing!'

'Plus you've hidden my child away from me, depriving me of precious time with him,' Damon continued as if she hadn't spoken. 'I don't think any court is going to look too kindly on you at all. In fact, I think you will be the one who is judged unreasonable.'

'You're twisting the facts!' She pushed a distraught hand through her blonde hair. 'I didn't know I was pregnant until after you'd gone. I didn't hide anything. And will you stop pretending that you give a damn about having a child? We both know that you would still have walked away from him even if I'd told you I was pregnant.'

'Do we?' Damon's voice grated with sarcasm. 'You don't know the first thing about what I would have done, because you don't really know the first thing about me.'

'I know that you are a playboy who likes to roam the pleasure fields.'

'Certainly.' He inclined his head. 'And I never planned on having children of my own. But you've changed that.'

Damon looked at her pointedly. 'Enlighten me, Abbie.

What were you planning on telling my son when he gets older? That his father is dead? Or that his father didn't want to know him?'

Abbie hesitated. 'I wouldn't have lied to him. I'd have handled it.'

'Believe me, no matter how you handled it, it still wouldn't have been right.' Damon's voice was heavy. He remembered all too well what it was like growing up without a parent. His mother had walked out of the family home when he was eight. It was so easy to screw up a child's life. Maybe that was why he had avoided settling down and having children. The responsibility was awesome, and he believed implacably that a child deserved two parents and a stable home.

'You had no right to keep Mario a secret from me.' Damon's eyes burnt into hers. 'Any court will tell you that.'

'He wasn't a secret. And will you stop talking about courts and judgements!'

He shrugged and took another sip of his drink. 'Courts and judgements are very much the reality; you better get used to it.'

'Why are you being like this?' The question sprang from her lips with anguish.

'Like what?'

'So…brutal…as if you want to punish me.'

He looked at her then, and gave a short, mirthless laugh. 'Why do you think?'

The sardonic question tore at her. 'My father was right— this is all about revenge, isn't it?' She made herself say the words, her voice trembling with emotion.

He took another sip of his drink, and then threw the remaining contents of the glass down the sink.

'You're angry about what my father did, and I understand that.' Abbie tried very hard to remain calm. 'And I'm sorry for my part in it. But as I tried to explain long ago, it wasn't my fault I—'

'Of course not. But then shallow, spoilt socialites like you don't believe in taking responsibility for your actions, do you? You think you can do what you want, and sorry is just a word.' His voice grated with sarcasm. 'But let me assure you that angry is a bit of an understatement for how I'm feeling right now.'

Abbie glared at him furiously. 'I am none of the things you have accused me of being.'

'And Father Christmas really does slide down chimneys on Christmas Eve.'

The scorn in his voice made Abbie's temper soar. But, as much as she would have loved him to know the truth about the past, she knew she could never tell him about her mother now. She had tried to explain her actions to him at their last meeting. She had braved the contempt in his eyes, and had haltingly started to open up to him, only to have him laugh scornfully in her face and cut her off. She couldn't go through that again. The pain of trying to tell him something so raw, so deeply personal, was beyond endurance. And why should she put herself through that when it was clear his opinion of her hadn't changed? He thought she was a liar, and he wouldn't listen to any explanation—wouldn't believe her, anyway. It all hurt far too much.

Some things were best left in the past, she told herself firmly. What mattered now was her child's welfare.

That fact made her swallow her fury and keep her cool. 'So you want to punish me,' she forced herself to continue. 'I can handle that. But going to a court to get access to a child you don't want—that isn't going to make this right. Please don't take this out on Mario.'

'How do you know I don't want him? You're making sweeping assumptions.' Damon's voice was cool. 'What did you think was going to happen when your father told me I had a child? Did you think I'd just throw money at you and disappear? If that's what you want, then you are dreaming. Because, believe it or not, I'm thinking about what is best for my son now. Something you seem incapable of.'

'I have always put my son first,' Abbie told him fiercely. 'And I don't want anything from you.'

He fixed her with a look that told her in no uncertain terms that he didn't believe her.

She swept an unsteady hand through her hair. Obviously he was never going to believe that she was anything other than a scheming witch. 'So what are you going to do?' she asked quietly. 'What do you consider *best* for Mario?'

Damon didn't answer her immediately. He appeared to be thinking about his options. Abbie could feel her nerves twisting and stretching. Was he deliberately trying to torment her? Was this part of his revenge? Maybe she should be flinging herself on his mercy instead of being confrontational.

But on the other hand maybe that was what he wanted. Her father used to enjoy controlling her through fear. When she'd tried to rebel, he'd reminded her of what he could do, and she would be yanked quickly back into line.

The memory made her angle her chin up defiantly to meet Damon's cool gaze. She had sworn that no one would ever have that power over her again. 'If you go for custody, I'll fight you every step of the way.'

'That's your prerogative.' He shook his head. 'I admire your spirit—but of course I will break it.'

He watched the bright glitter of fury in her eyes. She was so very beautiful—more so than she had been at eighteen; her father had been right about that. The thought stole, unwelcome, into his mind and he found his gaze drifting down once more over her body. He could see the firm curves of her breasts through the thin silk of the gown, and because the bright lights of the lounge were behind her he could also see the long, shapely outline of her legs.

She had always been attractive, but she had matured into a stunningly desirable package. Pity about her cold, mercenary heart, he thought dryly.

Abbie noticed the way he looked at her—noticed, and bizarrely felt her body throb, as if his eyes were actually touching her. She tried to ignore the feeling, tried to pretend it wasn't happening. How could she feel like this when her mind was racing with fear—when she hated him? 'Maybe you just have rage issues that need to be readdressed, Damon,' she said evenly.

He laughed. 'Maybe you are right.' He put his glass down on the draining board with a thud.

'So what are you going to do?'

'Right now, I'm going to bed,' he said calmly.

'You can't!'

'Why not?'

'Because you can't make statements like that and just leave things! I need to know what your intentions are regarding Mario. You are not really thinking of fighting me for custody, are you?'

Damon stared at her for a moment. When John Newland had told him he was a father, he had been shocked—then he had been furious. All kinds of emotions had been racing through him ever since. Some of the feelings had come as a complete surprise to him—such as the feeling of protectiveness when he had looked down at his sleeping child.

Yes, he'd decided a long time ago that he wasn't going to settle down and have children. But the fact was he had a child, and abandoning him wasn't an option. He couldn't walk away from that responsibility; he strongly believed in doing the right thing.

But what *was* the right thing in this situation? His eyes flicked over towards Abbie, and for a second he found himself thinking about her father's words to him in the boardroom.

Abbie could be of use to him.

The words sizzled provocatively through his consciousness. Abruptly he tried to dismiss them. 'I'll sleep on the problem, and we'll discuss terms in the morning,' he grated tersely.

He was so arrogant! So infuriating! She watched as he walked past her towards the lounge.

'I don't want to discuss terms in the morning. I want to discuss terms now! And it may have escaped your notice but there are no spare beds in the house. All the rooms you looked into tonight are empty. The only other bed in the house is mine.'

He turned slowly and looked at her. 'Is that an invitation?'

He watched the flare of heat under the creaminess of her skin with detachment.

'You know it's not.'

'Do I?' He shrugged. 'Nothing you would stoop to would surprise me. In fact, when I faced your father in the boardroom at Newland he made me a very bizarre offer.'

'What kind of an offer?'

'The deal was that I help him retain his place on the board, and in return I get you.'

'What do you mean, you *get* me?' Her voice was stiff.

'Just what I said. In return for my help getting him back on the board of directors, he said he could arrange for you to… Well, accommodate me in whatever way I saw fit, really. I'm not sure if he was selling you as a trophy wife who would have very useful business connections, or the convenient mistress there to entertain me in bed, plus play hostess when required—

that kind of thing. Of course, the second option caught my interest more at first. As you know, I'm not the settling-down type. But then, I didn't know I had a child at that point.'

He watched the colour flooding back into her cheeks. 'Don't worry, I turned him down. My motto has always been to cut out the middleman. Dealing direct is a much more satisfactory solution, don't you think?'

'What I think is that you are just as vile as my father.' Her voice trembled alarmingly. Just when she thought her father couldn't get any lower in her estimation, he sank to new depths. She felt degraded and humiliated by him—soiled by association.

'Dear me, have you had a fall-out with darling Daddy?' Damon walked back towards her and reached out to trail a finger down over the smoothness of her skin. 'What's the matter, are you annoyed because he can't bankroll you anymore?'

She flinched at the touch of his hand. She didn't know what hurt more, her father's disgusting business proposition or Damon's glib acceptance that she would be in any way amenable towards it!

His eyes held with her glittering gaze. 'Never mind. Although I've cut your father out of the equation, I'm still weighing all the possibilities up, I assure you. Trophy wife versus convenient mistress…' He shrugged. 'Or should I just take custody of Mario and walk away… The choices are endless.'

'You wouldn't get custody of Mario,' Abbie told him heatedly. 'And I wouldn't marry you if you were…if you were the last man left on the planet and lived in a gold-plated palace.' She angled her head up proudly.

Damon laughed at that. 'Oh, but we both know that you would.'

'You always did have an inflated opinion of yourself.'

'I just know how Ms Abigail Newland's gold-digging mind works.'

'You know nothing about me. I would rather die than go along with the idea.'

Damon smiled 'You didn't pass away with righteous indignation when you got involved with your father's deals last time.'

He watched her lips part noiselessly, watched the shadows flicker across the beauty of her eyes. 'That was different.'

Damon shook his head. She was a good actress, he'd give her that. 'You go where the money is—your father told me that about you over two years ago.'

He watched as her hands clenched and unclenched at her sides. She had such slender hands. Everything about her was so feminine; even her rage was simmering, contained—lady-like. Although, he remembered that in bed she hadn't been quite so restrained—not once he'd taught her what he liked and how he liked it.

He wished he could stop thinking about that. But the fact was he couldn't.

From the moment she had opened the front door to him tonight, he'd known that sexually he still wanted her.

He wanted her now. The strength of that need totally infuriated him. How could he feel like this when he knew her for what she was—disliked her, even?

He hated that. But it was a fact, and no matter how he kept telling himself to ignore it he couldn't. So what the hell was he going to do about it?

His eyes moved up over her body slowly, appraisingly. He had no doubt in his mind that she had known about her father's offer to him and had been hoping to play it for all it was worth.

Maybe the best thing to do here was to take control and play her at her own game. The more he thought about that idea, the more he liked it.

'So…' His tone was measured, his mind ticking over his options. 'You want to talk terms? Let's talk terms.'

The way he was looking at her was anything but clinical, yet the tone of his voice was detached, objective. What the hell was running through his mind now? Abbie wondered nervously. She moved her hands to draw her gown more tightly around her body, unaware that the instinctively protective gesture only showed her figure to clearer advantage.

She wanted to tell him to get out, that she wouldn't talk to him after the things he had said to her—the things he had insinuated. But she forced herself to calm down and think about what was important. And that was Mario. 'My terms are that my child stays where he belongs, and that's with me. Let's face it, Damon, you are a businessman who jets off around the world at a moment's notice. You sit in meetings that run on until the small hours. That doesn't fit with looking after a twenty-one-month-old baby. He's a full-time commitment.'

'Yes, he is. And that's the one reason I'm prepared to offer you a good deal.'

'What kind of a good deal?' The words were out before she could consider them, and she instantly regretted them as she saw the way his lips curved in a cool smile.

'You see? The Abigail Newland I know is never far away, is she?' he hissed. His eyes swept over her body again with a hard gleam of male appraisal. 'In a nutshell?' He shrugged. 'I guess your father's idea isn't completely off the wall. I suppose you would be a convenient package. You are the mother of my child and we understand each other. And, I have to admit, the whole idea of having a lady in the lounge and a whore in the bedroom does appeal.'

Fury swept through her at those mocking words. 'Well, maybe you'd better put an advert in the paper, because I sure as hell am not interested.' Her eyes flashed fire at him. 'The thought of you laying one finger on me makes me nauseous.'

She would have marched past him and out of the room at that point, but he caught hold of her arm and pulled her back.

'We both know that's not true.' Although his hand was holding her firmly, the touch of his skin against hers was like an electric shock sending weird little darts through her body, intruding on her rational mind—making her tremble deep-down inside.

He was right—it wasn't true. It was a long time since they had made love, but she remembered how much she had liked it—remembered how blissful it was to lose herself to the masterful dominance of his caresses, his kisses.

Why was she thinking like this? She hated him, she reminded herself fiercely. He had just insulted her beyond belief—hurt her beyond belief. Had she no self-respect?

'Let me go.' Her voice was harsh with reaction.

'You haven't heard the terms of the deal yet.'

'I don't want to hear the terms of the deal. I'm not interested.'

'Of course you are.' Damon smiled, but his eyes were singularly lacking in amusement. 'Your father has lost everything, and that means you have lost the goose that lays the golden eggs—you've even lost this place. But I can make everything better again.'

'All I have to do is prostitute myself to you—is that it?' Her voice was raw.

'Actually, as the mother of my child I'm prepared to offer you a better deal than that.' Damon spoke calmly, but his eyes seemed to bore down through hers. 'All you have to do is come back to Sicily with me and play at being the perfect wife and mother. Of course, you will have to share my bed. But in return I'll keep you in the style and comfort that you are used to.'

Abbie stared at him, her heart thundering against her chest. She just couldn't believe what she was hearing, or the fact that he was saying these things to her in such a clinical and calculating fashion.

'You'll have to sign a prenuptial agreement, of course. But as long as you abide by my terms and stay in the marriage you will have everything you want.'

'That's supposed to be a good deal, is it?' Abbie suddenly found her voice, but she was almost spluttering with rage. 'You really think I'd marry you? You've got a high opinion of yourself, haven't you? I don't even *like* you.'

'It's the best deal you are going to get, Abbie. The prenuptial agreement is non-negotiable.'

The harsh tone took her breath away.

'Your arrogance is incredible. You think I'd tie myself into a loveless marriage for...for—?'

'For wealth, security and all the baubles and trappings of luxury you could possibly want?' Damon cut across her dryly. 'Yes, I do. So let's just cut the pretence, shall we?'

'Yes, let's.' Her voice trembled. 'Because the truth is that even for all the money in the world I wouldn't want to share a house with you, never mind a bed. The very thought leaves me cold.'

Damon laughed.

'What is so funny?' She glared at him.

'You are. We both know that there's nothing cold about you. Maybe we don't like each other very much.' He shrugged. 'But we have a certain thing called chemistry. When I touch you, you come alive. Sex was always good between us.'

'As I said, you are the most conceited, arrogant man I have ever—' She broke off as he started to pull her closer.

'What are you doing?' She tried to wrench away from him, but he wouldn't let her go.

'I'm going to kiss you and prove a point.'

'Don't you dare!' Her eyes blazed up into his.

He smiled at her. 'The sooner you accept the fact that I'm calling the shots now, the easier it's going to be all around.'

'I will accept no such thing!'

Her breathing was coming in short, uneven gasps from anger and from the effort of struggling against him.

'You are just making life difficult for yourself.'

'No, you are making my life difficult! But that's what you want, isn't it?'

'No, Abbie, right now that's not what I want.'

There was something husky about those words, something strangely inviting. His gaze moved to her mouth.

And suddenly, as his head moved lower, she stopped struggling. She wanted him to kiss her. It was as if a tidal wave of desire suddenly hit her out of nowhere, flooding her entire body, pulling her under into very dangerous currents.

His lips touched against hers, gentle at first, and then as they tasted her acquiescence they became hard, demanding and brutal. She found herself kissing him back with equal strength, as if she couldn't get enough of him, as if she were intoxicated by his strength, by his passion.

Then suddenly, as she reached up to touch him, he pulled back from her.

She looked up at him, dazed by what had just happened. His gaze moved from her lips, down to the plunging neckline of her robe.

She noticed the look, and was suddenly very aware of the fact that if he reached out with his other hand he could pull her robe down from her shoulders, leaving her naked to his gaze.

For a shocking moment she wanted him to do that! She wanted him to touch her intimately, wanted to melt in against the powerful contours of his body. The feeling of longing overwhelmed her, rendered her helpless.

His dark eyes returned to hold hers, and there was a gleam of satisfaction there. 'You see, Abbie? You don't need to like me to make this *arrangement* work. All you need is to be your hot-blooded self and, of course, the perfect mother for Mario.'

Shame washed through her in waves. Why the hell had she kissed him back like that? *Why?*

She angled her chin up and forced herself to glare at him defiantly. 'I kissed you.' She shrugged. 'So what? Maybe I just wanted to give you a taste of what you are missing when I walk away from…from your offer.'

'Well, well,' he drawled softly. 'You really are—how is it you English say?—a chip off the old block, aren't you? Trouble is that, like your father, you have very little ground for negotiation. I'm not going to up my offer, Abbie. The prenuptial agreement is non-negotiable. You take what's on the table or you walk away.'

Her lips parted in a gasp as she realised he thought she was trying to make him increase his offer to her.

'You really are insufferable.' She grated the words unevenly, furious that he should make such an assumption. 'I'm not remotely interested in your offer, or in you.'

The sensual line of his mouth curved into a smile as his eyes once more moved down over her body, to where her breasts were straining against the satin material. She knew he could see the hardness of her nipples through the thin material, shamefully giving away the fact that even though his hands hadn't touched her she had been totally aroused.

'But you are interested, Abbie, because power and money are powerful aphrodisiacs for you. You want me more than you can say.'

She shook her head. 'I hate you!'

For one wild moment she thought he was going to pull her back into his arms to prove otherwise.

His lips stretched into even more of a mockingly amused smile. 'Of course you do, and you hate my money even more.'

To her relief, he stepped back from her. 'Well, why don't you run along to that bed of yours? That's if you really do want to go up there on your own.'

She didn't need telling twice; she almost fell over herself in her haste to get away. 'And why don't you get out of my house?'

He ignored that, merely smiled. 'Nice talking terms with you,' he called to her as she moved through the lounge towards the stairs. 'Think about my offer, because I'm only going to leave it open until tomorrow. After that, you will be doing all your negotiating with my lawyer. And, believe me, he won't be nearly as accommodating.'

CHAPTER FOUR

ABBIE lay on top of her bed, staring up at the ceiling. Outside the weather was deteriorating; she could hear the wind starting to whistle around the house with an eerie intensity. Strange how she had been so concerned about that this morning. But now even the threat of a hurricane outside wasn't as disturbing as the presence within.

Why had she kissed him like that? The question kept pounding through her senses along with the memory of his offer.

All she had to do was go back to Sicily with him and play at being the perfect wife and mother.

He could go to hell. She turned over and thumped her pillow. How she had ever once believed that he was a decent human being, she didn't know! And as for imagining that she had been in love with him! Well, she must have been out of her mind.

He'd made no attempt whatsoever to leave the house. A little while ago she had heard his footsteps coming up the stairs, and she had stiffened, her heart thundering against her chest. There was no lock on her bedroom door, and if he'd come in...

But he had merely gone into the bathroom next door, and the next moment she had heard the forceful jet of the shower being turned on.

She wasn't sure what would have happened if he'd come into her room. Yes, she hated him, but something really strange happened to her whenever he touched her. He made her lose control of her emotions so easily, turned her into somebody she didn't even recognise. And it had nothing to do with his damn money! Just what it was about him that affected her like that she didn't know. All she knew was that it scared her.

She heard him come out onto the landing again and she sat up straight, listening intently. But he turned away from her room and she heard him opening the linen cupboard at the top of the stairs.

He was obviously going to sleep on the sofa and was helping himself to some sheets and a pillow, making himself at home. But then the house did belong to him now. Every time she thought about that her anger soared.

The stables had been her refuge from the world, her place to run to. They had belonged to her mother, and it had always been understood that upon her death they were to revert to Abbie.

Obviously her father had got there first, and had taken the deeds as security.

Abigail's hands curled into tight fists as she thought about her father and his latest trick. Offering her to Damon as if she were a piece of property that could be traded! It hurt so much.

She took a deep, shuddering breath and told herself that it wasn't exactly out of character. John Newland excelled at using people.

Her parents' marriage had been a sham. Her father had married her mother because she'd been a member of the aristocracy and it had suited his purposes to play on that fact. As for her mother, although she had been a member of the upper classes she had been practically penniless when she'd met John Newland. Death duties had forced her to the brink of bankruptcy; she had been contemplating selling the house in Surrey that had been in the family for generations, and the riding stables in St Lucia, when John Newland had appeared in her life and offered to rescue her.

Her mother should have known better than to accept his proposal of marriage, but at the time she had believed that she loved him. It hadn't taken long, however, before she'd realised that far from being rescued she had been trapped in a loveless marriage, and her house had been lost, sold off to the highest bidder.

John Newland had been a controlling man, a bully and a womaniser. He had used his wife's connections and her name unashamedly, and at the same time he had despised her weakness in tolerating his behaviour.

As the years had gone by the relationship had deteriorated; even the birth of their only child, Abigail, had not softened John Newland. In fact he had grown worse, parading his women in front of his wife, and heaping scorn on her if she dared to complain.

Abbie had been six and they had been living in America when she'd first witnessed the full extent of her father's rage— a rage that could come upon him from nowhere and for no reason.

She had been packed off to boarding school in England afterwards, but she hadn't forgotten the scene that night.

Why her mother had put up with such a controlling husband for so long, she didn't know. It was Abigail who'd persuaded her to leave. On her sixteenth birthday, she had helped her mum pack a few belongings and had fled with her to St Lucia.

They had told John Newland that they were just having a few days' break to celebrate her birthday, but they hadn't gone back. And from there her mother had filed for divorce.

John Newland's rage had been fierce. Nobody crossed him.

Nobody walked away unless he said they could go. But Abigail had stood firm by her mother, and when her mother had started to get sick she had given up her chance of a university education to help her build up the stables so that they weren't in any way financially reliant on her father.

Things might have worked out. The stables had started to pick up. They had been selling rides to tourists and doing quite well. They might finally have been free of John Newland if her mother's illness hadn't been serious. The type of treatment she had needed hadn't come cheap, and they hadn't been able to afford it.

Nothing short of a life-and-death situation would have forced Abigail to go back cap-in-hand to her father. She had hated doing it, but she'd had no choice.

And of course John Newland had loved it. He had agreed to help his ex-wife by flying her back to the States and making sure she had the best medical help, but as usual the price of his rescue had been high. He'd blamed Abigail for the fact that his wife had ever felt strong enough to leave him, and he had set about making her pay for that betrayal over and over again. He had even threatened to withhold the medical care for her mother if Abbie didn't comply with his wishes.

Abbie had been forced to return to him in Vegas—to dance attendance and play along in his deals.

The worst of which had been the deal with Damon Cyrenci.

When her father had found out that she had fallen in love with Damon he'd seemed to take even greater delight in making sure, when it was all over, that Damon knew she had been complicit in his schemes.

Abbie lay back down against the pillow and stared into the darkness of the bedroom.

To be torn between doing the right thing for a dying parent and the man you thought you loved was a situation she would never forget. It had been pure torture, and of course there had been the guilt that if she walked away her mother might die. The guilt for the fact that Abigail had encouraged her mother to leave her father in the first place and, if she hadn't, John Newland would have paid whatever it had taken to get her better. Money had never been the issue.

So she'd been trapped in a situation that had felt strangely as if it was all her fault. However, when she had sat next to her mother's bedside and tried to say this, her mother wouldn't have it. 'I had more happiness in the few years of freedom we had in St Lucia than in my entire married life,' she had said firmly. 'I'm glad I left him.'

But then her mum hadn't known that behind the scenes Abbie was being torn apart.

At first her dates with Damon were chaste. With difficulty she drew back from his kisses, and deliberately kept him at arm's length, not because she didn't want him but because she wanted him too much and it scared her.

And she was right to be scared. Anything that involved her father always had a dangerous price attached. He'd drop little lines over to her: 'make sure you see Damon tonight,' 'make sure he's not back till late'. At first she did as she was told without question—the consequences of defying her father were too bleak to do otherwise.

But as she fell further under Damon's spell she was torn more and more inside. She desperately wanted their relationship to be untainted by the association with her father and his requests. She tried to reason with her father, but he didn't want to listen—in fact he was angry that she dared to question him. He told her that there was a weekend coming up when he wanted Damon out of town with his mind off business. 'Take him to my ranch in Palm Springs,' he ordered lazily. 'Entertain him until I tell you it is OK to come back.'

She knew her father was trying to pull a shady deal on Damon's father, also that he would only get away with it if Damon wasn't around to spot what he was doing. So for the first time ever she refused a direct command. But with just one cancelled cheque, her father reminded her that it wasn't her life that was held in the balance.

She wanted so much to fling herself on Damon's mercy at that point and tell him what was going on. She knew he would have been horrified, but at least he wouldn't have blamed her.

But then what would happen? She couldn't expect him to foot the bills for her mother.

Nor could she expect him to go away with her to Palm Springs. Maybe he would even confront her father. Either of those things meant her mother would suffer.

So she decided it was safer to say nothing, and she did as her father requested, and invited Damon away for the weekend. But Damon wasn't the walkover that her father was expecting. He was a shrewd operator, and brought in a lawyer to help oversee the dealings with her father.

She remembered Damon casually imparting this information as they sat alone, dining at the ranch. She remembered her relief; she felt as if someone had removed a death sentence from her. Everything would be OK, she told herself reassuringly. Damon hadn't allowed himself to be duped, and her father wasn't going to win this time. That knowledge made going into his arms so much sweeter.

She remembered undressing for Damon, and the strong, sure touch of his hands on her body. She remembered the wild passion that took them over. She remembered lying cradled in his arms afterwards, believing that she was deeply in love with him…

What an idiot! She couldn't believe now that she had been so stupid. Damon had only been interested in sex, not in love.

He'd enjoyed the thrill of the conquest—taking her over and over again. There had been no soft words, no promises.

And, as Damon enjoyed taking her that weekend, her father was busy buying off his lawyer.

Everyone, it seemed, could be used and bought. Everyone had a price. That was what men like her father seemed to thrive on, but she hadn't realised Damon was like that.

She wiped fiercely at some tears that dared to spill down her cheeks.

She had made a mistake falling in love with Damon, but the one good thing to come out of it was Mario. And no matter what it took she wasn't going to let Damon take him away from her. She was going to fight him.

She had been three months pregnant when her mother had died. It had been her lowest ebb. But she had proved then that she was made of strong stuff. She had picked herself up and she had fled back to St Lucia.

With her mother's death her father hadn't had the same hold over her, and she had shut him out of her life completely. She had started to build up the business in the riding stables again.

It hadn't been easy. Being a single mum with a struggling business had been tough—but she had managed.

No matter what Damon Cyrenci thought about her, she could look him in the eye and know that she was a hard working, decent person, not the money-grabbing gold-digger that he believed her to be.

But hard work and decency didn't help when you had lost your home to the devil.

The truth was that although she had managed to be self-sufficient she didn't have enough money for lawyers if Damon chose to play rough.

A violent roar of thunder tore through the night, and it seemed to echo the anger that tore through her.

He was probably bluffing, she told herself soothingly. He wouldn't want a baby cramping his style. And as for all that talk of offering her marriage—that was probably a bluff as well. Maybe he was just winding her up.

Maybe she would get up in the morning and find him gone.

Abbie buried her head into the pillow and tried to sleep, but it was impossible.

As the first light of dawn crept into the room it was a relief to get up, throw on a pair of jeans and a T-shirt and go across the corridor to see to Mario.

He was awake, and he smiled at her as she walked in.

'Hello, darling.' She bent to pick him up and he gurgled with delight.

Everything was going to be all right, Abbie told herself as she cuddled her son close. The storm outside seemed to be abating; the sun was starting to come out. As she busied herself with her usual morning routine of dressing Mario, the night before started to feel like a bad dream.

Maybe Damon would be gone this morning.

Holding on to that thought, she crept quietly downstairs, carrying Mario tightly in her arms.

The house was silent. The only sign of Damon was a neatly folded sheet and a pillow at the end of the sofa.

He'd gone. Her heart started to soar with relief until she walked into the kitchen. The back door was open, and Damon's tall, powerful body was silhouetted in the frame as he nonchalantly looked out at the morning.

He turned as he heard her. 'Good morning.' His eyes swept over her slender frame and the child in her arms. 'How did you sleep?'

How did he think she had slept? Anybody would think that this was a normal everyday situation, she thought angrily. Anybody would think that he hadn't issued her with an absurd ultimatum last night that threatened to upturn her whole life.

'I slept just fine, thank you,' she lied. She wasn't going to let him know she had spent the night tossing and turning and worrying. 'I thought you would be gone by now.'

'I don't know what made you think that. I made my intentions pretty clear last night.'

Abbie swallowed hard. She really didn't want to think about his intentions. If last night had been some kind of bizarre wind-up, he was taking it a bit far.

She settled Mario in his high chair, and then moved to organise his breakfast and switch on the kettle. Pointedly she tried to ignore Damon, but it was hard because she was aware that he was watching her every move.

Like her, he was wearing jeans and a T-shirt this morning. The casual look suited him, made him look younger than his thirty-one years.

She wished she didn't find him so attractive…but she did. She wished she could stop herself from darting a glance over at him as she walked past…but she couldn't. And as their eyes connected she found herself thinking about the way he had kissed her last night, the way he had made her want him. Abruptly she looked away from him again.

How could you hate someone yet find yourself drawn to him at the same time? It was a mystery. A mystery she could do without, she told herself angrily as she heated some milk for Mario and opened a packet of coffee. Maybe a strong shot of caffeine would help unscramble her brain.

'It looks like we missed the worst of that storm last night.' Damon shut the kitchen door. 'The weather seems to have settled again.'

She couldn't believe that he was talking about the weather now. 'Great,' she said dryly.

'Yes, it is.' He walked across and hooked a chair with his foot to sit down at the kitchen table. Mario smiled at him, one of his big, beaming smiles that made dimples appear in his cheeks. Damon smiled back and reached across to ruffle his son's dark hair.

'I've phoned the airport, and my private plane will be on standby this afternoon.' He glanced over at Abbie again. 'All restrictions on travel have been lifted.'

Abbie had been trying to spoon ground coffee into a pot, but her hand shook alarmingly at those words and most of it ended up on the counter-top. 'You're leaving!' She swung around to look at him.

'Yes. This afternoon at four o clock.'

So everything he had said to her last night *had* been just a wind-up. Relief surged through her. 'Look, Damon, I know it must have been a shock finding out about Mario the way you did. And a lot of things were said last night in the heat of the moment—'

'Were they?' Damon held her eyes steadily. 'I never say anything I don't mean.'

She frowned. She'd been going to tell him that maybe they could put the past behind them, and that he could see Mario when he wanted, because after all he was his father. But she left the words hanging in the air as she sought clarification. 'But you *are* leaving?'

'Yes, I'm returning home to Sicily, with or without you.'

'*With?*' There was a horrible silence for a moment as she digested this. 'You mean, you meant all that stuff about— about marrying me and the prenuptial agreement... Everything?'

'Everything.'

Abbie felt her heart bounce crazily against her chest at the look of cool determination in Damon's eyes.

She swallowed hard and turned away from him.

'I'll have a coffee while you're there,' Damon instructed calmly.

She wanted to say 'make your own coffee', but she didn't dare. She just poured the boiling water into the pot and got down some cups.

'You accept my offer and come with me to Sicily today, or I leave on my own and put things into the hands of my legal team. It's up to you.'

The decisive tone stirred up a sizzling kind of fear inside Abbie. She had never felt more out of her depth in all her life, and she just didn't know how to play this. So she kept her back to Damon and pretended to be engrossed in making Mario's breakfast.

Damon watched her as she moved around the kitchen. He'd thought long and hard about this situation last night, and the more he mulled it over the more sense his offer seemed to make. He wanted his son—wanted him with a strength and certainty that had taken him completely by surprise. But he knew he couldn't tear him away from his mother. No matter how much he threatened, that just didn't feel right. A child needed his mother. But he needed a father too.

So what should he do?

Offering Abbie marriage had been truly inspirational.

Mario would have his mother, plus he would have Abbie exactly where he wanted her.

She stretched up to an overhead cupboard, and his eyes drifted over the narrow hand-span of her waist to her bottom, noting its sexy curve in the tight jeans. *And he knew exactly how he wanted her.*

It was lust, of course—but there was an easy remedy for lust. He was going to make Abbie Newland pay in his bed for her gold-digging, deceiving ways, and at the same time he was going to rid himself of this thirst for her by taking her over and over again at his leisure.

'So, what's it to be?' he grated harshly. Now he had made up his mind about what he wanted, he wasn't going to wait around.

'I'll have to consider my options.' She tried to school her voice, rid it of all emotion, but there was a tremor there that she knew he would pick up on.

'You haven't got any options.' Damon smiled calmly. 'I've been looking through your accounts. They make dismal reading.'

'You've done what?' Her glance flew towards the small office that led off the kitchen. She noticed now that the light was on, and her papers were spread out across the desk.

'How dare you look through my private papers?' She swung around to face him.

'There's nothing private from me regarding the business here, Abbie. I own it. The sooner you accept that, the sooner we can move on.'

'I'll accept nothing of the sort.' From somewhere she found a flare of her old fighting spirit. 'I shall be seeking legal advice.'

'And what are you going to pay your legal team with?' he enquired with amusement. 'Washers?'

'I have some rainy-day money,' she told him shakily.

Damon laughed. 'Abbie, it's pouring down so hard that you have been washed away, and you know it.'

Abbie swallowed down on the knot of fear that told her he was right. The little money she had would be no match whatsoever against Damon's might.

'I've offered you a way out. Holding out in the hope that I'm going to increase the terms isn't going to work,' he continued smoothly. 'In fact, if you don't accept today, I will pursue a custody claim for Mario—because let's face it, Abbie, you can't even put a roof over our son's head now. He will be better off in Sicily. I can give him everything you can't—a wonderful education, a comfortable home, a good future.'

'And what about love?' The question broke from her lips in anguish.

Damon regarded her steadily. 'I'll be a good father. You have my word on that.'

'That's so reassuring,' she ground out sarcastically.

'Well, if you are worried come with us. You know my terms.'

'I can't just leave—especially at such short notice! I have the horses to sort out, and responsibilities.'

Damon smiled. Things were turning in his favour; he sensed she was starting to crack. 'I'll employ more staff and a manager, and review the situation at a later date. Believe me, this place can be sorted out in a few hours—money has the advantage of making any situation run smoothly.'

'Don't I know it?' Abbie's voice croaked bitterly. Pitted against Damon's wealth and power, she could possibly lose a custody battle…lose Mario for ever. But the alternative was letting him buy her like an extra member of staff. Her mind whirled around and around, searching for an escape route, but she couldn't find one. Instead his words were playing mockingly through her mind. *You can't even put a roof over our son's head.*

He was right. She'd lost the house and the stables, and there was no way she could fight that. What would she do? Where would she and Mario end up?

Was giving in to Damon now her only option? An over-whelming feeling of powerlessness descended on her as she thought about walking away from the home and the animals she loved. And what about her staff here? What would happen to their jobs? Then there was her beloved horse, Benjo, a three-year-old gelding that she'd rescued from a life of grim abuse. He had stolen her heart away with his trusting eyes and his gentle ways. 'I can't…' Her voice broke with anguish.

Damon's eyes narrowed. She seemed so vulnerable, so fragile. He remembered, when they had first been dating, he had sometimes caught that haunted expression deep in the beauty of her blue eyes. He'd seen it that first day when they'd met by the pool. He'd made some joke about her being a social butterfly, and she had looked at him strangely—almost nervously—a million shadows chasing across the beauty of her expression. It had brought out a feeling in him that he couldn't explain, it had made him want to reel her in and hold her tight. No woman had ever made him feel like that before. What a fool he had been. She'd been the one reeling *him* in. She *had* been just a social butterfly—a devious one at that!

Remembering just how devious brought him firmly to his senses. She had played him for a fool once. He wasn't going to be taken in by her ever again. 'Abbie, I haven't got time for your fake emotional outbursts. I don't know whom you think you are fooling. I can see right through you.'

Abbie slanted her chin up and tried to pull herself together. He was so cold—so ruthless—and she was damned if she was going to give him the pleasure of knowing that he was hurting her.

'Coming back to Sicily with me will be the best thing for our son. He will have both his parents, and all the advantages in life that you wouldn't be able to give him. Plus, I shall put a ring on your finger.' Damon shrugged. 'It's a good deal. I'm prepared to be more than generous to you.'

'And I'm supposed to be grateful?' Abbie's voice trembled with anger. 'The ring you want to put on my finger will mean nothing more than a band of possession.'

Damon conceded the point with a curt nod of his head. 'But a band of possession that will entitle you to certain privileges.'

'In return for certain favours.'

'Favours?' Damon looked amused at the term. 'Oh no, Abbie, that's not how our arrangement will work at all.' He stood up from the table to walk towards her. 'The fact is that you like what I can do for you.'

He stood close to her and reached out a hand to trail it down the side of her face. The caress sent a tremor racing through her entire body—but it was a tremor of desire, not repulsion. A tremor that said he was right, she did like what he could do. And that fact disturbed her deeply.

'We're good together, and what's more now we understand each other.' Damon's tone was matter-of-fact, but his eyes were burning over her body. 'You'll just be my good-time girl, but on a regular basis and on a more honest basis than in the past. I hope we are clear on that?'

'Oh, I think you've made yourself more than crystal clear. But there's nothing *honest* about this,' she said huskily.

'It'll be more honest than what happened between us last time.' Damon tipped her chin up so that he could look into her eyes.

The words hurt her so much. She'd loved him in the past—or *thought* she'd loved him. 'Damon, I didn't have a choice, I—'

'There are always choices in life,' he cut across her firmly.

'Like my choice now, you mean?'

For a second the tremble in her voice stole under his defences. He noticed the shadows in the beauty of her eyes, noticed how they changed from deepest indigo to violet-blue.

'Damon, what happened between us was—'

'What—a regrettable mistake?' Reality swirled in around him. It was amazing how for just a moment she could still get to him. Obviously it was because he still wanted her sexually and that clouded his judgement—that had always been his weakness where she was concerned. His lips twisted wryly. 'I suppose from your point of view you could look at it like that. You made the wrong choice, you backed the wrong horse, Abbie—your father can't bankroll you now. But I can.'

It was strange how his voice was so brutal, yet the touch of his hand as he trailed it down her cheek was so seductively gentle. It sent conflicting signals racing through Abbie's body.

'You forget that I know you. I know how your mind works.' His eyes were on her lips.

She felt a lick of heat stirring through her body, the kind of heat that made her long for him to move closer.

How could she feel like this when she was so appalled by his words? She tried desperately to make herself move away from him—but she couldn't.

'This pretence of yours has gone far enough. Let's just cut to the chase shall we? Have we got a deal?' As he asked the question he grazed his thumb over the softness of her lips. The caress made the longing inside her grow stronger. She wanted him to kiss her, to hold her…

She couldn't understand it. How was he able to turn her on like this? How could he make her ache inside with this deep, burning anguish? Of all the men in the world, why *him*?

'Abbie, have we got a deal?' His voice was insistent, and as he spoke he moved his other hand to her waist, pulling her a little closer. She could feel the heat of his body only centimetres away from hers, and the touch of his hand at her waist was like a sharp brand of ownership.

She imagined being owned by him, sleeping with him in the deep comfort of a double bed every night. Her eyes closed on a wave of weakness as she imagined his hands on her body, his lips crushing against hers.

Sex had been so wonderful with him. He was right, there was chemistry between them. And she did like what he could do to her, liked it so much. That fact made her ashamed of herself. But, as much as she despised herself, she wanted him.

'Abbie?'

Weakness was flooding her body; she felt trapped by her circumstances—but also by her own emotions.

'Abbie, have we got a deal, yes or no?'

She shook her head against the deluge of longing that threatened to overwhelm her. She couldn't tie herself to a man who didn't love her.

But what choice did she have?

The question brought back some semblance of sanity. Her eyes flickered open. All she could do now was some damage limitation. 'What about the staff here?'

Damon frowned That wasn't the kind of question he'd expected from her. 'Their jobs will be safe.'

'And I need to read the contract you want me to sign before I can agree to anything.'

She was like a fish emerging from the water, wriggling on the end of a line. Damon's lips curved. 'Ah, at last, the real Abigail Newland!'

'Don't be smart with me, Damon.'

'The contract will state that financially the world is your oyster, just as long as you stay with me and abide by my terms.' Their eyes met and held. 'And you already know my terms.' He enunciated the words clearly. 'So, I'll ask the question for the last time: have we got a deal?'

Her heart was thundering against her chest so hard that it felt as if it were filling the room with sound. There was nothing she could do. He had her exactly where he wanted her, and he knew it. 'Ok…' She shrugged wearily. 'Yes, we've got a deal.'

She saw the flicker of triumph in his dark eyes. 'At last, an end to the pretence.'

CHAPTER FIVE

THE door of the aircraft slammed shut with all the finality of a cell door closing behind her.

Abbie shut her eyes and told herself that she was being fanciful. If she was going to prison, it would be a very luxurious one. It would be a place where her son would be given a good education and a wonderful life.

She was doing the right thing for Mario. She couldn't have fought against all of Damon's might and power. The one thing she had learnt from the years with her father was that if you had a plentiful supply of money it bought you anything you wanted…even people.

And now she had allowed Damon to purchase her.

But what else could she have done?

She still felt a bit dazed from the speed everything had moved at. One moment she had been standing close to him in the kitchen, the next she had been sent upstairs to pack her things.

'Just bring what you can fit in a small suitcase,' he had ordered. 'Essentials to tide you and Mario over. Everything else can be replaced by new things when we get home.'

Home?

Would she ever feel that Damon's house was her home?

Somehow she didn't think so. And she didn't want new belongings. She wanted her old things. She wanted to feel safe. She wanted to feel like she had her integrity back.

But she had the horrible feeling that her integrity had been left behind in her house along with all the belongings she had once cherished.

She could try to make herself feel better by remembering that she had no choice but to accept Damon's terms—which she hadn't. *But that didn't excuse the fact that she had liked the way he'd touched her—had wanted him to draw her closer—kiss her, caress her.*

The aircraft engines roared and Mario wriggled on her lap. She held him close. 'It's OK, baby, there's nothing to worry about,' she whispered soothingly against his ear.

Liar. There is everything to worry about, she mocked herself.

As the aircraft thundered down the runway she could think of a million worries. And number one on the list was how she was going to give herself in marriage to a man who was going to use her purely for sex.

She remembered how he had sought her out when he had discovered her deception in Vegas. How he'd refused to listen to anything she'd had to say. And then, as his rage had died, the coldness and the clarity in his voice as he'd told her the truth of how he had really felt about her all along. *'As far as I was concerned, our time together was all about sex—I felt nothing for you, other than the pleasure of taking your body. Nothing at all.'*

Those words had never left her. She wished they still didn't hurt. She wished she could forget them—*especially now*.

What future happiness could there be for her with a man who just wanted to possess her body and cared nothing for her?

Had she made the worst mistake of her life in accepting his terms now and getting on this plane?

The aircraft left the ground and soared away from the island of St Lucia. If she looked down she might be able to see her house nestled by the palm-fringed bay. She might be able to see her horse galloping out in the paddock, or Jess taking a group of holidaymakers down to the beach for a long ride across the sands.

Life would go on there without her. Whether she had made a mistake or not, she was on the path to a new life now.

She opened her eyes, and her gaze connected with Damon's.

He was watching her with a cool detachment that made her heart start to beat unevenly. Hastily she looked away from him again.

Where would she be sleeping when they arrived at his house? Would he expect her to just move straight into his bedroom?

The question tormented her.

It was two and a half years since their weeks of wild, abandoned passion. But she could still remember it like yesterday. Could remember the way he had made her feel—as if she'd come alive for the first time. And afterwards being held by him had been the most wonderful sensation. She had felt cherished and protected, and he'd made the loneliness deep inside her melt away.

Of course those feelings had just been an illusion, she reminded herself angrily. But, even so, in the intervening years she had failed to find them again. In fact, dates with other men had failed to stir any spark of excitement inside her. She had wondered if perhaps that side of her was dead. If it had been extinguished by the pain and the fear that if she got too close to someone she might be hurt all over again.

And then Damon Cyrenci had walked in through her front

door and had blown all those theories to smithereens. He could turn her on with just a glance.

It was a cruel twist of irony that the man who had smashed her heart, the man who cared nothing for her feelings—who despised her, even—was the one man who could turn her on.

She couldn't sleep with him tonight, she just couldn't. Fear shot through her in violent waves. She didn't know what frightened her most: the fact that she wanted him so much, or the fact that once he took her to bed she would reveal just how vulnerable she was where he was concerned. He already had such a powerful hold on her; giving him the satisfaction of knowing he was right, and she was his for the taking any time he pleased, was more than her pride could bear.

The aircraft levelled out and the seat-belt sign was switched off.

'Do you want a drink?' Damon stood up and headed to the back of the plane.

'No, I'm all right, thank you.'

She watched as he poured himself a coffee in the galley kitchen, and she tried to direct her thoughts away from what was going to happen between them. This was a lengthy overnight flight. They wouldn't be landing in Sicily until the early hours of the morning. The sleeping arrangements were a long way off.

She glanced away from him around the interior of the plane. She had never been in a private jet before. The last flight she had taken had been a scheduled one from Vegas when she had fled from her father. That flight had been full, and the seats had been jammed close together.

By contrast they were alone on this flight. The deep leather seats were soft and luxurious and placed far apart. There were personal TV screens that could be pulled down from the ceiling above her, and phones concealed in the armrests. There was also a recline button that would fully adjust and transform the chair into a bed.

Damon returned to sit opposite her. 'Do you want to put Mario down on the seat next to you?' he asked. 'Now that we are airborne it might be more comfortable. There is a booster seat, and you can put a blanket and the safety belt around him.'

'Thank you, Damon, but we're fine,' she assured him stiffly. Somehow she didn't want to relinquish the warm little body close to hers.

'Please yourself.' Damon shrugged and reached for some papers in the central armrest. 'I have some work to do,' he murmured.

Abbie looked out the window. How could he be so relaxed about this situation? How could he study his sheets of figures and concentrate on high finance when he had ridden rough-shod over her, made her homeless, torn her away from every-thing she knew?

Because he didn't care, she thought tiredly. Retribution was all he cared about.

Abbie leaned her head back and closed her eyes. Somehow she would get through this, she told herself fiercely. She had to, for Mario's sake.

Silence fell between them, filled only by the drone of the aircraft and the rustle of his papers.

Damon didn't look up from his work until a few hours later, when Mario made it known that he was hungry.

He watched as she soothed the child and moved him into the seat beside her.

She was good with him, he thought, as he watched Mario smile at her suddenly.

But then Abbie could charm the birds off the trees.

His eyes moved down over her figure. She was wearing the jeans she'd had on this morning, but she'd changed her T-shirt for a clinging black top with spaghetti straps. It kept riding up at her waist as she bent to secure Mario in his seat. Her skin was firm, and tanned a golden honey. Her hair swung silkily around her shoulders as she moved.

How he itched to take her; the need for her was burning him up inside. When he'd pulled her close to him in the kitchen this morning he'd wanted to unfasten those jeans and pull off her T-shirt to reveal the soft swell of her curves. And it would have been so easy to have her there and then. He'd seen the flame of desire in her eyes—a flame she had desperately tried to hide behind the pretence of being hurt by the crudeness of his offer.

'OK, sweetheart, dinner is coming.' She bent close and kissed the child. Then she glanced over at Damon. 'Watch him for me, will you, while I heat him something up?'

'Sure.' He inclined his head. Oh yes, she was sweetness personified—nobody would ever guess that her only qualm about selling herself to him had been how good a deal she would get from him.

Well, as soon as she signed his prenuptial agreement her game would be over and his would just have begun.

He put his papers to one side and reached to pick up one of Mario's toys that had fallen on the floor. He smiled at the child as he handed it back. Mario smiled back at him.

Pleasure intensified inside Damon. Oh yes, things couldn't be better. He had his son, and this was all working out very well.

Abbie returned a few moments later, and knelt down beside the little boy to help him with his dinner. Darkness fell outside the windows. Damon returned his attention to his work. He had a backlog to deal with, and he wanted to be sufficiently up to date when he returned to Sicily to be able to take some time off—time that he intended to spend making up for lost time with his son, and enjoying himself with his newly acquired wife…over and over again.

The sun was rising slowly in the east when Damon finally put his work away and the private jet started to make its final descent. Abbie leaned forward and watched as they skimmed in low over the Mediterranean. She noticed the golden glitter of sun on the water beneath them, and the dark shapes of fishing boats. As they approached the land she could see cypress trees and steep mountains silhouetted against the pink of the morning sky.

The touch-down was smooth, and within a few moments they had taxied to a halt and the seat-belt sign was switched off.

They were on the island of Sicily. Abbie wondered if she would suddenly wake up and find herself back in her own bed, find the last twenty-four hours had all been a wild figment of her imagination.

But as she turned her attention back inside the plane and her eyes met with Damon's she knew that this was real. There was no peace of mind to be found. Her future started here.

'Home sweet home.' His lips curved in a slightly mocking smile, as if he could read her consternation.

'If you say so.'

His smile merely widened at that. 'At least we are off to a good start.'

She looked at him enquiringly.

'You realise that what I say goes.'

'Very funny, Damon.'

'Who's joking?' He flicked her a wry look before standing up to gather their belongings from the overhead locker.

She angled her chin up and forced herself not to give him the pleasure of knowing that she could feel every nerve-ending inside her stretching and shaking under the tension.

The door of the aircraft slid open, and Abbie picked up her bag and gathered Mario up into her arms. It was a pleasure to step outside. The morning air was fresh with the promise of a hot day to come, and as Abbie followed Damon down the steps towards the tarmac she took deep breaths as if she were emerging for the last time into freedom.

There was a group of authorities waiting for them by the base of the steps, and behind them a uniformed chauffeur stood patiently next to a stretch limousine, the passenger doors open, ready for them.

'I need both your passports, Abbie.' Damon held out his hand and she scrabbled in her bag to find them and hand them over.

As the formalities of customs and immigration were observed smoothly and within minutes, it suddenly struck Abbie that this was a way of life for Damon Cyrenci.

He was used to people treating him with respect—used to his path being eased, to getting everything he wanted. She noticed their luggage being efficiently loaded straight into the boot of the waiting limousine.

She had to admit it was impressive, as were the warm tones of his accent as he spoke in his native tongue. It was the first time she had heard him speak in his own language, and she liked it. It gave her a strange, liquid feeling in her bones. The trouble was that it was a feeling that annoyed her intensely.

She didn't want him to have that effect on her, because that was giving him power over her, and Damon had enough power. He was arrogant and insufferable, and she wasn't going to be a walkover for him—no matter how attractive she found him. Maybe everyone else bowed and scraped to him, but she wasn't going to. Pride was the only thing she had left now, and she was going to hold on to it at all costs.

Trying to keep that thought firmly to the forefront of her mind, she walked across towards the waiting car.

A few minutes later they were speeding away across the tarmac, out of the terminal and onto the main road.

Damon talked to the driver in Italian for a few moments before closing the glass partition. 'Won't be long, and we'll be home.'

Abbie turned away from him and tried to pretend that she was interested in the scenery. 'You've still got our passports,' she reminded him curtly.

'They are with the rest of the documentation.' He stretched his long legs out. 'I don't know about you, but I could do with a shower and a lie down.'

His words prickled against her senses. Would he expect her to 'lie down' with *him*? 'They say the best cure for jet lag is to stay awake as long as possible, and try to sleep at the normal time,' she told him stiffly.

'Do they?' She could hear the underlying amusement in his tone. 'We'll have to try and think of a way to keep awake, then.'

Abbie bit down on the softness of her lower lip and kept her gaze averted from him. She watched as the Sicilian countryside flashed by in a whirl of colours. She noticed the baked, hard terracotta soil, the silver green of olive trees and the fierce blue of the sky. But all she could think about was the sleeping arrangements at the end of their journey.

The driver turned the car up through the winding, mountainous roads before dropping them back down towards dazzling views out across the coastline.

Then they slowed down and turned into a hidden entrance. Electric gates wound back to allow access to a long driveway that wound its way through lush Mediterranean gardens. As it curved around, Abbie had her first glimpse of the place that was to be her new home.

Her lips parted in a gasp of admiration, for it was more beautiful than she had ever imagined. It had the size and grandeur of a mansion, but it also had a character that stole her heart away.

Vines tangled across the warmth of the red bricks, jasmine and bougainvillea vying for position over the elegant arch of the front door.

'This is a beautiful house, Damon.' Despite the fact that she had been determined to make no comment about her surroundings, her enthusiasm would not be curbed, and it broke from her lips before she could check it.

'I'm glad you approve.' By contrast, Damon's voice was dry. It was as if he had expected her admiration, which of course she supposed he had. After all, his home had all the trappings associated with the residence of a multimillionaire: an infinity swimming-pool sparkled and merged into the deep, hazy blue of the Mediterranean, tennis courts were towards the other side and vast lawns sprawled out at the front.

As the car pulled to a halt by the front door a slim, smartly dressed woman in her late fifties stepped out of the house to greet them. She had dark hair swept into a chignon, and high cheekbones that gave her a regal air.

'This is my housekeeper, Elise,' Damon informed her as he climbed out into the heat of the day. 'Elise speaks good English, is a great cook and runs the house very efficiently. So there will be no problems for you to deal with.'

Abbie frowned. In St Lucia her days had been packed—she had worked long hours, and sometimes it had been difficult juggling motherhood and running the business. There had been days when she had longed for some time and space just to be able to spend time with Mario. But she had also enjoyed the challenge.

How would she fill her days here? she wondered.

Elise welcomed her with a friendly smile, and then cooed and fussed over Mario in Italian.

They stepped into the entrance hall where a grand, curving staircase led up to a galleried landing.

'I have a few business calls to make, Abbie,' Damon informed her curtly as the chauffeur carried in their bags. 'Elise will show you up to the bedroom. Go and make yourself at home. I'll be up presently.'

Abbie's heart was starting to thud so hard against her chest that it hurt. It sounded like he was ordering her to go upstairs and prepare for him!

Maybe he imagined, because she'd agreed to his terms, that all he had to do now was snap his fingers and do as he pleased with her. Well, he could think again. She had far too much self-respect to allow him to use her like that.

Oh no, Damon Cyrenci, you are not getting everything your own way, she told herself fiercely as she followed Elise up the staircase. She may have agreed to his obnoxious terms, but it didn't mean she was going to be a complete pushover.

The room Elise showed her into was palatial. Two arched windows allowed sunlight to flood in. One looked out towards the glitter of the pool and the sea, the other looked over the side gardens. But it was the bed that took her attention. It was a massive king-sized four-poster swathed in white, and it totally dominated the centre of the room.

'There is a dressing room through here.' Elise opened another door. 'I have placed Mario's cot in here, as Signor Cyrenci instructed.'

Abbie followed the woman and glanced into the room. Sure enough, a large cot was placed next to some walk-in wardrobes. Damon had been busy. All those phone calls before they'd left St Lucia had obviously paid off.

But then, as Damon had said, when you had money the way was smoothed very easily.

She felt suddenly exhausted.

'And there is an *en-suite* bathroom through here.' Elise opened the door next to the dressing room. 'Now, is there anything else I can get for you, Ms Newland?'

Abbie shook her head. 'No, everything is fine, thank you.'

With a nod, the woman took her leave. Abbie sank down onto the side of the bed and put Mario down beside her.

The little boy was delighted to be free, and he pulled himself up and toddled off to explore. She allowed him to run unhindered across the soft white carpet; there was nowhere for him to go, nothing for him to harm himself on, and the freedom was probably just what he needed after being confined for so long.

But what freedom was she going to have now? Obviously Damon didn't expect her to do any housework, which meant she would have no say in the running of the house. Was her only role to be that of mother and bedmate?

She noticed the long bank of wardrobes against the far wall. If she opened them up, would she find Damon's clothes hanging inside? Was this his bedroom? It was hard to tell from just glancing around; there were no personal items on the dressing table or on the bedside tables, not even a book or a clock.

Mario toddled back towards her, and she swept him up into her arms. She didn't have the energy to investigate or even think about this situation any longer. She would bath Mario, have a shower herself and deal with everything else a step at a time.

It took Damon a while to sort out the paperwork in his office. He read through the prenuptial agreement that he had asked his lawyer to draw up. He'd done a good job. Satisfied that everything was in order, he pushed his chair back from his desk and went in search of his quarry.

But when Damon stepped into the bedroom he found Abbie lying on top of the bed, fast asleep. He glanced through into the adjoining room and saw that Mario was also sleeping in his cot.

So much for getting her to sign his contract straight away! He crossed the room and sat down beside her on the edge of the bed. She didn't stir. She was lying on her side, her long, blonde hair slightly obscuring her face in a silky curtain. His eyes travelled down over her body, noting the fact that she'd changed into a white pencil-skirt, a white short-sleeved top and that her long legs were bare.

She looked achingly beautiful. He reached out a hand and stroked a strand of her hair back from her face. She moved a little at his touch but she didn't wake.

It was hard to believe that someone who looked like her had such a cold, mercenary heart. Hard to believe that the only thing that really turned her on was money.

He felt a dull ache of something swirling inside him. She looked so innocent in sleep, almost virginal, her lips parted softly, and her long, dark eyelashes thick and sooty against the soft perfection of her skin.

He remembered how he had felt when he had discovered that she was complicit in his father's destruction. She had played the game so perfectly—luring him in, drawing back from his kisses as if scared by the intensity of passion that had sprung between them, teasing him with her tremulous smile and her innocent, big blue eyes. But all the time she had known exactly what she was doing.

There was nothing innocent about Abbie. The knowledge stabbed through him fiercely as his eyes travelled lower over the soft curves of her body. She knew exactly how to use that beautiful body of hers to maximum effect. Knew exactly what she wanted.

Well, so be it—she could use her beautiful body to full effect, she could even have everything she wanted…but at a price. Their roles had been reversed. The huntress was now the prey. He was in control this time.

'Abbie.' He stroked a hand down over her face. 'Abbie, wake up.'

Her eyes flickered open. She looked disorientated for a moment, as if she didn't know where she was. And as she looked up at him the intensity of her kitten-blue eyes seemed to mock his determination to be cool and ruthlessly in control.

'So much for staying awake,' he said softly.

'I only meant to rest my eyes for a moment.' She stretched sleepily and his eyes followed the lissome movement. He noticed how she was very clever at showing her body to full advantage. The round-necked top was in a silky material that emphasised the curve of her breasts in a tantalizingly provocative way, especially when she put her hands over her head like that. The skirt showed how tiny her waist was, and how curvy her hips.

'Good job I've come to your rescue and woken you up,' he grated sardonically. 'We don't want jet lag interfering with our fun, do we?'

As sleep faded from Abbie's mind, the realization of her situation flooded back in. How long had Damon been in the room? How long had he been sitting beside her, watching her sleep?

She drew herself up. 'Damon, what are you doing in my room?'

'Your room?' His lips twisted with amusement. 'This is *our* room, Abigail. This is our marital bed.'

'Well, we are not married yet!'

Although her eyes flared with fire, she sounded flustered—almost nervous—and he laughed at that. 'Such old-fashioned virtue from such a modern—shall we say to be kind, less than virtuous—woman.'

'When were you last kind where I'm concerned?' she croaked huskily.

'Dear me, are you panicking already about how generous I intend to be?' He looked at her with a raised eyebrow. 'Now I understand the reason for the display of innocent virtuosity.'

He watched as the pallor of her skin flooded with colour. He had to hand it to her, she was a superb actress. 'Don't worry, I will be kind, you will get everything your heart desires.'

He reached out a hand to trail one finger down over her cheek. She flinched away from his touch. 'I don't want anything from you, Damon.' She was smarting from his words, from the touch of his hand. She knew his opinion of her, and it shouldn't hurt so much—but strangely it did.

'Drop the pretence, Abbie—we're past that now.'

The mocking tones lashed across her. She swallowed hard.

There was the sound of a car pulling up outside, and Damon stood up from the bed to go over towards the window. 'Ah, right on schedule. Put your shoes on, Abbie, and come downstairs. We may as well get business out of the way now.'

'I can't leave Mario. He might wake up and need me.' Abbie swung her legs off the bed. She didn't want to go anywhere with him—in fact all she wanted right now was to run away.

'Mario will be fine. There is a child-monitor installed. Switch it on and we'll hear him in my study if he cries.'

'You've thought of everything, haven't you?'

'I hope so.' He moved towards the door decisively. 'Don't be long. I'll be waiting for you downstairs.'

There was no alternative but to do as she was told, so she slipped on her high heels and went to check on Mario.

She tried to tell herself that dealing with Damon in the study was preferable to dealing with Damon in the bedroom. But somehow it wasn't much of a reassurance, and her feelings of vulnerability only intensified as she went down to join him. If it hadn't been for Mario, she might have been tempted to keep on going, out through the front door. But, even with Mario in her arms, where would she go? She had no money and no passport.

The knowledge made her heart thump unevenly as she found Damon's study.

'You've still got our passports,' she reminded him as soon as she entered the room.

'Have I?' He was sitting behind a large desk, flicking through papers, and he barely glanced up.

'You know you do.'

Damon shrugged. 'Well, they are not going to be a lot of use to you now anyway. Why do you want them?'

The calm question disconcerted her. 'Because I just do! You can't keep me prisoner here!'

He laughed at that. 'I've no intention of keeping you prisoner here, Abbie.' He sat back in his chair and opened up a drawer to take out some keys. 'In fact, these are for you.'

'What are they for?'

'One is the front-door key to this house and the other is the key for the brand-new silver-blue sportscar waiting outside on the drive for you. It's just been delivered.'

'Oh!' She was taken aback by the gift.

'Oh indeed.' He smiled. 'You see, I do intend to be generous, and you can come and go as you please. As long as you're here for me when I need you.'

The words were said in a certain, seductive way that made

her heart start to hammer even more fiercely against her chest. She noticed the way his eyes slipped down over her figure—assessing, warm.

'Have a look out the window if you want. You'll be able to see the car from here.' He leaned back further in his chair and watched her lazily. He was curious to see her reaction.

Her hands curled into tight fists at her sides. He was treating her like the mercenary little gold-digger he thought she was, and she wasn't going to play. 'I don't want your damn car,' she told him tightly.

'Abbie, don't be coy, it doesn't suit you and it doesn't fool me.'

'I want the passports back.'

He shrugged. 'And you can have them. But they will be utterly useless. They are out of date.'

'No, they're not!' She stared at him mutinously. 'They have years left on them—'

'Abbie,' he cut across her crisply. 'Mario's passport says that he is Mario Newland. That is not his name. His name is Mario Cyrenci. The error will be made right as soon as possible.'

Damon watched impassively as shadows flickered across Abbie's eyes. 'And, as for you…' He smiled coolly. 'I've arranged for a special licence. We will be married tomorrow afternoon.'

'Tomorrow!' Her eyes widened, and the panic inside her intensified. She felt as if she was backed into a corner with no way out. 'Isn't this all a little rushed?'

'Why wait around?' He leaned forward in his chair. 'All you have to do is sign this.' He tapped the papers that were lying on the desk. 'And then you can have these.' He picked up the keys and dangled them.

'Is this the carrot-and-stick approach?' She tried to make a joke, but her voice rasped huskily.

He smiled. 'You could call it that. And, speaking of carrots…' He picked up a small box from beside the papers. 'I suppose you should also have this.'

He opened the lid, and a magnificent diamond-solitaire ring blazed fiercely as the light caught it.

'You don't need to worry—despite the fact that it's an antique, it's worth a lot of money. It's flawless, and it's set in platinum.'

Abbie swallowed down on the shaft of pain inside her 'Why do you want to think the absolute worst of me?' The trembling question broke from her lips involuntarily.

'You know why.'

She wished he knew the truth—wished she could make him believe that what had happened wasn't her fault. 'Damon, I am not a mercenary person. I had no choice but to go along with my father…' Her voice was full of emotion as she tried to reach him. It was so painful even thinking about the past and her mother. 'I—'

'Save it Abbie,' he cut across her ruthlessly. 'I don't want to hear your excuses. Because only a fool doesn't learn by their mistakes, and I'm no fool.'

She stared at him wordlessly. You couldn't make someone believe you when they were just determined to think the worst.

'Now, are you going to sign these so we can move on?' He picked up a pen and tapped the documents in front of him.

What would happen if she said no? Abbie wondered suddenly. Would she be put back on a plane—without Mario? And a plane to where? She had nowhere to go, and nothing except for the one small suitcase she had brought with her.

'I never sign anything without reading it.' She tilted her chin up proudly. She was damned if she was going to make this easy for him. She wouldn't let him see she was beaten. 'You'll have to leave it with me for a few hours.'

'Fine.' He drummed his fingers on the desk impatiently. Then he picked the ring up out of the box. 'In the meantime, in an act of good faith, should I slip this onto your finger?'

She hesitated, and then shrugged. 'I suppose you could. I can always take it off again.'

Damon's dark eyes gleamed with a moment's annoyance. Every time he thought he had her just where he wanted her, she managed to do some kind of sidestep. 'I've really had enough of your games, Abbie.' He stood up and walked around towards her with a purposeful look in his eye, a look that made her heart race. Then he reached to take her hand in his and slip the ring firmly into place.

It fitted perfectly.

'There.' Instead of letting go of her hand, he sat down on the desk behind him and drew her closer.

'Now, you've had some tokens of my intentions. I think it's time I had some token from you.' He said the words roughly, but bizarrely there was nothing rough about the way his fingers stroked over her hand.

'What kind of a token?' She pretended not to know what he meant—but she understood all too well. She could hear what he wanted in the deep rasp of his voice, see it in the dark flame of his eyes.

'I think you should undress for me, Abbie, and show me exactly what *you* can offer *me*…'

CHAPTER SIX

THE command sent a strange pang of emotion shooting through her. There was a part of her that was horrified by his words, and another part… Well, the other part was weakened by the fact that he had pulled her very close and one hand had moved to her waist. He was so close to her and she could feel the heat of his body, smell the familiar scent of his cologne.

His eyes were dark and commanding as they held hers. Then they moved down towards her lips, and she felt something inside her turn over.

This was the father of her child—the man she had loved so passionately once, the man who had made her cry with pleasure when he'd brought her to climax. The man who had chased away the loneliness inside her and held her so tightly against him that she'd thought she would die from happiness.

The memories swamped her, just as they did every time he came too close.

She didn't want to feel like this. But somehow she just couldn't help herself.

'Don't, Damon.' She whispered the words unsteadily.

'Don't what?' He reached up to stroke a stray strand of hair away from her face.

The strangely gentle caress was like pure torture. 'Don't torment me!'

His eyes gleamed with a moment's dark humour. 'Darling Abbie,' he grated sarcastically. 'Why should I listen to that plea when you torment me so well?'

'Do I?' She looked into his eyes, startled by the remark, and he laughed.

'You know, if they were handing out Oscars for this performance you'd get one. You play innocent so damn well.' His words rasped with a slightly uneven edge.

'Now you're mocking me!' Her eyes clouded.

'Now you're going for the "best actress" award as well as "best newcomer".'

'Leave me alone, Damon. I'm not going to allow you to insult me like this—I deserve better!'

'Really?' His tone was sardonic. 'Well, show me what you think you deserve, then.' He let go of her suddenly.

The challenge riled her—riled her almost as much as the fact that he wasn't holding her now. She wanted to feel his arms around her.

She frowned as the realization struck. She wanted him to treat her the way he had when they were lovers; even if it was just an illusion of love, it was better than nothing.

She shut her eyes and leaned closer, and before she could think better of her actions she kissed him. It was gentle at first, almost tentative, but as she felt the warmth of his lips moving against hers she deepened the kiss. For a while she was in control, and she liked it—liked the feel of his body against hers, liked the way he responded to her.

Memories licked through her body, heating her up, making her ache. There had been this tenderness between them in the past, this tentative yet highly inflaming spark. She could feel it now, burning against her lips, sizzling through her consciousness.

His hands were on her waist again, drawing her closer. She could feel his arousal pressing against her.

She wanted him…wanted him so much.

His hands swept upwards and over her breast, caressing her gently, finding the hard peaks of her nipples and stroking them, teasing them into tight, throbbing buds that strained against the satin of her clothing.

'Now, this is better…' His words cut through the warmth inside her.

She closed her eyes and strove to cut the cynical tones from her mind. 'Damon, we were so good together once.' She whispered the words huskily. 'Maybe we could be like that again.'

When he didn't answer, she pulled away from him a little so that she could look into his eyes. 'Maybe we could put the clock back to the way we were together that weekend in Palm Springs?'

'When I didn't know the truth about you?' His eyes held hers steadily. 'I don't think so, Abbie.'

The sudden coldness in his tone struck her uncomfortably.

'I just thought… We have a child together, and if we are going to make this…situation work, then maybe we should try to forget the past.'

'Nice thought.'

Still the coldness was there in his tone.

'At least we could meet each other half way?' She looked up at him with beseeching blue eyes.

'And after we've met half way—then what?'

'Well, I told you, we could put the clock back, start again.'

'Just like that?' He snapped his fingers.

'We could, if it was what we both wanted.' Her heart was thundering against her chest. 'And it would be better for Mario if there wasn't this tension between us, if we could trust each other.'

He didn't answer her immediately, but his hands dropped completely away from her, leaving her aching for him.

'Well go on, then, show me how much you mean all this, hmm? Prove your undying devotion.'

She frowned, unsure of what he wanted from her. 'Well, we would have to take it a day at a time, but we could try.'

'Well, let's take it a minute at a time now. Do as I ask and undress for me.'

She took a step back from him. 'You're serious, aren't you?' Her voice trembled slightly. She wanted his tenderness so much, but he kept bringing it back to this.

'Why—aren't *you*?'

He sounded so cold, so ruthless, and yet when he'd kissed her, when he'd touched her, she had imagined she'd glimpsed the man she had thought she loved once.

It was as if a veil was down between them now, and it didn't matter what she did, she kept getting tangled up in it. Maybe she always would. Maybe no matter what she did or said he would always think of her as the mercenary gold-digger who had deceived him.

And then, before she could analyse what she was doing, or why, she started to take off the white silk top.

Her blonde hair fell in disarray around her shoulders as she pulled the top over her head. She was wearing a plain white bra, not overtly sexy, just plain white cotton trimmed with satin. Yet its plainness made it the sexiest piece of underwear Damon had seen in a long time, due in no small way to the pert voluptuousness of her curves.

Her eyes held with his as she unfastened her skirt and let it fall to the floor.

His gaze travelled slowly down over her body, taking in

every detail. She was wearing a pair of white satin pants that curved prettily over her hips. Her figure was as toned and sensational as he'd remembered, her legs long and shapely.

'You still look as good as you did back then,' he told her gruffly. 'You always were an incredibly sexy woman.'

He watched the flare of colour in her skin. She looked embarrassed and shy, yet she stood straight and met his gaze with guileless, clear eyes. 'But I'm not the same,' she told him softly.

'No?' He felt his insides tighten and his need for her scream out as her hands went around to unfasten the bra.

'No. I've had a baby since then. It changed my body.'

The bra fell to the floor.

Her breasts were fantastic—large, yet so perfectly shaped and firm, her nipples still hard and erect from his touch.

'It changed you in a good way,' he told her softly. 'A very good way.'

Her hand played with the thin satin of her pants, and she cast him a look that shot molten heat through him. She looked so vulnerable, so nervous. He couldn't stand her looking at him like, that it ate him away.

'Come here.' Before she could take the underwear off, he reached and caught her arm and pulled her closer.

'I thought you wanted me to take all my clothes off?' The soft yet tremulous question tore at him. Was she close to tears? He felt like someone had struck him. He pulled her closer and into his arms, and allowed her to bury her head against his shoulder.

'No, it's OK.' His hand stroked down over the softness of her blonde hair and then the smooth, naked skin of her back. She felt good in his arms, too damned good. 'I know it's as you English like to say: collar and cuffs all match.'

He just held her for a moment, his mind racing. What the

hell was the matter with him? Why did he feel so bad? She was a teasing, tormenting witch! She deserved a bit of humiliation.

She turned her head slightly and cuddled in against him. His thumb brushed gently over the side of her face. Was it wet with tears?

'Abbie?'

The rasp of his voice aroused her so much. She turned her head, and suddenly they were kissing with a heat and a need that tore her apart. It was as if the spark had ignited, and everything around them had caught fire.

His hands caressed her naked body, finding her breasts, grazing over her nipples, his fingers teasing them, squeezing them until she gasped for pleasure. She found herself turned around, so that she was the one against the desk, and the next moment she was lying over it and she could feel the cold leather against her back.

His mouth moved to kiss her neck and then trail a blaze down to her breasts, finding her nipples, sucking on them, licking them.

She wound her arms around his neck. All she could think was that she wanted him urgently, wanted him now!

His hands stroked down over the satin material of her pants, stroking her through the material.

'Damon, have you got anything?'

'Hmm?' He lifted his head to look at her.

'Have you got any protection?'

He smiled. 'Yes…somewhere.' As he moved away from her slightly, the contracts on the desk slithered to the floor.

'Maybe that's an omen.' She looked up at him through the darkness of her lashes, her eyes sparkling and seductive. 'Maybe we don't need those contracts now.'

He stilled.

'I mean, we don't need to rush into getting married,' she

explained softly. She reached up to run her hands through the darkness of his hair. 'We can take our time, recapture the past, get to know each other again and—'

'Stop it, Abbie,' he cut across her roughly. 'We don't need to get to know each other again. And I certainly don't want to recapture the past. I know you well enough.'

The brutal words cut through the illusion of their tender love-making. Nothing had changed, she realised dully. She had been fooling herself to think that Damon could ever forget what she had done.

She watched as he zipped up his jeans, and then bent to pick up the contracts from the floor.

'You are not going to get round me—you will sign the contracts, Abbie. Otherwise there is no deal.'

His voice was perfectly controlled, and it was all a million miles away from the passion of just a few moments ago.

She shouldn't have mentioned the contracts. Why had she said anything? 'I wasn't trying to get round you,' she said softly.

'Of course not.' By contrast his voice was almost contemptuous, and her skin burned as his eyes flicked over her naked body.

'I did as you asked,' she reminded him, putting her arms over her breasts to shield them.

'And now you can do as I ask again.' He put the contracts down beside her and picked up a pen. 'Sign on the dotted line.'

Her breathing felt constricted. She had been so turned on…and his cold, merciless manner hurt so much.

'Fine!' She snapped the pen out of his hand and stood up from the desk. 'Show me where you want me to sign and let's just get it over with.'

'Very wise.' He turned the pages over for her and pointed to the last line. 'And don't forget to date it.'

He was unbelievable! Abbie's heart thumped fiercely against her chest as she scribbled her name and the date.

Damon watched her detachedly, and then he couldn't help but let his eyes wander over her figure.

She looked so good, her blonde hair swinging around her shoulders, brushing against her breasts. She still had on her high heels.

The erection that had been straining against his jeans earlier suddenly intensified.

'There.' She slammed the pen down and turned to look at him, her eyes filled with vehemence. 'Satisfied?'

'No, not yet.'

The tone of his voice had changed; his eyes were like liquid fire.

To her consternation, the look turned her on. She was furious with herself. Couldn't she just learn her lesson where he was concerned? She tried to move away from him but he caught her arm.

'Now we can consummate the deal,' he said softly.

She shook her head. 'Oh no, you don't get everything your own way, Damon.' To her horror her voice trembled with feeling. 'You want the *deal*—as you like to call it—done correctly. You marry me first.'

'You're such a spitfire when you want to be.' He paid no attention to her words, just pulled her closer. 'But at least now we've cut through all that rubbish about turning back the clock. If you think I'm going to forget what you really are, then you are mistaken.'

'Fine, have it your way.'

'Oh, don't worry—I will.' His eyes drifted down over her body, and to her dismay she found the way he looked at her made her breasts instantly harden and throb with need.

'I'll have it my way over and over again.' He smiled, but he let go of her. 'And I'll look forward to that tomorrow.'

She glared at him with a mixture of fury and regret. She

didn't want things to be like this between them. She didn't want to yearn for him…but she did.

Rather than bend to pick up her clothes, she left them on the floor and fled from the room. She would rather take her chances bumping into Elise than give Damon the pleasure of watching her gathering up her clothing wearing just her pants.

Luckily she made it to her bedroom without bumping into the housekeeper.

Mario was still fast asleep. The room was tranquil and silent, but there was no solace to be found for Abbie. In fact that very tranquility seemed to mock the tempestuous emotions swirling around inside her.

How could she have allowed herself to think for one moment that they could turn back time? Damon would never forget what she had done, and he would never, ever even consider the fact that he might be wrong about her.

He was so damned smug and superior! She kicked off her shoes and took off her pants, then went to stand under the cool, forceful jet of the shower.

Well, he could go to hell—she hated him!

But as her face turned upwards to the jet of water she remembered how he had so easily turned her on. And she knew that she didn't hate him at all. One moment she had been lost and desolate…the next he had stoked up a fierce longing inside her that had allowed her to return his kisses without reserve, had allowed her to speak without thinking.

She should never have mentioned those contracts. She was such an idiot. But she really had thought that maybe they could start to put things right. She kept remembering how good it could be between them.

Wrapping herself in a towel, she returned to the bedroom to get dressed. She found a black linen skirt in her bag, and a white T-shirt, and hurriedly put them on.

She needed to forget the way Damon made her feel and concentrate on reality, she told herself crossly. But as she reached to pick up a brush to tidy her hair the diamond ring on her finger flashed fire, reminding her that the reality for her was, from tomorrow onwards, she would be Damon's possession.

Mario woke up and started to cry. 'It's OK, honey. I'm coming.' Glad of the distraction, she put the brush down and hurried in to pick him up.

Mario was hungry, which meant going downstairs and facing Damon again. Her stomach tied into knots as she carried the child out into the hallway and down the stairs.

She peeped her head around the door of the study, but there was no sign of Damon. Her clothes, she noted, had been placed on a chair. Part of her wanted to go in and get them, then run back upstairs with them, but Mario was fidgeting in her arms. He needed something to eat, and he was starting to grizzle about the delay.

So, ignoring her discarded clothing, she carried on down the corridor in search of the kitchen. She found it without too much effort. It was at the back of the house, next door to a dining room that looked as if it was big enough to be used as a banqueting suite.

The kitchen was also massive. It had a black-and-white tiled floor and black counter-tops against pale-beech units. Elise was standing at the far end of the room, peeling and chopping vegetables, before throwing them into a pan on the black range cooker. She looked around with a smile. 'Ah, the little one is refreshed now?' Leaving her work, she came over to fuss over Mario. 'He is adorable, and he is so like his father!'

'Yes...' Abbie felt her heart contract at those words. 'But he's a bit crotchety because he's hungry.'

'Put him down.' Elise drew out a high chair from beside the kitchen table. 'I'll make him some lunch.'

Cots and now high chairs, Abbie noted dryly. *Damon has got himself organised.*

'Thank you, Elise, but I can manage. You continue with your work. I don't want to disturb you.' As Abbie put the child into the chair, she spotted the bag she had brought with her that contained all the paraphernalia Mario needed for meal times. Their driver must have brought it in—or maybe Damon. 'Have you seen Damon, by the way?'

She tried to sound nonchalant as she asked the question, but inside she felt taut with tension.

'He came in a few moments ago to tell me he's going over to his apartment in town to sort a few things out.' Elise glanced over at her with a smile. 'Congratulations on your engagement, by the way.'

'Thank you.' Abbie wondered if Elise found this situation as strange as she did. A whirlwind wedding and an un-expected child all catered for in the space of forty-eight hours—it was a lot for anyone to get his or her head around. And, in fairness to Damon, he must still be in shock himself from learning he was a father. 'Did Damon say when he'd be back?' She wanted to see him, to try and make things better again.

'I rather assumed he wouldn't be,' Elise answered with a frown. 'He said he would be sleeping there tonight as it might be bad luck to see his bride on the eve of the wedding.' She must have seen the look of surprise on Abbie's face because she immediately looked concerned. 'He didn't tell you?'

Abbie shook her head.

'Maybe you both have a touch of pre-wedding nerves, hmm?' Elise looked over at her with sudden sympathy.

She thinks we've had a lovers' tiff and Damon has marched

off, Abbie realised. She wished suddenly that it were that simple. 'Perhaps.' She shrugged evasively. She couldn't possibly begin to tell the woman what was really going on; it was far too embarrassing.

'Damon has been a bachelor who has enjoyed his freedom—this is a big step,' Elise said soothingly. 'He's bound to be a bit apprehensive…'

'Yes, I'm sure.' Abbie's tone was dry. She knew exactly what Elise meant when she said Damon was a bachelor who enjoyed his freedom—no doubt he'd enjoyed more women than there were days in the year. She'd seen the way women looked at him. He was like a magnet for them. As for feeling apprehensive now—she didn't think Damon was in the slightest bit worried. As far as he was concerned, he would be gaining a legalised mistress tomorrow, nothing more.

'And it is difficult for you too,' Elise was continuing smoothly. 'You have come to a new country, given up everything you know. It's exciting, but also scary. There is bound to be tension.'

'Yes.' Elise had definitely got the last bit of that statement right. 'I don't even know him that well,' she found herself admitting softly.

'Signor Cyrenci is a very honourable and decent man. He's had a lot of sadness, with the death of his father. Watching someone you love die…' Elise shook her head. 'Well, it was terrible for him. His father was such a good man, and so strong and vital until illness struck.'

'When was that?' Abbie asked softly.

'Must be over two years ago now.'

'Around the time he lost his business?' Abbie felt an ice-like chill start to seep through her.

Elise nodded. 'It was some time after that, yes.'

'I didn't know!' Abbie felt distraught. Had the stress of losing his business made Damon's father ill?

Elise shrugged. 'Well, it's in the past—Signor Cyrenci probably doesn't want to remember it. Things are happier now, and you are getting married tomorrow.' Elise smiled. 'I'm so pleased for you both. Signor Cyrenci deserves this chance of happiness.'

But the reassuring words didn't help at all; Abbie felt sick inside.

'Are you OK?' Elise was looking at her strangely now.

'Yes.' Abbie tried to pull herself together, but she wasn't OK—she was anything but OK.

No wonder Damon wanted to punish her. Maybe he blamed her for not only helping to ruin his father financially but also for contributing towards his death.

'Do you want to sit down? I'll look after Mario.'

The housekeeper's kindness made her want to cry. She didn't deserve any kindness. She was guilty. Guilty by association…guilty of having a father who wrecked lives. 'I don't want to put you to any trouble.'

'Nonsense, it is no trouble. I told Signor Cyrenci I will be glad to help with Mario. I have had three children of my own; two boys and a girl. They are all grown up now.'

Abbie was grateful for the cheerfully efficient tones soothing over her, and grateful when the woman took over from her to heat Mario's lunch. She really didn't feel capable of anything right now.

'Thank you, Elise.' She smiled tremulously at the woman. 'If you are sure, maybe I'll go into the garden for a few moments and get some fresh air.'

It was a relief to step outside the back door, a relief not to have to pretend that everything was all right. It sounded as if Damon's father had died as a result of her father's actions. She walked around the side of the house, the gravel crunching beneath her feet whilst her mind crunched over and over the past.

There was sweet warmth to the summer morning, but Abbie felt cold inside. Her father had ruined so many lives.

She remembered the emotions that had swamped her as she'd watched her mother's life ebbing away. The helplessness of the situation, merged with the anger—then the guilt. If she hadn't helped her mother to escape from her marriage, she would have got treatment sooner and then maybe she could have got better.

Did Damon feel like that when he looked at her? Did he think if he hadn't gone away with her to Palm Springs that his father might be alive today?

If so then he would never forgive her, because he could never forgive himself. Those kinds of feelings could eat you away inside.

She paused as she reached the front of the house and saw the silver-blue sports car that Damon had given her the keys to that morning. She didn't want his gifts. She didn't want his money. All she wanted was to make things better between them again. But that hope seemed further away than ever now.

'Come out to admire your new acquisition, I see.'

Damon's mocking tones made her whirl around in surprise. He was standing a few yards away from her on the front doorstep, watching her. She noticed he'd changed into a pair of black jeans teamed with a black T-shirt. He looked heart-wrenchingly handsome, every inch the haughty Sicilian, master of all he surveyed.

Tomorrow he would be her husband. The knowledge drummed inside her with insistent force.

And then what would happen between them?

'Actually, I was just getting some fresh air.' She hastily tried to pull herself together. 'Elise told me you'd gone to your apartment in town.'

'I have one or two loose ends to tie up here first.'

She nodded and looked away from him. 'At least you've got the business side of things taken care of for our wedding tomorrow.' She tried to sound nonchalant.

Damon watched her through narrowed eyes. There was something poignant about the way she said that. She looked so innocent, so…

He swore under his breath. What the hell was the matter with him? She looked sad because he'd forced her to sign his contract, and she knew now that she wouldn't be able to have a quickie divorce in a few months' time and walk away with his fortune.

That was the type of person she was, and he couldn't allow her big blue eyes and gorgeous figure to cloud that reality in his mind.

He couldn't believe that in the office this morning he'd been filled with remorse for what he was doing to her—filled with shame for making her undress. And all the time she had been the one trying to seduce him into throwing away the prenuptial contract!

And now here she was, out surveying her car—weighing up how much it was worth, no doubt.

She was treacherous!

'Yes, the business side of things is in place,' he replied coolly. 'All we need now is the piece of paper from the registrar.'

She nodded and moved to push her blonde hair out of her face as a soft breeze caught it. The silky tumble of her hair around her shoulders made him think about how she had looked when she'd pulled her top off this morning.

He'd wanted her so much. He'd never desired any woman as much as her. How he had managed to regain his control and pull back from her, he didn't know. All he did know was that tomorrow he would make up for lost time; he would take her again and again until he'd purged some of this need for her out of his body.

'So it's to be a civil ceremony?' She maintained eye contact with him, and tried not to flinch from the fire in his eyes as he watched her.

'Of course it is. Were you hoping for a big high-society wedding? A white dress, your father giving you away perhaps?'

The derisive tone hurt. 'I wasn't hoping for anything.' She tried to angle her chin up a little further. 'I tried to tell you that this morning, that we could just live together…' She struggled for the right words, but she couldn't find them.

As she looked up into his eyes she wanted to tell him that she was sorry about his father—that she was desperately sorry for the part she had played, that she would try to make things up to him…in any way he wanted. But she couldn't say any of it; the words were stuck amidst a well of tears lodged deep inside.

Damon shook his head and came closer to her. 'No, darling Abbie, I think it's best that our arrangement is written down in black and white. You will marry me tomorrow and become a dutiful wife and mother.'

The scorn was sizzling, but she didn't rise to it. 'I'll do whatever you want, Damon,' she said softly instead.

Damon felt a flare of exhilaration as he realised he'd finally brought her to heel.

CHAPTER SEVEN

IT WAS her wedding day.

As Abbie stood in her bedroom and surveyed her reflection in the cheval mirror, she still couldn't quite believe that it was happening—that she was going to marry Damon Cyrenci.

As a little girl she had always maintained quite staunchly that when she grew up she would never get married. She supposed her parents' marriage had put her off; John and Elizabeth Newland had certainly not been a glowing advertisement for the institution.

She remembered telling her mother once when she'd been about ten that she didn't even want a boyfriend let alone a husband. Her mother had laughed. 'Abbie, when you grow up and find someone you truly love then you will change your mind. And I hope when you do that you find the kind of man who is protective and tender and strong—someone who lets you find your wings and soar. With that kind of love, you can conquer the world.'

Why was she thinking about that now? Abbie blinked back the tears. She couldn't think about her mother today—this was already hard enough.

Her eyes drifted down over her suit. She was wearing an ivory silk pencil-skirt that finished just under the knee, teamed with a matching nipped-in jacket that showed off her tiny waist and the swell of her breast.

On Damon's insistence she had allowed his chauffeur to drop her into town yesterday afternoon so that she could buy something to wear.

'Buy some new lingerie as well,' Damon had instructed as he'd peeled some notes out of his wallet.

She'd turned away from him before he'd been able to press the money into her hand. 'I can afford my own dress and underwear, Damon,' she had told him forcefully.

'But we both know that what you really want is to spend this…don't we?' He'd pulled her back and tucked the notes down into her bra.

Just thinking about that now made her upset and furious all over again.

He really thought that she was just interested in money. She bit down on her lip. She understood why he thought that. From his point of view she had lived off her father's ill-gotten profits without shame or remorse. She was calculating and mercenary. There was nothing she could say that would change the past. She had done what she had done and Damon's father had died a broken man. She could only hope that once they were married he would get to know the real her, would realise she had never meant to hurt him, and that deep down she wasn't a bad person.

Damon hadn't been there when she'd returned from her shopping trip. He'd spent the night at his apartment in town. Elise had told her that he would meet her today at the town hall, where they would be married.

She wondered how he had spent his last night as a bachelor, and how he was feeling this morning. What was he thinking? Had he spent the night with another woman?

That thought brought a punch with it that really hurt.

There was a knock on the door. 'The car is ready and waiting whenever you are,' Elise called out cheerfully.

But would Damon be ready and waiting for her? Maybe he'd decided that a marriage without love wasn't worth having, and maybe he was right except the thought of him walking away from her now hurt so much she could hardly breathe.

'Abbie?' Elise knocked on the door again. 'You're running a little late.'

With difficulty Abbie pulled herself together and went to open the door.

'Oh, you look so beautiful.' Elise smiled with delight as she saw her.

'Thank you.' Abbie reached to take her son from the woman. 'Has he been good for you?'

'A little angel,' Elise said quickly. 'Now, you mustn't worry about him this afternoon. I'll take good care of him.'

Abbie nodded. She'd wanted to bring Mario with her to the ceremony, but Damon had insisted that he stay behind with Elise.

'A few minutes and it will all be over,' he'd told her firmly. 'Why disrupt his routine? He has an afternoon nap, is that not so?'

'Yes, but—'

'Then we will leave him to his sleep. He is a baby, Abbie. He won't know what is going on. What happens between us tomorrow is between consenting adults. The only thing that will be important to Mario is that he has both his parents with him as he grows up.'

Abbie hugged the child close now, and he wriggled in her arms. He was tired; she could see his eyes starting to close.

'I'll put him down in a few minutes,' Elise told her soothingly. 'Then I'll turn on the baby monitor and listen out for him.'

'Come up and check on him as well,' Abbie said. 'Just in case…'

'Yes. Please don't worry. I know all about taking care of babies. I'm not just a mother, I'm also a grandmother.'

With a smile Abbie handed her baby back over to the woman. She knew Mario would be fine with Elise. She was capable and kind, and Mario seemed to like her. Her real worry was what lay ahead of her.

Elise accompanied her back down the stairs, and stood framed in the doorway with Mario in her arms as she watched Abbie getting into the limousine.

The white-hot heat of the afternoon made the atmosphere strangely silent, as if everything was lulled into sleep. The scent of lavender and jasmine was heavy in the air. The chauffeur closed the door and climbed behind the wheel. Abbie waved at Elise and Mario, then settled back into the empty silence of the car.

She watched the scenery pass by. For a while there was an arid landscape of cacti, then dazzling mountain villages surrounded by lemon-and-orange groves against the backdrop of a cerulean blue sky.

The limousine pulled into a village square and ground to a halt under the shade of a large tree. Abbie thought that they would be getting married in the city where she had shopped for her outfit yesterday, but this town was quaintly charming, and had almost a surreal, romantic feel about it.

She smiled sadly at the thought. She was sure Damon hadn't chosen this location for any reasons of the heart.

She looked around. The buildings were painted a dazzling white and the narrow streets were cobbled. Somewhere a bell was chiming. But there wasn't a soul about. Abbie wondered where Damon was. Maybe he had stood her up. Maybe she'd been right about last night.

A black cat asleep under the shade of the tree uncurled to watch with curious green eyes as the chauffeur opened the car door for her.

Then as she stepped into the heat of the afternoon she looked up, and her glance met with Damon's.

Abbie felt her heart dart with a burst of pure pleasure.

He was standing at the top of some steps leading into an impressive-looking building. He looked so handsome in the formal suit, his dark hair glinting in the sun, that she found herself rooted to the spot just drinking him in, committing this moment to memory.

The car door slammed closed behind her, bringing her back to reality, and she walked slowly across to where he was waiting.

Although he was leaning nonchalantly against the pillar of the doorway, there was nothing casual about the way he was watching her. She noticed his dark Sicilian eyes held that blatantly bold look—a look that took in everything about her from her high heels to the way she had secured her hair up. A look that practically undressed her and made her sizzle inside with tension, but also with an answering need, a need that she didn't even want to try and acknowledge right at this moment.

'Hello.' As she reached his side, she smiled up at him uncertainly. What did one say in this situation? 'Am I late?' She cringed—that sounded absurd given the circumstances.

But he smiled back, his lips tugging in a crooked line. 'As a matter of fact, you are. But you were worth the wait.'

The husky undertone made her warm inside. 'That's all right, then.' She tried to sound nonchalant.

'I suppose it is.' He held out a hand. 'So, shall we go get this over with?'

She hesitated for just a moment before putting her hand in his and allowing him to lead her inside.

The possessive touch of his skin against hers made her even more nervous. It was dark inside the building, dark and cool. Her high heels echoed on the marble floors as he led her towards another door and opened it.

The room they walked into had a high ceiling and an ornate upper gallery. A large stained-glass window filtered sunshine in shafts of red and blue across the large wooden table at the top. Behind it there was a throne-like chair and a stand that held both the Sicilian and the Italian flags.

Wooden seating was arranged in the auditorium, probably enough for fifty people. But only a group of three waited for them at the top of the room, a woman and two men. All were dressed smartly. The men wore grey suits and the woman, who was an attractive brunette of perhaps forty, was wearing a blue business-like trouser suit.

'Signor Cyrenci.' The woman reached to shake his hand, and Damon let go of Abbie to greet her. For a moment the conversation was in rapid Italian and then the woman smiled at Abbie. 'My apologies, Ms Newland, I didn't realise you didn't speak Italian. The ceremony today will be conducted in English. We have two witnesses for you, Luigi Messini and Alfredi Grissillini, both clerks who work here.' The woman smoothly introduced the men to her, and they nodded their heads in acknowledgement. 'Now, shall we proceed?'

As Abbie and Damon moved to take two chairs placed before the table, the woman took the throne-like seat behind.

This all felt unreal, Abbie thought as she listened to the woman talking about the institution of marriage whilst at the same time taking out some documentation from a drawer.

She glanced over at Damon, who was listening intently. Her eyes moved over his rugged features, taking in the firm, square jaw, the sensual curve of his lips, the aristocratic nose. His thick hair gleamed an almost blue-black streaked with just a few strands of silver at the temple; it was brushed back from his face in an almost careless manner. She loved his hair, loved running her fingers through it when he kissed her.

The thought of him kissing her made her stomach do a weird flip of desire.

She glanced away from him hurriedly as the woman asked them both to stand.

'Abigail Newland, do you take this man, Damon Allessio Cyrenci, as your lawfully wedded husband? Do you promise to love, honour and obey him and for all time stay true only to him?'

Abbie looked over at Damon. He was watching her with an unfathomable expression in his dark eyes. She felt her heart speed up, hitting against her ribcage with a fierce intensity that was almost painful.

'I do.'

He smiled, and she tried to pull her thoughts together as they jumbled together inside her in the craziest of emotions.

'Damon Allessio Cyrenci, do you take this woman, Abigail, as your lawfully wedded wife, to have and to hold from this day forward?'

It wasn't lost on Abbie that the vows he took were different from hers. He'd written what he wanted. He'd made her promise to obey him—whilst he'd promised only to have and to hold. Damon did what he wanted, and was asserting that this was the way it would be from now on.

She felt a surge of pure anger. But as he took her hand in his, and slipped the plain gold band into place, he smiled at her and this time there was something in his eyes that stilled her anger.

'I now pronounce you man and wife.' The woman smiled at them. 'May I be the first to congratulate you on your new life together.'

'Thank you.' Damon didn't break eye contact with Abbie as he answered, and for a moment it was almost as if he were saying thank you to her.

'I suppose we should seal the deal with a kiss…hmm?' he asked her softly. He didn't wait for a reply. He leaned down, and his lips grazed tenderly over hers.

The sensual feeling sent shivers of desire racing through her entire body. She kissed him back tentatively, yet she desperately wanted more, wanted this place and these strangers to melt away and leave them alone to finish what they had started such a long time ago.

Damon pulled back from her, and then it was time for them to sign the register.

Abbie watched the coloured shafts of light slant over the papers, the light turning them to rose pink then to gold as they were moved for her signature. A few minutes later they were outside again in the fierce sun.

Had that really happened? Was she really married? Abbie looked up at the handsome Sicilian beside her. He was a stranger to her in so many ways, and yet so achingly familiar.

Damon glanced down at her and smiled. 'So, how are you feeling, Mrs Cyrenci?'

Abbie didn't know how she was feeling. 'Shell-shocked, I think,' she admitted softly.

Their chauffeur opened the doors of the limousine for them, and it was a relief to slip into the air-conditioned cool.

A bottle of champagne waited for them on ice, and Damon sat opposite her to uncork it as the vehicle glided smoothly out of the square.

He handed a glass across to her, and then sat back to give her his undivided attention.

How was it that he only had to look at her like that and the adrenalin started pumping wildly through her body? Was it something about his eyes? He did have the sexiest eyes of any man she'd ever met. Or was it his aura? He did radiate a powerful magnetism. Whatever it was, it really got to Abbie, made her temperature soar so much that she wanted to melt, made her heart race, made her body tingle with pleasure, made her think about the pleasure he could give her...

Hurriedly she looked away from him. Silence stretched between them. She felt awkward. She felt like she needed to say something to break the tension rising inside her.

'I can't believe that we actually got married,' she managed at last.

His lips curved in a smile. 'Well, we did. And you made a very sexy bride. I like the outfit.'

'Thank you.'

'Your hair also looks good like that.'

His eyes moved over her face, noticing the velvety softness of her skin, the blush of her cheeks and the peach-satin sheen of her lips.

She'd taken his breath away when she'd stepped out of the car. He'd never wanted anyone as much as he'd wanted her at that moment. The suit was perfect: sexy yet sophisticated. And her hair was also perfect—also sophisticated, but the tendrils that had escaped to curl around the beauty of her face gave her softness and a fragile vulnerability that tore him up inside.

She raised her blue eyes towards him now and he felt the same wrenching feeling inside. He wished he could rid himself of this sensation. He wanted to feel lust for her, nothing more...

'I told Frederic to drive us back to my apartment in town. The staff there will have laid us out a late lunch. And then I'm taking you to bed for the afternoon.' He said the words in a low, commanding tone and watched as her skin flared with colour. 'Are you hungry?'

Abbie hurriedly glanced away from him. Her heart was racing. She didn't want to eat. She didn't know what she wanted…

The thought of spending the afternoon in bed with Damon was infinitely exciting, yet terrifying, all at the same time.

'Not really.' She didn't dare look over at him. She felt foolish and unsure of everything. 'And don't you think we should go back to the house, not to your apartment? I want to check on Mario.'

'Mario will still be asleep.' Damon reached across and topped up her glass of champagne. 'And Elise is very trustworthy.'

She couldn't argue with that.

Would he ask her to undress the way he had yesterday… Would he be gentle? In the past Damon had always been a passionate yet sensitive lover. She remembered the tenderness in his kiss yesterday, and a floodgate of feelings for him opened up that truly terrified her.

She took a few hurried sips of her champagne and then put the glass down in the holder next to her.

Damon watched as she nervously fiddled with a couple of buttons on her jacket.

'You should take that off now,' he instructed.

Something about the instruction made her nerves stretch even more. 'Damon, I know you got me to promise that I would obey you, but I have to inform you right now that it is not a promise I intend to keep.' She suddenly angled her chin up and sent him a look of fierce defiance from her flashing eyes.

To her disconcertment he merely looked amused at her outburst. 'Breaking your vows already?' He mocked her with dark eyes. 'Dear me, Abbie…' He shook his head. 'That simply just won't do.'

'No, it won't!' She lowered her tone but her voice trembled alarmingly. 'I may be your wife, but I have my own mind, Damon. There are certain things that I will not be told about.'

'And what are they?' Damon sounded like he was enjoying himself—as if she were the most entertaining of women.

'What to wear, what to do—and on the subject of Mario—'

'On the subject of Mario we will confer and decide things together,' he cut across her firmly and smiled. 'You are his mother, and I respect that.'

The words took her aback, took the fire out of her argument.

'But as for what you wear and what you do especially in the bedroom…on that you will defer to me.'

His arrogance inflamed her senses, yet the melting eyes that held with hers made the warm darts of desire increase inside her.

She looked away from him, annoyed with herself.

'And by the way when I told you to take your jacket off it was because I thought you looked uncomfortable,' he added. 'I wasn't going to tell you to take everything else off as well.' He glanced at her. 'Well, not yet, anyway.'

'Very amusing.' Abbie fought down the flood of heat inside her. He thought he was so clever. 'And I can't believe you made me promise to obey you.' She shook her head.

Damon laughed. 'Well, you were late. I thought I'd fill the time waiting for you in a productive manner.'

The limousine pulled up by a marina. Luxury yachts bobbed on tranquil clear water, and there were some upmarket boutiques and restaurants. The place had a very sophisticated feel. It was obviously a playground for the moneyed, yet it still retained a charm and character from the past. Fisherman sat mending their nets by the harbour wall, and the new buildings along the quay merged seamlessly with old.

'My apartment is just here.' Damon pointed to a modern building.

It was all very swish, Abbie thought as she followed him into the foyer. A security guard greeted him by name, and then they stepped into a lift.

Damon's apartment was at the top of the building. By contrast with his house, it was ultra-modern to the point of minimalist. A bachelor's playground, Abbie thought as she glanced around, all tubular steel and appliances of science. Wall-mounted TV's, remote-control gadgets for everything, probably even the cooker. And the bed… Her eyes skimmed past the room that held the enormous king-sized bed.

Damon opened doors that led out to a large terrace. They were high up, and the view was spectacular across the harbour and the alluring blue glitter of the sea.

Someone had gone to a lot of trouble, and had set a table outside for lunch. The table was covered with a crisp white-linen cloth, and was laid with silver and crystal ware. An ice bucket held a bottle of champagne, and there were balloons everywhere across the wooden decking.

Damon shook his head as he surveyed the scene. 'I made the mistake of telling the staff that it was my wedding day—they must have thought balloons were a nice touch.'

'They are.' The fact that someone had gone to that trouble somehow touched Abbie. She met Damon's steady gaze and shrugged. 'Well, I like them…it's lovely.'

His lips twisted in an amused smile. 'There's something you'll probably like a little better waiting for you on the table.'

She saw the jewellery box sitting on the white place-setting, but didn't go to pick it up. 'What is it?' she asked him huskily.

'A little bauble to mark our wedding day. Go and have a look.'

Before she could answer, the ring of Damon's mobile phone interrupted them. He glanced at the dial before answering, then disappeared inside for a few moments.

Abbie could hear him talking in Italian, but she was barely listening. Why couldn't he get it through his head that she didn't want his gifts? She opened the box and glanced inside. Nestling on velvet was an exquisite necklace, a single diamond teardrop on a gold chain. It was probably worth a fortune.

For a moment her mind ran back to their conversation when he'd first suggested they get married, and she had rounded on him in outrage. *'You think I'd tie myself into a loveless marriage...?'*

'For wealth, security and all the baubles and trappings of luxury you could possibly want? Yes I do.'

She snapped the lid closed and put the box down as if it had burnt her. Then she moved towards the balustrade to look down at the harbour, but tears blinded her eyes.

'So, do you like the necklace?' Damon appeared behind her again.

She didn't answer him, couldn't answer him.

'It is real,' he told her dryly.

She closed her eyes. She understood why he thought of her the way he did—she just wished it didn't hurt.

His phone rang again, and after a moment's hesitation he took the call. 'Sorry about that,' he murmured a moment later. 'I've got an important deal going through soon.'

Abbie had been glad of the interruption; at least it had given her a moment to pull herself together. 'That's all right, you've got to get your priorities in order.'

'Well, today *you* are my priority—so I've switched the phone off now.'

She wished he meant that. She stared pensively out across the expanse of sea.

'So, shall we have something to eat?'

'I told you, I'm not really hungry.' She felt too tense to eat, too tense to even look around at him. 'I don't know what we are doing here. We should really have just gone back to the house.'

'You know what we are doing here, Abbie,' he told her softly.

She closed her eyes. 'Mario will be waking up soon.'

'Mario will be fast asleep.'

Abbie didn't say anything. She knew he was right, she knew she had no need to worry about Mario. She just wished that Damon hadn't bought her that necklace; she just wished that things between them were different. That the silly balloons meant something to him! What on earth was the matter with her? How stupid was that? she mocked herself fiercely.

She pulled herself together and blinked the tears away. Then, steeling herself, she turned to look at him.

'Elise told me about your father,' she said suddenly.

'What did she tell you?' he asked coolly.

'About his death—you know, soon after him losing the business, and…I just wanted to tell you how sorry I am. And I never wanted any of that to happen.'

The sincerity in her voice and in her eyes perplexed him.

'Well, I suggest we forget about the past and about the outside world for now, and relax.'

'But you can't forget about the past, can you?' she asked softly. 'And your father died because of it!'

'My father died because he smoked heavily all of his life,' Damon said with a frown.

'Oh! I thought… I thought it was the stress of losing the business.'

Damon watched the emotions flicker through her eyes. She looked like she had been genuinely distressed by the notion— but he only had to remember how cold-blooded she had been in the past to know that it was another of her little acting ploys. A woman who cared about hurting people didn't go around deceiving them, lying to them, didn't deliberately use her body to hurt others and get what she wanted.

'Abbie, you didn't contribute to his death, but you are right about one thing—I can't forget about the past or what you are. Because I'd be a fool to forget it.' His eyes swept over her suddenly and the contempt in them lashed at her.

'Feeling like that, I'm surprised you went through with the wedding,' she whispered rawly.

'On the contrary, when you stepped out of the car today and into the square I knew positively that I was doing the right thing.'

'Did you?' Her eyes lifted to his. 'Why?'

He looked at her for a long, considered moment and she could feel her heart racing against her chest.

'Because we have a child to look after. Mario has to come first now.'

Given the circumstances she knew she should be content with that, but the coldness of his response added to the ache inside her.

She watched as he turned away from her and lifted the bottle of champagne.

'Let's have a drink.'

He was so cavalier and nonchalant, and it made Abbie's temper rise. 'It's very noble of you, putting your needs to one side for your child's security,' she grated sardonically.

'Who said anything about putting my needs to one side?' He flashed her an amused look and she felt herself blush. 'I have absolutely no intention of doing that.'

He passed her the glass of champagne, and she was annoyed to find that her hand wasn't quite steady as she accepted it.

'But I want things to be right for Mario,' he continued smoothly. 'I know what it's like to grow up without a parent, Abbie. My mother walked out when I was eight, and… Well, I always vowed that I'd never put a child through that. A child needs stability. Bringing up a family is the ultimate commitment.'

'Is that why you decided to just play the field for all these years?'

He looked over at her wryly. 'Being a bachelor was something I was good at,' he said, his mouth curved with amusement.

Abbie remembered her suspicions earlier that morning, that Damon had been out last night enjoying himself, had brought someone back here to bed.

'And, now that we are married, do you *still* intend to play around?' She forced herself to ask the question even though she wasn't sure she wanted to hear the answer.

Damon watched the way her chin slanted up. What was she thinking? he wondered. Despite the valiant angle of her chin, there was a husky tone to her voice, and that look in her eyes…

He frowned and dragged his thoughts away from the absurd wayward direction they wanted to go in. Abbie's greatest concern was probably only the fact that, if he found someone else, she might lose her golden ticket to riches.

'I thought I made my intentions clear—I want a stable home for Mario.' He held her gaze steadily. 'So I intend to amuse myself playing around with *you* from now on.'

She flushed a little and he smiled. 'I think you will manage to keep me satisfied. You are very attractive, very beautiful, Abbie—but then of course you know that don't you.'

The compliment sat painfully with her.

Damon watched the shadowy, dark glints of sapphire in her eyes. She was so desirable, he felt his stomach tie up with the thought of having her now…felt himself harden. He just wished she didn't stir up these other emotions inside him.

Like now, for example; something in her expression made him long to forget what she was and reach out to hold her tenderly. It had been the same today when she'd stepped out of the car into the square, and also when she'd looked up at him whilst taking her vows.

She wasn't going to get under his skin ever again, Damon reminded himself fiercely. When he touched her, when he held her, it would be to take her, possess her, use her the way she had once used him.

He picked up his own glass of champagne. 'So what shall we drink to—the future, hmm? Our new arrangement?'

'How about your new acquisition?' she supplied, her eyes sparkling with that mixture of defiance and rawness that he was starting to know so well.

'Or to Mario?' he suggested. 'The one thing we got absolutely right?'

She smiled at him suddenly, and it was like the sun had come out from behind the clouds.

His eyes moved over her slowly. 'So, here we are, Mrs Cyrenci…alone at last.' His voice was teasingly sexy.

'Are we?' She tried not to sound apprehensive. 'Where are the staff?'

'All gone. We have a very good arrangement that gives me maximum privacy.'

'Everyone around you is very cooperative.'

'Apart from one…' His eyes moved down over her body with a possessiveness that made her pulses race. 'My wife. The woman who has already informed me today that she intends to break her wedding vows.'

She tried not be affected by the way he was looking at her, but she was. And his teasing tone brought her skin out in strange little goosebumps. She liked the way he referred to her as his wife in that warm way, as if it did mean something to him.

But it doesn't, she tried to remind herself fiercely. He'd already made that clear. She didn't mean anything to him.

Even so when he reached out and trailed one finger along

the side of her face she felt herself melt inside. 'You belong to me now, Abbie,' he said huskily. 'And that means keeping the promises you made today.'

Her heart hammered fiercely against her chest as she looked up at him. 'I'll keep the ones that are most important,' she whispered.

Something about the way she said that, the way she looked at him seared him to the bone. He watched as she put down her glass, reached to unfasten the buttons on her jacket and then slipped it off.

Underneath she wore a peach satin camisole with spaghetti straps. It emphasised the firm upward tilt of her breasts.

Abbie looked up at him and saw the flare of desire in the darkness of his eyes. She liked the way he looked at her. But she knew he didn't love her. She knew what he thought of her.

Still, he did want her. And she needed him to want her. Needed him to fill the aching void inside her. He was the one man she had never really got out of her system. She didn't understand why, and she didn't want to dwell too deeply on the questions. All she knew was how he could make her feel. And she wanted to feel like that again.

'How private are we out here?' She looked up at him from under dark eyelashes.

'About as private as you can get. Why don't you put on the gift I bought for you and take off everything else?'

The seductive comment inflamed her senses. 'I don't want your gift, Damon.' She continued to looked up at him through cloudy blue eyes.

He reached out a hand and stroked it softly down the side of her neck. The caress made her tingle inside. 'Well, I want your gift to me…and I want it right now.'

His fingers moved lower, teasingly stroking her along the edge of the camisole top.

The touch of his fingers brushing against her skin felt so good. She knew what he was talking about, and she didn't try to misunderstand him. There was no point in pretending, not when the gravelly command had made her body burn with a need to comply.

'So…what do you want to do?'

Damon liked the question—liked the way she matched it with a shy, almost faltering look in her big eyes.

'Should I do this…?' He watched as she unfastened her skirt and let it drop to the floor. She was wearing hold-up stockings, and she looked so sexy that he felt he wanted to burst with the intensity of his need for her.

'You should definitely do that,' he told her quietly.

'And how far do you want to go?'

'You know how far I want to go, Abbie,' he instructed. 'All the way.'

CHAPTER EIGHT

HER top followed her skirt onto the floor.

His eyes moved over her body. Her underwear, unlike yesterday, was deliberately provocative. The bra pushed her up, showing the round peaks of her breasts to perfection, her lace pants were hipsters but see-through and as for the lace-top stockings… Well, they were just too sexy for words.

Hell, he wanted her, wanted to fill her completely…possess her completely.

The way he was looking at her made Abbie feel taut with need. She wanted him to take her into his arms, wanted desperately just to be held. 'So…shall I help you out of your jacket?' It was an excuse for her to move closer to him. 'Perhaps unfasten your tie for you?' Her hands slid up over his chest to smooth the jacket away from the breadth of his shoulders. It fell to the floor with her clothes.

She looked up into his eyes as she reached to unfasten his tie.

Before he could think about how or where he wanted her, he was picking her up and turning her so that her back was against the wall. 'You know exactly what you do to me, don't you, with those big blue oh-so-innocent eyes…?'

Her eyes locked with his as she looked up at him breathlessly, and then she trembled as he slowly and deliberately ran his hands over her body, stroking over the curves of her breasts, his fingers finding her nipples through the lace of her bra and squeezing them. The caress shot exquisite darts of pleasure through her body, and like shots of an addictive drug the feelings made her long for so much more.

He smiled as he heard her gasp with need. Then his mouth moved to possess her lips. The kiss was like nothing she had ever experienced before, masterful, fierce; it sent a feeling of passion so strong, so fierce, racing through her that she felt dizzy…possessed, almost. She opened her mouth and let him plunder the softness inside. All the time she could feel the hard warmth of his body pressing against the aching need of hers.

Just when she thought she was going to die with the desire to be closer, to be possessed totally, he pulled back.

'Don't stop!' Her eyes were wild with tumultuous feelings of desire. 'Please, Damon…' She didn't have to go on because suddenly she felt his fingers stroking her through her knickers.

She was wet and ready for him, and as he stroked her some more she shuddered.

'You like that, don't you?' He whispered the words against her ear.

She closed her eyes. Her breasts felt so tight, so hard; they were throbbing with the demand to be touched. Her body was telling her that she had to have him…it was telling her with such insistent force that she couldn't think straight.

Then suddenly she felt him pushing her knickers down and moving her legs further apart, touching her in a way that took her breath away.

She moaned with pleasure when at the same time he pulled her bra down and bent his head to suck on her nipples.

Her body convulsed with enjoyment, and she raked her

fingers through the darkness of his hair, giving herself up to him with a total lack of control.

Just as she thought she was going to die of sheer pleasure, he left her.

'Damon?' The momentary uncertainty in her eyes was almost his undoing.

'We'll continue this inside.'

He took hold of her hand to lead her through to the bedroom.

It was taking every inch of his willpower not to lose control. He wanted her. Just watching her in those high heels, the stockings lovingly curving around her slender thighs... He needed to contain himself, he reminded himself fiercely. But as she sat down on the bed he could hardly wait to get rid of his clothes.

She noticed that he tore his shirt whilst unbuttoning it... She'd made him do that. The knowledge gave her a flip of exhilaration, but it was nothing to the way she felt as her eyes moved over the sheer perfection of his physique.

His body was toned and strong, tapering down to the perfect six-pack. Abbie remembered his body very well, remembered having been in awe of him when she had first seen him naked. Those feelings hadn't changed.

He joined her down on the bed and she made to take off her stockings, but he lifted her up and moved her back against the satin pillows. 'Stay as you are.' He growled the words against her skin as his mouth moved to capture hers again.

His kiss was ragged with need, his fingers insistent as once more they found her nipples, rubbing over them, pushing her bra down further so that they were forced upwards for his mouth to take possession of them again.

He straddled her, and then reached for some contraception before his body captured hers with fervent, demanding thrusts.

She writhed and gasped with pleasure, and then he pulled back from her a little, stroking her tenderly, finding her lips and kissing her with such sweetness, his hands stroking her hair.

He murmured her name almost incoherently as his body dominated hers, taking her with almost ruthless determination and yet at the same time with an exquisite care, possessing her with ardent warmth that made answering warmth flood her body.

He looked down into her eyes and murmured something to her in Italian.

'I like the sound of your voice when you speak in your own language,' she murmured breathlessly. She moaned and arched her back, and ran her fingers down over the powerful muscles of his back.

He said something else that she didn't understand…then took her lips with his, before grazing down her neck to her nipples to suck on them, lick them, and rock her towards a climax that was so forceful and shattering in its intensity that she cried out. Only then did he join her, releasing himself as wave after wave of sheer joy racked through both of their bodies, fusing them together as one.

For a long time they just lay there holding each other. Abbie felt like crying, not with sadness but with sheer joy, because making love with him had been as incredible as she'd remembered. Once again he had conjured up all the crazy feelings of belonging, and had strangely given the power of his love-making a sense of such sweet tenderness.

But this wasn't love, it was just sex, she tried to remind herself fiercely before she got too carried away on flights of fantasy. But the trouble was it didn't feel like it was just sex. She frowned and cuddled a bit closer to him. When he held her, especially like this, the feeling was blissful. It was like the real thing…like she never needed to be lonely again because he was her soul mate.

She closed her eyes and tried to stop analyzing things. It was enough to be in his arms.

He stroked his fingers through her hair almost absentmindedly, and then kissed the top of her head.

It was such a tender gesture that she let her breath out in a sigh. 'Making love with you is so…so good.'

'Yes, the chemistry is as powerful as ever between us. I knew it would be.'

She rolled over a little so that she was looking down at him. 'It is powerful, isn't it?' she breathed huskily. 'You turn me on so much.'

'I noticed.' He smiled at her suddenly, his eyes teasing.

'I kind of noticed that I had a similar effect on you.' She snuggled against him. 'Apart from the obvious—I think you ruined a perfectly good shirt.'

He laughed. 'So how are you with a darning needle, Mrs Cyrenci?'

She smiled. The connection between them felt so strong, the outside world had ceased to exist. Surely he couldn't have made love to her with such searing passion if he felt nothing for her? She wondered, if she took the risk of telling him a little of how she felt right now, would he meet her half way? 'No one's ever made me feel the way you make me feel,' she admitted.

Their eyes locked together, and for a heart-stopping moment she thought he was going to say something similar back to her. She felt so close to him, not just physically but emotionally.

Damon hesitated. She sounded as if she'd really meant that, and there was no doubt that her responses to him had been wildly passionate—she really had wanted him. Making love with her always had been incredible, and it had been better now than he'd even remembered. He felt like he couldn't get enough of holding her, teasing her to arousal, caressing her, kissing her... He frowned. But of course this wasn't making love—there was no emotion involved, he reminded himself fiercely. He had to remember exactly what Abbie was.

Yes, she enjoyed sex, but even the most mercenary of creatures did. Probably what aroused Abbie so much was the thought of all his money.

He ran a tender hand down over the side of her face. That knowledge was difficult to accept when she was looking at him with such sultry blue eyes. But he had to accept it. And at least she did enjoy sex with him—because if she didn't, well, he'd never forced a woman in his life and he certainly wasn't going to start now. 'And that's why our arrangement is going to work so well.' He growled the words against her ear.

Pain spiralled inside her from nowhere. She hadn't expected a declaration of undying love—but she hadn't thought he would remind her quite so dismissively that this was just an arrangement. She could be so stupid sometimes where he was concerned. She pulled away from him abruptly.

'Yes, I suppose you are right.' She tried to match his flippancy so that she could hang on to at least a small shred of pride. She should have known better than to risk lowering any barriers.

Damon watched as she moved away from him, and he was aware of a sudden sharp feeling of regret, as if a precious moment had been lost.

What the hell was the matter with him? He was supposed to be using her for his own pleasure—not making passionate declarations! But for one wild moment he wanted to pull her back, wanted to tell her that she had the same effect on him. That no other woman could make him feel the way she could.

He was losing it, Damon told himself furiously. It had been the same when they were making love: one moment he had been totally enjoying himself with her, and the next she had sighed and cuddled into him and the feelings inside him had completely changed with a swiftness and a power that he'd had no control over. He'd wanted her so much…wanted to hold her close and pleasure her.

He watched as she sat up from him. Her hair had escaped from the pins that had held it up, and it was tousled and sexily dishevelled around her shoulders and her naked breasts, her nipples slightly pink and engorged from the heat of his caresses.

He wanted her again. She was like some kind of nymph who could put a spell on him with just a glance, lure him so easily away from rational thoughts. Well, he wasn't going to allow her to control him with her perfectly staged words and her come-hither looks—he'd fallen for that the first time around.

Abbie was aware that the silence between them was stretching tautly. 'We should be getting back to the house now.'

'You're not going anywhere, Abigail…' He pulled her back towards him suddenly and kissed her again. It was a kiss that sent tingles flooding through her entire body.

It was strange how his lips told her one thing, with their seductive, possessive kisses, and his words told her something completely different with their commanding, slightly mocking edge.

The mix set wildly conflicting thought patterns racing through her. Part of her wanted to pull away from him with a toss of her head—part of her wanted to melt into him. She swallowed hard. She didn't want to stop making love with him. The adrenalin was charging through her veins, changing her into somebody she hardly recognised. She hated herself for being so weak.

'Damon, I need to get myself a drink of water.' She pulled away from him abruptly and he let her go, and watched how she pulled her bra up to cover her swollen nipples, before picking up his shirt from the floor and pulling it on to cover her nakedness.

It swamped her, but it also looked incredibly sexy with her stockings and high heels.

He watched her walk away from him towards the kitchen. How was it that just when he thought he had her tamed and submissive she could so easily turn the tables on him? Damon wondered edgily. He got out of bed and threw on a towelling robe that was hanging on the back of the door.

She was pouring herself a glass of water from a bottle she had found in the fridge.

'I'll have one of those while you are there,' he directed softly.

'OK.' She didn't look round at him but reached to get a glass.

'You look good in my shirt, by the way,' he remarked as his eyes moved down over the long length of her legs. 'Even the way it's ripped is strategically enhancing.' He noticed as she turned that he could see the top of her thighs.

She flicked him a slightly nervous glance. She was good at looking at him with just that mixture of uncertainty and desire. It drove him crazy.

'All you need now is the necklace that I bought for you,' he murmured suddenly.

'I told you, Damon, I don't want your gifts.' Her voice trembled slightly.

'Of course you do.' He disappeared for a moment to pick up the jewellery from outside on the patio. Maybe if she wore this hunk of expensive, beautiful stone around her neck it would remind him of what she was, he thought forcefully. Because every time she looked at him in that raw, almost vulnerable way of hers he was in very real danger of forgetting.

'I don't want that necklace, Damon,' she told him softly

when he came back into the kitchen. 'I don't want you to put it anywhere near me.'

'What's the matter, isn't the diamond big enough to satisfy you?' he rasped.

'Don't, Damon!' The look she shot him was so beseeching that it cut.

It would be so easy to forget what she was. She was so gorgeously desirable, all kitten-warmth and come-to-bed eyes.

But he couldn't allow himself to forget…he just couldn't.

'Abbie, I bought this for you as a wedding present, so the least you can do is damn well wear it on our wedding day.'

'Sorry, but I'm not going to.'

'You are so stubborn!'

'So are you!' She glared at him as she walked across towards him with his glass of water. 'You don't listen to me. I don't want your money or your gifts!'

Who the hell did she think she was fooling? he wondered angrily.

'Come here.' He caught hold of her hand as she approached and pulled her towards him. Then, putting down the water on the kitchen bar, he pulled her towards one of the comfortable chairs in the lounge area and brought her down so that she was straddling his knee.

'Now, hold your hair up out of the way.'

She held his gaze with a mutinous stare.

'Do as I ask, Abbie—it's just a necklace.'

'But it's not, is it?' she asked softly. 'It's *not* just a necklace, it's a symbol of what you really think of me.'

He ignored that and opened up the box to take out the necklace. It flashed fire in the sunlight. 'Lift up your hair,' he ordered again.

When she still didn't comply, he placed it around her neck and fastened it over her hair. Then he reached and pulled her hair up, letting it trail through his fingers like liquid gold as he released it.

The chain fell around her neck, the diamond heavy and cold against her skin. He sat back to look at her. 'There… It looks good.'

She hated it, but she left it where it was and just held his gaze defiantly.

'Abbie, don't look at me like that.' There was rawness in his voice for just a second, a note that was at odds with the arrogant dominance of his actions. 'I'll buy you another necklace tomorrow, one that you can choose for yourself, all right?' As he spoke he trailed a hand over her chin, down the line of her neck.

It wasn't all right, but she couldn't speak, her throat felt too choked. She trembled at his touch; she felt so cold inside, yet just the slightest stroke of his hand made her warm again, stirred up a heat she didn't want, couldn't handle, couldn't control.

'Now, where were we?' He started to unfasten the buttons on the shirt, and then as it fell apart he pulled her bra down, exposing her breasts to the darkness of his eyes.

Her heart was thundering painfully against her chest. She wanted him too, so much it hurt.

His fingers played with her nipples, squeezing them, stroking them until they were hard peaks of need. Her hands moved to rest on his thighs, and his fingers became rougher yet inflamed her all the more.

Then suddenly he was inside her, bouncing her on his knee, watching how her breasts moved with each of his thrusts. He put his hands on her slender hips, controlling her, watching how she writhed, how her hair swung silkily around her shoulders, how the diamond sparkled as it nestled between her cleavage.

As she climaxed she called out his name, and he leaned forward and took one breast into his mouth, sucking on her, until he also reached his own climax.

She wrapped her arms around him and buried her face in the dark softness of his hair, holding him tight against her. Her body was convulsed with pleasure, throbbing from the aftermath of a sensation so pleasurable it had exhausted her totally.

They were wrapped so tightly in each other's arms and he was still inside her, still a part of her, so that it was almost as if they had become one.

He stroked her hair back from her face, and as she pulled away from him a little he captured her lips in a dominant, yet tremendously sensual kiss. She wanted it to go on and on, but he pulled away from her after a few moments.

Spent and exhausted, she cuddled in against him.

She tried to remind herself that part of her should still be angry about the necklace—about his dominant, insensitive ways. But try as she might she couldn't rekindle that anger. It felt too good being held by him.

He doesn't trust me—he doesn't love me—but when he's with me like this he is mine…totally mine, she told herself firmly. And for now that was enough, because she loved him so much.

The thought made fear and shock race through her so violently that she shivered.

'Are you OK?'

The concern in his voice caused even greater emotional waves to smash through her body. 'No, not really.' She buried her head into his neck. She couldn't allow herself to be in love with him—he'd never return the feelings, and it hurt too much. And yet she knew now that she was in love with him. Maybe she had never really stopped loving him, and had just tried to persuade herself that she had because it was the only way she'd been able to cope with losing him.

'I didn't hurt you, did I?' He sounded mortified. 'Abbie, I never intended to hurt you.' He gathered her closer, stroking her hair.

She squeezed her eyes tightly closed against the tears that wanted to flow. 'You didn't hurt me. I just had a momentary pang of…something.'

'Of what?' He held her away from him and looked at the bright glitter in her blue eyes. His heart turned over as a tear spilled down over the pallor of her skin.

She shrugged. 'I don't know, I'm being stupid.' She brushed the tears from her eyes harshly and pulled away from him to stand up. She was going to have to pull herself together. She couldn't possibly tell him that she loved him. She remembered his earlier response to her unguarded comment, and she couldn't risk seeing contempt in his eyes now—couldn't risk losing the little pride she had left. 'Maybe I'm just tired. I didn't sleep well last night and, well, it's quite an emotional business getting married, isn't it?'

He frowned. 'I guess it is. Abbie, I—'

'Are you hungry?' She cut across him firmly and smiled. It was the kind of smile that made his heart drum wildly against his chest. The kind of smile that made him question everything he'd done—everything he'd said to her in the last couple of days.

'Because I am,' she continued swiftly. 'I haven't eaten anything all day. I was too tense this morning for breakfast.'

'Were you?' He watched as she pulled his shirt over her curves.

'Of course. Marriage is a big step and, like you, it's something I said I'd never do.'

She moved away from him. In truth she wasn't in the slightest bit hungry, but she needed to do something—needed to change the direction of her thoughts to pull them away from the dangerous edge where they were poised precariously.

She opened the fridge door and looked in. 'There are all sorts of goodies in here—do you want something?'

Damon belted his dressing gown and stood up. Was it his imagination, or was her voice too bright? 'I'll have whatever you are having.'

Abbie brought out some smoked salmon and some salad and put it on the breakfast bar.

'Shall we sit here to eat? I know the table is laid outside, but I just want a snack, and somehow this seems more relaxed.'

'Yes, that's fine.' Damon pulled out one of the breakfast bar-stools and sat opposite her.

The glasses of water from earlier were beside them. 'I'll top these up with ice,' he said as he leaned over to the ice dispenser. 'They might be warm now.'

'Thanks.'

He noticed that she avoided his eyes as he put the glass down beside her again.

Why had she cried? The question burnt through him. Now he thought carefully back over their love-making, he didn't think he'd been rough. She'd seemed to enjoy it, had moaned, with pleasure not pain. Had called out his name with a little husky moan.

Just thinking about it made him want her all over again. How was it that even now, after a wildly passionate afternoon, he still needed her?

He forced himself not to think about that now.

'So you were nervous this morning?' he asked quietly.

'A bit.' She reached for the water and took a long swallow. 'Weren't you?'

There was a moment's silence, and she shook her head. 'Sorry, silly question.'

'It's not a silly question. I had a few last-minute qualms.'

'Really?' She looked at him then.

'I've been a bachelor a long time. Of course I thought deeply about what I was doing this morning.'

She nodded. 'Did you go out last night?' She tried to sound casual, as if she didn't really care what he'd done. But she did care, she cared way, *way* too much about everything.

He shook his head. 'I worked. I had a lot to sort out so I could have a few days off with you now.'

'Oh!' She smiled at him and felt some of the tension inside her easing as he smiled back. He had such a gorgeously sexy smile...

She reached for her glass of water again.

'Thirsty?'

'Yes. I know it's air-conditioned in here, but I feel a bit hot.'

'Again?' He looked at her with a mixture of warmth and humour, and she blushed prettily.

'Well, let me eat something and get my strength back first,' he murmured softly.

She liked the look he slanted across at her, liked the provocatively teasing tone in his voice. It made her sizzle inside.

It was nice sitting here with him like this. If she didn't think too deeply about things, she could pretend that they were just a regular couple—just married and too much in love to keep their hands off each other.

'You know what's missing in here?' he asked suddenly.

'Some music?'

'No, but that could be arranged.' He smiled. 'No, I was talking about the view.'

'You have a spectacular view.' She turned her head to look out the window across the dazzle of the blue sea.

'But it could be better.' He leaned across and unbuttoned the shirt she wore so that he could see the full curves of her body in the lacy bra.

The touch of his hands against her skin made her flare with a deep longing for him.

'And maybe we should get rid of this.'

To her surprise, he reached and unfastened the necklace from around her neck and set it down to one side.

Their eyes held across the table.

Her heart was thundering wildly against her chest as he smiled at her.

'Is that better?' he asked huskily.

She nodded. 'Infinitely better.'

CHAPTER NINE

ABBIE was pretending to read a book as she lay next to the pool, but really she was watching Damon. He was playing in the water with Mario. They'd got some water wings for the child, and he loved being in the pool with his father. He was laughing with delight now as Damon allowed him to kick his legs and make a splash whilst he supported him carefully in strong arms.

She smiled as she watched him raise the child into the air then dip his toes down again in the water, and she loved hearing Mario laugh. She loved watching the muscles ripple powerfully in her husband's arms as he moved. He really had a dreamily wonderful body, she thought distractedly as her eyes moved over his bronzed torso, noticing how his skin gleamed in the bright sunshine.

He looked like he worked out every day. There was a gym down in the basement of the house, but Abbie had never seen him use it. She'd asked him last night as they'd lain together in the deep comfort of their double bed if he ever used it, and he had laughed. 'Not enough hours in the day—anyway, I'm saving all my energy to work out with you.'

They certainly had 'worked out' a lot together this week. Just thinking about it made Abbie's heart race. Since Damon had taken that necklace from around her neck, it was as if they had turned some kind of a corner in their relationship.

She knew nothing had fundamentally changed—deep down he still distrusted her. But it was as if some sort of unspoken truce had occurred, as if a line had been drawn under the past. And Abbie was glad of it, because this had been the most wonderful week of her life. She loved the way Damon could make her feel.

She loved the way he couldn't seem to get enough of her, because she felt exactly the same. Even now, watching him in the pool playing with their son, she wanted him. Yet just a few hours ago he'd taken her back to bed for a siesta. Just thinking about that 'siesta' now made her melt with longing all over again.

She also loved the way he was with Mario, protective and gentle, yet fun. She'd noticed how over the week the little boy had fast grown attached to him, his dark eyes lighting up whenever his father walked into the room.

Damon looked up now and caught her watching him. 'Why don't you come in and join us?'

'No, it's OK, you carry on.' She smiled at him. In truth she didn't want to get too close to him, because she was feeling extremely aroused just watching him. And she didn't want him to know just how much she wanted him *again*.

'Come on, the water is lovely.' He splashed some of it in her direction and the cold hit the heat of her skin, making her jump.

'Ow! It's freezing! I'm definitely not coming in!'

'Don't be such a chicken.' Damon lifted Mario out of the water.

The little boy chuckled as Damon splashed Abbie again.

'Damon, stop!' She swung her long legs over the edge of the sun lounger and put her book down.

Damon's eyes swept over her body with bold approval. She was wearing a very skimpy black-and-white bikini and it looked sensational on her. 'Come into the pool with us,' he said firmly. 'We need you.'

'No, you don't.'

'Yes, *I* do.' He smiled with that half tug of his lips that made her go hot inside.

She watched as he hoisted himself out of the water, his muscles rippling powerfully as they flexed, water gleaming on his broad chest. He slicked his dark wet hair back from his face and grinned at her. 'So are you coming in of your own accord, or do I have to carry you?'

'Don't you dare!'

'Is that a challenge?' He laughed, and before she could say another word he had swept her off her feet and up into his arms. His body was cold against the heat of hers, but he felt so good. She wrapped her arms around his neck.

'Put me down.'

'Amazing how words can say one thing and the body another,' he teased.

'Yes, I often think that about you.'

'Do you? And what is my body saying now, hmm?'

'It's saying, *I adore you, Abigail Cyrenci.*' She whispered the words against his ear. *'And I wouldn't dream of putting you in that cold water…'*

The rest of her words were drowned out as he jumped with her into the pool. Water swished over her head, and the world was a blur as she surfaced, gasping with the shock of the cold.

She glared at him furiously, and he laughed.

'A good cooling-off is just what you needed.'

'That's not what you were saying to me earlier.' She slanted him a provocative look, and he smiled.

'True.'

She pushed her wet hair back off her face, and as she raised her arms it emphasised the firm tilt of her breasts. 'Maybe I'm the one who needs cooling off,' he added gently.

She saw the fire in his eyes, and it lit an answering one deep inside her.

Damon glanced over at Mario, who was happily sitting by the side of the pool playing with some toys. He caught hold of Abbie and turned her until her back was towards the child and pressed against the side of the pool.

'Now, where did we leave off this afternoon, hmm?' He bent his head and kissed her very slowly, very deliberately, on the lips. The sensation was blissful, and she curved her arms around his shoulders and gave herself up to the pleasure.

She could feel his body pressing against hers in the water, could feel the heat of his desire warming her.

One hand moved to pull her bikini top down.

'Damon, someone might see!' Her protest was half-hearted; she was facing the ocean, and she knew there was no one around—besides, she loved the feel of his fingers running over the cool of her skin in the water.

'Who's going to see us?' he murmured with a grin. 'A passing seagull would have difficulty in seeing anything. It's Frederic's day off, Elise is in town, Mario…' Damon's eyes flicked over her shoulder to where the child was busy making a tower out of some plastic bricks '…is otherwise occupied.'

'Even so.' She shivered with need and with pleasure as his fingers found the hard peaks of her nipples.

'Even so, we need to enjoy every moment we can…' He lowered his head and licked at her breast. His tongue was warm against the coldness of her skin and it inflamed her senses wildly.

She leaned her head back against the pool and looked up into the dazzling blue sky, luxuriating in his caresses.

'Because tomorrow I'm back at work.'

'Really?' Her head jerked upwards.

'Yes, really…'

He looked at her with a gleam of amusement in his dark eyes. 'As much as I enjoy taking you to bed morning, noon and night, I've got to get back to reality some time.'

'I suppose.' The words brought a coldness swirling inside to meet the warmth of her desire. She wished he'd said 'making love' and not referred to it as just taking her to bed. She supposed the truth was she really didn't want reality; she liked the dreamy world of desire she had inhabited this last week. What did getting back to reality mean? Was it a return to his cynical manner? Would he be travelling away on business? What would she do all day while she waited for him to come home to her?

'I want you so much…' She whispered the words softly. Her fingers moved tenderly over the strength of his back.

His mouth moved to capture hers, catching her shuddering sighs. His tongue probed her mouth as he pressed against her, invading her senses on every level.

The water swished softly around her body, stroking against it with satin warmth as the sun beat powerfully down.

'You were just getting out of a pool the first time I met you—do you remember?' Damon asked softly as he nuzzled in against her neck.

'Of course I remember.' She closed her eyes as his lips moved upwards towards her ears, the sweet kisses making her shiver with pleasure.

'You looked so beautiful.' He breathed the words against her. 'It was as if you cast some kind of a spell on me that day as you rose out of the water, and I just couldn't get you out of my mind after that—all I could think about was wanting you.'

'I felt the same, Damon,' she whispered tremulously.

He pulled away from her suddenly, his hands leaving her body.

'Damon?' Her eyes met with his. 'I wanted you too…'

Her heart crashed painfully as she noticed that the mocking light was back in the darkness of his eyes. 'And was that before or after your father told you how much money was riding on *wanting* me? Hmm?'

'It wasn't like that.' Her voice shook slightly.

But he wasn't listening, he was moving away from her, swimming with hard, powerful strokes down to the far end of the pool.

Abbie adjusted her swimming costume. She shouldn't have said anything. They couldn't talk about the past—she should know that. But she wished desperately that they could, and that he would know the truth about her feelings and about what had really happened in the past. But trying to cut through his scorn and derision was too hurtful.

She felt pain spiralling through her as she watched him get out of the pool and walk along towards Mario.

With a deep breath, she hoisted herself out of the water and reached for a towel.

'Elise is having a night off tonight.' She tried to keep her voice normal, as if nothing had happened, as if everything was fine and her heart wasn't splintering. She just wanted to put things back to the way they had been earlier.

'Yes, she usually has Sunday off.' Damon reached to take off Mario's armbands. He didn't look up at her. 'We can go into town to eat, if you want—there is a very trendy new bistro you would probably like, and if we go early enough we can bring Mario.'

'Actually, I thought I'd cook dinner for us.'

He glanced up then, and his lips twisted in that cynical way that tormented her so much. 'Can you cook?'

'Yes, actually, I'm a very good cook.' She slanted her chin up defiantly.

He shrugged. 'Well, if you want to make dinner that's fine.'

'Good.' She smiled at him. 'Because I do.'

Mario reached out with a red building-block and handed it to Damon. 'Dada,' he said with a smile.

'Hey, Mario—that's right—Dada.' Abbie crouched down beside the child and smiled at him. She'd been saying 'Daddy' to him a few times this week as she'd handed things over to Damon, but this was the first time he'd said the word himself. 'Clever boy.' She kissed the top of his head, and as she straightened her eyes connected with Damon's. This time there was no hint of mockery in his eyes, just warmth.

Mario's tower toppled over as he tried to put another two bricks on top at the same time.

'Oh dear.' Damon turned to help him pick them up. 'You've got to work at things slowly, Mario. One brick at a time.'

Maybe it was the same with their relationship, Abbie told herself firmly. If she tried really hard and took one minute at a time, one day at a time, then maybe one day there would be a framework for Damon to trust her. She couldn't give up on that hope—she just couldn't.

Damon put some paperwork to one side and glanced at his watch. Abbie had told him that dinner would be at eight, so he'd taken the opportunity to catch up with some work in the study. It was the first he'd done for a week and he really needed to get back into it. He definitely needed to go into his offices in town every day next week, probably some evenings as well.

Trouble was that for the first time in his life he didn't feel driven by work. The overwhelming desire in his heart these days seemed to be spending time with Abbie and Mario.

It was good to feel like that about his son—but his feelings for Abbie were troubling him. She only had to look at him in a certain way—touch him in a certain way—and he was in danger of forgetting the lessons of the past. It was dangerous territory.

But he wasn't a fool, he reminded himself sharply. He knew what she was. And today when she'd tried to pretend that she'd had feelings for him back when they met… Well, he couldn't allow her to think he was falling for that.

He was going to have to watch his emotions carefully. It was probably just as well that work was beckoning. Distance was probably what he needed to think things through.

Damon glanced at his watch again and put away the papers. For now work could wait. He was a bit early for dinner, but he was curious to see how Abbie was getting on. Domesticity wasn't her style. Why she wanted to cook dinner, he didn't know. He could have got someone else in to cater for them, or he could have taken her out and wined and dined her in style. He'd offered both before retiring to his study but she had been adamant.

The clock in the hallway said seven forty-five. He went quietly down towards the kitchen and then stopped by the door through to the dining room. She was standing by the table, lighting some candles. The place looked lovely. She'd lit a fire in the big open-cast fireplace, and laid the table with the best china and silver. Candlelight reflected softly over the polished surface of the table.

As he watched she smoothed a hand almost nervously over her black dress and checked her appearance quickly in one of the large gilt mirrors. She looked stunning, Damon thought as he leaned against the door and watched her with leisurely approval. She was wearing very provocative high heels, and her black dress hugged her slender figure. The square neckline plus the fact that she had put her hair up showed her long neck and her soft curves to full advantage. Her handbag was sitting on the sideboard, and she reached into it and took out a lipstick to apply a red gloss to her lips.

Damon wanted her so much that he ached. He watched as she put the lipstick back into her bag, and he was just about to step into the room to tell her just how much he wanted her when she took out a mobile phone and opened it.

He watched with a frown as she hurriedly started to key in some numbers.

Who was she ringing? he wondered. A part of him wanted to step forward and let her know that he was there, but he didn't. Curiosity rooted him to the spot.

Abbie pulled out a chair and sat down. She had two missed calls on her mobile—both were from the stables. All she could think was that something had happened to her horse. She knew all the business dealings with the stables had to go through Damon now, but Jess knew how much Benjo meant to her and if there was something wrong she would want to tell her personally.

It seemed to take for ever before someone picked up the phone. It was Jess and she sounded out of breath as if she'd just dashed in from outside.

'Hi, it's Abbie here. Have you been trying to ring me?'

'Yes… Oh, Abbie, I'm so sorry!'

The genuine distress in the other woman's voice struck horror into her. There *was* something wrong with her horse!

'It's your father.'

The words stilled Abbie's mind.

'He's been here, and he's been insisting I give him your mobile phone number—he wouldn't go away. I know you don't want to talk to him, Abbie, but in the end I had to give it to him, and I had to tell him where you were. He was—bullish.'

'I can imagine,' Abbie said dryly. She closed her eyes. At least it wasn't as bad as she had thought. She'd rather deal with a few phone calls from her father than hear that something had happened to her horse. 'Don't worry about it. I'll sort it out. How's Benjo?'

'He's in good form. We all miss you here, Abbie. But the stables are fine; you don't need to worry about them. How's Mario?'

'He's well—fast asleep, tucked up in his cot. We miss you too.'

The clock out in the hallway struck eight and Abbie remembered about dinner. 'Listen, I've got to go.'

'OK—and I am sorry, Abbie. I feel like I've let you down, giving your father that information, but honestly I had no choice. Oh, and after I told him where you were he rang someone called Lawrence.'

'Lawrence Woods,' Abbie murmured uncomfortably. She had hoped she'd never have to hear that name again. He was her father's very dodgy accountant.

'That's right, and he told him where you were and talked about some business deal.'

Abbie pushed a hand tiredly through her hair and wondered what her father was up to. Why couldn't he just leave her alone? 'Did he say what the deal was?'

'No, just that he was sure it would be in the bag now.'

'Don't worry about it.' Abbie tried to lighten her tone to make Jess feel better. 'I'll sort it out. No problem.'

'I hope so. That man is a bully.'

'I know. But I also know how to handle him. You take care, and keep in touch.'

As the connection was cut, Abbie's false bravado also died. The last thing she wanted was to deal with her father.

She sat quietly for a few moments, trying to pull herself

together, then she got quietly up from the table and pushed the chair back in. John Newland couldn't hurt her any more, she told herself fiercely. He was miles away, and she'd do what she had done in St Lucia and just ignore his calls.

'So…how is dinner going, Abbie?'

The voice from the doorway made her whirl around. Damon was standing there watching her.

'Fine.' She smiled at him, but he didn't smile back; he was watching her with deep, unfathomable eyes. 'I didn't hear your footsteps,' she said nervously. 'How long have you been standing there?'

'Not long.' One dark eyebrow lifted quizzically. 'Have you been on the phone?'

She hesitated for just a moment, wondering if he'd heard her. Then she realised he'd asked her because she was still holding her mobile in her hand. Even so, for a split second she debated telling the truth—and then she panicked. Her father was such an explosive subject between them, and things were shaky enough without any reminders of the past casting even more shadows. Besides, why let John Newland ruin a perfectly nice evening?

'I was just…checking my messages.'

Damon watched with a frown as she went to drop her phone back into her bag. And he knew exactly why she was lying.

At first he'd thought her conversation had sounded banal enough. He'd presumed, because she'd asked about a horse, that she was just talking to someone at the stables.

But then she had mentioned a name that had brought a red-hot wave of fury sweeping over him: *Lawrence Woods*. Damon remembered that name very well. Lawrence Woods was the accountant John Newland had used to help rip off his father in Vegas. He was her father's right-hand henchman.

And then she had asked what the deal was.

John Newland didn't do a deal without his crooked accountant. *She'd been talking to her father.*

The very thought turned his stomach. But the more Damon thought about it the more likely it was. Things had moved pretty fast since he had last seen Newland, and he'd probably been out to the stables looking for his daughter.

And he was probably very impatient to learn what kind of financial deal she had cut. He was probably looking for some money to invest in one of his shady deals.

Damon advanced further into the room. 'And were there any messages?'

She turned, and for a second he glimpsed a decidedly uneasy light in her blue eyes. 'No, nothing. Now I really had better get back into the kitchen.' She smiled up at him. 'Why don't you sit down, make yourself comfortable?'

But Damon didn't sit down, and as she walked over towards the door he was blocking her way, looking at her with those dark eyes in a way that made her very apprehensive.

She looked up at him questioningly. 'Is everything OK?'

'You tell me, Abbie.'

The grating, sardonic tone disconcerted her completely. 'Yes. I just need to turn the oven off…'

Still he didn't move out of her way.

On impulse she reached up and touched his face softly, then stood on tiptoe to kiss his cheek. He made no attempt to touch her, and that took her aback. Usually if she kissed him he would kiss her back, touch her. 'I want us to just relax and enjoy tonight.' Did she sound as tense as she suddenly felt?

Of course, he should have realised immediately that she was up to something when she'd offered to cook for him, Damon thought wryly. After all, he'd already heard via the grapevine that John Newland was searching around for money, trying to set up a shady business deal with an old associate of his. Abbie probably wanted to invest—she'd probably been re-assuring her father that she would be able to siphon money away from her new rich husband to send to him.

The more he thought about it, the more obvious it was. There had to be something in it for her. That was why she'd been suddenly so keen to cook him dinner. That was why she was looking up at him so seductively. Abbie wasn't the domestic type, but she was the seductive, temptress type who knew how to use every feminine wile in the book to get what she wanted. She'd proved that long ago.

Rage started to pound through him.

'Damon?' Her hands moved to rest on his chest, and she looked up at him, perplexed by the fact that he still hadn't made any attempt to either move out of her way or pull her closer and kiss her.

'So tell me, Abbie, what's this really all about?' he asked quietly.

'Sorry?' She frowned. 'I don't know what you mean.'

'I mean this.' He nodded towards the beautifully laid table. 'What was really running through that pretty head of yours as you lit those candles and played at being Ms Domesticated, hmm?'

The mocking tone made colour flare in her cheeks, and her hands dropped from his chest. 'I wasn't playing at anything. I told you, I want us to have a nice relaxing evening—after all, we are still officially on our honeymoon.'

His heart drummed ferociously against his chest. Her acting abilities were too good. But then of course that shouldn't come as any surprise to him; he'd experienced her acting skills before. He remembered how easily she had convinced him that she was vulnerable and shy as she'd given herself to him that first time in Palm Springs. Would he never learn where she was concerned? He didn't know whom he was angrier with—

himself for ever questioning the truth about her when he had held her in his arms, or her for being the gold-digging hussy that she undoubtedly was.

'You know, Abbie, if you want something you don't need to go to these great lengths. I've told you, you can have anything you wish for. All I ask is that you follow the terms of our agreement. And it goes without saying that I want you to have no contact with your father, and certainly no involvement in his shady deals.'

The sudden blunt statement took her very much by surprise, and it hurt. 'I've told you, Damon, I don't want anything from you!' She tried to pull away from him, but he put his hands on her waist suddenly and held her firm.

Her eyes burned as she looked up at him. 'Damon, I can assure you that I've had no contact with my father.'

'Just like you assured me that you were just checking the messages on your phone a few moments ago?' he demanded tersely. 'I know you were lying to me, Abbie. I heard you talking.'

He watched as her face drained of colour.

'So, are you going to tell me what it's all about?' he asked lazily.

'There's nothing to tell.' She was furious that he had tried to catch her out like this.

'Really?' Damon's tone was scathing. 'So, if it was such an innocuous phone call, why lie about it?'

'Because I didn't want to ruin our evening together!' She looked up at him, and for a moment her eyes shimmered with feeling. 'You always like to think the worst of me, don't you?'

His gaze held with hers steadily. 'I'd just prefer it if you didn't try to pretend, Abbie.'

'I wasn't pretending about anything.' She bit down on her lip. 'The phone call wasn't worth mentioning.'

'But worth lying about.'

'Because you never trust me!' The cry broke from her lips. 'Why can't you just trust me?'

Damon watched her, his eyes dark, cold and uncompromising. He wasn't going to be drawn in by her plea, or by the beauty of her eyes. He'd been stupid to ever doubt himself where she was concerned. She could lie her way out of anything. 'Why should I trust you?' he asked coldly. 'I only married you because you are the mother of my son—and also for your body, of course. "To have and to hold" I think was the deal…nothing more.'

The words shouldn't have come as any great surprise. She knew what the deal was, she knew how he felt. Yet after their week of glorious love-making they struck her as painfully as if he'd physically hit her. She had dared to hope that he was softening towards her, that if she was patient he would perhaps start to see her in a different light, but she knew now how stupid those dreams had been.

'So, let's drop the pretence, hmm?' he suggested now.

She shrugged. 'If that's how you want things.' Her voice was numb.

'It is.' He dropped his hands from her waist. 'Now, run along and see to whatever it was you were doing in the kitchen before you burn the house down.'

Anger shot to her own defence. 'If the house burns down it will be your fault, not mine.' How dared he talk to her like this? Who did he think he was?

She marched past him, glad to escape into the kitchen, but to her consternation Damon followed her and lounged against the door, watching as she moved towards the oven to turn it off.

'So, tell me about the phone call,' he demanded. 'And I don't want to hear any more lies.'

'Go to hell, Damon.'

'I want to know exactly what you were planning, Abbie.'

'I wasn't planning anything. And I certainly wasn't speaking to my father! We haven't spoken in over two years!' Almost before she could finish what she was saying, she heard her mobile phone ringing again in the next room.

'Well, well, I wonder who that could be?' Damon asked sarcastically, and watched as her skin once more flooded with colour. 'What's the betting, if I go and answer that, it will be Newland again with some instruction he forgot to give you?'

Abbie shook her head, but she couldn't find her voice to answer, because she was terrified that it could very well be her father, and Damon would never believe that she hadn't solicited the call. 'I don't take instructions from my father,' she managed shakily instead.

'Of course not.' Damon's tone was cynical. 'But it could be him?'

She shrugged helplessly.

'So, shall I answer it for you?' He made as if to turn away, and her eyes widened anxiously.

'No! Don't, Damon—please!'

He turned back slowly. 'So now we are getting to the truth.'

To Abbie's relief the phone suddenly stopped ringing. 'I suppose he wants money for some deal,' Damon said tensely into the ensuing silence. 'I had heard he was up to his old tricks.'

'I don't know what he is up to. I don't want anything to do with him.' She raised her chin and met his eyes steadily. 'And that is the truth.'

'You really are a great actress, Abbie.' Damon's lips twisted with bitter amusement.

He was never going to believe anything she said, Abbie realised dully. And could she blame him after what had happened in the past? She turned away from him, and tried to busy herself taking the dinner from the oven, but she felt like she was just running on some kind of automatic pilot. She didn't care about dinner now, and there was a knot of pain inside her that just wouldn't go away, no matter how she tried to swallow it down.

Damon watched as she bent over and took out the last of the dishes. He was furious with her, yet at the same time through the mist of his fury he couldn't help noticing how her skirt rode up as she crouched down to pick something up. Then she smoothed a hand over her dress as she straightened, and he found his attention wandering down over the soft curves of her figure.

She was an enticing witch, he thought, raking a hand through the thick darkness of his hair. But he'd known that from day one this time around, he reminded himself fiercely. Any weakness that he had felt for her as she had looked up at him with those kitten eyes had been entirely his own stupidity.

Of course she would be conniving with her father if she got the chance—that was what she did. *He knew that*.

All he could do was watch her carefully, and stick to his original plan—use her the way she had once used him.

'So what is on the menu tonight?' he asked suddenly as she straightened up and put the trays out on the racks to cool.

She shot him a look of uncertainty. 'I decided I would try some Sicilian recipes,' she told him tremulously. 'And I asked Elise what you liked.'

'Really?' Damon shook his head. 'I have to say that, even though I know it's just one of your little ploys, I like the idea, and you do suit the guise of the domestic goddess.'

She closed her eyes and tried to cut out the mocking scorn of his voice. 'It wasn't a ploy. I wanted tonight to be special.'

'You can still do something special for me.' His voice held a commanding, sensual edge that wasn't lost on her.

She bit down on her lip and shook her head. If he touched her she felt sure she would break down.

'Come here.'

'Damon, I—'

'Come here, Abbie,' he cut across her firmly, and after a moment's hesitation she did as he asked, stopping at arm's length from him.

'Don't ever lie to me again.' His voice rasped harshly as he reached out and pulled her closer. He put a hand under her chin, tipping her face so that she was forced to look up at him.

'You belong to me now, Abbie, body and soul. Don't forget that.'

How could she forget it when even the lightest touch of his hand against her face was like a burning brand of possession making her whole body tremble with longing?

He leaned closer and kissed her. There was anger in his kiss, but it was also searing, and achingly passionate. Before she could stop herself she was moving closer and responding. How could he give her so much pleasure and at the same time stir up so much pain inside her? she wondered hazily.

She hated the things he said to her, yet she still wanted him, she still loved him. She hated herself for her weakness.

She felt his hand hitching up her dress.

'Do you want to go upstairs?' She whispered the words breathlessly as need overtook all other emotions.

'No.' He found the lace of her knickers and pulled them down, then turned her around towards the kitchen counter. 'I want you here.'

CHAPTER TEN

DAMON stared up into the darkness of the bedroom. He hadn't been able to get enough of Abbie last night. He'd taken her ruthlessly, and she had responded totally to him, her fire matching his ardour.

And once upstairs the same thing had happened all over again. He'd taken her with a cold-blooded determination, as if trying to purge the need he felt for her. Yet the strange thing was that, no matter how many times he took her, that need was still alive.

He thought about the way she had given herself to him—that shy look in her eyes, and then the fiery, wild, uncontrolled way she had responded to him as he'd kissed her.

Afterwards she had taken a shower in the *en-suite* bathroom and had returned wearing a white satin nightdress. She'd looked so pure in it, her face fresh and scrubbed of make-up, and her blond hair lying in loose, glossy curls around her shoulders. Oh yes, she'd been the picture of beautiful innocence, which went to show how deceptive looks could be, he thought with a wry twist of his lips.

'Take the nightgown off,' he had murmured as she had reached the side of the bed.

'Damon, do you have to be so cold with me?'

She had sat down at the edge of the bed and looked at him with an underlying sadness in her eyes that had torn him up inside. Just thinking about it now made his stomach clench. He didn't know what bothered him more—the anger he felt for still allowing the way she looked at him to affect him, or her for playing her games so damn well.

When he'd made no reply she had taken the nightdress off, her eyes holding with his gaze, her chin tipped up so that there'd been a hint of defiance about her acquiescence. Then, as she'd slipped into the bed beside him, she had been the one to reach for him.

She'd rolled over on top of him and had looked into his eyes before kissing him deeply, opening her mouth and allowing him inside. 'I wasn't lying to you earlier, Damon. But you've proved your point,' she had whispered softly. 'I'm yours totally.'

She rolled over in the bed now, and he felt the warmth of her body against him. The soft sincerity of those words had plagued him all night. A part of him hated himself for taking her body the way he had. If she'd tried to pull back from him he would have stopped, but she had given herself so freely...so lovingly. He frowned.

She had given herself freely and lovingly in Palm Springs too, he reminded himself angrily. She was a con artist.

Dawn was breaking outside now, and the first rays of sunshine started to slant across the room. He turned on his side and looked down at Abbie, and impulsively he stroked a stray strand of hair away from her face so that he could see her more clearly.

Her skin was perfect; her lashes were long and dark, and her lips infinitely kissable. There was almost an ethereal loveliness about her, a delicate-rose vulnerability.

But of course all roses had very sharp thorns, he reminded himself tersely. But she was achingly beautiful…

Her eyes flickered open suddenly and connected with his. 'What time is it?' she murmured sleepily.

'Almost six.'

'You're awake early.' As she slowly focussed, memories from the night before came flooding back: Damon taking her again and again, his attitude demanding and ruthless. Yet just now as their eyes had met there had been something else. She frowned as she tried to place the expression in the darkness of his eyes. Regret?

'I've got to go into the office early.' He rolled away from her onto his back.

She didn't want him to go. More than anything she just wanted him to reach out to her and put an arm around her, wanted to close out the harsh memories of last night and the demanding way he had taken her body. Maybe he wanted that too. Maybe he regretted his coldness.

'Do you have to go?' she ventured softly. 'We could spend the day together, and—'

'I don't think so,' he cut across her firmly. 'I need to make sure my businesses are ticking along smoothly. And, anyway, I'm sure you'd rather I got my priorities straight—you don't want the money to dwindle, do you, Abbie? You wouldn't like that.'

She closed her eyes against the pain stirred up by those sizzling, scornful words. So much for him regretting anything! 'Don't, Damon,' she whispered huskily.

'I'm just being practical.' That was the way he had to be around her, he told himself forcefully. 'Why don't you go shopping today? Your credit card has arrived. You just need to sign it.'

'There's nothing I need.'

'I'm sure you'll think of something.'

The hard edge to his tone hurt. She took a deep breath and

tried to pull herself together, tried to face up to the reality of her life. She needed to stop lying to herself and recognise the truth: Damon would never love her; their marriage was purely a convenience for him. He'd made that abundantly clear even in the way he had taken her body last night.

He had pleasured himself callously with her and yet, through all of that, she had imagined she had tasted something in his kiss—something more than just raw sexual need.

It was known as 'grasping at straws', she told herself now scornfully. Or maybe she had just been trying to excuse the way she had responded to him.

'What time will you be home tonight?' she asked softly.

'I don't know, Abbie. I'll be late.'

'Fine.' She frowned and swallowed hard.

Something in the tone of her voice made him look over at her again. 'Go and have some fun spending money on yourself, Abbie. The credit limit on your card is high, and—'

'I don't want to spend your money, Damon!' she cut across him furiously. 'Why won't you ever listen to me? I want to spend time getting to know you, I want…' She trailed off as she realised that it didn't matter what she wanted. She was just grasping at more straws.

'You want to spend time getting to know me?' He leaned up on his elbow to look at her better. He sounded very amused now, and that annoyed her. 'What exactly do you want to know?'

'I don't know…everything.' She shrugged. 'You could take me on a tour of the island. Show me where you grew up.' She threw the suggestion at him wildly.

He laughed. 'And you'd be disappointed.'

'Why?'

'Well, my old family home would probably tick all your

boxes, I suppose, although it needs a lot of work doing to it as it's been empty a long time. But I only actually lived there until the age of eight.' He rolled over onto his back again. 'My father lost everything at that point and we had to move. I don't think you would be in the slightest bit interested to see where I lived for the next ten years. It was a bit of a slum area, to be honest.'

'So your father had lost everything once before?' She looked at him in surprise.

'Yes, and then made it all back. Bought back his old house. Only to lose it all again in Vegas. Bizarre, isn't it?' Damon stared up at the ceiling. 'He was a bit of a gambler. Not in the cards-and-horses sense, but in an entrepreneurial way. He liked to take risks in business. You'd think he'd have learnt first time around, that when something seems too good to be true it generally is.'

'So your mum left him when he lost all his money first time around?'

'Yes. I don't suppose he was easy to live with, and my mother—well, my mother likes luxury.'

'Likes? Is she still alive?' For some reason Abbie had assumed his mother was dead.

'Oh yes, she's in the south of France now, I believe. Hooked herself another millionaire and got married again about three years ago.' There was silence for a moment. 'I can understand her leaving my father. Living with someone who takes risks all the time can be hard. But he was a good man in other ways.'

Abbie sat up a little to look at him, and saw the shadows of pain for just a fleeting second in the darkness of his eyes. His childhood must have been tough, she thought with sympathy. She could understand a woman leaving her husband, but not her child. And she guessed Damon had had trouble accepting that too. No wonder he was so determined to give Mario a secure upbringing. Damon saw the expression of concern in her eyes. 'You don't need to worry,' he grated sardonically. 'I don't take wild gambles in business.'

'I wasn't worried.'

'No?' One dark eyebrow lifted in disbelief. 'Well, you can rest assured, the risks I take are all very well calculated.'

'I know that already, Damon. Your risks are calculated in marriage as well as in business.'

He didn't say anything to that.

She wondered if she had inadvertently struck Damon's Achilles' heel. Maybe, because of his mother, he thought most women were more interested in money than love, and his theory had been compounded by what had happened between them in Vegas.

Mario was waking up in the next room. Abbie could hear him happily talking to himself, but she didn't move immediately to go to see to him. It was the first time that Damon had ever opened up to her about his past and she didn't want to lose the moment. 'I would be interested to see where you lived, Damon, both before and after things went wrong in your parents' marriage.'

For a second he looked at her with an odd expression in his eyes. Then he shook his head. 'Maybe another day.'

He pulled away from her and pushed back the duvet. 'I've got to shower and get to work. And it sounds like our son needs his breakfast.'

She watched as he disappeared into the bathroom. Then with a sigh she reached for her dressing gown. The precious shared intimacies had been nothing more than illusion. The reality was that Damon probably regretted telling her anything.

Damon left for the office half an hour later, and Abbie, bathed and dressed in a skimpy pair of shorts and a T-shirt, carried Mario to the front door to wave him goodbye.

Although it was early, the air was already shimmering with heat. It promised to be another scorching day, and Damon felt a frisson of reluctance as he got into his limo and glanced back at the perfect tableaux of his wife and son framed in the doorway.

Abbie looked so beautiful and so young. He forgot sometimes that she was only twenty-one, because in some ways she was so mature for her years. But everything about her was deceptive, he reminded himself forcefully—she knew how to play innocent so well.

As Frederic drove along the twisting, mountainous roads, Damon took out some files and his mobile phone to try and get ahead with some work. He had several intense meetings lined up for this afternoon, and needed to get a handle on things well before then.

But somehow the columns of figures he was supposed to be studying seemed to blur as he read them, and his mind seemed to wander. He was remembering the way Abbie had curled in beside him this morning.

I would be interested to see where you lived, Damon, both before and after things went wrong in your parents' marriage.

The words teased him provocatively. Of course, it was all part of her act. She would be horrified to see where he had grown up. After his father had divorced, he had ploughed all the money he could back into starting again in business. Corners had been cut—and living accommodation had been one of those corners.

However, experiencing that poverty had strengthened Damon's character. Everything he had achieved in life, he'd worked for. Abbie wouldn't understand that—wouldn't be interested, even.

So why had she seemed so interested?

He frowned and tried to return his concentration to his papers.

Women like Abbie lived for shopping and luxury; they didn't want to delve too deeply into anything else.

So why hadn't she just grabbed her credit card and headed happily into town this morning?

Her words played through his mind over and over... *I don't want to spend your money, Damon! Why won't you ever listen to me? I want to spend time getting to know you...*

Damon frowned and closed the words out. She was just clever, that was all. She believed in playing the bigger game— she wanted cash to invest in her father's schemes, not a credit card that could be checked on.

The traffic increased as they approached the outskirts of town.

But she hadn't actually asked him for any cash, he reminded himself suddenly. Well, not *yet*.

And she had looked at him with such feeling in her eyes when she had come to his bed last night. He found himself remembering how he had taken her again. He remembered how pale her skin had looked against the dark-granite worktops in the kitchen. Then he found himself remembering again how she had looked in the white-satin nightdress.

I wasn't lying to you... Her tremulous whisper replayed in his mind.

Why the hell was he thinking about that? Of course she was lying—and why should he take any kind of risk on her? A marriage of convenience just suited him fine. She was good in bed and she was a good mother to Mario. That was all that mattered to him.

Your risks are calculated in marriage as well as in business. He frowned as he remembered those words. She had a point.

The feelings Abbie had generated in him the first time around in Vegas had troubled him even before he'd found out

exactly what she was up to. Because he didn't trust easily—
he never had. Marrying Abbie on his terms, cutting away the
emotion and just making it a practical arrangement, had suited
him. She was right about that.

The truth of that sat uncomfortably with him.

They were gridlocked in traffic now. It looked as if there
had been an accident up ahead.

Damon leaned forward and opened up the partition between
him and his driver. 'It looks like we are going to be stuck here
for a while, Frederic. Turn the car around.'

'You want to find a way around this?'

'No. Just take me back to the house.' Damon frowned. He
needed to find his way around the thoughts plaguing him
before anything else.

Abbie felt lost when Damon left. She stood on the doorstep
for a few moments and watched as the car disappeared from
sight.

Then she returned to the kitchen to give Mario his breakfast. Elise was already there, and the two women chatted as
Abbie sat down to spoon-feed Mario his cereal. The little boy
seemed more interested in playing with the food rather than
eating it, and he wasn't happy when she took the spoon away
from him.

The shrill ring of the doorbell took them both by surprise.

'I'll go and see who it is. Won't be a moment.' Elise put the
bread she had been making into the oven and hurried out. She
returned a few moments later, and Abbie could hear her talking
to someone in English.

She frowned, wondering who it could be. Then she heard
a familiar male voice that made her heart freeze.

'Yes, I've just flown in this morning. I have some business
here, so I thought I'd drop by and say hello.'

The kitchen door swung open. 'Abbie, it's your father.' Elise led the man in with a smile. 'That's a nice surprise, isn't it…?' Her cheerful words trailed away as she saw the shock on Abbie's face.

'Hello, sweetheart.' The drawled words held a veiled sarcasm that wasn't lost on his daughter.

She hadn't seen John Newland since she had fled from Vegas a few months before Mario had been born. But he hadn't changed much. He'd never been what you would term attractive. Due to his love of excessive living he was a portly man, and he looked older than his fifty years, with greying hair and sharp eyes. He was dressed for business in a grey suit and looked like he'd just stepped out of his office.

'Shall I make a pot of tea?' Elise ventured gently into the silence.

'No thank you, Elise, my father won't be staying.' From somewhere Abbie managed to find the strength to get to her feet.

'Of course I'm staying—I want to see my grandson. Don't worry, I have plenty of time,' John contradicted her firmly, and then turned to Elise with a charming smile. 'But perhaps you'd give us a few moments alone? I haven't seen my daughter for a while and we parted on, well, unfortunate terms.'

'Unfortunate terms?' Abbie was incensed, and her voice was sharp with disgust. 'It was a lot more than that!'

'You obviously have things to talk about and need some privacy,' Elise said quickly. And before Abbie could say anything to the contrary she left them.

'Nice place you've got yourself here.' John walked further into the room. 'You've done well.'

It spoke volumes that all her father was concerned about was the wealth of her surroundings. He had hardly even glanced at his grandchild.

'You've got a nerve, coming here.'

'I think I've got every right to come here,' he replied calmly. 'And, well, frankly I expected a bit more gratitude than that.'

'Gratitude?' Abbie's voice rose slightly. 'Why on earth would I be grateful to you? All you've ever tried to do is ruin my life, like you ruined my mother's.'

'Not that tired old refrain.' John shook his head. 'Change the record, Abbie. If it wasn't for me you wouldn't have any of this.' He spread his hands out to indicate the house. 'I was the one who prompted Damon into doing the right thing by you. I suspected he'd take the bait. He always did like to think he was the honourable type—they are always quite easy to sucker.'

'He *is* the honourable type. You haven't suckered anybody!' Abbie moved to the back door and opened it. 'I want you to go. You are not welcome here.'

'Now now, Abbie, that's not very respectful!' Instead of moving to the door, he sat down in the chair she had vacated and looked at Mario. 'So this is the heir apparent. He looks like his father.'

'Just get away from him.'

Mario reached out a hand and smiled at his granddad, and Abbie watched with a stab of horror as her father took the little hand in his. 'Hello, little fellow.'

'Get away from him!' She stepped back into the room to pick him up, but her father stopped her by standing up and placing himself in front of the child.

'I'm just saying hello to my grandson. There is no need for these hysterics.'

'You haven't come to say hello. You haven't been interested enough to even bother enquiring after him until now.'

'Well, I tried to ring you just before you left St Lucia, Abbie, and you didn't take my calls.'

'You wonder why?' Her eyes glared stonily into his.

'Come on, Abbie, things don't have to be like this between us.'

He put a conciliatory hand on her arm, and she shook it away angrily. 'What do you want?'

'Well, like I said, I think a little gratitude is in order for setting you up here so well. You know I've always had your best interests at heart.'

Abbie stared at him, nonplussed. 'Best interests at heart? You blackmailed me into going along with your vicious deal in Vegas—told me that you wouldn't pay for Mum's treatment in hospital unless I did what you asked. You got me implicated in something that ruined Damon's father financially, a ploy that tore our relationship apart, and you think I should show you gratitude?'

'Well, you're happy now, aren't you? It all worked out for the best.'

'No, it did not work out for the best!' Abbie blazed with fury. 'I can't believe you are saying this! I knew you were evil, but I didn't think you were mad. You tried to ruin my life!'

'You know what? You sound just like your mother,' her father spat contemptuously.

'Good, because I loved my mother.'

'Don't I just know it—you made a laughing stock of me when you encouraged her to leave!'

'And you never forgave me, did you? But she needed to get out from under your thumb. You made her deeply unhappy with your womanizing, and—'

'Let's just cut to the bottom line, shall we?' John Newland sliced across her in a bored tone. 'I'm currently in the middle of some business negotiations that are doing well—but as you know, thanks to your husband, I am a little bit strapped for cash.'

'You've come here for money?'

'Yes. I've been talking to Lawrence, and he thinks a nice, round five-figure sum should get the deal in the bag…' John mused for a moment before naming his sum exactly.

Abbie stared at him in shock. 'I haven't got any money, and even if I had I wouldn't give you a single penny.'

'I think your attitude is a little unreasonable, Abbie. After all, we are partners in this…marriage arrangement. I suggested it—I told you how to play it. I set the ball rolling by sending Damon to you. I think the least you can do is settle your account.'

'I'm not partners with you in anything. I never have been and I never will be. And I haven't spoken to you since my mother died over two years ago!'

'I was hoping you were going to take a more realistic line than this.' John shook his head. 'I could make your life very uncomfortable here, Abbie. I could stir things up with a lot of force. Damon believed me once before, when I told him you were my willing partner in that deal involving his father. He swallowed it hook, line and sinker when I told him you are nothing but a little gold-digger. I could throw a few more curve-balls into his mind. A few telephone conversations—a few well-placed remarks.'

Abbie knew he was right. One well-worded sentence was all it would take to ruin her fragile marriage. That much had been more than obvious last night.

'All I need is that money then I'll be out of your hair.' Her father's tone was wheedling now. 'You won't see me again.'

'Until the next time there's some big deal and you need some more money,' Abbie answered quietly. She loved Damon, and she didn't want her marriage to fail, but she couldn't do this. 'As I told you, I don't have any money, but even if I had I wouldn't pay you a penny. You've blackmailed me once and I won't let you do it again.'

John Newland looked genuinely taken aback.

'Go—do your worst, dad. I'll take my chances with Damon.'

'You're not thinking this through.'

'On the contrary, my thinking has never been clearer.' A noise from behind them both made Abbie turn, and she froze with shock as she saw Damon standing in the open doorway. His features were grim as his eyes moved from her towards her father, and he looked truly menacing.

'Well,' he drawled. 'Look what's crawled out from under a stone.'

John Newland turned to face him. 'Nice to see you too,' he said in a falsely bright tone. But Abbie could see that, although he tried to sound as if he wasn't intimidated, he shrank a little as Damon took a step forward.

'Damon, this…this isn't what it looks like!' Abbie's voice was distraught. How much had Damon heard? He looked so angry—maybe he thought she had invited her father here. If that was the case, her marriage really was over.

'Get out of my house, Newland.'

'You can't throw me out. I have a right to be here.' John tried to pull himself up to his full height and face Damon down, but his voice wasn't steady. 'This is my daughter and my grandson.'

'No, this is *my* wife and *my* son. Now get out of here, before I call the police and have you arrested for trespassing.'

'Don't be ridiculous! You are making a big mistake…' For just a moment her father blustered. 'Abbie invited me here—'

'No, *you've* made the big mistake,' Damon grated, and as he took another purposeful step closer her father turned and ran for the door.

As soon as he'd gone, Abbie sank down onto the chair in shocked reaction. Her legs were shaking and she felt sick.

'I didn't invite him, Damon, I didn't!'

Damon didn't reply. He just stood by the door. She noticed his hands clenching and unclenching at his sides as if he was trying to get a grip on his emotions.

'You don't believe me, do you?' She covered her face with her hands. After last night and the phone call, he probably assumed she was indeed back in business with her father.

Mario started to cry suddenly, long, wailing sobs that brought Abbie instantly back to her feet. 'It's OK, darling.' She bent to look at the child and then, as she picked him up to comfort him, Damon walked past her and out of the room.

'Damon, we need to talk—' she called after him, but he'd gone, and a few minutes later she heard the front door closing.

CHAPTER ELEVEN

ABBIE had wanted to run after Damon, grab hold of him and beg him to listen. But instead she had stood immobilised until she had heard him driving away.

It was now nearly three in the afternoon and he hadn't come back. He was either still furiously angry with her or else he didn't care and was just carrying on with his work. Either way, any hope she had of making this marriage work was now effectively over, she realised with a heavy heart.

Even if he had stayed and talked to her, it wouldn't have made any difference. Damon would never believe that she hadn't invited her father to this house. He probably thought that the moment he'd left for work this morning she had been on the phone to him again, and that she was hatching some plot with him.

Mario was crying again. He'd been fractious all day, and hadn't settled at all to have his afternoon nap. She went to see him now and lifted him out of the cot.

'It's OK, darling,' she whispered softly to him, and buried her face against his. She felt like crying the way he was crying, giving in to loud, noisy sobs. But that wasn't going to solve anything.

He was very hot, she noticed. Maybe he was teething. She

reached for his soother and put it to his lips to see if it would help, but he pushed it away.

'You are out of sorts, aren't you, Mario?' Abbie pressed a kiss to his cheek. 'Come on, let's give up on sleep and go downstairs and sit quietly, see if we can settle you.'

But, down in the lounge, Mario seemed even more restless.

Elise came into the room as she heard his wails. 'This isn't like Mario,' she said with concern.

'No. I don't know what's wrong with him. I thought he was teething, but I think it's more than that now.' She put a hand to his forehead. 'He's running a bit of a temperature. I think I should make an appointment with the doctor for him. Just have him checked over to be on the safe side.'

'Yes, it might be best.' Elise nodded. 'Do you want me to ring up and make the appointment? Signor Cyrenci's doctor's number is on the diary in the study.'

Abbie nodded. 'If you don't mind, Elise, just in case I have any difficulties with the language.'

'No problem.' Elise bustled away and was back a few moments later. 'All fixed for half-past four this afternoon. Is that OK with you?'

'Yes, great, thank you.' Abbie was trying to put a cooling cloth to Mario's face but he kept pushing it away.

'Do you think we should ring Signor Cyrenci?' Elise asked suddenly. 'Tell him that Mario isn't well?'

'He's probably dealing with important business,' Abbie responded rawly, then thought better of the reply. She was angry and hurt with Damon for just walking out on her, for not caring enough to even talk to her about what had happened— for not loving her.

But he did love his son. And there would be nothing more important to him than Mario's welfare. 'But maybe you'd better ring him,' she added softly. 'I'd probably get his secretary who can't speak English or something…'

'Not if you phoned him direct on his mobile.' Elise picked up Abbie's phone, which was sitting next to her on the table, and passed it over.

She hesitated for a moment before taking it. It wasn't that she didn't want to speak to Damon—it was more a case of being afraid of speaking to him, afraid of losing the last shreds of her dignity and breaking down whilst he remained unmoved and uncaring. She didn't think she could bear that.

But this wasn't about them, this was about Mario, she reminded herself staunchly as she took the phone.

Elise smiled at her, and then reached to take Mario from her. 'I'll look after him for you while you do that.'

Even though she was left alone and in silence, it took Abbie several minutes to gather up the courage to make the call.

Damon answered almost immediately, and before he could say anything she took a deep breath and launched straight in.

'I wouldn't have rung you at work, only there's a problem with Mario and I thought I'd better let you know.' She heard the cold note in her voice, but she couldn't take it out. And why should she, anyway? He didn't care about her.

'What kind of a problem?' Immediately Damon sounded concerned.

'He's been crying all day and he's running a temperature. I've had to get an appointment for him with your GP.'

'What time is his appointment for?'

'Four-thirty.'

'Right, I'm on my way. I'll pick you both up at four.'

'There's no need, Damon. I can manage on my own.' Even as she said the words she ached for him. But she had stopped hoping for any kind of miracle in their relationship. If it wasn't for his concern over Mario, he wouldn't even have bothered talking to her now, never mind rush home.

'I know you can. But I'm still coming.'

He'd hung up before she could argue further.

However when Abbie went through and joined Elise in the kitchen she didn't have time to think again about Damon, because it was very obvious that Mario's condition was suddenly deteriorating fast. He was very lethargic, as if he was passing in and out of consciousness between bouts of crying.

'You know what? I don't think I can wait for that doctor's appointment, Elise,' Abbie said in panic as she took the child back into her arms. 'There's something really wrong with him.'

'Maybe you should take him to the hospital,' Elise agreed instantly. 'Shall I get Frederic to bring the car around?'

'Yes…and tell him to be quick.' Mario looked so weak, so unlike his usual robust self, that her heart squeezed with fear just watching him struggle to keep his eyes open. This wasn't good.

Damon arrived at the hospital ten minutes after the doctors had swept Mario away from her. She saw him striding down the corridor, his face gaunt with anxiety, and her heart welled up with emotion. Nothing from the past mattered at that moment, all that counted was the fact that she was so fiercely glad that he was here, as if somehow his very presence was going make their son better.

He looked up and saw her, and for just a moment there was a powerful expression of pain in his eyes. 'How is he?'

'The doctors have taken him away to do tests.' Abbie's voice caught with fear. 'Damon, he looks so ill I'm so afraid…'

She didn't get to finish her sentence, because the next

moment Damon had pulled her in close to his chest to hold her.

She melted against him, so glad to be in his arms again, and trying to draw strength from his presence. 'Do you think he'll be all right?' she whispered, desperate for reassurance. 'It all happened so quickly. I didn't know what to do.'

'You've done the best thing, getting him here so quickly, and he's going to be fine—he *has* to be fine.'

They stood for a while, just holding each other and holding on to that thought.

One of the doctors came through to the waiting room and looked around for her, and they broke apart. 'Is there any news?' Abbie asked anxiously.

The doctor didn't answer her immediately, but looked over at Damon. 'This is my husband, Damon Cyrenci.' Abbie introduced him quickly. 'How is our son? Is he going to be OK?'

'We are doing—more tests.' The doctor's English was halting, and Damon spoke to him in Italian.

It was deeply frustrating not to know what was being said. They were speaking so quickly that there was no way Abbie could even pick up on a few words, so she kept watching Damon's face nervously to try and figure out if this was good or bad.

It was hard to work out. Damon looked tense, but seemed like he was very much in control of the situation.

'So what is he telling you, Damon?' she asked as the doctor broke off to consult a chart in his hand.

'They are running a few more tests. Nothing is conclusive yet.'

'What are they testing him for?'

'Come on, let's sit down.' Damon nodded at the doctor and thanked him.

'But I want to see him, Damon. I need to be with him.'

'Not just yet. Come on, let's sit down.'

'Oh God, this is bad, isn't it?' She was suddenly terrified, and sank down into the chair that Damon had brought her towards.

'They suspect that he might have meningitis.' Damon sat down next to her and reached for her hand.

As he looked into her eyes, he saw the way her pupils dilated in fear at the word. 'Mario is really strong, he'll fight this.' Damon squeezed her hand. 'And the good thing is that you've got him here quickly.'

Although he was being positive, Abbie could see a muscle ticking along the side of his jaw. She looked down at the hand that held hers.

'I don't know what I'm going to do if I lose him, Damon, I can't bear it.' Her eyes misted with tears.

'We are not going to lose him.' Damon squeezed her hand tightly. 'He is receiving expert care, and the results of the tests aren't even back yet, so let's not cross bridges until we have to, hmm?'

She bit down on her lips and nodded. She knew he was right, but it was so hard not to let her imagination start running ahead.

They seemed to sit there for ages like that, just holding hands.

A nurse came by and asked if they would like a coffee, but they both refused.

'It's going to be all right, Abbie,' Damon said softly. He stroked a thumb over the back of her hand. 'He's a survivor, like his mother.'

She tried to smile, but couldn't. The touch of his hand against hers was so wonderful, so deeply comforting and reassuring, and yet so painful. Because if it hadn't been for their mutual love of Mario he wouldn't be holding her like this.

Damon looked down at the fragile hand in his and felt more helpless than he had ever felt in his life. He wanted to take away her pain, make this better, and have his son back in his arms.

The last few hours had been hell. Finding John Newland in his house like that had been a shock. Hearing their conversation had been even more shocking.

At first he hadn't been able to take it in. Part of him wondered angrily if it had all been staged, if somehow Abbie had known that he would come back to the house. But how could she have known?

And she had looked so scared. His heart had wrenched when he'd seen that look on her face, that anguish in her eyes. He'd had to get out of the house, had to take stock and think about things deeply. He didn't want to make any more mistakes, because he'd already made enough to last a lifetime.

A few doctors walked towards the door, and Damon and Abbie both looked up anxiously, but the doctors didn't come in. They were talking to the receptionist outside.

'This is hell,' Abbie grated, and he squeezed her hand even tighter.

The doctor who had spoken to them earlier suddenly appeared in the doorway and they both got to their feet.

This time the doctor smiled at Abbie. 'It is—how do you say?—good news.'

'Thank God.' Relief flooded through Abbie, and she leaned weakly against Damon as she listened to him questioning the doctor more closely in his native language.

'He has a viral infection, Abbie, but it is not meningitis and it can be treated,' he translated for her swiftly. 'They say he'll be fine in a few days.'

'Thank you.' Abbie smiled at the doctor, her eyes shimmering with gratitude.

Then impulsively she turned and went into Damon's arms.

It was so wonderful to be close to him, and the feelings of happiness and relief mingled with the sharp pain of knowing that this bond they shared was only one of mutual love for their son—nothing else.

'Can we see him?' Hastily she pulled away from him. Now that the worst was over and Mario was on the road to recovery, she knew that she couldn't allow herself the luxury of being in his arms.

CHAPTER TWELVE

Abbie stepped outside the hospital front door and took a deep breath of the early-morning air. She and Damon had sat next to Mario's bed throughout the night, neither of them wanting to leave until their son's fever had broken.

Finally, at six o'clock that morning, Mario had smiled at her and she had seen the healthy colour returning to his skin. Then he had settled down into a peaceful and exhausted sleep. That was when she had allowed Damon to persuade her to go home.

She felt worn out as she waited for Frederic to bring the car around. The emotional turmoil of the last few days, added to her fears for Mario, had taken its toll. She knew she probably looked washed out, and she felt wretched. But she didn't intend to be away from Mario for long. She would just have a shower and freshen up and then go straight back. For one thing, Damon deserved a break as well. Sitting across the hospital bed from him, she had realised that the worry over Mario plus losing a night's sleep had also affected him—he'd also looked shattered and drawn.

The car arrived, and as Abbie settled into the comfortable seats she closed her eyes. It had been such a strange night. She and Damon had been at pains to be polite with each other after the worst had passed. It had been as if they had never held each other moments earlier or sat holding hands.

He probably was still furious with her for allowing her father into his house. They couldn't go on like this, she realised sadly. It was tearing her apart and it was probably tearing him apart, too. He didn't trust her—*couldn't* trust her. The situation was no good for either of them.

But what was the alternative—a divorce? For the first time she allowed herself to admit that might be where they were headed. She raked a hand in anguish through her hair as she imagined that situation—a polite distance from each other maintained at all times, except in periods of emergency.

At least she knew he would be there for his son no matter what. But living in close proximity to him like that and yet not being with him would be torture.

But what choice did she have? If they divorced she couldn't go back to St Lucia. She'd lost everything there, and anyway it wouldn't be fair to deny Mario regular access to his father. And it was obvious how deeply Damon felt about his son. Even after the doctor had told them everything was going to be all right, the bleak expression hadn't completely left his eyes.

No, her only option if they decided on a divorce would be to try and get a flat and a job somewhere nearby. She didn't want it to end like this, she really didn't. The pain in her heart felt overwhelming. But to love someone and know that there was no hope of them ever loving you back was also too painful to bear.

The car pulled up outside the house, and she went inside. Everything was quiet and the kitchen was deserted.

'Elise?' she called to the housekeeper as she went through to the hallway, but there was no reply. Maybe she'd gone for a lie down, Abbie reflected. She knew she had been very worried about Mario, and although Damon had rung her as soon as they had known he was going to be OK she had probably had little sleep.

Going upstairs, Abbie stripped off in the bedroom and went for a shower. It was bliss to stand under the hot, pounding water.

She was just pulling on her dressing gown when she heard a noise from downstairs.

'Elise?' She opened the bedroom door and looked out. 'Elise, is that you?'

'No, it's me.' To her surprise Damon appeared at the top of the stairs. 'Elise arrived at the hospital a few moments after you left, so I decided to take the opportunity for a quick break.'

'I see.' He did look like he needed a break—in fact, he looked terrible. 'But everything is all right with Mario, isn't it?' she asked anxiously.

'Yes. I saw the doctor again before I left, and he told me they might discharge him later today.'

'Thank God for that.' Abbie smiled at him tremulously.

'Yes.'

For a moment there was an odd silence between them. His eyes moved down over her figure. 'You were wearing that dressing gown when I arrived at your door in St Lucia,' he recalled suddenly. 'Seems like a lifetime ago.'

She nodded. 'Well, a lot has happened since then. Marriage, and now…' She trailed off brokenly. 'Now it's all such a mess.'

'You want a divorce, don't you?' He asked the question bluntly, and there was a very sombre look in his eyes now.

She yearned to tell him that a divorce was the last thing she wanted—that what she wanted was for them to make things work, and for him to trust her. But pride kept her silent. What was the point in telling him that? He wouldn't believe her anyway. When he'd found her father in his home, he had probably come to the conclusion that he couldn't continue with this charade.

So she shrugged helplessly. 'I think we both know deep down that we can't continue like this—' she whispered brokenly.

'Abbie, I can't bear it,' he cut across her suddenly. 'I know I have absolutely no right to ask you this—but I really can't bear for you to leave.'

Abbie frowned. She'd never heard that raw note in his voice before. He'd always been so much in control of the situation, and of her. 'Well, you know I can't go anywhere unless you allow me to leave. I have nowhere to go, Damon…' Her voice broke for a moment.

Damon raked a hand through his hair. He couldn't believe that he had done this to her—trapped her here against her will—used her.

Yesterday when he'd left the house he'd needed to put space and time between them, had needed to be alone when the blinkers had finally lifted from his eyes—because the guilt had been so damn overwhelming that he just couldn't bear it.

Overhearing the conversation between Abbie and her father yesterday had made him sick to his stomach. Hearing the truth had opened a pit of guilt and despair inside him that he didn't think he would ever be able to close. Now he knew the reason for the sadness in her eyes when she looked at him: she was innocent of all the charges he had laid before her. She was as much a victim of what had happened in Vegas as his father had been.

The conversation had confirmed what he'd wanted to believe. She didn't have a bad, selfish or mercenary bone in her body.

But the revelation had come too late.

He'd hurt her so much, trapped her in a marriage she didn't want, in a place she didn't want to be.

She had tried valiantly to make the best of the situation, and to make things work, but she didn't want to be here.

He remembered the way he'd tried to punish her—the way he'd talked to her, the way he had taken her body so ruthlessly. And he hated himself.

'Damon?' The soft, questioning note in her voice tore into him. 'Damon, I need you to believe me when I tell you I didn't invite my father to this house—'

'I know you didn't invite him. I heard every word.' His voice cracked for a moment under the weight of emotion that was tearing him up inside.

'You heard?' Her voice was stiff with disbelief. 'But you blamed me—you walked away.'

'I couldn't bear to look at you.' His voice was husky with a strange note that she couldn't place. 'I hated myself too much for what I'd done to you. And when I looked at you and saw the distress in your eyes… Oh, Abbie, I couldn't bear it— couldn't bear the knowledge of what I'd put you through—of what you'd been through before I met you.'

For a moment she stood silently, hardly daring to believe what she was hearing. 'So you believe I didn't lie to you? You believe I would never have done anything deliberately to hurt you? That my father forced me into a situation that I didn't want?'

As he listened to the pain in her voice, Damon's heart smote him once more with the horrific guilt of what he had put her through, what he had accused her of. 'Yes, I believe it,' he whispered. 'And I'm so sorry, Abbie. I've behaved so badly towards you. I believed the worst—I wanted revenge… And all the time you were an innocent victim of your father as well.' He shook his head, and she could hear the self-disgust in his voice. 'Abbie, why didn't you tell me about your mother?'

'I tried…' Tears sparkled in her eyes. The relief that he knew the truth was so tremendous, as if a weight of a hundred boulders had lifted from her. 'But you didn't want to listen or believe anything I said about the past. And it hurt so much, Damon, to try and talk about something so deeply personal and painful and have everything I said twisted and scornfully dismissed…'

'I should have listened and believed you, but I was so sure that you were lying—'

'Damon, it's OK.' She cut across him, hating to hear his voice crack like that. 'I understand why you couldn't believe me.' She took a step closer. 'All the evidence was against me. And I know you had trust issues, as well, from your past.'

Even now, after the way he had hurt her, she could still find it in her heart to excuse him. Somehow the fact that she was so gently forgiving made him feel worse. He'd got it wrong so badly—had ignored all the voices of caution and believed the worst of her. He didn't know if he would ever forgive himself, let alone expect her forgiveness. Hearing her tell her father how this situation had ruined her life had been gutwrenching.

'I don't deserve your forgiveness, Abbie. But I'm going to put everything right, I promise. I'll tear up the prenuptial agreement for a start. You can have whatever you want.'

'You don't have to do that. I don't want anything.'

'I know you don't want anything! But I need to do that—don't you understand? I couldn't live with myself knowing…' He trailed off. 'And I'll move out of the house, if that is what you really want, while we decide how best to proceed.'

'Move out?' Her voice was cold suddenly, and the feeling of relief inside her quickly started to turn to fear. 'Why would you do that?'

'Because I want to do the right thing by you and make amends.' He broke off and spoke in Italian for a moment.

'Damon, I don't understand.' She shook her head.

'I'm saying I always thought of myself as an honourable man, and I've treated you so badly that I'm ashamed. I've forced you into a marriage that you don't want.'

'Damon, I…'

'There's no excuse for what I've done. Yes, I wanted to give Mario the best and most secure of family lives, but instead I've just brought misery and acted selfishly.'

Abbie stared up at him, her heart thundering painfully. 'So you want a divorce?'

'No! That's the last thing I want, Abbie!' His voice grated harshly and there was such torment in his eyes as he looked at her that she wanted to reach out to him. 'I'm a proud man, Abbie—possibly too proud.' His lips twisted cynically. 'But I'm not too proud to beg you now. Please don't end our marriage.'

'Damon, don't!' She took a step closer to him. She hated to see him like this. 'You didn't need to beg. I know how much you love Mario. I won't take him away from you. I couldn't live with myself, knowing how much he means to you—'

'Yes, he means a lot to me.' Damon reached out and touched her face. 'But so do you, Abbie.'

'Do I?' The heart-wrenching question made Damon's insides turn over with regret. He murmured something in Sicilian, before shaking his head. 'I've been such a fool where you are concerned. I believed what John Newland told me about you, when he was an obvious charlatan.'

'Well, he could be very convincing,' Abbie murmured. 'When my mother got sick and I had to ring him for help, I believed for one crazy moment that he felt some compassion for her circumstances.' She shook her head. 'But that man doesn't appear to have an ounce of compassion in his soul.'

'Unlike his daughter—who has too much, who has forgiven me against all the odds.'

'You were hurt by him too.'

'Abbie, can we try again?'

The sudden question made her heart almost stop beating.

'I've been such an idiot,' he rasped. 'I've never deserved you. And I know I've made a mess of things. But we are married now…and we are good together, aren't we?'

The question tore her up.

'You mean the chemistry is still good between us,' she corrected him huskily.

'Yes.' For a second his eyes moved towards her lips. 'There is no denying that. Is there?'

She shook her head; there was no way she could deny that.

'And we've got the most wonderful son in the world who we both adore.'

She smiled at that. 'Yes.'

'So let me try and make amends by being the best husband you could wish for.'

For a second Abbie's eyes shimmered with tears. She wanted to say yes, she wanted to go back into his arms so badly. But she knew she couldn't. She just couldn't give herself to him again, knowing that the love between them wasn't there. That he would only be doing this for his son. It was too painful, and she loved him too much to be able to bear it.

'Damon, we were good together, and the chemistry between us is strong.' Her voice shook alarmingly. 'But it's not enough.'

'Don't say that, Abbie, please!' His eyes held hers steadily. 'I'm nothing without you. Please say you will be my wife for ever this time. For richer or poorer, in sickness and in health, all the days of our lives I want to cherish you and love you and be with you.'

'You want to love me?' Her heart skipped a few beats.

He nodded. 'Abbie, I love you more than you could ever know. I've just been too proud, and…' His lips twisted in a rueful way. 'Maybe too frightened by my feelings for you to admit it—even to myself.'

Abbie couldn't find her voice to say anything for a moment; she was too overwhelmed by what he had just told her. 'You really love me?' she managed at last. 'Really?'

'With all my heart.'

A tear trickled down her pale face. 'Damon, I don't know what to say, I…'

'Just say that we can stay together and give our marriage a chance. That's all I'm asking for, Abbie. I know you don't love me—in fact I know you've downright disliked me sometimes, and I've deserved it. I've said some terrible things, done some terrible things, and I'm deeply sorry. But let me try and make things up to you, please.'

'I've never disliked you,' she murmured. 'It's just something I said to cover my real feelings. To lie to myself.'

He frowned. 'But I've made you so very sad sometimes.' He wiped her tears away with a tender hand. 'On our wedding day, for instance, I made you cry.' His voice cracked with fierce emotion. 'I hated myself for that.'

'I didn't cry because you made me sad, Damon,' she whispered softly. 'I cried because I realised how much I loved you. I've always loved you. Right from that first moment we met in Las Vegas and I looked into your eyes out by the swimming pool.'

'You loved me?' His voice sounded strange as if he hardly dared to believe what she had said. 'But I heard you tell your father that what he had done had ruined your life. That everything hadn't turned out for the best.'

'I was talking about the fact that he'd turned you against me—that we had wasted precious years apart, that even now you didn't trust me. And I loved you so much.'

'Oh my darling.' He pulled her close and held her. 'My darling Abigail. I'm so sorry…for putting you through that torment. I misunderstood, and all I could think was that I had ruined your life by bringing you here. I felt so wretchedly guilty that I had to get out of the house—I didn't know what to do, where to put myself.'

She leaned against him and wound her arms around his neck. 'Damon, I love you, and I want to make this marriage work more than anything in this world.'

'I want that too, more than you will ever know.' He pulled away from her for a moment and then kissed her, a long, sensual, burning kiss that made her heart turn over with longing. He murmured something to her in Italian.

'I don't understand what you are saying,' she whispered.

'I'm saying that I love you so much,' he whispered hungrily. 'Need you so much.'

'Me too.'

He kissed her again and then, sweeping her up into his arms, carried her back into the bedroom.

Abbie laughed tremulously. 'We haven't got time for this, Damon, we need to get back to the hospital.'

'Yes, but first we have some more making-up to do.'

'And secondly?' She looked up at him playfully as he put her down on the bed.

'Secondly there are a few Sicilian phrases I need to run by you. Phrases like "I love you" and "I adore you" and "I will always be here for you"…'

'I'd love to learn those words, Damon.' She reached up to kiss him, knowing that for the first time in her life she was truly home, truly happy.

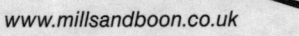

Celebrate 100 years of pure reading pleasure with Mills & Boon®

To mark our centenary, each month we're publishing a special 100th Birthday Edition. These celebratory editions are packed with extra features and include a FREE bonus story.

Plus, you have the chance to enter a fabulous monthly prize draw. See 100th Birthday Edition books for details.

Now that's worth celebrating!

July 2008

**The Man Who Had Everything
by Christine Rimmer**
Includes FREE bonus story *Marrying Molly*

August 2008

Their Miracle Baby by Caroline Anderson
Includes FREE bonus story *Making Memories*

September 2008

Crazy About Her Spanish Boss by Rebecca Winters
Includes FREE bonus story
Rafael's Convenient Proposal

Look for Mills & Boon® 100th Birthday Editions at your favourite bookseller or visit
www.millsandboon.co.uk

FREE

4 BOOKS AND A SURPRISE GIFT!

We would like to take this opportunity to thank you for reading this Mills & Boon® book by offering you the chance to take FOUR more specially selected titles from the Modern™ series absolutely FREE! We're also making this offer to introduce you to the benefits of the Mills & Boon® Book Club™—

- ★ **FREE home delivery**
- ★ **FREE gifts and competitions**
- ★ **FREE monthly Newsletter**
- ★ **Books available before they're in the shops**
- ★ **Exclusive Mills & Boon Book Club offers**

Accepting these FREE books and gift places you under no obligation to buy; you may cancel at any time, even after receiving your free shipment. Simply complete your details below and return the entire page to the address below. You don't even need a stamp!

YES! Please send me 4 free Modern books and a surprise gift. I understand that unless you hear from me, I will receive 6 superb new titles every month for just £2.99 each, postage and packing free. I am under no obligation to purchase any books and may cancel my subscription at any time. The free books and gift will be mine to keep in any case.

P8ZEE

Ms/Mrs/Miss/Mr..Initials ....
BLOCK CAPITALS PLEASE

Surname ....

Address ....

....

....Postcode ....

Send this whole page to:
The Mills & Boon Book Club, FREEPOST CN81, Croydon, CR9 3WZ

TOKEN OF DRAGONSBLOOD

Damaris Cole

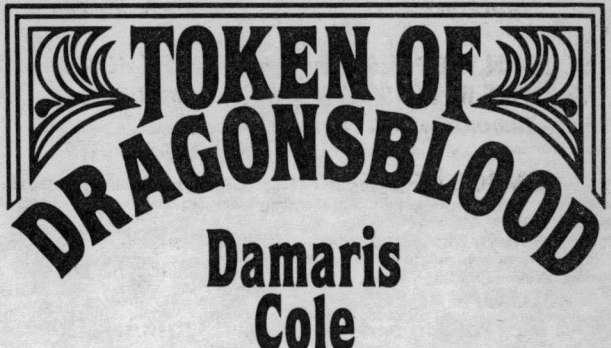

TOKEN OF DRAGONSBLOOD

When she awoke, blackness surrounded her. It was pierced only by a thin sliver of moonlight through a tiny parting in the window hangings and the glow of embers in the fireplace. Noressa lay still, trying to determine what had awakened her.

From near the fireplace came the quiet shuffle of someone approaching, and a figure passed across the slice of moonlight. Recognizing the dwarf's silhouette, Noressa clasped a handful of bedding and waited. As the dwarf reached a hand out toward her, she flung the coverlet over him and wrestled him to the floor. He gave no struggle but lay passive as Noressa sat astride his legs and pulled the cover from his face.

"You play a dangerous game, dwarf. What brings you to my bedchamber at this hour?"

His voice was soft but urgent. "I came to warn you. If you wish to live past the morrow's sunset, you must leave here tonight! Now!"

Other TSR™ Books

For Brandon, a very special boy

PROLOGUE

On the world of Yerel, in the land of Sidra, an arcane war was fought between eldritch sisters.

Once a flourishing nation, Sidra lay in the deadly grip of an invading evil. No more did her merchant ships ply the waters of the Taserel and Evorli seas, their gold and white sails promising the delivery of rare treasures. No longer were her fields covered with ripening crops of zalia grain, nor did her forests shelter herds of fattened yarja. Her markets and ports, her river landings and trade routes, once thronged by outlanders come to vie for her goods and riches, lay desolate and empty.

The evil that had descended on Sidra was borne on the wind. It seeped into the earth, seeming to leech the very strength and will from both land and people alike. Women faltered at their weaving looms, men plodded despairingly behind their plows, and children huddled, pale and silent, before their hearth fires. Such had become the land of Sidra.

But there were those few who continued in their fight against the oppressive malignancy, and on a clear, dark night, they made a desperate stand in the fortress of Ac'talzea.

On that night, black smoke hung thick and heavy, a pall over the countryside. It snaked out across the land, its dark bulk fed by the rolling coils writhing forth from the village turned inferno. The screams of dying men and the shrieks of things not human mingled with the clash of sword against shield and the angry roar of the fire.

On a hill overlooking the village, Castle Ac'talzea stood as the final defense against the approaching army. Atop the walls, grim-faced soldiers watched as black soot obscured the pale moon and blotted the stars like a hungry black beast that devoured all light in its path. Fearful yet defiant, the warriors awaited their destruction.

In the darkness below, two mounted figures slipped from the castle. One rider clasped a wriggling bundle. Keeping the fortress between themselves and the village, they fled along the shallow valley toward the river.

CHAPTER 1

She was a gilded vision of death. Her silken gown accentuated the sensual curve of her breasts and hips, its dusty violet hue matching that of her eyes. Unbound and free-flowing in the manner of her people, her figure-length hair was a mantle of gold.

With a double column of soldiers at her back, Felaya strode in triumph through the ruined keep into the great hall and paused to survey the room. It had been the final stronghold of the battle, the place most heavily guarded, and it lay undisturbed by the fighting. The walls were hung with tapestries depicting magnificent battles and coronations. To the left sat the *shill bae*, the lords' council table, each of its five empty chairs draped by a silk banner emblazoned with a different family crest. To the right sat the *shill kren*, the judges' table, also empty.

Beyond the tables on a three-tiered dais, six men, three on either side, flanked a throne of dark, carved wood. Swords drawn, they waited with impassive faces to defend the woman seated between them. Behind the royal chair stood an elderly maidservant.

Felaya felt the dissipating vestiges of an arcane energy and smiled, moving in arrogant fashion toward the royal figure. Her inner self continued to probe for any remaining sign of the power that had held her besieging army from the castle for four days, but she found none. The woman before her was strangely empty.

Felaya stopped before the dais and inclined her head in a mock bow, the movement sending shimmering ripples through the golden hair cascading to her heels. Her eyes reflected the cool amusement of her smile. "Queen Breann, how kind you are to grant me this audience."

The women regarded each other in silence. Breann's emaci-

9

ated figure seemed lost in the confines of the throne. Her once-lustrous dark hair was dull and gray-streaked. It hung unbound, framing her thin face, held back only by a delicate jeweled crown. Fatigue underlined her gray eyes in dark smears, and she appeared scarcely able to sit upright.

Felaya knit her brow in reproach. "Come, come, little Sister. Have you no welcome for me? No cool wine to slake my thirst or soothing balm for my travel-weary feet?"

Breann maintained her silence. Her gaze moved dispassionately over Felaya's figure—past the witch's dagger suspended at her waist by a silver belt, then upward to linger on the tiny gold medallion at Felaya's throat, at the bloodstone glowing softly scarlet.

A glimmer of apprehension pricked at Felaya. She sent a thought into Breann's mind and found . . . nothing. Her apprehension grew. "Where is Salet that she does not attend you, Sister?"

There was a moment of fright in Breann's face, then her eyes narrowed and she looked past Felaya to the black-robed wizard advancing imperiously through the double row of soldiers. His handsome face was twisted by a look of contempt.

The old maidservant behind the throne drew a hissing breath and tottered forward to spit at his feet. "You dare to enter this hall? Traitor! Killer of kings! Do you think for one minute the illusion of your past youth will hide the blood on your hands or the truth of the diseased and dying old fool you truly are, Tylek of Eksorm?"

"Ah, but you are wrong." Felaya laughed. "His youth is no illusion. One night in my bed was proof of that." Her voice became a caressing enticement. "A strong young body is only one of many gifts I can offer, old mother."

"Call me not mother, soulless whore. I will die a thousand deaths before I become such as you!"

"And you shall, old hag! But first you will live to see your precious queen draw her last breath." Breann's guards stiffened in anticipation of attack as Felaya turned her angry gaze to her sister. "Your flattened belly tells me you are delivered of your child, Breann." A cruel smile rested on Felaya's lips. "It is regrettable that you will not live to see it grown, but fear not, for I shall raise the orphan as my own."

Breann leaned forward, a flush of anger on her face. Pointing a quivering finger at Felaya, she sent a flicker of blue flame dancing between them. Felaya stood smiling, unscathed, and answered the attack with a vermillion bolt that pitched Breann backward.

Seeing their queen so abused, the swordsmen charged. A look and a word from Felaya halted them in midstride, her enchantment forcing them to watch their queen's downfall in helpless silence.

"Foolish Sister. Did you think to goad me into granting you an easy death? When I am ready, I will choose the time to release your Companion."

Breann's lips curled into a grim smile. "You are wrong, Sister. You have worked your sorcery too well. Already death sucks the breath from my lips. But my death will avail you nothing, for I no longer possess what you seek."

It was not Breann's words so much as the desolate emptiness in her eyes that stripped Felaya's triumph from her, setting in its place a cold fear. Breann reached to brush away the hair from her neck, revealing a throat of pale, bare skin.

Felaya stared, incredulous, a hand pressed to the medallion at her own throat. "Where is it? Where is the Token of Dragonsblood?"

Breann's look was almost pitying, and she leaned wearily against her maidservant's arm. "Believe what you see, Felaya. Have you not sensed my emptiness? I am . . . alone."

At once, Felaya reached through her own token to the alien mind that so long ago had bonded with hers. She felt the familiar pulse that was her Companion, Kael. Felaya drew slightly on that bond, feeling Kael's strength become her own, and her fright became anger.

"You lie, Sister. No one could bear to put away the power of her Companion. But I know how to find the truth." She whirled on the wizard behind her. "Bring me the child!"

Tylek's look was one of self-assurance. "My men are searching even now. They will find the child."

Felaya approached the dais, one hand clenched on the hilt of her dagger, her voice almost a whisper. "You will not trick me into believing the child has received the Companion, for I know it is not of an age to petition a joining. But you will give me what I seek, or you shall watch your babe die."

Breann smiled again. "You have taken my husband, my land, and my life, Sister. But you will have neither my Companion nor my child." With her final words, all strength went out of her. She sighed, letting her eyelids flutter closed.

Sobbing, the old maidservant fell to her knees. With gentle touches, she pressed her queen's lifeless hand to her cheek. "Oh, mistress, mistress!"

Felaya ascended the dais. Her face flushed with restrained fury, she took the golden circlet from her sister's head. "Be silent, old woman. I am mistress now!"

Soon Tylek's men returned to report that no child was to be found. Only then did the castle reverberate with Felaya's screams of rage.

*　*　*　*　*

They fled through the days and nights that blurred one into the other, a gray-bearded elder and a dark-haired woman with an infant. From Sidra, they traveled across the Bourne River into Dromund and to the city of Tarragon.

Leaving the elder as a shield for her back, the woman continued west toward the mountains, searching.

Deep within the Skellen Mountains, a peasant woman lay raging with birthing fever while her husband mourned at the grave of their stillborn child.

CHAPTER 2

Light filtered through the shuttered cottage windows, to be lost in the darkness of the surrounding forest.

Inside, Noressa paced nervously, stopping on occasion to peer through the shutters into the night. Uneasy, she fingered the black, waist-length plait of hair falling across one shoulder. The restless feeling that had plagued her through the winter was now like a wild animal snapping at her heels. She bit her lip and folded her arms tight against herself to keep from flinging the door wide and rushing headlong into the darkness.

Noressa stopped to check, yet again, the traveling provisions that lay ready on the small trestle table. Inspecting the bindings on the food pack and the herb pocket roll, she laid them aside and tested the weight of the small leather sack heavy with coins. Beneath her long cloak and clothes bundle lay her bow, quiver of arrows, and hunting knife.

Assured that she had forgotten nothing, Noressa wandered through the cottage, pausing to examine different items. The table linens her mother had woven, her father's favorite pipe, the footstool she had helped him make—all would be left behind come morning. Touching each object, she tried to fill her mind with the memories that must last her a lifetime, memories that would be her only companions when she left at dawn.

But cutting under the grief and loneliness evoked by these thoughts was the anger that gave her sorrow a bitter edge. "Why?" she demanded of the empty cottage. "Why did you not fight harder? You both gave up too easily."

Eyes burning with tears, Noressa stumbled to her room. But she stopped short of flinging herself onto the bed. She was afraid that if she gave way to her tears at this moment, she also might give up.

Standing in the doorway of her tiny sleeping room, Noressa wiped her eyes and looked about the cottage. Realizing how little it had changed through the years brought a fresh surge of pain.

Before the fireplace sat the long, high-backed bench where she had spent many winter evenings listening to her parents' stories. Dominating the rest of the room was the wooden eating table. In its center, a daxet tallow candle flickered, adding its yellow light to that of the log fire.

Watching the shadows dance, Noressa could see again her mother and father at the table. Memory washed over her, and she was back in her eighth year. She remembered crouching in her room, peering through a tear in the cloth that served as her door. She listened to her parents argue and wished the *knowing* could have warned her of this, too.

The *knowing* had wakened her early in the morning, sending her into the forest to bring down a meirmek for their supper. And it had been the *knowing* that had sent her halfway down the mountain to meet her father in late afternoon.

The evening had been a pleasant one. After their meal, she had presented him with the meirmek's feathers, knowing he would use them to fletch more arrows. Then she helped him unpack the gifts he had brought from Tarragon. She enjoyed unrolling the lengths of fine linen cloth and pieces of exquisite lace, but the last gift, she had felt, was the best. It was also the crux of her parents' argument.

Her parents sat at the table, where her mother glared at the heap of linens and lace. Her father sat counting a pile of coins before him. Setting aside a smaller pile of silver and copper, he tossed in three gold coins. The rest he returned to the thick leather sack hidden beneath the loose flagstone on the hearth. The silver and copper he placed in a wooden bowl on a high shelf.

"There is nothing to be said, Rina. It is already done."

Her mother stood to face him, her anger making Noressa flinch. "It is too much for me, Rolf, too much! Each year I am alone for a full cycle and more while you make your mysterious trip to Tarragon. Each year you return with gifts and sacks of gold, saying it is for services given, but what services you will not say. And now you return, saying we must send away our own child. It is too much for me!"

"I am not sending her away. Only down to the village for schooling. She is old enough now to learn more than hunting or roaming the mountain like a wild daxet."

"But what need has a huntsman's daughter for scrolls and curtsies?" her mother objected. "She needs to be here, with me, learning about spinning and herbs and the proper care of a man's home for when she marries. It is shameful enough that you teach her fighting and hunting as if she were your son. Now you would fill her mind with the useless fripperies of a village noble until she will be such a contrary girl that no man will have her."

Her father only shook his head and bent to kiss her mother's face. "She will go."

Noressa knew by the quiet authority in his voice that the matter was settled. Her mother knew it, also, for she let herself be led off to bed with only her tears as further argument.

Noressa returned to her own bed, snuggling into the warmth of her embroidered blankets, also gifts from one of her father's trips, and waited eagerly for morning. Outside, Diml's faint glow softened the darkness of the night sky. Before Diml's cycle waxed full and bright, Noressa had become a student and member of the kren-hold, the judge's house.

Noressa sighed as the memory faded, leaving her with the reality of being alone now, a reality she did not want to face. She moved to the table and fingered the smooth curve of her bow.

The weapon brought back images of her father's lean, sure hands shaping a piece of wood or in the delicate process of fletching an arrow. How strong he had been. And how she had loved him for it!

Secure in his strength, he had ignored the villagers' scorn for teaching her the way of the huntress. Once he responded to a castigation from a village leader, "Less than feminine it may be, elder, but when I am dead, my child will never be at the mercy of village charity to put food on her table." He glowered at the throng of smirking young men who were enjoying his public chastisement. "Nor without a means to ensure her privacy and virtue."

At times, Noressa often wondered if he were not compelled

in some way to teach her, so great was his determination that she learn. But whatever his reason, she had been an eager pupil. She loved the mountains and the excitement of the hunt and, most of all, being with her father.

Those had been the good days, days full of her father's laughter and independence, and also his strange journeys to Tarragon. Her mother would cry and watch him out of sight down the mountain, frightened that her man was off to face wicked temptations. Noressa watched him go and ached to join him on a wonderful adventure.

Then came the sickness. Slowly at first. Mornings when her father rose with a stiffness in his legs, a lingering pain in his back. Too soon came the crippling that swelled his hands, twisting them into useless, gnarled lumps, twisting his spirit as well into something small and frightened.

In the four years since the crippling, he had not made his yearly trip to Tarragon. He spent his days hunched before the fire, haunted eyes staring into the flames. Then death had come with this past winter's first snowfall. Diml had not completed a full cycle before her mother died as well, as much from heartbreak as from the coughing sickness.

Settling onto the fireside bench, Noressa shook her head to clear away the painful thoughts. "Sorrowful memories are not what I need to begin a journey." She tossed her head in defiance of the pain that lingered. "My parents are dead. I am a woman now. I must begin my own life!" Leaning back, with eyes closed and legs outstretched to the fire, she forced all thought from her mind. Eventually she drowsed, until a half-forgotten childhood nightmare returned. . . .

She wandered on a misted plain, stumbling, searching out the sweet, distant voice that called to her. It beckoned, offering sanctuary from the horror that rushed and snorted behind her. Blinded, she struggled through the darkness, her mind whirling with her efforts to lay name to the voice. An instant from full realization, she was overcome. A shadow of fear and hatred passed overhead, pressing her to the ground. All-enveloping, it gnawed at her until it had consumed all but her despair.

Her own scream awoke her. As a child, she had wakened to the safety of her father's embrace. But tonight she was alone;

there were no strong arms to comfort her now.

"You gave up too soon, Father. I still need you." Her whisper seemed to echo about her as Noressa sat trying to slow the frantic drumming of her heart. She rose to pace rapidly in a short, tight line before the fire.

The dream had heightened her need to be gone. The summoning, that unexplained yearning that had plagued her since her mother's death, was strong in her mind. Once again she fought the urge to run blindly into the night.

Common sense held her back. Should she race through the darkness until she plunged off some precipice? Perhaps she could run screaming to Dolaes for sympathy. She knew the smug self-assurance that would greet such behavior, and her agitation became anger as she remembered his arrogance.

Only two days after her mother's burial, he had swaggered into her cottage with his proposal of marriage. He let her know that, as a peasant girl already twenty years of age and unmarried, she should be grateful for the chance to wed the judge's eldest son.

Enjoying her astonishment, he also made it clear that he would enjoy removing her from the status of *til bren*. Disgusted by the thought of herself, or any maiden, being brought to womanhood by Dolaes, Noressa had driven him from the cottage. Even so, she knew that he spoke the truth; if she stayed, Dolaes would be the best she could do. In that moment, she had made the decision to leave at winter's end.

A light tapping on the door sounded through her musings. Noressa hefted the long hunting knife from the table and went to answer the knock. "Who is there? What do you want?"

An old woman's voice answered. "I bring news for Noressa, daughter of Rolf the huntsman." Noressa hesitated, then scolded herself mentally. It was only the memory of the dream that made her suspicious.

She unbarred and opened the door.

Firelight poured out to reveal an old woman, her thin shawl and patched dress scant protection from the cold night. She stood rubbing her bony hands together and glancing uneasily over her shoulder. Noressa peered into the darkness behind the woman but could make out only the dark mass of trees surrounding the cottage.

"I am Noressa, old mother. You have news for me?" The woman nodded, edging forward. "Then come in and warm yourself."

"Thank ye, child, thank ye!" The woman entered but waited until Noressa had closed and barred the door before hurrying to the fire. Her smile was rueful when she turned to find Noressa watching her with great curiosity. "Spring has come to the land, but winter lives deep in an old woman's bones."

Noressa smiled, motioning her to the table. "Sit down, grandmother, and I will bring you some tea." She poured the tea, then brought a thick shawl, draping it over the woman's shoulders.

The woman smiled her thanks and pointed to the traveling provisions. "Ye are leaving soon?"

"Yes. At dawn."

"The powers be thanked, I have reached ye in time!"

Noressa pushed back the sudden uneasiness crowding into her mind. What harm could an old woman bring to her? She took a seat across from the woman. "You are a stranger here, old mother. What news can you have for me?"

The woman wrapped her hands tight around the mug of tea, then glanced about as if to be sure they were alone. "I am Edell from the village of Athelwayte. Some days ago, during the last heavy rain, a woman came to me door beggin' a bed for the night. She beguiled me with soft words and a gold coin, so I took her in. I did not know her to be a witch until too late."

Noressa shivered at the woman's words and wished she had started her journey yesterday. She had no wish to become entangled with witches and a crazy old woman on the eve of her new life alone. Still, she was intrigued to discover how Edell's story of a witch might somehow lead to news for her.

Edell paused, squinted at the door, and gulped her tea before continuing. "When I awoke the next day, I found she had taken a fever and could not travel. I tended her as best I could, and for a time, she rallied. But then she lapsed again."

Once more the woman's gaze darted around the room, and Noressa's unease increased. Clutching the shawl with one blue-veined hand, Edell went to peek through the shutters, checking to see that they were securely fastened.

"You seem to be expecting someone, mother Edell."

Edell returned to her seat and leaned forward, speaking in a low voice. "As I told you, she was a witch. When she knew that she was dying, she charged me with delivering her message. She cursed me, saying I would not rest easy until I had done her bidding. I want only to deliver the message and be on my way."

Edell closed her eyes and recited carefully. "Find the tree in the crossroads, in the markets of Tarragon. By the Token of Dragonsblood, he will know you are the one." She opened her eyes and stared hard into Noressa's face. "She said you must follow your dream-call."

Noressa sat in stunned silence while the woman fumbled in a pocket of her skirt and withdrew a knotted piece of cloth. Edell pushed the object across the table to Noressa, then leaned back and sighed, as if relieved of a great burden.

Noressa untied the cloth. It fell open and she stared at the treasure it held. Linked on a delicate silver chain, a small gold medallion winked back the fireglow. Chased along the outside rim was the slender form of a two-horned dragon, wings furled against its body. She marveled at the wonderful detail, the tiny clawed feet and minute scales. In the medallion's center, a tiny red drop glistened. Noressa reached to touch the droplet, and a jolt of power surged through her. She snatched her hand back, trembling, letting the pendant fall.

Noressa fought down the panic threatening to engulf her. The energy she had felt revived the terror of her nightmare. It compounded the restlessness of the past winter and awakened a heavy foreboding in her. She pushed the medallion, on its cloth, back toward Edell. "You have mistaken me for another. I am not the one you seek."

Edell shook her head, refusing to touch the cloth or its contents. "It is you I seek. The witch searched for a gray-eyed girl with hair as black as a moonless night, living in a cottage above the village Moaak. I sought for Noressa, daughter of Rolf the huntsman, and so you have named yourself." The woman shook her head again when Noressa would have argued. "I have discharged me duty. I'm free of it. It lies with you now."

Noressa swallowed the angry words on her tongue. "Very

well. You have done me a service, old mother. Ask what you will, and I shall give it if I can."

The woman's eyes darted around the room and came to rest on the food cupboard. "It has been a long journey for old Edell. Me provisions were poor and few to begin with."

Indeed, Noressa thought to herself. And what of the gold coin the witch gave you? And whatever else she left behind at her death.

Still, a meal was a small enough price to pay, even for such unsettling news. In silence, Noressa set out the remains of her own supper—bread, cheese, boiled thaga leaves, and roast yarja. It all disappeared as Edell fell upon it. Noressa questioned her as she ate.

"Is there nothing more you can tell me of this witch-woman? What was she called? From whence did she come?"

Edell shook her head, wiped her mouth on a grimy sleeve, and gulped the last of her cold tea. Noressa rose to refill the cup.

"There is little else, child. Her name was Salet, but that is all I know. She rambled often in her fever, talking of babes and wars and strange things."

Noressa had many more questions, but Edell could answer none to her satisfaction. When the woman had finished eating her meal, Noressa led her to the tiny room that had been her own.

Edell's eyes widened at the sight of the bed piled high with thick, warm blankets and a plump down pillow. She stepped gingerly onto the multicolored woven mat that covered most of the dirt floor. Edell gawked for a long moment at the tapestry of Diml, Lady of the Moon, recumbent on a silver couch. "Ye live well for a huntsman's daughter."

Noressa did not answer, but turning to leave, she stopped in the doorway. "Old woman, on the morrow I will leave this place forever. As I have no family, this house will stand empty. You are welcome to all I leave behind, and you may stay here or go, as you wish." Then she dropped the curtain and left the old woman standing openmouthed in the midst of her new-found wealth.

Noressa paced most of the night. She stopped often to gaze down at the medallion, fascinated by its intricate beauty but unwilling to experience again that strange surge of power. So the medallion lay untouched while questions chased themselves through her mind.

What was the strange power the token held? Why had it been sent to her? What had made the witch-woman certain that she, Noressa, would make the journey for her? And why Tarragon?

That name conjured the loneliness she had worked so hard to put away from her. It brought back memories of the stories her mother had told while they sat carding the long sirre hair for spinning or stringing shaba roots to dry in the summer sun.

She remembered the faraway look in her mother's eyes when she described the clamor and bustle of the port city's markets. Noressa had marveled that any place, even a thriving port such as Tarragon, could boast three full markets, Clar, Sten, and Lont, each market named for the trade route that fed into that portion of the city. Noressa had long wanted to see the Molevean klasers lumbering into the harbor, their hulls painted with bizarre multicolored designs to ward off evil sea spirits and their holds filled with exotic cargoes.

But it was the Plains of Bada-shi that had most intrigued Noressa. Surrounded by her towering mountains, she had never seen anything like the grasslands where her mother had been raised.

"Between Tarragon and the hills," her mother would say, "in every direction—unlimited measures of rippling emptiness." And if her father were present at the moment, her mother would add, "Nothing to be seen save a sima tree and a self-proud huntsman."

Then they would smile together, each remembering the tale of a young Rina, who for three years watched the mountain huntsman traverse the grasslands to win the archer's tournament in Tarragon. In the third year, she accompanied him home as his wife.

Noressa blinked away the tears her memories brought, scolding herself. "You are a child no longer, and tears will not change what is past." Her brave words lost their strength in the empty room.

Perhaps the journey to Tarragon will give my leaving a purpose, she reasoned to herself. Then, having seen something of the land, I can decide what direction my life should take. What place there is for a huntsman's daughter, I do not know. But I will find it—or make it.

And there was the summoning that drew her mind eastward. Tarragon stood to the east. Perhaps, in delivering the amulet, she might learn more of the strange call that compelled her.

Noressa continued to argue with herself until, toward morning, she slept for a time on the bench before the fire. When she awoke, gray dawn was paling the sky.

She rose and stretched her cramped legs, her gaze falling on the pendant. For just an instant, it seemed that the dragon moved, writhing on the edge of the medallion. Noressa shook her head, staring hard at the gold piece, but the dragon was still and the center droplet was only a dull red stone.

Noressa wiped the sleep from her eyes and stirred up the fire, casting frequent worried glances at the pendant. She was preparing fresh tea when the old woman emerged from the bedchamber, a blanket clutched around her. Hesitant, Edell smiled and joined Noressa at the fire.

After a moment, she turned to Noressa. "Did ye speak me true last night when ye gave me hold to this house?"

"Yes, grandmother, the offer was true. If you decide to stay, I will bring down a yarja and dress it that you will have meat for a while."

Edell turned back to the fire, trying to hide her tears. "I will stay."

Noressa donned her hunting cloak, took up her bow and quiver, and slipped from the cottage into the forest. The sky was lightening quickly, but the ground was still deep in shadow; in a moment, she had become one with the shadows.

Not far up the mountain, Noressa came upon a pack of dakwi ravaging the body of a yarja. The stiff white bristles along their otherwise hairless backs flared upward. The dakwis' short, heavy bodies twisted and jerked as their fangs tore chunks of meat from the carcass.

Noressa shivered. The yarja's still-moist eyes and the scent of warm blood told her that this was the dakwis' own fresh kill. Carefully she worked her way around them, leaving the squealing animals to their feast. The usually timid scavengers were in a breeding bloodlust, and she had no wish to attract their attention to herself.

Moving farther uphill, she soon found spoor of another yarja. Tracking the slender-legged beast, Noressa was passing a deadfall when movement caught her eye. She saw a brown sirre perched atop a fallen log. His glossy fur, fluffed up, made him appear twice his size. She grinned at his angry chatter and pursed her lips to answer. Suddenly the creature flattened itself against the log, its long nose twitching in panic. Then it turned and disappeared into the burrow within the fallen tree.

Noressa felt strangely exposed in the hush that followed. No bird trilled, no insect chirred. Something drew her gaze upward, and she searched the sky, finally picking out two dark forms.

On great black wings filled with the dawn wind, two manshapes came gliding out of the sun. They banked in a lazy circle above the village far below her. Then, like iac hounds finding a blood scent, they wheeled and flew toward the cottage nestled on the mountainside.

Noressa watched in horror, while below, a lone figure dropped its burden of firewood and scampered inside. Screaming in triumph, the creatures folded their wings and dove earthward. With a strangled cry, Noressa plunged down the mountain.

Heedless of the brush that snagged at her clothes and whipped her face, she ran, intent only on reaching the house below her. From the cottage, Edell's terrified screams spurred her on.

The instant she broke into the clearing around the cottage, the two creatures emerged from the house, dragging Edell's limp form between them. One creature threw back its dark, furred head and howled exultantly, holding aloft the silver-chained medallion.

Noressa screamed her rage. Taking up a length of the discarded firewood, she hurled it at the beast. The log struck, causing the creature to stumble. Noressa drew back at the hatred contorting the fiend's dark, pointed face as it whirled to face her. The pendant fell from its grasp as the creature lunged, its taloned claws reaching for her.

Stepping back in that instant of attack, Noressa thrust aside her emotion, becoming once more a hunter facing her prey. With quick, familiar movements, she drew and nocked an arrow. She sighted, released, and watched the fiend stagger from the force of the arrow suddenly sprouting from its throat.

Fingers clawing at the shaft, the monster's thin body writhed. Leathery wings flapped convulsively as the creature collapsed in a twitching heap.

Noressa drew a second arrow and braced for an attack from the remaining fiend. But though it hissed and gnashed its teeth, the beast continued to drag Edell with it. Huge wings beat in a frantic but useless effort to rise with its victim. At last the fiend released Edell and rose, screaming, into the air. But it did not rise quickly enough to escape the arrow that drove deep into its chest. Wailing its pain, the creature lurched through the air, then plummeted into the forest.

Noressa ran to Edell and cradled the woman's battered body in her arms. She brushed the gray hair back from the pale, bruised face. Hot tears blurred her sight, but not enough to hide Edell's pain-filled, questioning look.

"Why . . . why? I did me charge. They . . . made for the token straightaway. . . . I didn't try to stop them. Why?"

Noressa could not answer. She held the old woman close until the staring eyes and lolling head told her that Edell was no more.

Grief and anger raged inside her. What wretched treasure was this that forced an old woman from her home under threat of curse and then destroyed her once the mission had been faithfully completed? Noressa laid the woman down and moved to retrieve the medallion. Again she felt the surge of power spreading through her, but it quickly subsided when she looked toward Edell's body.

Why? The question spun itself over and over in her mind. A dying witch-woman, enchanted tokens, jumbled riddles. What did it all mean? And what had it to do with her?

An acrid stench assailed her. She turned to the body of the first fiend, but all that remained was a pool of foul black tar. She remembered the creature's savage hatred and wondered if there were yet others like it. But she knew there was only one place that held any promise of providing an answer to her thousand questions—the markets of Tarragon. Slipping the medallion around her neck, Noressa turned to the task of preparing a grave.

* * * * *

The burial was done. Noressa stood beside the grave. "I'm sorry, Edell, that you must lie in strange ground with none but me to mourn you. Were it in my power, I would give you a proper ceremony with a hundred wailers to cry you to your rest."

Instantly Noressa felt strength being pulled from her, and she stood in the midst of a crowd of black-shrouded women. She watched as the women cried. They moaned and lamented in a manner that would have paid homage to a queen.

Noressa roused herself and reached out a hand to the wailer nearest her. At her touch, the woman and her companions vanished, leaving Noressa alone with her surprise and a fading warmth where the medallion pressed against her skin.

CHAPTER 3

arly on the twelfth morning of her journey, Noressa crested the final mountain peak. She gazed down into a tiny valley cupped between the forested mountains and the smaller rocky hills. Near the far end of the valley, she was relieved to see the vague form of a village lying at the base of a gray fortress. There she would be able to purchase a new kifera to replace her mount, which had fallen prey to a dakwi pack the day before.

Looking past the village, Noressa felt her relief fade. Beyond lay the Plains of Bada-shi, the measures of open grassland her mother had spoken of so many times. Beyond that lay Tarragon. Standing on the trail, Noressa shivered. She couldn't help but feel that once she had left the familiarity of her mountains, she would have left behind the real world.

She looked up into the branches of the jerjal tree beside her and spied the clusters of tiny green fruit. She smiled as she thought of the fruit, small and nut-hard now, dangling heavy and ripe by early summer, each one as long as her thumb. Reaching up, she scored a fleshy leaf and inhaled its pungent odor. It reminded her of the spicy freshness that filled their cottage when her mother would wrap each fruit in zalia dough, then bake them beside the coals until the fruit burst to fill the bread with sticky sweetness.

Staring down into the valley again, her memories faded, leaving her alone and a little afraid. There was a duty to be performed before she could follow the strange summoning that pulled her eastward. She gave the jerjal's smooth trunk an affectionate rub. Reluctantly she headed down into the valley.

It was midmorning when the clouds that had threatened rain for two days fulfilled their promise. The cold downpour sent Noressa scurrying for shelter in a leafy stand of swayle brush. She wriggled into the protection of the thickly matted leaves and frightened a covey of bata birds. They whirred away on stubby wings that were scarcely strong enough to lift their plump bodies. Their sharp beaks sounded the clacking *bata-bata* noise that earned them their name.

Noressa had just settled herself when she felt a tremor in the ground. A feathery touch of fear at the nape of her neck made her peer cautiously through the brush. Hidden from the road, she watched the rapid approach of kifera-mounted soldiers.

The kifera trotted quickly, with long, sinuous necks held close to their hairy bodies and large, round eyes half-lidded against the rain.

The riders, a group of six, were arrayed in full battle dress. Four were swordsmen, wearing rounded helms, shirts of mail beneath back and breast plates, and calf and thigh greaves to protect their legs. In addition to broadswords, each carried a lance, shield, and short dagger. The remaining two soldiers were archers, each with heavy crossbow and wearing leather armor.

Noressa forced herself to remain still and silent, ignoring the panic that demanded she flee. She watched them pass while the *knowing* beat a painful warning in her mind.

They were a great danger. But why? For the *kalr-bae*, or holder lord, to send fully armed men out could only mean a threat of war. But if they rode to protect their hold, what danger were they to her?

The rain ended soon after they had passed, but it was a long while before Noressa left her sanctuary. Then it was with many backward glances that she continued on the road.

By early evening, she was very near the village. Behind her, the sun was slipping beyond the mountains, and Noressa watched the tattered clouds ahead being streaked orange and pink as they scurried before a brisk wind. On the ground, trees threw long shadows across the road and the wind tugged at her cloak.

Once during the day a young child had stood beside a mudstone cottage, watching her until a woman emerged to whisk him inside. There should have been men plowing their fields, Noressa knew, or perhaps a peddler, and surely a few travelers to the village market. Yet, except for the child and the soldiers, Noressa had encountered no one. A silent warning had nagged at the back of her mind the whole day. Now, seeing the light was almost gone, she quickened her pace in the hopes of reaching the village before full dark.

She hadn't gone far when the foreboding increased and she recognized the sound of kifera approaching. She wished desperately for another stand of swayle brush in which to hide. But aside from the few trees spaced at random along the road, the land stretched away on either side in partially plowed fields that the morning rain had turned to sticky mud.

Noressa paused and touched the medallion at her throat. Drawing on its power, she began weaving the illusion she had practiced during the journey.

Noressa closed her eyes, holding in her mind the image of a young man. Tall, fair-skinned, and beardless, the figure easily appeared. He stood before her, faintly at first, then with more depth as she added details. A tiny scar emerged over his left eyebrow, small calluses on fingers accustomed to pulling a bowstring, a rogue curl among the layers of straight black hair. She continued adding small touches here and there until the figure stood complete before her mind's eye.

He could have been her brother, so close was the resemblance between them. Indeed, his was the face of an imaginary childhood playmate she had often envisioned.

It was a simple illusion she had developed with the aid of the medallion, one that had made passage easier several times in villages where a lone young woman dressed in men's clothing and bearing arms would have drawn unwanted attention.

The weaving of the illusion had taken only a few breaths' time, and Noressa resumed walking. Deliberately she ignored the sounds of the mounted group behind until they were nearly on top of her. At the last moment, she stepped to the side of the road and turned to face them, afraid but confident of the image she presented.

The group reined to a stop. The lead rider was red-bearded with a wide chest and a hard set to his mouth. From his mount, he measured the handbreadth of distance between Noressa and the field. Then he exchanged a slow grin with the rider next to him and called out, "You there, stranger. Stand aside and let pass the men of Wigram's Keep!"

Noressa's reply came soft and low. "Kind sir, it would be better for all concerned if you were to pass me by and allow me this small portion of the road." She watched his face flush with anger, and he reached for his broadsword. Noressa continued, indicating the field. "Were I to step off the road, I would surely fall and begin to flail my arms and cry out loudly, making a fool of myself. This would surely upset your mount, causing him to throw you into the mud. Then not only would I be cold and wet, but you would beat me as well. And you would return home in a foul mood and be unable to enjoy your supper."

For a moment, there was silence, the rider staring in surprise. Then he threw back his head and laughed. "By the powers, this beggar will never do without. He has a tongue of silver." He leaned forward with an appraising eye and nodded toward Noressa's bow and quiver. "But then you are no beggar, eh? Where are you bound, stranger? And which master do you serve?"

Fear knotted her stomach, but Noressa forced her words out slowly, calmly. "I follow a private quest. Tonight I am bound for the village to seek a night's lodging. As for my master, I serve myself."

Again there was a silence while Noressa accepted the scrutiny of the soldier's pale blue eyes. Though her clothes were the simple garb of a hunter, they were of good quality and Noressa carried herself with a noble bearing. She wanted to make it clear that here was no peasant set out to seek his fortune, but someone of good blood with a definite purpose in mind.

The soldier smiled, though his eyes remained cold. He gestured one of his men forward. "Very well, my silver-tongued seeker. Come, ride with us to the keep. My lord would be pleased with your wit, I think."

Noressa nodded and took the offered seat behind the second soldier. When she was mounted, the lead rider introduced himself. "I am Jaaben of Hamden, captain of the guard to Lord Pashet, master of Wigram Keep."

"I am . . . Noren."

It had been slight, but the captain's eyes narrowed at her hesitation. Then he smiled broadly and turned his kifera toward the castle, his voice booming into the cool evening air. "Welcome, Noren, to our little band."

They rode quickly, despite the muddy road and fading light. They passed through the darkened village, arriving soon after at the keep. Coming from the cold darkness of the road into the smoky light of the torch-lit courtyard, they were greeted by the raucous shouts of their comrades-in-arms. Without a second look, the captain dismounted and left his kifera standing in the courtyard. Brushing past the stableboy rushing to take his mount, Jaaben led Noressa into the keep.

They stopped in a small chamber off the entrance hall, where a servant divested Jaaben of his armor. Rather than watch the captain undress, Noressa admired the room's ornate furniture and skillfully carved insignia embossing the wooden-tiled ceiling. "The craftsmen of this valley provide well for their lord."

"And well they should." Jaaben ran thick fingers through his dull brown hair, which contrasted sharply with the fiery vibrance of his beard. "Lord Pashet is worthy of the best in any place he conquers."

Surprised by the daring boast, Noressa made no answer. But when they left the small chamber, she understood why the servants passing in the hall took care to leave a wide berth between themselves and the captain. One old woman was not quick enough. When she stepped, head bent, from a doorway with an armful of linens, Jaaben gave her a push that toppled her load and sent her staggering against the stone wall. "Stupid woman! Stay out of my way!"

The woman sank to her knees and began gathering her sheets, while Noressa fought back a wave of anger. Ignoring the woman, Jaaben grinned. Clapping a hand to Noressa's shoulder, he gave her a friendly shake. "Come, boy, we mustn't keep our lord waiting. Besides, I'm hungry and, as you said, this land provides well." He leered at a buxom young maid who blushed and scurried past. Laughing in derision, Jaaben continued down the hall. Noressa followed, head bowed to hide her own flushed cheeks.

Entering the dining hall, Noressa found herself in a large, high-ceilinged room lit by many torches lining the walls and finely wrought candelabra that stood as high as a man. The far end of the room was taken up by three long tables set in an open-ended square. The tables were set with rich, steaming platters of food and crowded round with noisy soldiers. While the soldiers ate, servants moved among them, keeping up a steady flow of dark, red wine. Too warm, the hall reeked of hot wax, roast meat, and stale sweat.

Noressa was almost overcome by the heat of the room and the smell of food. She had eaten little of her bland journey food that day, promising herself a large hot meal at the village inn. Now platters of roast yarja and stuffed meirmek with t'li sauce crowded close amongst bowls of fried shabas and thin, sugar-crisped slices of ticy, while loaves of zalia bread yielded a soft whiteness beneath tender brown crusts. She was forced to concentrate completely on holding her image of Noren.

Noressa wrenched her gaze from the food and looked ahead of Jaaben as he led the way through the room. A large, red-haired man, who bore a striking resemblance to Jaaben, presided over the center table and watched them approach. To either side of him were seated more officers, but the space directly on his right was empty.

"You there." Jaaben barked an order at a wine server. "Bring a chair and wine for my guest!" Motioning the other officers to move down, Jaaben bade Noressa sit beside him and seated himself next to the red-haired man.

"Brother Pashet, see what I have brought you," Jaaben addressed the warlord. "A silver-tongued seeker. A freeman on a quest; for what, I do not know."

Pashet nodded, not speaking until Noressa had divested herself of weapons, then he turned to his brother, speaking low so that she was unable to hear. Noressa busied herself with settling into the chair that had been brought. Her cloak draped across the back of the chair, she bent to lay her weapons at her feet, and her eyes met those of a small, squat figure huddled under the table at Pashet's feet. Surprised, she straightened in time to hear Jaaben speaking to his brother. "If the boy can use his bow half as well as he uses his tongue, he'd be a boon to any master."

Seeming impressed with his brother's report, Pashet addressed Noressa. "It isn't often that a man, especially one so young, can charm my hot-blooded brother. You are to be congratulated." He gestured for more wine. "What is your quest, young Noren? A fortune? A title? Mayhap you could find it here in our fair valley. There is always a place for a good fighter."

Noressa considered a moment, aware of the many pairs of eyes that watched her. "I do not feel, my lord, that I possess the qualities that you require in a soldier. And as I am on a quest, I could not give myself fully to any master until it is done. Also, I do not enjoy killing."

Pashet snorted in surprise among a few scornful chuckles from some of the officers. "If that be true, then what use have you for so fine a bow?"

Noressa smiled. "A necessary evil, my lord. It keeps me fed while I travel and discourages those who would do me harm. It has been my experience that most men who choose to fight do so either for the enjoyment of inflicting pain or to take that which is not rightfully theirs."

Along their table, activity ceased. Noressa felt the captain stiffen beside her, and the wine servant who had been filling her cup scurried away. Noressa helped herself to a portion of meat as she continued. "But in the case of your great army, my lord, the inducement must surely be your fine hospitality and obvious leadership. For in truth, it is not every man who would take a stranger to his table and give him the best of his bread and wine." Raising her wine cup, Noressa faced Pashet. "Though I must decline your generous offer of position, kind sir, I thank you for your hospitality. To your health, Lord Pashet."

The last words were said loud enough that they attracted the attention of the soldiers at the other tables and brought a noisy chorus of agreement. Slowly Noressa sipped her wine, her gaze locked with Pashet's until the warlord began to grin, then burst into laughter. "You choose well, brother! Never have I been so elegantly insulted. Your guest will entertain us all this night. And speaking of entertainment—" Pashet kicked sharply.

A dirty bundle of rags rolled from under the table, sprouted arms and legs, and jumped to its feet. Before them stood a dwarf. His dark brown eyes flicked over Noressa quickly before fixing themselves on Pashet, the square-jawed face a blank mask.

Pashet speared a small chunk of meat from his plate and sniffed its warm aroma. He smiled and offered it to the dwarf. "Would you like something to eat, Bydawine? A bit of meat or some wine? I am sure I can spare it; a little man such as you would not require much." Pashet tossed the scrap, and the dwarf's eyes followed its course through the air to land at his feet. "Come, Bydawine, eat your supper. Then you must play for our guest." With a contemptuous smile, Pashet sat back and watched the dwarf's indecision.

Jaaben laughed and turned to Noressa. "Our jester is an accomplished creature. He sings and plays, makes dire predictions of doom, and can survive on a morsel a day."

The dwarf tried to stand resolute. He held his fists clenched at his sides, and his hatred of Pashet was obvious in the angry twist of his mouth. But it was obvious, too, that his hunger betrayed him. He bent to pick up the meat.

Noressa sat rigid, feeling her own anger build. She heard the derisive chuckles of the soldiers and saw the pitying looks of the servants who turned from the scene. Standing abruptly, Noressa pushed back her chair so that it grated harshly on the stone floor. Her action brought all eyes to her and a breathless silence to the chamber. Pashet's look was cold. Jaaben's hand rested on his dagger. Many of the officers mirrored their captain's pose as she faced the warlord.

Swallowing her anger somewhat, she managed a disdainful smile. "I pray you will forgive my impudence, Lord Pashet, but I find no pleasure in simply watching a man starve. I prefer instead to create my own entertainment. If you will allow me, I believe you will find it an interesting diversion."

In answer to his brother's questioning look, Pashet nodded and smiled. "If the stranger wishes to amuse us, let him have his chance."

Noressa went to stand in front of the table with the dwarf. A quick kick from her leather-booted foot sent the small bit of meat flying under a table, where it was pounced upon by a long-snouted hound. The dwarf's gaze followed it, and he swallowed hard as the hound gobbled down the unexpected treat.

She stepped to the nearest table and cut a large slice from a haunch of yarja, then took half a loaf of bread. Returning to the dwarf, she bade him hold out his two hands. As they stood thus, Noressa addressed the assembly. "It has been shown that Lord Pashet is a man of generous hospitality. Never let it be said that any man was denied food in his hall. So I say, Bydawine, eat your fill and be satisfied."

At these words, a fury twisted Pashet's face and he rose from his seat. But he stopped short as Noressa placed the food in the dwarf's outstretched hands and stepped back. At once, a wet, marshy stink filled the room, and Bydawine held not bread and meat but a black toad in one hand and a large brown rat in the other.

Bydawine made to hurl the creatures from him, but Noressa stepped forward and commanded, "Do not drop them here; I have not finished my own meal! Take them away!" And she pushed the dwarf toward the door.

Bydawine ran from the hall, followed by the foul smell and the jeering calls of the crowd.

Pashet took his seat slowly. "So, Brother, you have brought us a wandering magician."

Noressa shook her head. "I am no magician, my lord. It is merely a simple trick taught to me by a wise woman who could not pay for my services in coin. I thought it might amuse you."

Pashet inclined his head thoughtfully when he spoke. "Such a feat would prove a great boon to an army, young Noren. Had you thought on that?"

"In what way, my lord?"

Jaaben broke in eagerly. "Imagine what advantages an army could have if the enemy's entire food supply could be turned to rats and toads! Or their weapons! The man who could do such a thing would be an important man."

Noressa smiled an apology and returned to her seat. "I am not that man, then, for my trick is a simple illusion, limited to my immediate presence and the belief of those who see it. If any attempt is made to deal directly with the subject, the illusion is broken."

"Then the creatures you gave to my dwarf were only bread and meat?" Pashet's voice was soft, and his gaze was intent on a guttering candle at the end of the table.

"So it was," Noressa answered. "But it may be that even

your hungry dwarf will hesitate to eat meat that only a moment before had squirmed wetly in his hand."

Pashet's smile was a tight upturning of lips in his fiery bush of beard. "Still, it would be a useful thing to know. I would pay you well, Noren, to instruct me in such a trick. If you can spare the time from your travels."

"I could not accept your coin, my lord, but I could spare a day from my journey to a man worthy of the knowledge." Pashet smiled his acceptance while Noressa wondered how she might escape the castle by dawn.

The rest of the evening Noressa spent in idle conversation among the officers. She amused them with visions of treasure and tiny ga'hee women sensually parading along the table and other fantasies. And always she was aware of Pashet's thoughtful gaze and the pain throbbing in her head.

The night was late before she was taken to her bedchamber. It was a large, well-furnished room, one end filled by a high feather bed. The walls and window were covered with rich tapestries, and a fire blazed in the grate. Colorful woven rugs brightened the somber hue of the stone floor.

Noressa stood in the center of the elegant room, pondering a question that had plagued her throughout the evening. How could Pashet, even were he a military genius, have taken over this valley so completely without arousing the ire of his neighboring lords or the king? The servants' clear hatred of Pashet and his court gave strong support to Jaaben's boast of conquest, yet in her journey through the valley, she had seen no evidence of war. There had been no destruction of crops or homes, no sign of men having died at the hands of an invading army.

Noressa reflected on these things while she inspected her room. Finally certain that she was alone, she secured the door and removed her boots. She lay down, still dressed, and held the guise of Noren until she was safely under the coverlet. Undressing would be a waste of time. She intended to rest only a short while before attempting to leave the keep. Pashet had been friendly enough, but she understood that if Jaaben's claim to conquest were genuine, she would never be allowed to leave.

The exertion of the evening's illusion weaving had left a

whining pain in her skull. Coupled with the nagging insistence of the summoning and the silent danger cry of the *knowing*, she was exhausted.

I'll rest only a few moments, she promised herself. Just until the rest of the keep has settled for the night.

But after too many nights spent on cold, rocky ground or lumpy tavern cots, the feather bed was a wonderful change. And despite the thoughts and worries tumbling through her mind, she slept instantly.

When she awoke, blackness surrounded her. It was pierced only by a thin sliver of moonlight through a tiny parting in the window hangings and the glow of embers in the fireplace. Noressa lay still, trying to determine what had awakened her.

From near the fireplace came the quiet shuffle of someone approaching, and a figure passed across the slice of moonlight. Recognizing the dwarf's silhouette, Noressa clasped a handful of bedding and waited. As the dwarf reached a hand out toward her, she flung the coverlet over him and wrestled him to the floor. He gave no struggle but lay passive as Noressa sat astride his legs and pulled the cover from his face.

"You play a dangerous game, dwarf. What brings you to my bedchamber at this hour?"

His voice was soft but urgent. "I came to warn you. If you wish to live past the morrow's sunset, you must leave here tonight! Now!"

"Why would you come to warn me of danger? I mean nothing to you."

"You showed me a kindness, and I would repay you."

Noressa eased back, allowing the dwarf to sit upright. Invoking the guise of Noren, she rose and pulled wide the window hangings. Diml's light gleamed on the dagger in her hand. Despite the seriousness of the situation, Noressa couldn't keep the amusement from her voice. "You think it a kindness to be driven like an idiot before a jeering crowd with only a handful of filth for your supper? You are indeed a strange man, Bydawine. I am not sure I would wish you to repay me."

A half-smile flitted across the little man's face. "Strange is how your filth became a most tempting meal once I had left the hall. And stranger still is why Pashet would employ such deception to keep you here as an honored guest when he plans to have you imprisoned on the morrow."

"Imprisoned? Why? He seemed most eager to learn my little trick."

"Pashet has no need of such a trick—he has Tylek. Tylek would have laughed at such a child's game. And surely you do not believe that your wit was sufficient to excuse the liberties you took with Pashet's pride."

"I wondered, but—" Noressa shrugged. "Who is Tylek?"

"Tylek is Pashet's magician. But there is no time to talk now. I will explain as we go."

He made to rise but was brought up short by the dagger point under his chin. "Go where, little man, and why?"

"Out of the keep. No stranger who has come to Pashet's hall has ever left alive. They are always imprisoned at once and then presented to Tylek. Then they are killed—usually very slowly. Tylek waits for someone special, and no chance is taken that he might be warned."

"Who is this special one?" Noressa asked, but the prickle of apprehension along her arms told her the answer before the man spoke.

"No one knows what he is called—not even Tylek. But he will be known by an amulet, a gold chain chased round with a winged dragon and set with a blood-red stone." He cocked his head at Noressa. "Jaaben has told Pashet that you possess such a charm."

Noressa reached down and assisted Bydawine to his feet. In silence, she laced on her boots and gathered her things. When she was ready, the dwarf led her to a rectangular hole gaping beside the fireplace. Motioning her ahead of him, he followed, turning to swing the stone panel shut.

They were in a narrow tunnel. By standing with her back to one wall, Noressa could just touch the other wall with her fingertips. Bydawine fumbled in the dark beside her, and a sudden ray of light streamed across their path. He reached into a deep, narrow slot, carefully removing a lighted candle, then replaced the stone cap that had shielded the candle in its niche.

He turned to face her, the candle held high. "I will get you away from the castle if I can. In return, I want you to take me with you. Let me travel with you for seven days, and I will ask no more of you."

"Agreed."

He turned and led the way down the passage, which soon brought them to a flight of stairs. Noressa recognized the curve of the great stair leading from the entrance hall to the upper chambers. When they came to the bottom step, Bydawine motioned for silence.

"Now we will cross to the passageway on the other side of the hall, but we must wait until the guard has passed. I will go first and open the passage, then you will follow." He indicated a small stone jutting out from the wall. "Tell me what you see."

Noressa grasped the stone and pulled. It came away in her hand, and she was peering through the slotted visor of a fighting helm affixed to the other side of the wall. In a moment, there came the sound of footsteps, and a soldier sauntered into view. She waited until he was gone and his footsteps could no longer be heard. "The guard has passed."

Bydawine handed her the candle, opened the panel, and hurried across the hall to disappear behind a tapestry on the far wall. Immediately a corner of the tapestry was pulled back, and he beckoned her forward. Noressa replaced the stone and followed.

The second passage took them down past several branching tunnels and at last through a final panel, where they felt the cold night air and were assailed by a strong animal smell. They were outside the castle, but still within a passageway.

Bydawine whispered. "We are passing under the stables. Behind them is a small gate. It will be our only chance to leave the castle. There will be guards, but I have a plan for them." He smiled a little, and his hand moved to a wine flask hanging on his belt beside a short dagger. He paused to wet his fingers and snuff the candle. "If we make it through to the countryside, we may be able to steal some farmer's kifera."

"Why not take a mount from the stables?" Noressa asked, pointing upward, though she knew he couldn't see her. "It will be faster and keep an innocent farmer from punishment when we are discovered gone."

She felt his hesitation and heard his regretful sigh. "No, I could not talk my way past that. The alarm would be raised, if not by the guards then by a stableboy afraid to face the consequences of a missing beast."

He moved away from her in the dark, and she followed, one hand trailing the wall, around a corner to what seemed a dead end. There was a low sound of stone against stone, and a short panel swung wide to reveal a trampled area of corral behind a long stable. Noressa touched the small amulet at her throat. "There is someone who can get us a kifera and access to the gate, Bydawine. But you must trust me as I have trusted you." She touched his shoulder, holding him back, and smiled at his surprise.

Bydawine gaped at the figure looming over him. Feeling the hand on his shoulder, he had turned, expecting to see the friendly face of the young man, Noren. Instead, he was looking into Jaaben's grinning, hairy face. "But how—?"

The figure shrugged in a self-conscious way that he had never seen in the true Jaaben. "Much like the rat and the toad." The words rumbled softly into the night. "But we have no time for explanations, Bydawine. I wish to take a late night ride. Fetch my mount."

Bydawine nodded once and set off to fulfill the "captain's" order.

A short time later, he was moving from the shadow of the stable toward the guards at the gate. They stood at the ready, weapons poised, and the senior man stepped forward, his sword menacing Bydawine's midsection. "Hold, dwarf. What do you want here? We have no need of your idiot riddles tonight."

Bydawine drew himself erect, trying to project an air of confident officiousness. "You are ordered to open the gate. Captain Jaaben wishes to depart."

"Do you think us fools like yourself, buffoon?" the guard snarled. "What trickery do you think to play on us?" He raised a fist to Bydawine, then stopped at the sound of an approaching kifera. Both soldiers came to surprised attention when they recognized the rider.

Jaaben of Hamden drew up before the group, swaying, and Bydawine was impressed yet again by the illusion's seeming reality. The sharp odor of wine was strong on the rider, and

Jaaben grinned, acknowledging the guards' salute.

"Take your ease, men. I will not trouble you long." The apparition chuckled, leaning so far down that he nearly slid from his mount. "I only wish to make a short visit to a certain farmwife."

The three men laughed together, the sound sharp in the darkness. Then Jaaben turned and waved Bydawine forward.

"Where is my wine, jester?"

Bydawine quickly unstopped the wine gourd and handed it up. In the act of raising the flask to his lips, Jaaben paused and, giving the guards a conspirator's wink, thrust the flask at the nearest man. "A good leader must see to his men's comforts first."

The guard hesitated and Bydawine smiled, enjoying the man's indecision. Then, seeing the frown coming across his captain's face, the soldier took the wine, drank a deep draft, and passed it to his companion. The second man drank and stepped forward to return the gourd. But it slipped from his fingers, and he joined his comrade facedown on the ground.

Bydawine and Jaaben exchanged exultant grins before the captain reached down to swing Bydawine up behind him.

A short time later, Bydawine glanced back in triumph as they entered the narrow hilltop pass. The lean-bellied moon just settling into the far mountains left the castle a dark bulk in the valley below them.

CHAPTER 4

Noressa and Bydawine spent the remaining hours of darkness pushing their mount to its limit. It was a strong beast, and because Bydawine was familiar with the trail, they put a good distance between them and the keep. It was still dark when they crested the hills ringing the valley, yet despite the rocky terrain, they had nearly reached the plains by early dawn.

With the dwarf seated behind and her face hidden by the hood of her cloak, Noressa had felt secure enough to drop the guise of Jaaben. But when they stopped in a narrow gorge to rest, she reclaimed the illusion of the young Noren before turning to face Bydawine. The kifcra was tied where he could forage the tiny clumps of hill grass from rock crevices, while Noressa and Bydawine breakfasted on bread and cheese from her supplies. Knowing there was no time for sleep, Noressa fought her weariness by questioning her companion.

"Who is this Pashet who rules your valley, Bydawine? He does not seem to be of your people."

"No. Pashet and his army followed Tylek from across the Bourne."

"The Bourne River? From the land of Sidra?" Noressa was intrigued. Her father, as huntsman and mountain dweller, had seldom shown any interest in things outside the sphere of home and village. Yet he had always gone out of his way to learn whatever news was to be had concerning the far-off country of Sidra.

Bydawine was nodding, on his face the angry, defiant look she had seen when he faced Pashet. "Yes. I have heard them speak of it often. The army would like nothing better than to stay here in Dromund. They were happy to leave their own desolated country to plunder our bountiful land."

"I have heard stories of Sidra from the people in my village," Noressa mused. "It is said that Sidra was once a land as rich and beautiful as our own until some plague of evil destroyed it."

"True," Bydawine answered. "For these many years, the lords of the northern borderlands have been alert to the possibility that it might spread to Dromund. Many times they have turned back raiding parties from across the river. That is why we were surprised to see so many of them as far south as our valley. It is clear now that Tylek and his magic brought them through. But when we finally understood this, there was no defense open to us."

"And this Tylek—" Noressa was remembering the dwarf's threat that she was to be given to this man—"he is a very strong sorcerer?"

Bydawine must have sensed her unease, for he didn't answer at once. Then he nodded, staring back up the trail. "He is very powerful. And dangerous, for he bears a shroud of grace and comeliness that belies his corruption. He insinuates himself into a place until . . ." Bydawine scuffed at a bit of gravel beneath his foot. "That is how Tylek came to us. A wasting sickness was upon my uncle, Lord Norwick. None among the court physicians could treat the malady until the appearance of an accomplished physician from the northern plains."

"Tylek." Noressa spoke the word, testing its sound on her ear.

Bydawine nodded again. "He affected a wondrous cure and soon became Lord Norwick's most influential advisor. But I knew he was not to be trusted, as did Berael, my uncle's magician. As a member of my uncle's military council, I tried to warn Lord Norwick, but he accused me of jealousy and would not hear it. Berael was most vocal in his distrust of Tylek and soon after fell victim to some unknown poison. It was not long until Tylek convinced Lord Norwick that members of his own guard were planning revolt." Anger came into his voice, and Bydawine shook his head as if he still couldn't believe it had happened. "My uncle was old and the fever had affected his mind, else he would not have agreed when Tylek offered his own army to put down the uprising!"

"Your land gave no resistance to a strange army marching

into his domain?"

"Resistance, hah! My uncle received Pashet with open arms in the High Council room. In the midst of the welcoming speech, Pashet's guards drew their blades, and my uncle and his son were Tylek's prisoners."

"But what of your own army?" Noressa asked. "Surely they would have been strong enough to retake the hold."

Bydawine shook his head. "Tylek had made his preparations. There were few of my uncle's officers well enough to keep their feet that day. Those officers who would not join with Pashet were imprisoned, or their wives and children were imprisoned to ensure their services. I was not jailed because, in my rage, I attacked one of Pashet's men, knocking him to the floor. Two others pulled me away. It so amused Pashet to see me dangling between them like a child's doll that he claimed me as the spoils of war to be his slave."

Bydawine sprang from his place and stalked away to stand beside the kifera.

Noressa kept silent, allowing him time to deal with the shame and anger she had seen in his eyes. Then she became aware of him watching her. His gaze, questioning, searched her face. Noressa shifted nervously, pulling her cloak tighter. "Why do you stare at me so?"

Bydawine glanced away, then back, confusion and apology in his look. "I know from what I have seen that you are the one Tylek searches for. Yet at times, when I look at you, I almost cannot see you. It is as if . . ." He shook his head but said no more.

She considered a moment, then spoke. "You will know eventually, and I weary of the disguise." Noressa closed her eyes and let go her illusion. She sighed deeply at the easing in her mind as she banished the image of Noren. Then she threw off her cloak to stretch long and hard. "Oh, it is good to be myself again!" Noressa opened her eyes and laughed at the dwarf's stunned surprise.

"But—but how . . . ?" Bydawine stammered. "Are you a witch?"

Noressa sobered. "No. I am not a witch. I am Noressa, daughter of Rolf the huntsman. It is not I but this that creates the illusions you have seen." From beneath her leather shirt, she brought out the tiny medallion.

"I knew you were the one when Pashet did not imprison you! How came you by this token?"

She told him quickly of her parents' deaths and her decision to leave and of Edell's arrival and subsequent death.

"It was there at Edell's grave that I first learned of the power in the amulet." She held the medallion tightly as she told him of the wailing women, almost forgetting his presence in the memory of that first wonder. The amulet held the slight warmth that had replaced the tingling surge of power in her earlier contacts. "I have practiced many hours while I have traveled, and I've found that I could create almost any illusion. But to hold the illusion for any long period taxes me greatly—almost as if the amulet draws its strength directly from me."

Bydawine was awed. "And a witch-woman you have never known sent you this charm?"

"Yes . . . and died in the attempt. Now I must find the one person who can tell me why. That is why I travel to Tarragon. Then—" she paused, her thoughts on the ever-present tug of the summoning "—then I have one other task to complete."

Morning sun filled their small gorge with warm light. Bydawine scanned the peaks behind them. "I think it best if we travel on. They will surely have discovered our absence by now."

By midday, they had left the hills behind and turned northeast toward the sea and Tarragon. Bydawine rode in front, guiding the kifera. They rode across the plains, skirting the main road and avoiding those few cottages they saw. Once Noressa made Bydawine halt the kifera, and they sat staring out at the grasslands. The grass brushed the bottoms of her boots, rippling in the wind, bowing before the breeze, then springing upright in a rhythmic, teasing dance.

"Is that a sima tree?" Noressa asked, pointing to a distant tall silhouette.

"Yes," Bydawine answered. "From the size, I would say it marks a large spring." He turned to look at her with some surprise. "Have you never seen a sima?"

"No. Nor these grasslands, either. I have never been down from the mountain. But my mother has told me of these things. She was born to the grasslands."

Noressa could not keep at bay the familiar sorrow. Almost angry, she kicked the kifera forward in a useless attempt to escape the memory the grasslands had awakened.

In the afternoon, a wooded stream afforded them a better cover, and at Bydawine's suggestion, they followed it until darkness fell, then made camp among the trees. Not willing to risk a fire, they ate once more from Noressa's cold provisions. Afterward, they sat together in a depression formed by the gnarled roots of a giant sima tree, with Noressa's cloak spread over them against the evening chill.

In an attempt to ease his obvious discomfort at their closeness, Noressa questioned Bydawine about his knowledge of Tartagon.

"Have you made this trip often, Bydawine?"

"Yes, many times. Of course, we always used the road and traveled at our leisure. The trip took four and a half days. But if we travel as fast tomorrow as we did today, we should reach Tarragon by evening tomorrow."

"Then you must know what was meant by the tree in the crossroads."

"Of course. It is an old landmark. When the port of Tarragon was settled generations ago, the tree in the crossroads *was* the market of Tarragon. It was the point where the three main supply roads met. Then the market was held under its boughs. Now that Tarragon has become a great city, it is only a meeting place for old men and young lovers."

There was silence for a time, and Noressa thought that Bydawine slept. But when she looked at him, he was staring up through the trees.

"What are you thinking of, Bydawine, that you seem so grave?"

"I was thinking of the creatures you say attacked the old woman. It could be that they were Tylek's fiends."

"Are you certain?"

"No. But there were things that happened about that time. There were two young men taken from the dungeons and sent to Tylek's chambers. Tylek was at his conjurations for many days, though their screams ceased after only two. Their bodies were never returned, and it was soon after that when Tylek gave orders to increase the patrols. Then—"

"Then I came."

He nodded, and Noressa shivered at the implications of his story. Great indeed would be the sorcerer who could wreak the terrible transformation of men into the loathesome creatures she had confronted. And it frightened her that this immense energy was now directed at her and the medallion. Her hand went to the slim chain lying warm against her throat, and she wondered at the power that must lie in the amulet to warrant such destruction.

Bydawine's voice broke through her thoughts. "Someone should keep watch. They will be searching for us."

"Who should watch, Bydawine? You are as tired as I. Go to sleep; they won't search in the darkness. Let's rest while we may, for tomorrow is another hard ride."

Bydawine shook his head. "I would rest more easily if someone kept watch." He looked to where her fingers still traced the silver chain. "Are there only illusions in your amulet? Has it no other power?"

She sighed, pulled the golden disc from beneath her shirt, and rubbed it gently. "I have felt a great power in it, my friend. But I do not know how to use it. I couldn't even summon a simple watch spell to keep us safe through the night."

They were silent then, each wrapped in his own weariness and lulled by the sounds of the night. Noressa, drifting in the gray fog that precedes deep sleep, seemed to hear her own voice as from far away. But the words were muffled and forgotten the instant they were uttered. When she roused enough to look about her, all was quiet. Slipping into the limbo of sleep, she counted as only a dreamshadow the small, dark-scaled dragon form sliding away into the trees.

Bydawine's restless movements brought her awake to the predawn stillness. They chewed pieces of dried meat washed down with sips of liet cider while they prepared to leave. When they were mounted and ready, Noressa sat for a moment breathing deeply of the faint, sharp tang in the cool morning air. The brisk sea smell was new to her and filled her with a rising sense of adventure, despite the pressing menace behind them. Her eagerness to reach the port city convinced her of their course of travel.

"We will make better time if we make straight for the port, Bydawine. I say we follow the road."

He disagreed. "It is better if we remain unseen as long as possible. We would have little defense if caught in the open. And it isn't only Tylek we must fear. What could we do against any band of ruffians—a dwarf and a mere girl?"

But Noressa was not to be denied. "No, speed is our best weapon now. They do not know which direction we travel. If they make for the north or east, we'll have at least two days before they discover their mistake. If they come this direction first, we still have half a day's lead—and I want to keep it."

So saying, she urged the kifera from the woods toward open ground. She paused at the edge of the grasslands to be sure they were not seen. They were alone. As they moved ahead, Noressa gave no thought to the black ebrot that rose from the trees, hooked beak open in a soundless cry, to wing its way back toward the hills.

CHAPTER 5

oressa's spirits lifted higher still as the sun burst, flaming through a thin frill of clouds floating on the eastern horizon. She was forced to make a conscious effort to refrain from urging the kifera to full gallop, such was her impatience to reach the port city. In front of her, Bydawine was stolidly silent, his fingers clutching the short thick fur of their mount. His face was set in a scowl of grim disapproval of Noressa's stubborn insistence to travel openly.

In the short time since gaining the road, they had passed several merchant carts and short family caravans bound for the trade city. As they passed each lumbering cart or caravan, they were stared at with open curiosity. Noressa knew they made quite a sight, a handsome youth clothed in simple but well-made clothing, in contrast to the dwarf's filthy attire.

In silent compromise to Bydawine's wish that they remain unknown, Noressa invoked the guise of Noren each time they approached any traveler close enough that her face could be seen. But by midmorning, the road was so congested with traffic that she was forced to maintain the guise constantly. After a time, her head began to throb, and she was reconsidering the wisdom of Bydawine's desire to travel alone when she detected the enticing smell of roasting meat. Bydawine, too, was roused by the smell.

"Not far ahead is an inn where we often took a meal on our journey," he said. "I have no money, but the innkeeper may remember me and give us a bit of meat and perhaps a mug of targ." Even as he spoke, the sweet aroma of meat blended with that of fresh bread, and Noressa urged the kifera forward.

They found the inn full to bursting. Many people sat outside in their carts or under the few trees scattered around the building while young boys waited upon them. At the far end of the hostel was a large dirt-packed yard with several open fires where red-faced young boys turned spits of roasting fowl and carcasses of yara and young spring daxet. The air was thick with the smell of spices and the heady aroma of warm targ.

Noressa pulled up short to avoid trampling a boy hurrying past with a tray of targ mugs. The boy quickly distributed his load among a trio of loud, dirty men. On his way back to the inn, Noressa called for the boy's attention.

Bydawine opened his mouth to speak when the boy stopped beside them, but Noressa spoke first. "Bring us a loaf of hot bread, cheese, half a rod of daxet, and some targ." The boy nodded and scurried away, leaving Noressa to deal with Bydawine's objections. Noressa waved away his protests while they dismounted and led their beast to a small bit of shade near the noisy group just served by the boy serving the ale. Noressa addressed her companion in feigned surprise.

"Bydawine, do you mean that you're not hungry? Or perhaps you would prefer the dried meat and stale bread in my provision sack. If so, you are welcome to it, and I will gladly accept your share of the daxet."

Bydawine, arms akimbo in exasperation, eyed her sharply. "Of course I would prefer the daxet. But how will we pay for this feast?"

Noressa laughed and patted his shoulder in comradely fashion. "Do not fear, my worrisome friend. I have a few coins."

She withdrew her coin pouch, chose several copper coins, and quickly returned the bag to its place. Nevertheless, she was aware of at least one pair of eyes that had seen and measured the pouch's hefty bulge. She pretended ignorance of the man's gaze and turned her attention to the boy who was returning with their food.

They settled on the grass for their meal. When she had finished, Noressa leaned against the tree, pulling her cowl close about her face. Then she dropped the image of Noren and allowed herself the luxury of a few moments' drowsing. But Bydawine couldn't relax as easily, and soon his agitation roused her and they continued their journey.

It was late afternoon when they came to the city proper. They passed through the city gates, leaving behind the patchwork order of freshly plowed fields for the jumbled hovels and grimy shops of the city's poor. Following Bydawine's direction, they soon came to a cleaner, more prosperous-looking street. Here Noressa stopped before a small tailor shop and gently addressed her companion.

"My friend, I have no wish to offend you, but I fear your clothes have seen their final service. People will mistake you for my slave rather than a traveling companion, and a badly treated slave at that!"

Bydawine said nothing, though his face flushed dark and he plucked at the kifera's short fur while Noressa dismounted. As he, too, dismounted, they were approached by a young street urchin. With a cunning look, he offered to watch their mount.

Bydawine scowled, motioning him away. But Noressa fished out a silver coin and held it before the astonished boy. "Take my mount to the nearest stable and have him fed and bedded down for the night."

The boy hesitated, then snatched the coin and hurried away with the kifera. Bydawine stared after him, incredulous, then whirled on Noressa, his brown eyes hard with anger. "It is clear that you are indeed an ignorant mountain peasant! You are a fool if you expect to see either boy or beast again!"

Noressa shrugged, unaffected by his vehemence, and spoke quietly. "It would be just as well, Bydawine, for I do not intend to claim the beast again. It was simply a measure to distract our friends."

Bydawine hesitated, confusion mixing with his anger. "Our friends?"

Noressa flicked her gaze back toward the direction they had come. "That surly trio from the inn this morning. I believe they have it in mind to relieve me of this troublesome burden." She patted her bulging coin pouch. "But never mind. We waste time, and the tailor will bar his door in a moment." With that, she led the disconcerted dwarf into the shop.

As predicted, the shopkeeper was preparing to close. He frowned at the dusty travelers and spoke sharply when Noressa settled her bow and travel pack in a corner. "I am closed for the night. Come back tomorrow!"

Noressa smiled and shook her head, gesturing toward Bydawine. "I am afraid we must trouble you for your services tonight, sir. As you can see, my friend has met with some misfortune and is in need of new traveling clothes."

The tailor shook his head stubbornly. "I don't have time. My wife awaits with my supper, and I'm weary from a full day's work." He took a wary step backward as Noressa approached. Then he stood gaping at the two gold coins laid on the sewing bench before him.

"We do not expect anything extravagant. Just breeches, a shirt that will wear well, and a warm cloak." Noressa tried to ignore the pain behind her eyes and to keep her voice that of a carefree young man with money to spend and no cares to wrestle.

The tailor suddenly remembered he might be able to shorten one of his son's shirts, perhaps. . . .

Noressa turned away and, leaving the man to his work, went to peer through the shuttered window. Darkness had fallen, and there was little traffic on the street. She couldn't see them in the gloom, but she knew the would-be thieves were concealed in the shadows. She sighed and rubbed her tired eyes. The exertion of the past two days, both mental and physical, washed over her in a wave of fatigue that left a heavy pounding in her skull. Hiding once more beneath her cowl, Noressa dropped onto a low bench. Some of the pressure drained away as she sloughed off her self-apparition.

Intending to rest only a few moments, she was surprised to feel herself jerking out of a heavy sleep when a hand shook her and a voice gently demanded her attention. She opened her eyes to find Bydawine standing before her, his large, square face pulled into a worried frown. He shook her once more. "Awake, Noren, and admire my new finery." Hearing how he addressed her, she remembered their situation. Stretching, "Noren" rose and surveyed the tailor's handiwork.

Bydawine stood awkwardly for her inspection. The breeches, somewhat loose, were made of a thick brown material. The hip-length shirt, not unlike Noressa's, was of a soft leather, laced closed at the throat. A thick black cloak was draped over one shoulder, and on his feet were a new pair of leather boots. She eyed the boots and looked a question at the tailor, then waved him aside when he launched into a tale about his son's tutor's nephew.

She sent Bydawine a look and motioned toward the tailor as she returned to the window. She watched over her shoulder to make sure that Bydawine had understood her signal. When the dwarf nodded and turned to engage the shopkeeper with some trivial question about his cloak, Noressa turned her concentration to the street.

Noressa blocked out their muted chatter as she worked to build a certain image in her mind. The medallion grew warm beneath her shirt as she willed life and depth into the figures and sent them out into the street. She watched with satisfaction as the images of Noren and his dwarf companion hurried from the tailor shop to disappear around the far street corner. Three dark shapes disengaged themselves from the shadows and followed.

Taking up her things, Noressa hurried to the door. "Thank you for your excellent services, tailor, but our time is short and we must move on." She opened the door and slipped out, forcing Bydawine to snatch his cloak and race to join her. Together they scurried into the night and for a time dodged through the streets in what Bydawine assured her was the general direction of the markets. When they felt they had put sufficient distance between themselves and their pursuers, they took refuge in a crowded hostelry.

Once he had collected their money, the proprietor scarcely glanced at them. He led the way upstairs to a pair of rooms at the end of a narrow corridor. He lit a single candle in each room and, nodding good night to them, left them alone in the dark hall. Noressa dropped her guise of Noren and, bidding the dwarf good night, slipped into her room and barred the door.

The room was small, containing only a low cot and a small scarred table. On the table sat a large jug of cold water and a chipped earthen bowl with the candle burning steadily beside them. She set her things on the floor and, turning back the covers, was pleasantly surprised to find the linens almost clean. Stripping off boots and cloak, she lay down and plunged her weary mind toward the welcome balm of oblivion.

But the nightmare awaited. It fell upon her with frightening swiftness. She battled the invisible mire of that darkened plain, unable to escape the hovering menace. She fought with desperation against the thing that would smother her. With an angry cry still ringing in her ears, Noressa flung herself awake to lie panting from her exertions.

In a moment, there came a tapping at the door and Bydawine called to her. She hurried to open the door and found him standing barefoot, candle in hand, the now familiar scowl tugging the corners of his mouth.

"What has happened? I heard you cry out. Are you ill?"

Noressa scrubbed at her eyes. They were wet with tears. "No, I'm not ill. It was only a dream." She peered down the hall but saw no one. "What is the hour, Bydawine? Is it time to leave already?"

He shook his head, the scowl deepening. "No. I had only just settled into my bed when I heard you call."

She sighed. The dream had seemed interminable.

"Well, if you are certain there is nothing . . ." He hesitated until she managed a tired smile, then returned to his room. He paused at his door, waiting until she closed and barred her door, then she heard the sound of his own bar slipping home. She shuffled back to bed, was asleep instantly, and this time slept the night through.

In his own bed, Bydawine lay staring into the blackness, thinking back on how he had been brought to such a position. He was a fugitive from his own home, dependent on the whims of an impetuous young girl. But how could he, or anyone, have foreseen the happenings to come when his uncle had been struck down by the mysterious ailment?

Bydawine's humiliation at his treatment under Jaaben and Pashet still grated inside him. But he was free now, and in a position to claim justice for that. As Norwick's nephew, he was well acquainted with most of the city's elite, many of whom could be trusted to give him sanctuary and assistance. On the morrow, he would present himself to one of his uncle's allies. He should have kept on through the city streets until they had found such a place, but Noressa's decisiveness had caught him off guard again. She had dragged him into this place by the arm and was haggling about the price of the rooms before he realized what she was about.

Restless, he tossed and struggled with this new dilemma:

Noressa. She was young, beautiful, and stubborn. Sanctuary was his for the taking, but he knew she would refuse such for herself until she had found the one who could explain the amulet. He also knew that Tylek would not have extended himself so far in the takeover of Wigram Keep only to let his prey slip away now. Being in the city did not preclude them from the danger of Tylek's pursuit. Time was short, and Noressa's mission might take days or weeks. With Tylek so near, he balked at leaving the girl on her own. In years and stature, she was a woman. But to her, the world was bright, new, an adventure to be explored. Her very innocence and enthusiasm could prove deadly. Although she had, so far, displayed a wisdom unusual in most girls her age, he felt that her stubborn impulsiveness would soon put her within Tylek's reach. Bydawine shivered at the thought of Noressa stripped of her amulet and subjugated by the sorcerer.

And what of the "other duty" she had mentioned? He was certain it was that duty which often sobered her smile and darkened her gray eyes. There were moments when her attention shifted away, and she appeared to be watching and listening for something that couldn't be seen or heard. Should she be allowed to undertake such a thing alone? If not, could he hold her against her will? Why did he even care? Three days ago he hadn't even known of her existence. She carried money enough to live well for years. She was protected by a magic amulet and had come to find one who would likely give her yet more power in teaching her about the amulet. She was a free woman, and he had no obligations to her.

Still, there was something different about her. She was . . . special. But how? And how best to deal with this situation?

He wrestled with his indecision until fatigue laid hold of him. Insinuating itself into his thoughts, it forced him down into the depths of sleep.

CHAPTER 6

The morning air was a cacophony of sounds and smells. Vendors, loud and brassy-voiced, cried out the virtues of their wares, and the pungent odor of exotic spices mixed with the heavy smell of the market animals. At every turn, banners of scarlet and saffron fluttered in the salty breeze to catch the attention. Tight-fisted buyers haggled with shrewd-eyed merchants. Dirty street children begged alms from passersby or snatched fruit from a stall and dashed into the crowd.

Noressa was almost dizzy at the delightful strangeness of it all. Her gaze darted from one new sight to another, and she breathed deeply of the unfamiliar smells. Her pulse raced with the excitement of ambivalent expectations. Pushing through the crowd, she followed Bydawine's short figure toward the ancient knobby trunk that she now knew to be the old tree.

She paused, eyes wide and admiring, to watch a cloth merchant display for a woman a cloth of palest green that rippled through his hands like woven water. When she was able to pull herself away, Bydawine had disappeared. She fought down a sudden panic and started once more in the direction of the old tree. She hadn't gone far when a hand closed painfully tight about her wrist. Half expecting to see Jaaben's cruel smirk, she whirled, short dagger in hand. But she saw, instead, Bydawine's angry face glaring up at her.

"I cannot lead you if you do not follow. Now, pay attention, or next time it may not be *I* who takes you from behind!" He released her and forged once more into the crowd.

Noressa stayed close at times, almost trodding on his heels and trying to ignore the baleful glances that his quick pace and peremptory shoves earned them. She watched him trampling ahead and pondered his strange sullenness.

She had been awakened soon after dawn by his heavy-handed knocking. Having ascertained that it was Bydawine, she hurried through her morning toilet. When she joined him, having assumed her role as Noren, he only mumbled a low reply to her cheerful "Good morrow." He preceded her down the stairs and directly out into the street. Startled by this abrupt departure, she hurried abreast of him. "Where are you going? Why do you rush so? We haven't even breakfasted yet."

His response was curt. "Do you wish to find the one who awaits you at the markets?" She nodded. "Then let us be about it. There is food in the marketplace if you are hungry." And she followed, trying to think what she might have done to upset him.

Perhaps he had been offended by her decision the night before to outfit him with new clothes. She regretted her lack of diplomacy in that situation, for she knew a man's pride was a fragile thing. But the pursuing highwaymen had left her no time for tactful persuasion.

She shrugged to herself. At any rate, she thought, he does look good in them.

He had washed sometime during the night. His skin had the appearance of one who is accustomed to many hours in the sun, and his face, despite its angry scowl, was almost handsome. His hair, now without the previous coating of grime, was a light brown, shot through with glints of dark gold where the sun struck it. Noressa smiled at the appealing way it curled round his neck and ears. The leather shirt did little to hide his wide shoulders; his chunky body was supported by thick, sturdy legs that carried him along at a surprising speed, despite their shortness.

Around them, the city seemed to exude people into the already crowded streets. Noressa was forced to follow behind Bydawine as the streets became ever more congested with morning traffic. Upon reaching the south market, they found it thronged with people.

Now, hurrying behind Bydawine, Noressa felt her stomach growling impatiently. Her mouth watered at the warm food smells carried on the sharp sea breeze.

At last they pushed through to the edge of the market square. Noressa stopped and drew a steadying breath, feeling the uneven cobbles of the square through her bootsoles. Like an ancient broken beacon, the leafless spire of the old tree rose above the jostling crowds. Beneath the lightning-blasted spire, freshly-leafed branches rustled in the wind. Around the tree, the crowd bustled. Heavily laden porters scuttled after their clients. A harried young girl watched as her mother disappeared into the markets, leaving her with two small children. Indolent young men lounged in the shade of the old tree, watching as young women passed by with shy, averted faces. Noressa stared out on the turmoil in dismay.

"There are so many people, Bydawine! How will we ever find him?"

"I had thought that he was to find you."

Noressa shrugged. "I was to bring him this." She pulled forth the medallion to let it dangle on the front of her shirt.

Together they walked the edge of the square, watching for anyone who showed more than passing interest in the amulet. When they had traveled almost the full square, Noressa cautiously broached the subject of breakfast again. This time Bydawine smiled and, tracking down a delicious scent, introduced her to keilan.

They left the vendor's stall cradling hollowed shells of a thick, chewy bread filled with spicy meat sauce. As they walked, Bydawine made an apology.

"I am sorry that I was angry with you this morning. I was contemplating a difficult decision and laid my frustrations on you."

Noressa couldn't keep the relief from her voice. "I had thought you were angry with me because of the clothes. I tell you sincerely that I meant you no insult."

Bydawine shook his head, chewing a gravy-soaked chunk of bread. "I took no offense. Indeed, I was grateful." He hesitated, then rushed on. "I have thought on the duties that have brought us both to Tarragon. It may be that we could each be of help to the other in fulfilling our tasks. You know that I must rouse my uncle's allies to help me retake our valley. It is a thing I should have done last night, but as we are here" —he motioned toward the crowd around them—"let us spend the morning searching for this one who awaits you. If we do not find him by midday, come with me. It may be that my uncle's friends may know better how to find him." He paused as though chagrined. "And one who could explain the amulet's powers must surely know something of sorcery. Perhaps he might be persuaded to assist us against Tylek. For the moment, I can offer you only the hospitality of my uncle's allies until I can repay you personally for all you have done."

Pleasure welled inside her. He was asking her to stay. His words spoke of a few days at most, but his manner said more. She bent to one knee.

"Friend Bydawine, I require no payment. You saved my life. A few meals and a suit of clothes cannot repay such a debt. As for this one whom I seek—" Noressa shrugged— "once he receives the amulet, he will become Tylek's target. He may be quite willing to have an army beside him in any battle that comes of it. But if he will not assist you, my service is yours to command. Even without magic, I am a fair archer in my own right."

Noressa couldn't say why she gave the promise so easily. Even knowing that its fulfillment would mean yet another delay in answering the summons, she felt no hesitation. Nor could she explain the strange bond that had grown between herself and this man in just the few days they had been together. Perhaps because he was so unlike the dwarves in childhood tales, protrayed as buffoons and comic slaves in traveling minstrel troupes. Different from her expectations, Bydawine was not a creature to be pitied. He was a man of drive and purpose.

Yet was that so strange? she wondered. She was learning that much of the world was different from her childhood expectations.

At her last words, Bydawine almost smiled. Possibly he was amused, as were most men, at her boast of expertise in arms. Then he looked away into the crowd behind her, and she saw his eyes narrow. He glanced about, as though wary of a trap, and Noressa caught his unease. She rose, searching the crowd, too. "What is it, Bydawine?"

"There . . . do you see him? The elder with the blazing staff. He comes this way."

Noressa did see an old man making his way through the crowd toward them, but she saw nothing about him to raise such consternation.

At first glance, his appearance was one of approaching dotage. His shoulders were covered by a gray, cowled mantle that brushed the tops of his sandaled feet and hung open to reveal a long gray gown of similar material. The gown was belted with a braided cloth belt, from which depended a square leather purse. Thick gray hair hung to his shoulders, mingling with the gray- and black-streaked beard that flowed to his chest. His forehead was furrowed by lines of concentration, and the webbing around his eyes spoke of much weariness and worry. But the gaze from his intense blue eyes was clear and sharp, and it flicked from the medallion to "Noren's" face and back. His sure stride denied any need of the long staff he carried. The wand, carved of some pale wood, was circled at the top by a wide gold band that reflected the morning sun in gleaming flashes, but not so much as to attract undue attention. But Bydawine hadn't ceased to stare at the approaching man, and now the elder stopped before them. He smiled an apology, and his voice was soft, well timbered.

"I pray you forgive this intrusion, but I was caught by the workmanship of your medallion. It is a fine piece. May I inquire as to how you came by it?"

Noressa returned the smile, one hand caressing the amulet. "It was a gift. And you are right, it is a fine piece. I doubt there is another like it in all the land."

"You may be wrong, lad." The elder stepped closer to scrutinize the chasing on the disk. "I know a woman who has an identical charm. She is a friend of many years, and each spring we meet beneath the tree in the crossroads to renew that friendship. This year she is overdue. When I saw your medallion, I thought perchance you might have news of her." He paused. "Her name is Salet."

Noressa hesitated, and a sadness filled the man's face.

"She is dead, is she not?" Noressa nodded and he sighed. "I had feared as much."

He leaned against his staff, head bowed. Noressa moved forward, worried that the news had been too much for him. But at her approach, he straightened, his left hand gently dismissing any need of offered support.

"This was not expected. But I had not realized how much I

had depended upon the hope of uncertainty." He shrugged, as if the gray cloak were an ill fit. "It falls to me now." The last words were spoken more to himself than anyone. Noressa watched as he stared away into the crowd. At last he seemed to come to a decision and turned his attention to her again. "You bear the amulet now. Will you tell me how this came to be?"

"Of course," Noressa replied. "But it is a lengthy story. It would be best if we found a quieter place."

The elder nodded. "I have a room at the Blue Pearl Inn. It is not far, and I will see to it that you enjoy a proper breakfast." He paused, as in afterthought. "I am called Medwyn."

Bydawine stepped forward. "I am called Bydawine, and my companion is Noren. We accept your offer."

Medwyn nodded once, turned, and moved into the crowd. Noressa and Bydawine thrust their unfinished keilan into the hands of a surprised street waif and hurried after the man.

CHAPTER 7

Once away from the heavy market crowds, it was only a few minutes' walk to the Blue Pearl Inn. It sat on a bluff overlooking the harbor at the end of a row of busy shops and taverns. Its weathered exterior gave rise to images of derelict ships cast ashore and half buried by sand. Above the street door, a carved wooden shingle sailed the morning breeze, displaying a fat blue pearl nestled on a half shell.

As they entered the darkened interior of the inn, it took only a look from Medwyn to bring a young boy hurrying forward. He listened carefully to Medwyn's orders, then was gone.

Medwyn led them upstairs to his quarters, a large airy room with windows on two sides affording a wide view of the city and its port. The room was furnished with a high down bed along one wall, with a small table and washstand beside it. A long table with benches and a single high-backed chair sat before the deep-hearthed fireplace.

Noressa and Bydawine settled themselves before the fire in silence while their host paced the length of the room. In a few moments, the tavern boy and another youth brought two trays and laid the table with thick, hot porridge, sliced meats, cheese, a bowl of sweet cream, and a pot of wine-steeped lirsa tea. Through most of the meal, Medwyn was lost in thought, and neither Bydawine nor Noressa were inclined to disturb him.

Afterward they talked, Noressa, then Bydawine in turn. Medwyn was surprised to learn Noressa's true identity, then sorrowed anew by her tale of Salet's death. But it was of Bydawine that he asked the most questions—questions about Tylek's powers and the army that was with him. When he was at last satisfied that he had learned all the dwarf could tell him,

Medwyn once more began to pace the room. Noressa had begun to fidget, curious as to when she would be asked to deliver the amulet and if the elder would be inclined to answer her many questions. The thought of surrendering the talisman brought an uncomfortable tightening of her jaw; a part of her fought against the idea. The strange sensation had built almost to an anger when Medwyn turned to her, his face stern.

"It is well that we have found one another, child, for you would have soon put yourself into Tylek's hands. Until you have learned to control the energies within yourself, you must not use them unless there is a need. It will be my duty to instruct you in this restraint."

Noressa bridled at the admonishment. "Teach me control? You speak as if I am to remain with you, but I have fulfilled my obligation to deliver the amulet. Now I have a journey of my own to complete." She tossed her head in satisfaction at the magician's surprise, then worked loose the catch on the chain as Bydawine spoke in her defense.

"Noressa has done well in mastering the illusions of the medallion. Its power has done much in assisting her this far."

Noressa stood, reluctantly offering Medwyn the amulet. Understanding dawned upon his face and he shook his head, smiling. "It was not the amulet that was to be delivered, but its owner. It is yours, girl, by right of inheritance." Then he turned to Bydawine. "It was not the medallion that gave life to her illusions. *She* is the power, the Talent. And it was her awkward use of that Talent that led me to her, as it has been leading Tylek." He faced Noressa. "Your disguises are pretty but useless. You are like a child fumbling with a new toy. I must teach you the proper use of this thing."

Noressa's defensive anger returned, marring her joy at Medwyn's words that she was to keep the amulet. "I am not a child! My illusions are perfect. They have fooled everyone— even you. If my first disguise is found out, then I will make another."

Medwyn smiled as an indulgent father will smile at a willful child, then turned to gaze through the window. "There is much you must learn, Noressa. You have inherited a great responsibility, and there will be—" He stopped, whirling to face her, his eyes narrowed, hard.

Noressa had taken Medwyn's moment of inattention to clothe herself in the illusion of a second Bydawine. Now she stood with Bydawine before the fire, a faithful reflection of her companion. She allowed herself a moment of satisfaction when Medwyn's expression told her he was unable to discern between truth and her new disguise.

So. Let him speak of control now! Her thoughts were smug, and she settled herself firmly into the illusion. She was not intimidated as Medwyn came forward, a warning anger in his voice.

"The Talent is not a bauble to be tossed about for your own pleasure. It is a treasure to be guarded zealously and used carefully when there is a need for it. Pride and vanity will be your greatest enemies and can destroy you as surely as any sword." He paused, looking from one dwarf to the other. When neither spoke, Noressa caught a flicker of sadness in his anger. "Very well, if you would play the game, you must accept the consequences. I regret that your lessons must begin so harshly."

Medwyn straightened, seeming to tower suddenly, and Noressa felt her confidence begin to wane. The elder's left hand described a quick pattern in the air, and he intoned strange words that filled her ears with their sound but slipped away from her mind's grasp. Then Noressa caught her breath, feeling herself enveloped in a crimson haze of pain. She fell to the floor, twisting from the searing heat that would not be left behind. Through her agony, she watched the true Bydawine spring forward, his short dagger in hand. But Medwyn, never taking his eyes from her, raised his hand and spoke a single word. Bydawine tumbled to the floor and did not move again. This terrified Noressa as much as the pain, and she screamed, "I submit! I submit! Take away the spell!"

Medwyn answered quickly. "I cannot. The magic is your own. You must release it."

Noressa flung the image of the dwarf from her mind. The pain ceased, and she curled herself tight against the sudden absence of the heat.

Medwyn dropped his hand and Bydawine rushed to her side. Taking a defensive stance, he leveled his dagger at the approaching wizard. But Noressa sat up, pushing the knife aside. "No, Bydawine, he is not to blame." Bydawine looked at her, confused, but made no objection when Medwyn helped her up and settled her in the high-backed chair.

Ashamed, unable to meet the elder's gaze, Noressa whispered, "How did you know?"

Medwyn patted her hand. "To one learned in the craft, as am I, you are undisciplined in the use of your talents. When you invoke them, the power flows from you in waves. My incantation merely reflected them back to you."

Noressa shook her head. "You were right. It was pride that made me think my little trick could give me superiority over any who came against me."

Bydawine brought her a mug of hot lirsa tea, boldly pushing himself between her and the magician. He stroked back a wisp of her dark hair and glared at Medwyn. "If she is so incompetent in the use of the power, then why was it entrusted to her? Tylek has killed more than once to possess this amulet. Why should a witch-woman seek out a peasant's daughter to carry it?"

Medwyn shook his head. "The amulet is of no importance except as a sign of membership in a specific family. It is the rightful wearer of the amulet that Tylek seeks."

Noressa looked up in surprise. "Then it is you he would kill, Medwyn, for I was sent to bring you the talisman!"

"Not I," Medwyn answered. "Though he would kill me gladly. But think, child, what was the message Salet sent you?"

Noressa remembered Edell's quavering voice and spoke the words aloud. " 'Find the the tree in the crossroads, in the markets of Tarragon. By the Token of Dragonsblood . . .' "

". . he will know you are the one.' " Bydawine finished the chant when Noressa faltered. "Impossible! It would mean Tylek and his army invaded our land and killed our people simply to destroy a peasant girl and possess a worthless medallion. It is ridiculous!"

"If the destruction of an impoverished huntsman's daughter is viewed as his goal, then, my passionate little friend, you are correct; it is unbelievable. But when the truth is revealed, you will see why Tylek and his mistress, Felaya, must see her dead."

Noressa kept silent during their exchange, but now she stood, fury warming her cheeks. She laid the medallion upon the table. "No man, be he lord or slave, has just cause to see me dead. And if, to possess this amulet, my life must be forfeit, then by the powers, I will renounce it and all that pertains to it!"

"Silence!" The sharp thud of his staff striking the floor punctuated Medwyn's command. "You will make no vows until you understand fully what it is that you would throw away." They shared a moment of silent anger, each assessing the other. Then Medwyn's face softened and there came again the fatherly smile. "You have taken your mother's beauty, Noressa, but also your father's quick temper."

"What can you know of my parents?"

"More than you would think." He motioned her to be seated. "You have struggled long and hard that I might explain the riddle of the amulet. That I cannot do. Salet held that key. But hear my story. When you understand it, you will be free to do as you wish."

Noressa looked to Bydawine, uncertain. He shrugged. "It is why you have come."

Noressa shrugged also. "Very well, magician. I will hear your story, but I make no promise that I will stay when it is done." She returned to her chair, and Bydawine seated himself nearby on a bench. Medwyn stared deep into the fire, composing his face into a blank mask before he spoke.

"It has been nearly one and twenty years since the night I fled my homeland of Sidra and the evil that polluted its very soil. I fled, not out of fear, but at the command of my queen, whom I knew would be dead before another quarter-cycle had passed."

A chill shivered through Noressa, and memories of her father's hunger for news of Sidra broke in upon her. Here was a true participant in a war that was, to her, only a frightening tale whispered through shadows on gloomy winter nights. She saw that Bydawine, too, shared her surprise.

Medwyn hadn't seen their reaction, for he kept his impassive gaze directed toward the flames as he spoke. "I served as First Counsel to Onath, King of Sidra, and then to his son, Brydon. Brydon was a good king and maintained the peace his father had founded. But he was young and soon grew restless. So it was that King Brydon sought to increase trade relations with the land of Turalain."

Medwyn withdrew a short parchment roll from his cloak and unrolled it on the table, weighting the corners with the cream bowl and tea mugs. Bydawine and Noressa moved to either side of him to peer at the parchment.

"It is an old map of the continent. Here is Dromund and, to the east, Sidra."

"And here—" Noressa pointed to the top of the drawing. "This space is marked Turalain, but there is no country."

"So it is with all maps of Turalain," Bydawine answered. "Legend says it was a country of sorcerers who isolated themselves from the world."

Medwyn nodded. "Yes. The Turalainians had devoted their entire society to the development of the Talents. They were self-sufficient in all ways save one—salt. Three times in the year, the salt traders of Sidra were permitted to enter the wastelands of Turalain. A journey of two days brought them to an oasis, where their salt was purchased. Each trader returned home rich with all manner of precious jewels, exotic spices, fine woods; the payment was always far in excess of the salt's true value. But no outsider was permitted beyond this point or allowed to mingle with the people of Turalain."

"And this your King Brydon would have changed." Noressa was intrigued by the story, despite her wariness.

"Yes. No argument could dissuade him. In the fourth year of his reign, Brydon assumed the guise of a salt trader and traveled to the Oasis of Turalain. He returned, not with greater trade agreements, but with a new queen. She was Breann, youngest daughter in the family Zibeth, companions in the Clan of Dragonsblood. With her came her handmaiden, Salet. Breann's family was angered that she would forsake them for a man of the Outer Lands and disowned her. This left the young lovers both prey to the vengeance of her sister, whose affections Brydon had spurned."

Bydawine arched a brow in understanding. "The deadly triangle . . . an ancient passion. More than once, a rejected suitor has sought to destroy that which she claims to love most."

"True," Medwyn answered. "But seldom is the result as

devastating." Pain glittered in his eyes, but his voice remained flat, unfeeling, as though the story were a difficult lesson he must tell by rote. "For two years, there was great happiness in our land. Despite her reputation as sorceress and shape-changer, Breann's gentle ways conquered the fears of the people as easily as she had taken Brydon's heart. Then came news that the queen was with child. Brydon's joy was boundless, but Breann was consumed by a black despair. She wanted the child, but her rune-castings augured great destruction before its birth. Her fears were thought to be only a sympton of her condition, but within a twelveday came word that the eastern borders were under attack."

On the map, Noressa traced the faded ink of Sidra's eastern boundary. "An attack from Turalain."

"Not Turalain." Medwyn's voice took a hard edge, and he seated himself stiffly on the bench facing the fire. "Felaya. The queen's own sister. She had fed on the gall of rejection and hatred while she developed the dark elements of her Talents. She had bided her time and struck while Breann was in her time of weakness. And it was a traitor in our midst that brought her in—our king's own Second Counsel, Tylek of Eksorm."

"But your king—" Bydawine said. "Surely he would not leave the defense of his lands to his queen alone."

"No. He took half the armies and met Felaya at the Southern Wasteland border. For three cycles, the moon waxed full and Brydon would gain an advantage. Three times the moon waned and Felaya pushed farther into Sidra. At home, I spent long hours assisting Breann in her conjurations against her sister. But it was not enough. The growing child drained Breann's strength, while Felaya was succored by powers my queen dared not draw upon. And our armies dwindled as Breann continued to send more troops to Brydon."

Medwyn rose and went to stand at the window, staring out at the jumble of rooftops leading down to the harbor. "When the queen was in her seventh cycle, there came yet another call for men. She had scarcely twenty score remaining. She sent half to Byrdon, then, leaving me to hold the keep, she journeyed to the northeast with the final portion of the army. I was hard put to quell rumors that she had deserted king and country. Two cycles passed before she and Salet returned . . . alone. There was no word spoken of the men she had taken, nor where she had gone."

"But what of the child?" Noressa asked. "This should have been her time of confinement."

Medwyn returned to his bench at the table. "I had no choice but to tell her that Brydon had fallen in battle and Felaya was marching on the castle, less than two days distant. It was clear that Breann had suffered an ordeal during her journey, and it was this final blow that sent her to her bed. The child was born that night."

"So you took the child away and left your queen behind." Bydawine could not keep a tone of accusation from his voice. But there was no anger nor guilt in Medwyn's gaze as he faced the dwarf, only a tired sadness.

"Breann knew she was dying. Already Felaya's advance troops were destroying the village of Lynget and would soon besiege the castle. Once Salet and I had gone, Breann planned to use what final powers she possessed and the few remnants of the army that had fallen back to the keep to hold Felaya's attention to the castle. Time and the symbol of her severed membership in the Dragonsblood clan were all the legacy Breann could offer her child."

"It is clear you made good your escape," Bydawine said. "What became of the child?"

Noressa took the amulet from the table, brushing her thumb over the rough features of its engraving. Medwyn had said the token was hers by right of inheritance. She squeezed it tightly and refused to meet his gaze, praying the elder's reply would not be as she feared.

"We made our way to Dromund and parted company, promising to meet each year in the markets of Tarragon. Salet took the child. When next we met, she told me the babe had been placed with a peasant family who had lost their own child. Whether Breann's child was son or daughter, I never knew. Nor even its name. Only that, like its mother, the babe was fair-skinned and gray-eyed, with hair like ebony."

Now it was Noressa who stood alone at the window. She stared out past the tall-sparred ships hugging the docks to the glittering swells of the open sea and felt herself awash with conflicting emotions. She experienced anger, sadness, even excitement. Medwyn's tale explained her father's journey to Tarragon each spring and the source of his ready wealth. She understood, too, his passion for any news of Sidra and his insistence that she learn more than a huntsman's daughter would ever need to know. And the strange moods that came over him in his later years. The times her mother would send her to fetch him in, and she would find him on the hillside behind the cottage, sitting beside a small pile of stones. She had thought little of the winter nights spent at his feet when he would stroke her hair and mutter, "You should have had a sister to keep you company on these lonely nights." When she denied being lonely, he would only smile and shake his head.

Bydawine came to stand beside her. "So you are of royal blood, Noressa. It is the dream of every girl, yet you act as though it were a shameful thing. Or do you blame your parents because they did not tell you of it? Perhaps they were afraid that, knowing the truth, you would seek to claim this birthright and be lost to them."

She sighed, remembering her father's patience and watchful tutelage. "My mother never knew of it. All those years— the loss of their child, the burden of my protection—my father carried it alone. He spent his life preparing me for this decision."

"Then it is clear what you must do," Bydawine said. "You must claim your birthright. Is that not so, magician?"

"She must choose her own path," Medwyn answered. "If she would claim the legacy, it will mean great danger, but also the promise of great reward. To deny it will certainly mean her death, for she is the living symbol of all that Felaya has tried to destroy. Felaya will not rest until it is finished."

"My father knew there would be only one path open to me." She felt the insistent draw of the summoning. "And it is a path that must serve two purposes."

Bydawine laid his hand on her arm. "We must both fight for what has been taken from us, Noressa, and we share a common enemy. I will raise an army to defeat Tylek. Stay with me until that is done, and I will help you defeat this Felaya as well."

Noressa smiled her gratitude, then moved to stand squarely

before the magician. "You prevented my vow before, Medwyn, but you will hear me now, for I speak it with a full understanding of what I say." Excitement pulsed through her, its intensity almost a hunger. The amulet lay cradled in her palm, radiating a warmth that should have been painful but only added to her ardor. "By the powers, I pledge myself and all that I am to this quest. By my breath, I will claim my birthright to the Clan of Dragonsblood!"

For a long, clear moment, the air vibrated with power and the token's bloodstone blazed scarlet.

* * * * *

Felaya was jolted from the empty splendor of her throne, pierced by the momentary tremor of a familiar call. In some faraway place, a Companion had roared its challenge. She settled herself once more upon the throne, lips drawn in a cold, tight smile of anticipation.

CHAPTER 8

ylek's appearance in Tarragon caused a stir.

Pashet could see that, even for a trade city accustomed to strange sights, the twenty soberfaced guards riding escort for the handsome nobleman were of interest to all. Any young girl bold enough to catch Tylek's eye was left breathless by the fine arch of his brow and the secretive smile that flitted between them. It was a talent Pashet had often envied, but today his dark mood did not allow such a waste of emotion.

He still brooded over his angry parting from Jaaben. His last words to his brother had been harsh ones, and for that, he blamed Tylek.

Jaaben had strode angrily to and fro in his tent, rattling his sword in its scabbard, while Pashet listened to his tirade. "I tell you, Pashet, one day Tylek will go too far, and I will have my satisfaction. I will see him stripped and beaten and run before the hounds. I will—"

"You will do nothing but follow orders, Jaaben. You have no other choice."

Jaaben whirled on him, his body taut with anger, and shook a white-knuckled fist at him. "Do not mock me, Pashet! I suffer enough arrogance from that soulless devil. I will not suffer it from any other—even my own brother!"

Pashet knew that Jaaben's threat came not from true anger with him, but out of frustration at his subservient position under Tylek. They glared at one another for a long moment, and Pashet saw once more how vulnerable his brother could be. How different they were, despite their close blood ties. True, they shared the same father, a drunken, red-haired lout who had spent a week's leave and a full cycle's pay with the two daughters of a brutish innkeeper. And though he was the elder by a mere two days, Pashet had carried the burden of Jaaben's well-being since childhood, so much so that at times he thought of Jaaben more as a wild twin rather than a troublesome half-brother. He read Jaaben easily, knew his moods and how to handle them. And he knew the danger in letting Jaaben's anger influence him now, even though he shared his brother's hatred of Tylek. Feeling himself drawn into that anger, Pashet drew a long breath, forced his shoulders down, and returned Jaaben's look with weary patience. Jaaben gave a snort of disgust and turned away. But Pashet followed and, with mock seriousness, took Jaaben by the back of the neck, propelling him toward one of two stools flanking a small camp table.

"Calm yourself, Jaaben. I do not offer you arrogance, only the voice of sensibility." Jaaben only grunted as Pashet poured them both wine from the jug on the table. "If you will think on it, you will see that Tylek is correct to separate us here. An army of this size will not be allowed entrance to the city of Tarragon. But a strange nobleman accompanied by his private retinue of guards will arouse only romantic interest, not military suspicions."

Jaaben emptied his goblet in one long draft, then sat staring at the floor. Pashet seated himself opposite his brother and quietly refilled the empty cup. He knew when to keep silent and let Jaaben wrestle with his own temper.

"Tylek deliberately set out to provoke me."

"Perhaps."

"You know it as well as I, Pashet! Why else would he take us a full day's ride toward the city, then tell us our group was too large? He could have divided us at the foot of the mountain. He did it to provoke me!"

"Only because he knows you can be provoked."

Jaaben said nothing.

"Even now you play into his hands, Brother. It is near midday, and still we are encamped; you should be at least three leagues nearer to Stagget's Keep. This will surely be reported to the mistress."

"I am in command of this army," Jaaben growled. "I will say when we march."

Pashet's own temper began to rise. "You command only under me! And I under Tylek. And we must all answer to *her*. It has been nearly two days since we let the boy slip away from us, and Tylek bears no blame in that. It is you and I who must answer for it. With help from my dwarf, the boy may have already reached the city. If he raises the alarm before we take him, then our army must fight and retreat all at once. Then it will be our men who suffer for this petulance. They will be forced to ride three days with no rest to reach the safety of our border. And that safety will be lean, indeed, if we must return to the mistress empty-handed."

"Do not lecture me, Pashet! I am not a child to be scolded!" Jaaben slammed a fist to the table, upsetting the jug. Pashet jumped from his seat as the dark, red wine splashed across the table into his lap and dribbled down his legs.

Pashet held himself in check against the violent urge to throw himself bodily at his brother. Instead, he let his voice deliver his anger. "If you were any other man, Jaaben, I would thrash you soundly, then leave you to wallow in your pool of self-pity. But you are my brother and a leader of men. Those two privileges demand a measure of responsibility. If you cannot carry that load, then there is nothing further I can do in your behalf. Tylek will find another who can fulfill his needs."

Pashet left Jaaben glowering into the wine-soaked mess on the table. Back in his own tent, Pashet poured and gulped two cups of wine to calm himself. He was pouring a third when a runner came with news that Jaaben's men were preparing to march. Before half the camp was struck, Pashet and his twenty best men had departed with Tylek for Tarragon.

Now their group moved in the direction of the harbor. Without seeming to, Tylek followed the flight of the ebrot, which soared unnoticed by most of the town's citizens. As they drew near the street's end, Pashet saw the bird perched on the sign arm of a large inn.

Word of their approach had gone before them. The innkeeper, a short, thick-bellied man, stood before his door among a group of gawkers. His bulging eyes widened even farther when he realized the nobleman had stopped and was beckoning to him. The innkeeper sprang forward, obsequious chatter tumbling from his lips before he reached Tylek's side.

"A pleasant afternoon to ye, m'lord. Welcome to the Blue Pearl Inn. I am sure that ye will be most comfortable in our care. If there is any way that I may serve . . ." He faltered before Tylek's upraised hand.

"I do not wish lodging here, innkeeper, unless I find what I am searching for. I seek two companions."

The innkeeper twisted his hands. "And ye think I should know of them, m'lord?"

"I was told they were here. A young man, a huntsman by trade, and a dwarf."

"A dwarf!" exclaimed the man, a grin splitting his face. "Yes, I do know of them, sir. A handsome youth with gray eyes so soft they could break a mother's heart."

"That is the one," Tylek answered. "I wish to see them."

The innkeeper cringed. "But they are not here, m'lord. They left early this morning."

"When will they return?" A hint of impatience edged Tylek's words.

Pashet watched with distaste as the fat little man wrung his hands. His bulging eyes darted up and down the street as if in hopes of spotting the missing travelers. "They will not return, m'lord. I do not know from where they came nor where they went."

Only the twitch of a tiny muscle in his cheek gave sign of Tylek's anger. Pashet took some satisfaction in knowing that Tylek's next words were carefully smooth and even.

"It may be that they left me a message in their quarters. If I may see their rooms, perhaps I may find it."

The little man's face went blank. "Their rooms, m'lord?"

"Yes, their rooms!" Pashet interrupted, tired of the man's inanities. "Where did they sleep?"

"In truth, sir, I do not know, but certainly not at *my* inn. I beheld them for the first time when they came to take breakfast with one of my own guests."

"What?" Tylek jerked to attention. "You say they came here to meet someone? Who?"

"A patron of many years, sir. An elder who comes each spring. This year he stayed longer than is his wont, but he left early this morning with the two whom you seek."

"His name?"

"Medwyn, m'lord."

"So . . ." Tylek looked eager and he smiled at the little

man. "You have served me well, innkeeper." Tylek nodded to Pashet and turned his mount back toward the markets.

Pashet tossed the startled fat man a gold piece and hurried his own mount as quickly as he dared over the cobbled street. Once more beside Tylek, he asked, "Who is this Medwyn? Why do they travel with him?"

Tylek's smile was grim, tight.

"Possibly you were too young to remember him, Pashet. He was First Counsel to King Brydon. It was he who helped the woman, Salet, spirit away Breann's child." Tylek's eyes glittered with a hard, hungry look, and he breathed softly. "Medwyn—still alive!"

That expression brought Pashet a sharp chill, but he steeled himself against the accompanying shiver. Faint childhood memories curled at the back of his mind. It seemed he did remember a Medwyn. There had been a magician who held higher rank than Tylek and who disappeared at the moment of Felaya's triumph. But there had been little spoken of this other magician. Most attention was directed toward the woman, Salet, and the missing child. But Pashet decided the omission had been for the best. More than once he had seen this kind of eagerness in Tylek. And he knew that if Tylek's fulfillment did not come soon, it would be those around him who would suffer. And usually Jaaben was a particular target for Tylek's frustrations.

The thought was disturbing, but Pashet contented himself with the knowledge that Tylek now faced a worthy rival. A rival who had once been more powerful than Tylek and might be even yet, to have survived unknown all these years. Pashet had no doubt that the combined talents of Tylek and Felaya would be a match for any who came against them. But knowing Tylek's love of power, Pashet understood that any battle in which Felaya played the winning move would be less sweet for Tylek.

Jaaben would be pleased with that thought.

Pashet smiled inwardly, though he kept his face calm. "So, now where are we bound?"

"Home."

"What?" Pashet was astounded. "Without them? The mistress will set our heads on the castle gates."

"Rest easy, Pashet. Your head is secure. By now, Medwyn will have told the boy of his heritage and offered his services as counselor. The boy, of course, will accept, and Medwyn will have regained his seat as First Counsel to the throne. His next move will be to install the boy as king, and there is only one place where that can be done."

"Sidra." Pashet's worry eased some as Tylek's point became clear. "But if they should seek allies here in Dromund—"

"So much the better," Tylek chortled. "Obviously they cannot return to Norwick. There is no sign that they have raised the alarm here in the city. The nearest help they could expect will be from Stagget, and they don't know that Stagget was our first conquest. So we will simply wait until they deliver themselves to us at Stagget's Keep."

It was the first time Pashet had seen the magician laugh out loud.

Several hours later, Pashet waited with his men. He listened absently to the familiar creak of leather and jangle of harness as a kifera stamped or a soldier stretched a tired leg. He turned his head only slightly when Yalst joined him.

Yalst stood in the stirrups of his riding pad, arched his back, then settled once more on the seat. "If Tylek is so eager to reach Stagget's Keep, why do we sit here while he plays games in the trees?"

"He wants to send a message ahead so that Jaaben will be prepared for the boy when he arrives. And Tylek is careful not to disclose even the simplest of his secrets of conjuration."

"And careful he should be." Yalst smirked. "With a magician's powers, any strong young man might replace him in the mistress's favor."

"Replace? I think not. Tylek and the mistress are of the same mind in too many ways. But he might be added to—provided the newcomer possessed sufficient stamina."

They laughed between themselves, knowing the rumors of Felaya's reputed appetite when it came to men. Then Yalst sobered.

"But if Tylek believed the mistress were even considering his replacement, his anger would be of the sort I wouldn't wish to see."

"True," Pashet answered. "And I think he may see this

young Noren as such a threat. It might be a thing to keep in mind should the need arise." Pashet said no more, but he couldn't help wondering if Tylek's eagerness to capture the boy and his talisman before they returned to Sidra had more to do with personal reasons than a desire to serve the mistress.

Seeing Tylek emerge from the grove, Pashet motioned Yalst back with the men while he rode ahead. Tylek appeared pleased with his efforts.

"All went well?"

"Yes. Your brother will be alerted tonight, and I have sent word to our forces across the river to expect us at the end of three days."

Pashet was surprised. "Three days? You expect to have it finished by then?"

"It is almost finished now. Jaaben should have the boy and his friends within two days. If we ride hard, we can make Stagget's Keep by afternoon of the third day. We will cross the river that night and be on our way home by morning."

"An excellent plan . . . if all goes accordingly."

"If it does not, you know who will be to blame, Pashet. The boy's capture is all that remains, and Jaaben must see to it. That is our only weakness."

Pashet remained silent as he watched two dark blots in the afternoon sky—ebrots, Tylek's messenger birds. He let Tylek's threat to his brother pass by while he concentrated on pushing his anger down until it rested, a hard, cold lump in the back of his mind. He, too, harbored a deep hatred of Tylek. But unlike Jaaben, he refused to allow his antipathy to place him in a position of frustrated servility.

Pashet signaled his men to resume their close formation. With an easy hand, he guided his kifera into step beside Tylek and hoped his face projected an attitude of watchful calm. It would be a long three days.

CHAPTER 9

Night had come, but still they pushed on across the eastern fringe of the Bada-shi. Bydawine had made it clear that they must reach Stagget's Hold as soon as possible. Finally, at moonrise, Medwyn called a halt to their forced pace. Bydawine made no objection to the stop, though Noressa could see he was not pleased that the magician had taken it on himself to make the decision.

They made camp in an abandoned cottage, its stone walls half obscured by the tall resa weed that made up the grasslands. The cottage offered some shelter, despite the gaping hole a fallen tree branch had rent in the rotted timber roof. A rickety lean-to afforded a place to tether the kifera out of sight.

Noressa sighed as she watched Bydawine lay out their meal of cold meat and cheese. The spring nights still held a chill edge, and a cheery fire would have been welcome. But even within the protection of the stone walls, they dared not risk it. Still, she couldn't help thinking of the packet of ydrosh tea in her herb belt. A cup of the hot, sweet drink was exactly what she wanted now. Bydawine caught her watching him and smiled, seeming to know what was on her mind.

"At least it is all fresh. I was getting tired of stale bread."

"As was I," Noressa agreed. She had cleared away the debris from one corner of the room, and gathering several armfuls of the tender resa weeds, she set each bedroll on its own grassy mattress. Her bed she set slightly apart from the others, then went to sit with Bydawine.

"Your friends were generous to give us supplies and mounts on such short notice, Bydawine."

"They know me. And they are old and trusted allies to my uncle. I only wish I could have stayed until they had assembled their fighting men, but that might take several days and Stagget must be alerted at once. If all goes well, Tabir's messenger bird will reach Stagget by dawn, but with Tylek on our trail, it would not be wise to depend solely on that."

Noressa accepted the bread he offered her, glad of the shadowed spot where she sat so that he wouldn't see her blush when she spoke next. "I'm glad you came with us, Bydawine. I have grown fond of you in these last few days. In truth, I wondered what I would do without your terrible frowns and scoldings to keep me straight."

"Then why will you not wait until we have retaken my uncle's keep? There is no reason for you to go into this quest alone. You may stay in the safety of Castle Stagget, then, with the combined forces of my uncle's allies, I am sure we can defeat this mistress."

"I cannot say why, Bydawine, but I must go on. Something there—" She gestured eastward. "Something strong calls to me, and there is a true need in me to answer. Besides, I will not be alone. Medwyn will be with me."

"Huh!"

She heard the disdain in his response and saw the mirroring expression as he leaned forward into a shaft of moonlight to reach a slice of meat. She pondered his continued dislike of the elder. She had no such qualms, having been drawn to the magician from the first. She guessed that Bydawine had not yet forgiven Medwyn for the sorcerously painful lesson he had given her at the inn.

"You still do not trust him, Bedawine. Why? Do you think he lied about my parents?"

"Perhaps not about that, but I have known men who would speak the truth—or pieces of it—for their own purpose. He may have said those things to gain your trust, all the while intending to deliver you to this mistress as soon as you cross into Sidra! How can he expect the two of you to prevail against this woman? What power will a once-defeated magician and an apprentice sorceress have over one who destroyed a king's entire army and killed her own sister? Him with his gaudy staff. If he—"

Bydawine stopped as the magician entered the cottage. Noressa looked down at the bread in her hands, feeling guilty but unable to think why. Joining them at their meal, it was Medwyn who spoke first.

"The animals are tended and will be comfortable until we are ready to leave." Bydawine didn't answer; Noressa only nodded, her mouth too dry to speak. Medwyn spoke again after another awkward silence. "Perhaps, Noressa, it would be best if we delayed our journey until friend Bydawine and his companions are able to accompany us."

"What are you saying?" Noressa exclaimed. "Why should we wait?"

"Because it is the one practical answer that I can see. An army of allies is our only hope to survive this ordeal. Alone, Felaya would destroy us the moment we were in her grasp."

"But I have the medallion, and you will teach me its use. Surely—"

"No. The medallion is nothing. Do not trust it to save you. Your mother also had this medallion and a lifetime of experience with her Talents, as well as a husband's army to defend her. And she was still defeated. What hope do a tired magician and a lone girl have against the power Felaya wields?"

"Then if the medallion is useless and you cannot help me, what is the use in either?"

Medwyn sighed. The moon was high, spilling in through the broken roof, its hard, bright light softened to a dreamy haze by the dust their movements had stirred up. Coming from behind him, it formed a silver nimbus in the dark. The momentary splendor was incongruous with the weariness in his voice.

"As I have said, it was the sign of your heritage and your claim to the throne. For me, it was a signal that the time had come to fulfill my promise to my queen. It may be that you will yet find a special power in the amulet, but if it is so, I do not know of it. It was to have been Salet's responsibility to instruct you in its history and use. Now—" he made a small gesture with his hand—"now I must teach you what I can after my own fashion."

Bydawine looked surprised at the magician's sudden support of his argument, but was quick to take advantage of it. "He speaks true, Noressa. You will need our help. It should not take long to reclaim my home, and I know the border lords will consider this invasion an open act of war. They will carry the fighting back to Sidra."

"In the meantime," Medwyn said, "you will begin your training as my pupil."

Noressa was confused; she stared through the open doorway at the silver-washed fields. The sense of urgency was strong, pulling at her. Yet she knew, also, the validity of Medwyn's argument. She closed her eyes against her fatigue. The strain of the day's discovery, the burden of responsibility she had accepted, and their flight all ran together until nothing seemed real save the need to go on. Perhaps it would be better if she simply went home, back to her cottage and the unimportant life of a huntsman's daughter, hidden away on her quiet mountain. But she remembered Edell and the horrors that had followed her. Her mountain was no longer a refuge.

If I feel this way now, when I have just begun, how can I hope to face any sorceress? she wondered.

"Very well, I can see that you must be right in this. I will wait and hope that when your endeavor is complete, Bydawine, your allies will be as eager to assist me as you."

"They will be! When I tell them of your needs, they will insist on it."

"Do not be rash with your promises," Medwyn warned. "You have a personal role in our plight; the others do not." He raised a hand to Bydawine's angry denial. "There are serious odds to consider. Is your king now willing to plunge his nation into war with a land of Sidra's reputation? You were too young to remember, but you will know the history of your own war council. You will know that Brydon appealed to his ally, your king, for assistance against Felaya, and none was forthcoming. Will your king now listen to the words of an old man and a peasant girl? Would it not be simpler to occasionally defend one's borders than to risk complete destruction?"

"And what say you now, magician? Should she go on alone because you do not feel that she can depend on me for help?"

"I have no doubt of your sincerity, young friend, but you cannot speak for others on a matter as grave as this."

"He is right," Noressa said. "You must let the others make their own choice. I have said I will wait until then, so, please, let us not argue amongst ourselves. We should eat, then rest;

and we shall need to set a watch."

"Yes, but let one watch who does not need sleep," Medwyn answered. He rose, took Noressa by the hand and led her to the doorway; Bydawine followed. All three stared out into the grassy fields, stretching away and around the cottage, as Medwyn spoke softly beside her. "Your illusions have been one manifestation of your Talents; a watch-spell will be another."

"But I have no knowledge of these things," she protested. "I have no incantations."

"Use your own. Words are only a tool to clarify your desires. A watch-spell is only an extension of your awareness. But remember," he warned, "you must learn to control and direct your power. Give only what is needed."

Uncertain, Noressa touched the medallion where it lay against the laces of her shirt. The power was there; she felt it begin to surge. She snatched her hand away, for she felt, too, the scorching heat that began to envelop her. Medwyn's enchantment was still in effect. She took a deep breath, exhaled, and tried again. This time she didn't focus entirely on the medallion but turned her attention outward, to the field, when the power began to stir. Surprised, she uttered the words that came silently to her mind. "Summon now the partisan form, the eyes to watch, the tongue to warn. Encircle now our time of sleep, guardian dark, this watch to keep."

She steadied herself against the cold stone wall when a strength moved out of her and the disciplining heat began to flare. Noressa let go her summons and the heat subsided. Her searching gaze swept the plain, but she saw nothing that didn't belong. It was Bydawine who saw the thing first.

"There . . . do you see it?" he exclaimed.

She followed his pointing finger. Her mind fumbled with the tangled memory of what she had thought was a waking dream. But here it was before her again, that thing which had haunted the edge of her vision only one night past under the sima tree.

The length of a tall man, with dark scales agleam, it sat near the lee corner of the house. The heavy, triangular head swung around, fixing them with a glittering stare; its tongue made one long, sibilant sound before the creature slipped away into the grass.

Bydawine stared at her with awe. "Why a red-eyed lizard?"

She could only shake her head and look to Medwyn for the answer.

The magician led them back to their meal. "Your summoning did not name a particular beast. What we saw was shaped by your own desires. You have called forth the form that will serve you best; do not fear it. It will be a guide and a strength in times of need. Now let us eat, for we shall have little time to rest before morning."

Noressa would have thought sleep impossible, knowing what waited just outside their doorless shelter, but she was scarcely settled into her blankets when sleep caught her in its welcome embrace. She slept peacefully for a time before the dream came again, and she started awake in panic to find Medwyn and Bydawine anxiously bending over her. Noressa sat up, assuring them she was well, that it was only a bad dream.

"Was it the same as last night?" Bydawine asked.

At her weary nod, Medwyn demanded to be told about it. Reluctantly she told him, pulling her blankets tight when she spoke of the desperate evil that always overcame her. She told them, too, of its tiresome repetition and the nagging urge of the summoning.

"Well?" Bydawine demanded of Medwyn. "What do you say of that? The dream must be important to repeat itself so."

"Indeed, but I cannot be sure," Medwyn mused. Noressa heard a mixture of curiosity and surprise in his voice. "It may only be a symbolic rendering of things as they stand or a warning of things to come." Of Noressa he asked, "Did these feelings begin after you received the medallion?"

"No. The need to be gone has plagued me only since my mother's death. The dream is one I suffered as a child. Is that of importance?"

She thought he smiled at her in the darkness. "Only because it tells me that you are indeed your mother's daughter. You knew without the medallion that there was a purpose for you elsewhere."

"Truly?" Bydawine's sarcasm made Noressa wince. "Could it not be, as well, a result of having lost all family and being left with no roots to hold her to home? Many people in such circumstances will feel the need to be elsewhere."

Medwyn stood up, a pale shape in the darkness, his stance rigid. He didn't answer Bydawine but turned away, saying, "It's time we moved on. The moon is set and dawn is not far off."

They had a hurried meal of dried meat sticks and bread while they readied their kifera. The eastern sky was fading to gray-rose as they mounted, and Bydawine again took the lead. But Noressa hesitated, searching the quiet grass. "Do you think we should leave . . . it? Will it harm any others after we are gone?" She shivered, thinking of the other she may have left prowling the streambanks.

Medwyn gave her a patient smile. "You must learn to understand the enchantments you weave, Noressa. The incantation held its own limit—a watch-spell for this night's sleep. It was enough, so that your awakening discharged it. But it is well that you should think of it. You will learn that magic, as with all other principles, exists within its own boundaries. It is when you would overstep these limits that you must be certain your own restraints will be strong enough to contain what you have loosed."

Then Bydawine took the lead again, and this time she followed, shaking her head. It was becoming clear that this new "talent" would require a great deal of work.

* * * * *

It was early afternoon when Noressa called to Bydawine that Medwyn had fallen behind. Most of the day had been spent traveling the dense forest along the edge of the grasslands. The spongy turf had kept their passage almost silent. Now, returning to Medwyn, they found him clambering stiffly from his kifera. He declined their proffered assistance with a regretful shake of his head and began to pace carefully between his kifera and a moss-encrusted stump.

"I am too old for such excitements," he muttered. "I should be ensconced in a peaceful keep, leisurely attending to the training of some obnoxious, eager apprentice."

"Oh, come now. You are not so old," Noressa chided gently.

But as she brought him the water bag, she couldn't help wondering if the journey might not be too much for him. "You have kept the pace very well."

"Not so old?" He smiled, raising a hand to the softness of her hair. "You forget, child, that I was counselor to your grandfather even before your father was born. But no matter. For now, you will be an excellent apprentice, and I will yet hope for that peaceful keep."

Noressa could see that Bydawine was about to speak and sent him a warning look. She had already scolded him earlier after he was impudent to Medwyn's remarks. He frowned an acknowledgment and moved his kifera nearer.

"You are a teacher of mysteries, elder. Why does it matter whom you apprentice so long as that one is trustworthy?"

"It matters because there are limits to the talents of both pupil and master. I will teach Noressa because the fates have decided it. But I fear my knowledge of the powers will not be enough to teach her all she needs. We are each born to a certain destiny. Hers is to rule; mine, to advise and support. Yet I may still be of use to her, since roles often intertwine. Perhaps if we survive, I may yet find my apprentice."

"How will you know when you have found him?" Noressa asked, intrigued by the prospect of learning all that Medwyn knew.

"The test will show him to me."

"What test?"

Medwyn only smiled and, leading his kifera to the stump, prepared to mount. "We must go on. Our young guide does not have time for an old man's pains."

Bydawine flushed and stopped his fidgeting. "I would as soon rest here with you, magician, but Stagget's Keep is yet another full day's ride."

Medwyn nodded amiably and mounted with great care.

They rode until night made the trail impassable. Making another cold camp, they ate quickly from their rations and were soon sleeping under the baleful watch of Noressa's night-time servant.

Upon rising, even Noressa and Bydawine were forced to begin the day slowly, a reluctant admission of the stiffness in their limbs. To shake her discomfort, Noressa turned to further exploring the elusive potency within the amulet.

After several hours on the trail, the forest thinned, giving way to grassy meadows sprinkled with wildflowers. It was at the edge of one such meadow, in a small copse of trees, that they stopped to rest. Noressa alighted first, giggling at the surprise she held for her companions. She brought the desired illusion to mind and felt the familiar warming of the amulet as she drew on its power.

She watched the men dismount; Bydawine tethered the beasts and called to her. When she didn't answer, he called again, more sharply. At her continued silence, he began searching the group of trees. Twice he rushed past her.

Medwyn waited, the fatherly smile again on his lips. At last he looked directly at her and scolded, "Enough is enough, girl. Friend Bydawine is too tired for games."

Bydawine stopped, staring blankly in her direction. His scowl was terrible when Noressa laughed and let go her new illusion. "I see no humor in frightening me half out of my wits, girl. I feared one of Tylek's fiends had plucked you from our midst! Why do you delight in tormenting me so?"

"She has her father's temperament," Medwyn chuckled. "Impulsive to a fault."

"Oh, Bydawine, do not be angry with me," Noressa pleaded. "You saw what has happened!" But the dwarf was silent and Medwyn only smiled. "Medwyn, do not laugh at me. Explain it to him!"

"Our young sorceress feels she has learned control of her Talents because she was able to hold her illusion and circumvent my enchantment as well."

Noressa nodded happily. "I have worked all morning to find the secret, and the proof was my green-yellow bird."

Bydawine was not impressed. "Then you had best find yourself another secret, for I saw a green bird, *then* a yellow bird."

"Oh?"

Medwyn nodded his agreement.

"Oh."

"Do not be discouraged, my dear." Medwyn chuckled yet again. "You are learning quickly."

CHAPTER 10

T he sun rode a clear, azure sky, warming the countryside and brightening all with the freshness and clarity that is seen only on such early spring days. Wildflowers nodded beneath newly budded trees, and birds entertained with their darting flights of courtship. To the east, the Little Bourne, a tributary of the Bourne River, glinted a dark silver-blue edged with gold from the late afternoon sun. The orange tint of the western sky promised another early sunset.

Noressa was uneasy. Bydawine glanced at her where she rode between Medwyn and him. She turned often to look behind them. She slowed her mount, then urged him forward in restless bursts, until now the creature was fretting the bit and becoming troublesome. Bydawine was about to scold her when she caught his eye and, frowning, moved her kifera close to him.

"Am I a fainthearted child, Bydawine, or do you sense a strangeness here? It seems I have felt this way before but cannot say when."

"All seems peaceful enough," Bydawine answered. He had kept them in the forest until the keep was in sight, then brought them across a muddy field onto the road leading into the village of Ymaarel. All was peaceful, yet Noressa's composure was fading the closer they came to the village. Bydawine felt himself catching her distraction. He, too, glanced about quickly. "Perhaps it is the emptiness of the road after the confines of the forest that seems strange."

Noressa drew to a stop, her face draining of color. There was true fear in her eyes. "We must go back!" Her words were almost whispered, but they couldn't have chilled him more if she had screamed them.

Medwyn reigned close to her, reaching to pat her arm. Bydawine's unease became jealousy as she gripped the magician's hand and turned pleading eyes to him. "I remember now. It was the same in Bydawine's valley—no one about, save Jaaben and his men."

From the village, a group of riders was moving toward them. Bydawine slapped his knee in anger, suddenly understanding what was happening.

"Of course! It's no wonder Tylek's army could slip so far as Wigram undetected. Not if he had taken Stagget's place first. I've been leading us into a trap!"

"And the trap is about to close. Look!" Noressa pointed to the approaching men, now identified as soldiers by the orange light of sunset on helm and shield.

"Back to the forest!" Bydawine shouted. "We may lose them in the darkness."

They raced back along the road, hearing the distant shouts of the pursuing men. The haven of the trees seemed impossibly far as their mounts pounded away. Then, from the darkening shadows of the forest, burst a second group of soldiers. They charged, quickly closing the gap between their two groups.

Bydawine veered his kifera away into a field, making toward the river. Their change of direction angled them closer to the soldiers riding from the village, and now they, too, were closing rapidly. Ahead, the Little Bourne was a stream of ruddy orange-black as the low sun blazed its departing light. Without hesitation, Bydawine urged his mount down the bank and into the shallow water.

The water was only knee-high to the beast, but it was cold and swift, fed by the spring melt from the western curve of the Skellen Mountain Range. The kifera snorted its protest at the icy water and fought to return to the bank. Bydawine was hard pressed to keep the animal facing in the correct direction while it struggled to keep its footing on the rocky streambed. He reined tightly, then had his arms nearly jerked from their sockets when a whooshing roar sent the kifera scrambling up the opposite bank. With Medwyn beside him, Bydawine sensed the water brightening in a dancing flare of red, and something in the angry shouts of the soldiers made him risk a backward glance.

Just entering the water, Noressa urged her kifera into the rushing current; their melded forms were a black silhouette against the line of flames that leaped and danced along the bank behind her. Beyond the flames, the soldiers struggled to control their terrified mounts. Noressa reined in beside her companions, her face exultant, a strange fervor in her eyes that was more than just a reflection of the flames. It was a wild beauty, and Bydawine found himself both frightened and fascinated.

Then Noressa's words took meaning in his mind, and fright was all that remained.

"We have no choice now but to cross the Bourne and enter Sidra tonight! Let us hurry so that we may use the confusion to our advantage." And without waiting for reply, she sent her beast in a wild gallop toward the main river. Of a necessity, the two men followed.

Before they had traveled halfway, they were accosted by armed men riding from a makeshift ferry landing on the river. Noressa laughed when the commander shouted for them to stop, but she pulled her trembling mount to a halt. Bydawine guided his own kifera against hers, trying to force her to move on. "What are you doing? We cannot stop here!"

"Leave this to me!" Noressa cried. The eagerness in the forward tilt of her body and the avid tone of her words chilled him. Through the loosened ties of her shirt, he saw a blaze of scarlet riding the curve of her breast.

He had no time to protest further, for the soldiers arrived, fanning out to encircle them. Beside him, Noressa's voice raised in a quick chant, though he couldn't make out the words, and her left arm swept out to fling a handful of something into the faces of the nearest soldiers.

Chaos was immediate. Soldiers shrieked. Kifera reared, screaming. Bydawine glimpsed scorpions, their black stingers held high; and chidd, the tiny white serpents writhing beneath the soldiers' armor. The company broke ranks, mounts and men plunging away in headlong confusion.

Noressa would have led them straight toward the river again, but Bydawine seized her arm. "I know this land better than you do. Follow me!"

He made for the river, careful to lead them away from the

bobbing lanterns moving along the water's edge. His kifera stumbled, and he leaned along its sweat-soaked neck murmuring encouragements, his legs clenched tight against its heaving sides. He concentrated on pushing the frightened animal to the river, deliberately not thinking of the fact that he had never crossed the river, or that once across, they would be cut off from any aid and in the enemy's homeland. The river was their only possible escape, and he knew its narrowest point. For the moment, that was enough.

He gained the top of the bank and sent his mount scrambling down into the water. The kifera reared and lunged, almost unseating him, again trying to fight its way out of the frigid water. It stumbled sideways, was caught by the swollen current, and swept downstream. Bydawine grabbed a handful of fur and gave the beast its head while he struggled to keep his own face above water.

It seemed an eternity that he tumbled in the icy river. He was too short to sit the kifera and keep his head clear, so that the first time he was submerged, Bydawine kicked free of the riding pad and spluttered to the surface. He was aware of his death grip on the kifera's short mane and the creeping dullness in his arms and legs. His chest felt tight, as if he were swaddled in a winding sheet. And it was difficult to know if he was gasping in air or river, but he decided the difference wasn't important. Far back in his mind, something told him this was a danger, yet he lacked the strength to listen to it or to the voices that called his name. He was too tired, too heavy, and his neck ached from craning to breathe. He would answer them later. After he had rested; when breathing was not such a struggle. Then darkness swirled him down to a warm repose.

CHAPTER 11

In the fading light of the flames behind her, Noressa saw Bydawine's kifera stumble as it entered the water. She saw him struggle to gain control of the beast, saw the current take them until they disappeared beneath the water.

Noressa kicked her own mount into pursuit along the bank, calling Bydawine's name. When they surfaced, Bydawine clinging to the creature's mane, Noressa turned her kifera into the river.

Her beast snorted its terror and would have turned back, except it couldn't fight two currents. Despite the cold of the river, the amulet was a brand at her throat, and Noressa rode a second, unseen flow. She was aware of Medwyn behind her, but her attention was on Bydawine. As she came abreast of the struggling pair, the kifera went down again, dragging Bydawine under. With blind knowledge, she reached into the water. Her fingers closed on something solid and she straightened, heaving a limp Bydawine over the front of her riding pad. Then she was past the center of the river, the current pushing her ahead and out toward the riverbank.

Sidra!

Noressa felt the welcome of the land itself as her mount floundered onto the bank.

Then, from the purpling shadows of some nether plane, she knew the silent keening of an outraged entity bearing down on her. Noressa recognized her dream predator as it seared itself into her mind, stripping away all that she was. It tore at her very concept of self. Her mind was laid bare, a raw, primal thing unfettered by learned taboos and misconceptions. That Other swept her down into the seething confluence of base desire, weakness, and fear that was herself. And submission was her only hope of freedom.

Yet there was something else. Trails of light by which Noressa discerned her own despair, rivulets of sparks that wound their way among the horrors. Flowing outward, crossing, merging, they formed a network of power that held at bay the darker side of her mind. And she saw the fountainhead from which these strengths flowed. Bright, hot, it welled fiercely in a plain of desolation.

The single remaining thought that was Noressa plunged into that font of being.

Noressa heard the Other scream, a sound of rage and hate. But it could not follow, and Noressa felt her attacker break away and flee as she dropped into the healing light that was her own power.

*   *   *   *   *

The air rippled, seeming to thin and shimmer. Felaya's breath came in mewling, angry gasps. Her *self* had touched the essence of that *other*, had almost conquered the one so long sought. She had expected resistance, yes, but never a power of such force and brilliance like that which had driven her back. She felt it still, piercing sharp, deep, making her tremble with a pain she hadn't known since childhood. Felaya hugged herself against the flurry of doubts railing at her. She hadn't been beaten, merely taken aback with surprise. She let anger and desire warm her against the cold of uncertainty. The next time she wouldn't be so careless; there would be no mistake now. That which she had hunted for so long was now within her realm, almost within her grasp. Felaya's breath came easier. There were plans to be made, and she could afford to wait.

*   *   *   *   *

Noressa woke strangling on her terror, unable to move. She lay staring up at the trees ringing the small clearing and tried to orient herself to the strange dry forest. The knobby bark of the log against which she lay pressed into her shoulder.

"The dream again?" Medwyn's voice startled her. He watched her from a position on a rocky outcropping at the edge of the clearing.

"No. Something else." She sat up, puzzled. How could he be so calm after last night's strange confrontation on the riverbank? Could he not have known it? Perhaps it was only a dream. Noressa shook her head. The attack had been real. Real, too, was the glorious power with which she had driven away that Other.

Beside her, Bydawine slept, arms folded tight, curled into a ball. She almost reached to touch him, tasting again her fear at believing him drowned. But she remembered he had wakened, retching and gasping, across her mount's withers. She let him sleep; after last night, he had need of the rest. She slipped from the warm spot beneath her cloak.

It was just past dawn, only a few hours since they had stopped at the clearing, a decision made as much by the kifera's refusal to go on as their own exhaustion.

"Was it only last night?" Noressa mumbled. She remembered their forced crossing of the Bourne and her panic at seeing Bydawine swept away. Then they had struggled up the bank into Sidra—and terror.

She closed her mind against that memory. The battle had seemed endless, but regaining her senses, she had seen that they still rode the banks, fleeing their pursuers. When her kifera refused to go on, the three of them had lain together beside the fallen log, Medwyn and Noressa sharing their cloaks with a damp and still shivering Bydawine. She scarcely remembered to set her watch spell before tumbling into the darkness of exhaustion.

Now she stretched, feeling the dissipation of the watch spell and, more slowly, the dream terror. One of the kifera, tethered on the opposite side of the log, stretched its long neck and lipped a strand of her hair.

"I am sorry, my friend, but I have no grain for you." She continued to murmur at the beast while scratching him under the chin. The creature half-closed his eyes, rumbling contentedly. Smiling a little, Noressa went to stand with the magician, hugging herself against the chilly dawn.

Her stomach grumbled, reminding her that she hadn't eaten since afternoon of the day before, but she refused to dwell on her hunger. There was, perhaps, a three-day ration of bread, cheese, and meat sticks in her food packet, but that wouldn't go far among the three of them. The bulk of their supplies had been lost downriver with Bydawine's kifera. As for weapons, she still had her hunting knife and her bow with four arrows; Bydawine still bore his short dagger. Medwyn carried nothing that she could describe as a weapon save his staff, which might provide minimal use as a club.

But then, he has his magic, she told herself. And I have some power of my own. But would that be enough to carry them to . . . where? For an instant, she knew exactly where she must go. And which path to take in getting there. Then hunger jabbed at her again and the knowledge was gone, leaving only the need to move eastward. Noressa shivered and scrubbed at her eyes with the heel of one hand.

"What shall we do now?" She didn't realize she had spoken aloud until Medwyn answered.

"I think it best if we return to Dromund as soon as we can find a safe crossing."

Noressa looked back in the direction of the river and shook her head. "I cannot. What I seek is here. It is stronger than it has ever been, and I must go on."

"What will you go on to, Noressa? Your death? That is the only certainty ahead should you confront Felaya alone."

"Then you must help me, Medwyn, teach me. Each day I grow stronger. You saw what happened last night."

"What did I see? That your illusions distracted our pursuers? That your power carried us across the river when we should have drowned? True. Yet I also saw you lose yourself to the thrill of the power you thought you controlled. But what you felt was the impetus of fear and sudden danger. That power is erratic and cannot be sustained.

"The Talents are real within you—that much you have taken from your mother. But you are rash and impatient, as was your father. He would not listen to counsel, and you see what has happened."

Behind her, Bydawine stirred from his sleeping place, and she guessed he had been awake for some time, for he added his voice to Medwyn's argument.

"The magician speaks true, Noressa. There is little else to be done. We have neither allies nor haven in this place, nor supplies. Retreat is our best move."

Noressa rubbed a hand over her eyes, trying to sort the jumble of her frustrations. She accepted, even desired, the logic of her friend's advice. But the eastward summoning scattered all orderly thoughts, leaving only the compulsion to follow. Whether it was greater now because she was drawing closer or because she was too tired to ignore it, she could not say. She only knew it had become suddenly stronger the moment she had left the river and entered Sidra. And what of her attacker last night, and the power she had found to drive it away? Had Medwyn felt none of that? She must remember to ask him. There were so many things she wanted to ask, if she could but think.

"My friends, you misunderstand me. Felaya is not important to me, nor is Tylek. There is another thing that I seek—a thing I cannot name even to myself. It holds me as strongly as any army could. I will not go back because I *cannot* go back."

In that instant, she saw the gleam of sunlight on metal behind Medwyn, then soldiers were charging in upon them. She sprang in a diving leap to reach the bow lying beside her cloak. Bydawine, standing between her and the weapon, was bowled over by her sudden move. She had a glimpse of him rolling onto his feet with dagger drawn, heard his cry of warning.

"Medwyn, behind you!"

The magician didn't have time to turn. Soldiers charged from all directions, one nearly atop Noressa where she lay fumbling with her bow. She watched as in a dream while Medwyn grasped a handful of air, spoke a word, and flung blue lightning. Noressa's attacker staggered, pain contorting his face, a charred, smoking hole in his chest. Then a backhanded blow with a sword hilt from another soldier sent Medwyn tumbling forward onto the ground, where he lay unmoving. She saw Bydawine dash forward, leaping over the magician's prone body, his movement taking him between two soldiers. He landed, turned, slashed, his blade slicing deep into flesh. The one who had struck Medwyn went down, clutching at the spurting gash behind his knee. Bydawine turned again, but too late, and the second soldier sent him sprawling with a well-aimed fist.

The glade rang with shouts and curses. Noressa abandoned

the bow, seized an arrow, and jumped to her feet, swiping at one of three men advancing on her. She felt the arrow tip grate along the man's cheekbone, then a resistance as it cut into his nose. He screamed and raised his hands to his face. Noressa's right knee jerked up to land with a solid *thunk* between his legs. The man's scream ended abruptly and he crumpled.

His two companions seized her, twisting her arms back until she felt they would be pulled from her shoulders. She cried out against the pain and in desperation sought the illusions of the amulet. The medallion became a quick heat at her throat, and the warning yells of her captors told Noressa her conjuring was successful.

Blinking through tears she saw two iac hounds leaping for them. The soldiers cried out at the sight of the yellow teeth bared in foaming snarls and claw-tipped paws digging the earth, but they didn't run as she had expected.

One man released her and readied his sword. He brought the swordpoint up into the belly of the first beast that launched itself against him, gasping when the creature vanished. The second hound he dispatched as easily and turned, grinning, to his companion. "Hah! A trick! The trollop plays at witchcraft!"

He laughed again when four men charged into the clearing, their leader a tawny, axe-wielding giant. "More games!" the soldier chuckled and raised his sword, one-handed, to parry the wide swing of the giant's battle-axe. The sword went flying from him, his hand still on the grip. He just had time to scream before the axe swung a second, unerring time.

A dark-haired youth rushed in behind the giant, throwing himself upon the soldier still holding her. Free, Noressa slumped forward, arms dangling uselessly at her sides. She heard herself whimper with the pain exploding in her shoulders and fought the urge to collapse completely. Across the glade, two more dark-haired men engaged Bydawine's attacker. She didn't have time to follow their progress, for the man whose face she had slashed sprang up, bearing her over backward, his bloody hands at her throat.

Panic tore at her as his weight pushed the air from her lungs and his fingers pressed into her skin. Then the brown-gold colossus towered over them, and she squeezed her eyes shut against the glittering downward arc of the axe.

There came a jarring thump, the man was lifted from her, and she rolled away, fighting the nausea that threatened to overwhelm her. A deadening silence held the glade, the only sounds her own ragged breathing and the drumming she knew to be her heart. Then someone was helping her to her feet.

She looked into the face of the dark-haired boy who had appeared with the giant. His blood-spattered shirt attested to his recent activity, but the brown eyes gazing at her were friendly. When she stood, he bowed with a flourish. "I am Jatrae, sweet lady, your servant."

Behind them, words rumbled quietly. "Be silent, Jatrae, and let her tend the elder." It was the axe-wielding stranger who spoke, and Noressa turned away when he placed a foot on the dead soldier's spine and heaved the axe from between his shoulders.

She moved carefully to where Medwyn, face pale, had been placed on his back. Pain still throbbed in her shoulders, but she was able to move her arms some. She knelt and watched, arms cradled against her chest, as Bydawine probed gently at the back of the magician's head. Noressa was relieved when the elder moaned and opened his eyes. "Medwyn, can you speak? Do you know me?"

He stared a long moment, then tried to smile. "Yes, child, I know you."

Bydawine assisted Medwyn to a sitting position. Noressa helped him drink from a waterskin that the boy, Jatrae, eagerly fetched from her mount. Bydawine stood by, scowling at the strangers.

"Who are you? Why did you assist us against the soldiers?"

"We are rebels, traitors to the queen," Jatrae answered flatly, then smiled. "But I helped because it offered the quickest way into the good graces of this most beautiful, dear lady." He honored Noressa with a second bow, and she blushed at his audacity.

One of the other men, older by several years but with the same friendly brown eyes, dragged the boy away. With his companion, he propelled him toward the forest. "You talk too much, Jatrae. Come help us gather the soldiers' animals."

Noressa watched them go, her hunter's eyes noting the

stealthy grace with which they disappeared into the woodland. Then she and her companions were alone with the man who, not truly the giant he had seemed in the fury of battle, was decidedly tall. He stood before them in silence, cleaning his double-edged axe with a dark-stained piece of cloth. Around them, the bodies of five soldiers lay in armor-clad heaps. Already scavanger insects were gathering on spots of drying blood. Noressa's distaste at the scene must have shown, for the rebel spoke, his deep voice startling her.

"We will remove the bodies into the forest before we leave, dajari. But we have neither the time nor the wish to bury them."

Noressa drew herself up and looked sharply at him. He had called her dajari—"honored woman." Did he mock her that he used the formal term of respect? She knew how she must appear: disheveled, dirty, a young girl in male clothing traveling alone with two men. She wasn't exactly the picture of a respectable noblewoman.

But she saw no mockery or disrespect in his face and allowed herself to relax somewhat. She inclined her head toward the sixth man-at-arms lying behind the rock where she knelt. "And what of him?"

He was the one who had struck Medwyn and in turn had been struck by Bydawine. He lay in a wide, dark pool of gore, his pained face as white as new parchment, his breath coming in slow, shallow gasps. But even as the rebel leader strode forward to examine him, Noressa saw the soldier's eyes glaze and his face went slack. The rebel stared down at the body. "This one as well, my lady."

She nodded, leaned forward resting one cheek against the cool rock, and tried not to cry. A hand touched her shoulder and she winced.

"Are you hurt, Noressa?"

She looked up, hearing the concern in Bydawine's voice, and shook her head. She tried to force a smile, wanting to clear the worry from his eyes. He could be quite handsome if he didn't scowl so often, she thought, then said, "It's only a little pain because they held my arms too tightly."

It was then that the others returned, each leading two kifera.

"Good news," Jatrae informed them. "Enough mounts for each to have his own, and one left over."

One of his companions added, "And enough rations to see us all home."

Noressa glanced at the speaker, then stared until she was in danger of being disrespectful. Save for his clothes, the rebel was identical to the man beside him. He smiled at her surprise and stepped forward with a slight bow. It was then she saw that his hair hung a bit longer than the other. "I am called Khelcri, lady. And this is my younger twin, Culric."

Culric smiled and inclined his head. "Little brother Jatrae you have met."

"And I am Brameth." The tawny-haired leader moved to join them as he spoke.

At once, Bydawine took charge as spokesman of their group. "This is the lady Noressa. The elder Medwyn, her guardian. I am called Bydawine." It was clear to Noressa that he wished to give no more information than needed, and she wasn't surprised at his next words.

"We are indebted to you for your assistance in our battle, but we must now return to our homes. Keep the soldiers' mounts; you have earned them. We will take our own and be on our way."

"No." Brameth's words were quiet, firm with authority. "You cannot return to Dromund the same way you left it. Tylek guards both sides of the river, and his men still search the forest for you."

"How did you know . . . ?" Noressa bit off her words.

"That you were from Dromund?" Brameth finished her question. "Our men have watched Tylek's movements since he crossed the Bourne more than two cycles ago."

Jatrae spoke proudly. "It was I who saw you cross over. Those idiot soldiers blundered across your trail more than once but were too stupid to see it. I slept there last night." He pointed to a large tree with closely growing branches near the clearing's edge. "Then I left early this morning to meet my kin, who also followed your trail. I would have left sooner, only—" Jatrae hesitated, and Noressa was touched by the quick shame that swept across his face.

Culric laughed and clapped a hand to Jatrae's shoulder.

"Only our brother was seeing lizard-demons and could not leave his tree."

Jatrae pulled away from his brother, anger in his voice. "It was real! I swear by the powers, it was there!"

"He speaks true." Noressa caught Bydawine's look that warned her to silence, but she couldn't bear the boy's agitation. "It was real, but it was no demon. Only a watch spell to guard our sleep."

"Then one of you is a magician?"

Brameth's question hung in the air. Noressa didn't answer. She refused to look at Bydawine and see his reproach.

Brameth looked from one to the other, his gaze finally resting on Medwyn. "It must be the elder. He is neither dressed nor armed for battle and has the look of a scholar about him. It will be interesting to learn why you are all of such importance to Tylek, but it will have to wait until we have returned to our village."

"No!" Brameth was moving away but stopped at Bydawine's exclamation. Noressa would have held him back, but the pain in her arms kept her from moving quickly enough. She watched Bydawine step defiantly before the man who towered more than twice his height. "We cannot travel with you. When Tylek came to Dromund, he invaded my uncle's hold and took power. We must be allowed to return to Dromund. I have an army waiting to defeat him!"

Most men would have found Bydawine's defiance amusing. Men were judged as much by their size and strength as by their deeds. That this small man could aspire to the task of leading an army to defeat a wizard such as Tylek would be a source of great entertainment. Noressa understood this, and she ached for Bydawine and the humiliation that would soon be on him.

But the rebel leader regarded Bydawine with no hint of laughter. His words were not those of one condescending to a child, but of one man to another. "I know nothing of what Tylek has done in your land, Bydawine. But this I do know: Even the great Tylek cannot rule your hold from Sidra. And Tylek returns here less than two days hence."

Bydawine hesitated, and Noressa knew that he, too, had expected a much less courteous answer. "How can you be so certain of this?"

Brameth smiled and drew his thumb carefully across one edge of his axe. "Those who told me of Tylek's return were not in a position to speak untrue."

Jatrae stepped forward, genuine worry in his face. "You cannot return to Dromund and you have no refuge in the forest. Would you have us leave you for Tylek's men?"

A short time later, the glen was cleared of bodies, and together fugitives and rebels moved deeper into the forest.

CHAPTER 12

Concealed behind the screen of osfo trees, Noressa leaned forward against her mount's neck, trying to ease the pain in her back and legs. She was unaccustomed to long stretches of riding, and the four-day journey was taking its toll.

If I hurt so much, she thought, how bad does Medwyn feel?

She turned and exchanged glances with Bydawine, who sat on his mount next to Medwyn, keeping watch over the mage. Bydawine shook his head to her unasked question, and Noressa saw for herself the pain etched into Medwyn's face. The mage sat with shoulders slumped, eyes closed, as he had through most of the journey.

Behind them, Culric kept a careful watch over all. He had spent much of the trip acting as rear column guard, while Jatrae and Khelcri roamed the forest like restless phantoms.

Noressa turned forward and found herself under the measuring scrutiny of the rebel leader. She blushed and dropped her gaze to the reins laying slack in her hands. Then, angry with her unfamiliar shyness, she raised her head and stared back in defiance. But he had already turned away, peering through the osfo foliage at the village.

More angry with herself than him, Noressa glared at his broad back. What was this strangeness that came over her whenever she knew he watched her? It was a nervous fluttering that made her pulse race, frightening but pleasurable all at once. She pondered this giant of a man who had named himself Brameth. Shaggy red-gold hair touched on hard-muscled shoulders. His topaz eyes held a quiet intensity that smoldered in her mind long after he looked away.

Stop this! she scolded herself. This is not the time to go soft over the color of a man's eyes.

She forced her attention through the midmorning glare

back to the village. Jatrae had called it home. But to her, it was only a circle of run-down cottages hunkered between the forest edge and a ragged pattern of half-plowed fields. There was a wrongness in the air, the same sensation of impotence that had nagged at her since crossing the Sidra. She let her gaze wander through the dry forest around them. Looking from the stunted new leaves of the osfo to the tiny patch of tohl flower seedlings at its base, she finally understood. This land had not yet wakened from its winter slumber.

The season was now late spring. Noressa knew that, had she stayed on her mountain, by now her cottage would boast a newly thatched roof. Her garden would be freshly dug and planted, and her sirre would have dropped the year's first litter of naked pink pups. When she had left Dromund four days ago, the land was quick and blooming. Many trees were already fully leafed and set with fruit, and plowed fields were greening with tender seedlings in rich, dark earth.

But she saw no such activity here. Where were the springtime voices of the forest? She heard no hungry peeping of chicks. She missed the barking call of mating daxets and the shrill chatter of the sirre warren. Here in Sidra, even the swayle brush and osfo, two of the earliest-budding harbingers of spring, were just setting out new leaves.

This land is all but devoured by winter. Noressa shivered at the thought, for it reminded her of that terrible hunger on the riverbank.

Desolation hung over the land. It was reflected in the weary shuffle of a tall woman crossing the village common. In one hand, she carried a basket; with the other, she led a small child.

Noressa watched Khelcri slip from the shadow of a nearby wall and approach behind them. The woman jerked around and, with a small cry, released basket and child to fling herself into his arms. She embraced him, hugging tight about his neck and kissing his face. The child pressed against them, arms raised, begging to be held.

Jatrae moved in beside Noressa, and she turned to him. "His wife?"

Jatrae nodded. "Soreen and their daughter, Grantha."

Then Khelcri swept up the child while the woman retrieved

her basket, and all hurried into a nearby cottage. A moment later, Khelcri emerged and signaled to the waiting party.

Noressa followed Brameth into the open, careful to guide her kifera around the gray-green patch of tohl seedlings. At the cottage, Jatrae and Culric half carried the unsteady Medwyn inside. Brameth assisted Noressa to dismount, and they waited for Bydawine as he fumbled with Medwyn's staff, which he carried wrapped in a soldier's cloak.

The reunion inside was quick. The woman, Soreen, embraced each of the men, lingering when she came to Brameth. She held his face in her hands, smiling up at him. Then she was aware that Noressa watched and she stepped back. She smoothed down a wisp of pale blond hair, and her attitude became one of prim courtesy. Her gaze took a quick measure of Noressa and Bydawine, then she looked again to Brameth.

"I am pleased that you have fared well these last weeks, Brother. There is much fieldwork yet to be done."

Brameth chuckled. "Only just home and you would make a plowman of me. But first, Sister, make welcome our guests."

Introductions were brief. Presented to Noressa and Bydawine, Soreen offered them the traditional welcome. She dropped her gaze and spread her hands to indicate the whole of the cottage. "Be welcome in our house. Let all within be yours."

Noressa was surprised by the greeting. She was accustomed to the more casual welcome used between neighbors and village people. The formality of Soreen's words and gestures was like that which Noressa had learned while studying in the kren-hold. It was an etiquette used by nobility. But Noressa kept enough presence of mind to bow her head and make the expected reply. "We are undeserving of your generosity."

Brameth motioned toward Medwyn, who lay upon a cot set against the cottage wall. "The elder was injured in battle." He hesitated, and Jatrae spoke.

"He is magician."

Brameth looked sharply at the boy, and Jatrae shrugged an apology. Brameth said softly, "He is called Medwyn."

At the word "magician," Soreen's eyes narrowed in suspicion. But when she heard Medwyn's name, disbelief showed in her face.

She turned to Brameth, a thousand questions in her eyes, but he held up his hand. "We must meet with Bohsra. There is much to report. We shall return by evening. Jatrae will stay nearby, should you need us before then." With that, he and the twins hurried out.

Jatrae looked downcast. "Always left behind," he muttered, then caught Noressa's eye. He brightened and flashed her one of his mischievous grins. "But I am left with the most pleasant task this time. How may I serve you, my lady?"

Soreen answered by taking his arm and guiding him toward the door. "By tending those nosy beasts I hear snuffling at my door. I shall see to our guests."

When he had gone, Soreen turned back to Noressa and Bydawine. An embarrassing silence followed as the three looked from one to the other.

"Please sit and rest yourselves." Soreen said at last, indicating the long benches before a rough trestle table. "I will make tea."

Bydawine bowed slightly. "Thank you, mistress, but we shall sit there." He pointed in Medwyn's direction. "The elder needs tending." Still holding the cloak-covered staff, Bydawine tugged at Noressa's sleeve.

She followed him and settled herself on a stool at the head of the cot. Medwyn's face was pale, and he lay very still beneath a dark woolen blanket. She probed, gently, the lump at the base of his skull, and the magician moaned softly.

What to do? Noressa wondered. Her worry over Medwyn was tinged with a second fear. Twice on the journey, she had tried to invoke her new power to ease the old man's pain. Twice the punishing heat of Medwyn's spell had enveloped her and the magician improved not at all.

Where was the wonderful strength that had sustained and protected her from the attack of that other at the river? Was it a power that could be used only for her benefit? Or had that sudden outpouring consumed all her magic?

Not at all, she reminded herself. Enough remains to trigger Medwyn's spell.

Bydawine's actions interrupted her thoughts. Without unwrapping it, he slid Medwyn's staff beneath the blanket between the mage and the wall. He shrugged at her curiosity.

"I'm sure he would want it near him."

Medwyn groaned, and Noressa calculated the time since early morning. She decided enough time had passed that the mage could again have something to ease his pain. She moved to the fireplace, where their hostess bent over a soup kettle.

"Mistress Soreen, may I trouble you for a cup of tohl?"

The other woman straightened quickly, her face twisted with fury. "We have no tohl here! You will find no soiled bribes from that witch in this house!"

Noressa was unprepared for the woman's anger. Before she could gather wit enough to answer, Jatrae entered, favoring all with a crooked grin.

"What is the trouble? Soreen, your words are loud enough to frighten the kifera in the next village."

Soreen held herself rigid, fists clenching the front of her apron. Her attention never left Noressa's face. "This snip of a girl dares to ask me for a cup of tohl as sweetly as if she bade me good day."

Bydawine stepped between the two women. "And what is the harm in asking her for a simple draft to ease an old man's pain? Do the people of Sidra know nothing of hospitality?"

Noressa lay a hand on his shoulder. "Please, Bydawine, not so harsh. A mistake has been made."

"Indeed, indeed!" Jatrae strode into their midst. "But being from Dromund, you could not know the price exacted for a pinch of tohl."

"What?" Surprise widened Soreen's eyes. "From Dromund? That cannot be!"

"Truth be sworn, Soreen. With my own eyes, I watched them fight across the river and flee into our countryside."

Soreen stood, head bowed, a flush creeping into her cheeks. "Forgive me . . . I did not know." She spread her hands in a helpless gesture. "But my answer is the same—I have no tohl to give. It is a bait, a temptation along with food and other magic the mistress gives to those who would betray our people."

Bydawine regarded her with suspicion. "How can that be, when tohl is free to any who would but pluck it from the ground?"

Soreen shook her head, and Jatrae nodded agreement with

her words. "Tohl no longer grows in Sidra, except in the garden of the mistress. Many things no longer grow in Sidra. That witch has blighted the land."

"But the lady Noressa has her own tohl," Jatrae offered brightly. "She has given the elder several doses on our journey."

"True," Noressa sighed. "But I have only seeds, and Medwyn fights their bitterness. I had hoped for a few fresh leaves." She shrugged. "Jatrae, may I ask you to bring in my pack?"

Jatrae's dark eyes sparkled. "Ah, sweet lady, my life is purposed only to serve you." He bowed with great exaggeration and was gone.

Noressa laughed self-consciously. "He has paid me such homage from the first moment. I am not sure what to make of it."

A tenderness eased into Soreen's face. "He is one of the few bright spots in our lives." She bent and scooped up Grantha from beside the hearth where Khelcri had left her. "And this is another." She planted a kiss on the child's pale brow. "Will you not greet our guests, my daughter?"

Warily Grantha peered at Noressa from beneath a fringe of tangled curls, then hid her face against her mother's shoulder.

Soreen smiled. "With time, perhaps. In her four years, she has learned to beware of strangers."

Noressa nodded in silence. She dared not speak for fear her voice would betray her consternation. Though the child bore her father's sign in the wide cheekbones and strong nose, she possessed her uncle's coloring. The same red-gold hair curled and tumbled down her back. The same topaz-colored eyes had met hers. Noressa remembered times on the journey when she had looked up to find Brameth watching her with those warm gold eyes. That strange pleasure shivered through her again.

When Jatrae returned, he offered to stay and help, but a small boy came and summoned him away. Noressa watched him go, missing his friendly banter before he was even out of sight. She mused on the strong affection she had developed for the boy in just four days. And there were similar feelings toward his brothers and Brameth. But not only these men were important, the country itself had captured something within her. The land was nearly desolate, and the summoning was a bothersome nagging, but a tiny hidden part of her rejoiced in being here.

She stared so long after Jatrae that Bydawine finally had to prod her to action. In a cup of boiling water, she steeped a few seeds from her precious hoard. Then, with Bydawine supporting Medwyn's shoulders, she spooned the tea into the mage, ignoring his grumbled protests.

That done, Noressa tucked the blanket close around Medwyn and busied herself reorganizing her pack while Bydawine strolled around the small cottage.

In moments, he returned to her side and said softly, "That soup is mostly water. I saw a few shabas and perhaps some izel, but no meat. I ate better as Pashet's slave." He moved closer, lowering his voice further. "That soup will not serve five, much less seven or eight. When she serves the food, we must refuse. Mayhap we will have some luck with hunting."

Noressa disagreed. "The food cupboard is also bare. If we don't eat now, we may faint from hunger before we can hunt."

Soreen spoke to Grantha, and the child scrambled onto a bench at the table. Soreen beckoned to Noressa and Bydawine. "Will you take supper with us?"

Bydawine's look forbade Noressa to accept, but she only smiled and gave his hand a quick squeeze. "We are grateful for your hospitality, Soreen, but we couldn't accept unless we are allowed to share our own provisions." Noressa carried her pack to the table and removed three cloth-wrapped parcels. She was apologetic, opening two parcels to reveal an almost whole loaf of bread and a thick slab of hard white cheese. "Hot soup will soften the bread, and the cheese is warm but only a few days out of the cellar." She handed the third packet to Soreen, who unwrapped it and stared a long while at the strips of dried meat. Noressa laid a gentle hand on her arm. "Perhaps boiled they will not be so tough."

In silence, Soreen gathered the packets and carried them quickly to the food cupboard, but not before Noressa had seen the woman's tears.

Throughout their meal, Noressa was aware of Grantha watching her. The child ate quickly, averting her gaze whenever Noressa sought to catch her eye. The first to finish, Grantha sat staring wistfully into her empty bowl. Noressa pushed her own slice of cheese across the table. "Will you finish my cheese, Grantha? I am too full." Only when Soreen nodded permission did Grantha take the cheese, giving Noressa a shy smile.

Afterward, Noressa woke Medwyn, coaxed him to take a little soup. Bydawine whispered that he would see what was to be seen in the village and slipped out. Soreen watched him go, but said nothing. Grantha stared after him with unabashed curiosity. Noressa was still wondering how to break the uneasy silence when the first visitors arrived.

They came in twos and threes, the women of the village. Quiet and courteous, they welcomed her. And all stared and whispered among themselves at hearing Medwyn's name.

With the women came their children. Thin and silent, they watched Noressa from behind the safety of their mothers' skirts. There was a lethargy among them that saddened her. It was a weariness born of long hunger and lost hope. Noressa watched this through the afternoon and felt an anger building.

These are my people! And they suffer because of me, she told herself. They suffer because this usurper, Felaya, would destroy an entire land to destroy me.

Noressa spoke with each woman, accepting their welcome and truly enjoying the company. But it was a real fight to keep the anger from her voice, and she was relieved when the last visitors departed and Soreen stepped out to speak with them.

Noressa dropped onto a bench, still struggling with her emotions. She glanced up to find Grantha watching her with that same apprehension she had seen in the other children. Noressa's anger drained away, and she was left feeling hollow and lonely. Memories of her mother holding her tight and murmuring soft assurances in frightening times made Noressa want to reach for the child. But Grantha's face held a wariness that forbade any approach.

Noressa raised a silencing finger to her lips and whispered. "I have a gift for you, Grantha." The child rose, eyes darting to the open door. But at Noressa's smile, she hesitated, though still poised to run.

Noressa held out her hand, her first finger extended. She drew power, so gently that the medallion did not even warm at her throat. At the end of her finger, a tiny light glimmered. A miniature star blazed, winked out, and in its place shimmered a scarlet windflier.

Grantha stared openmouthed as the insect fanned scarlet wings outlined in gold. Once, twice it spread its glorious wings, then it fluttered across to her, leaving a faded tracery of color in the midafternoon gloom. Grantha extended her finger, and the windflier settled onto it immediately, enveloped in its own radiance.

At that moment, Soreen returned and stopped short on seeing the common orange and brown windflier that rose from her daughter's hand and fluttered through the door. With a delighted cry, Grantha raced after it.

"How—?"

Noressa shrugged. Then she pulled a stoppered gourd from her pack and moved to press it into Soreen's hand. "This is for you."

"Your—your tohl seeds?" Soreen stammered, "but what of—?"

Noressa interrupted her. "I have kept enough to care for Medwyn, but I want you to have these. They are strong and fresh and mayhap will fare better in your soil. Though I think your blight is over, for I know I saw tohl growing in the forest this morning."

"You saw it?"

"Yes. I would have told you earlier, save that I did not wish to anger you further. Shall I show you?"

Soreen nodded and followed her from the cottage. Several of the women who had just left the cottage were speaking together in the common. Soreen beckoned to them. "She says there is tohl in the forest." The women clucked and whispered disbelief. But when Noressa led them around the osfo that had sheltered her that morning, all gasped to see the jumble of seedlings at the tree base.

" 'Tis True!" a woman whispered.

"Look there," another cried. "More tohl!" She pointed to a patch beside a fallen log.

The women scattered through the forest calling to one another about their discoveries. One called to them, her voice urgent. "Come! Come see this!"

All crowded round the woman who held a length of vine. It was dotted with dark purple lumps. Another woman began to cry and took the runner from her neighbor, gently touching the tender buds.

"The grelt berry has not grown since we were children." Blinking through her tears, the woman was awed. "The blight is ended!"

Noressa saw hope dawn in their faces before the women turned and hurried back to the village.

CHAPTER 13

The entire village knew of the tohl by evening. Those able hurried into the forest and returned wide-eyed at what they found.

It was after nightfall when Soreen's men returned, talking of the forest discoveries. They fell silent in astonishment as Soreen placed bread and cheese before them. When they learned from whence the bounty came, Noressa received a chorus of thanks. Jatrae saluted her with his wooden spoon before devouring the largest chunk of meat in his bowl. Khelcri hesitated until Soreen assured him that she and Grantha had both eaten.

"And," Soreen told him, "there was enough meat that I could give some to Heska." She turned to Noressa in apology. "Heska suckles a new babe and has need of the strength."

"The decision was yours, Soreen. I require no explanations." Noressa felt herself warm at Soreen's smile of gratitude. But it was Brameth's silent look of approval that made her cheeks flush. She turned away to hide her fluster, only to face Bydawine's scowl.

Her bewilderment must have shown, for Bydawine dropped his gaze and hunched his shoulders. He reached beneath Medwyn's covers, made certain the staff was securely hidden, and pulled the blanket a little higher around Medwyn's shoulders.

Knowing his dislike of the staff, she wondered at his sudden, protective interest in the thing. Several times on their way across the bada-shi, she had caught him muttering that the staff was too gaudy, too obvious. Yet after Medwyn was injured, Bydawine insisted on taking responsibility for it. He carried it wrapped in a dead soldier's cape. And though he professed such antipathy for the wand, he appeared at times entranced by it.

Why does he protect so well that which he dislikes so much? Noressa could think of no answer, but the pondering occupied her mind until the men finished their meal.

While Soreen cleared away the dishes, Jatrae hurried out. He soon returned, followed by a large group of men. Some were very young, scarcely out of childhood; others were bent with age. Noressa estimated their number near twenty, and when the last man was crowded into the small cottage, Brameth turned to her.

"These are the men of our village. They would speak with you."

He stepped back and a second man approached. He was shorter than Noressa by a head, with a body lean and hard. His face was long and thin, his generous mouth pulled into a tight line. He moved with the grace of a young man, but an abundance of gray shot through his dark hair, and deep lines around his eyes betrayed his years.

He stood with his arms folded, his gaze sharp, commanding, as he looked from Noressa to Bydawine and back to her. "I am called Bohsra, elder of this village."

Noressa was paralyzed with sudden fright. *He will surely want to know why we are here. What shall I say? I am your queen come to rid you of your tyrant mistress? I have no army, no power, and my court consists of an aged magician and an angry dwarf. Shall I say that I flee a nightmare while chasing a dream, and all should rally to me that I may claim my birthright?*

Noressa took a breath in readiness for her confession, but Bydawine was already rising to face the elder. He sent her a glance that warned her to remain silent.

"I am called Bydawine of Calet Den. This is the lady Noressa." He motioned toward the cot behind him. "The elder is Medwyn."

A murmur slipped through the crowd. Noressa heard Medwyn's name repeated amid whispers of prophecy and heirs. Bohsra raised a hand for quiet. Bydawine continued.

"We came into Sidra by happenstance, being forced into the river when we were attacked by Tylek's men near Stagget's Keep."

Bohsra's eyes narrowed. "Why would Tylek's men attack

you? And in such numbers as was reported?"

Bydawine raised an eyebrow, and Noressa almost smiled at his air of tolerant grandeur. "I am nephew to Norwick the Elder, Lord of Wigram Keep. Tylek invaded our hold. The lady Noressa and I escaped to Tarragon, where we raised the alarm among my uncle's allies. The elder Medwyn was accompanying us to Stagget Keep, where we were to raise the alarm and consolidate forces against Tylek. Surely your man Brameth told you as much."

"He did."

"But you chose not to believe your own man?"

At once, tension filled the air. Noressa spoke quickly, surprised at Bydawine's antagonism and amazed by the calm of her own voice. "It is always best to hear a story directly, Bydawine. There may be questions that Brameth's report couldn't answer." Now it was she who gave Bydawine a warning look before continuing. "Please forgive my companion's lack of subtlety, elder. The retelling of our escape has reminded him that he was unable to join the battle against Tylek to free his home."

Bohsra hesitated, then nodded slowly. "A frustration we understand, my lady. We share a common goal."

Behind Bohsra, Jatrae's grin confirmed the success of her peacemaking, and the admiration in Brameth's look rekindled her flutter of excitement so that Noressa had to drop her gaze and concentrate on Bohsra's next words.

"It is said the elder Medwyn is a magician and you are his apprentice."

She nodded.

Bohsra looked from her to Medwyn. "Years ago there was a Medwyn, First Counsel to the throne. Be this he?"

Bydawine nodded, stepping forward to take charge again. "So he claims."

Again the murmuring as Bohsra spoke. "And what of the child? Before our queen died, she was delivered of a babe that Medwyn and a maidservant carried away to safety."

Noressa's pulse sounded a rapid cadence in her ears. Would she be found out now? And even if she proved her royalty to these people, what had she to offer them? She held her breath, awaiting Bydawine's reply.

The dwarf scarcely hesitated before answering. "I was a child myself that many years ago and not active in the politics of other lands. If a babe was spirited away, you must ask the magician."

Bydawine hadn't given her away, and Noressa, wondering at her relief, said nothing. The whispers of the crowd held a tone of disappointment. Again Bohsra raised a hand for silence, and Noressa caught a glimpse of thick calluses. She could see this was not an elder who sat by his fire gleaning honors from past glories. His body spoke of a man accustomed to hard work. His words gave sign of intelligence. Strength and authority were evident in his bearing, and in the faces of his men she saw complete trust.

Bohsra spoke with some sadness. "Brameth's report that the magician, Medwyn, was returned had sparked hope that our true king had returned as well."

King? Will they be disappointed to find they have only an illusionist queen? Noressa wondered. But she felt pride at his words. King or queen, the people's loyalty to their rightful liege ran deep. For me. My people. A new feeling stirred in her—the warmth of homecoming. She belonged here.

Bohsra was speaking again. "We will wait until the elder is able to speak with us."

Bydawine nodded and answered. "And after that, we shall return to Dromund."

Noressa sat rigid and silent, mentally denying his words. No, my friend, I cannot go. If you return to Dromund, it will be without me. As if she had spoken, Bydawine sent her a startled look. Noressa dropped her gaze, but her heart whispered the promise, I am home. I will not leave. Bydawine, I cannot go! No, my friend, if you return to Dromund, it will be without me. Pain twisted in her at the thought that he might leave her, but she knew she would never follow. By my mother's blood, I must stay here and see this through, no matter the cost!

* * * * *

Noressa couldn't sleep. She was exhausted, but the tensions of the day's activities wouldn't let her rest. She tossed on her pallet beside Medwyn's cot. Again and again her mind played the scene of Bohsra's interrogation. Each time Noressa was sure her decision to remain in Sidra had been a good one. It was certain the thing she searched for was here.

She lay still, listening to the soft footsteps of the village sentry passing outside. When he was gone, only the sound of Medwyn's breathing and the sleepy call of a nightpeeper remained.

Noressa turned again, searching for a comfortable position. She yearned for sleep, but dreaded its approach. She was too vulnerable to the dream terror when asleep, and was loath to give herself over to the mental chains of sleep.

She sat up, arms wrapped around herself against the chill that came, not from the cool night, but from her own memories. Her head ached and her gaze swept the room, as if she might find an escape from her torment in the shadows.

Across the cottage, Bydawine lay before the hearth, curled into his blanket. Faint light seeped through chinks in the window shutters above her to outline the doorway of the sleeping chamber wherein lay Khelcri and his family. Medwyn lay within arm's reach. She was surrounded by people, yet felt completely alone.

It was impossible to keep still. Moving to the window, she unbarred the shutters and swung them wide, closing her eyes against Diml's brightness.

The Goddess of the Night rode high and full in her couch of darkness, nestled deep in the Consort Constellation. Noressa watched the swirl of stars that wreathed the moon and tried to let other, less painful thoughts fill her mind.

She breathed deep of the cool, spring night. On the breeze came the scents of newly plowed earth, a promise of rain, and the heavy sweetness of osfo blossoms.

The view faced east, and she stared over the top of the forest to the stormclouds beyond. The summoning came to her again, and she struggled to define it. She knew it to be a thing apart from herself, almost believed it held a sentience of its own. It was a yearning that touched on her mind as sibilant waves might lap at an empty shore.

She glanced around the room. The door was unguarded. She could easily evade the sentry. The yearning tided higher.

In moments, she could be into the forest and away. She was awash in the need to be gone. She swayed as the summoning tugged her mind outward. Only by gripping hard at the window ledge did her physical self resist the drawing.

I cannot! I have a responsibility to my people here. She cradled her head in her arms and fought back tears. She was so tired. She wanted to go home, to be in a place where people loved her, a place where she could rest and there was no fear.

But *this* was the place she belonged. The solid truth of that stilled some of the ache behind her eyes. She looked at the somnolent forms of Medwyn and Bydawine, then turned to stare toward the sleeping room of Soreen and her family.

A rush of affection filled her. She couldn't say why these people, so recently come into her life, were now of such importance. There was so much she wanted to do for them, but she was certain the amulet and the summoning had much to do with fulfilling this desire.

Tears threatened again, but this time she welcomed them. They carried away her pain and indecision. Noressa felt the weight of her fear slipping down her cheeks. She was home.

With the release of her tensions, Noressa opened herself to the night. Part of her moved out into the darkness until she could actually turn back and watch herself standing at the window.

She was exposed, accepting, infused with the fires of life hidden in the night. Perceptions shifted, blended, as she passed through the life forces around her. She touched the hunger of some newborn, knew the rising desire of a beast in carnal pursuit. She was drawn into the banked curiosity of a drowsing sirre.

Then, from far off, Noressa heard a scream of pain and knew it to be her own. Her mind raced back to the cottage, and she was suddenly, forcibly aware of her body and the agony quivering through it. Once again she was in the grip of the living dream terror. As on the riverbank, the attack was without warning, its ferocity devastating. But unlike then, Noressa did not succumb to its surprise. She turned at once toward the hidden well of power.

The entity sensed her intentions and leapt ahead, blocking her path. Noressa faltered. She hadn't expected to be denied her own strength. Her mind was becoming entangled among tendrils of fear and hatred that burned hotter than any physical flame. Enmeshed, body and mind, Noressa watched her nightmare play itself out. She struggled as the triumphant Other tightened its bonds. With a feral satisfaction, it fastened itself to her amulet, and Noressa felt the life being drawn from her. She cried out to the only hope left her.

"Medwyn, help me!"

The entity hesitated at her call. Then Noressa felt its pleasure as it traced her thoughts to the magician. She realized she had exposed Medwyn to a danger he could never withstand. She had doomed them both!

But in that moment, her memory went back to a stone cottage in a moon-silvered plain of grass and a scarlet-eyed apparition. Medwyn's words sounded faintly: "You have called forth the form that will serve you best. It will be a guide and strength to you in times of need."

Before the Other could block her from this last hope, Noressa invoked her familiar. "Guardian dark, I summon thee, send thine earthborn power to strengthen me!"

The entity raged a denial, pulling back from its pursuit of Medwyn to tighten its bonds on her, but Noressa ignored it, plunging into the new power flowing over her. She spread her arms in defiance, arms that suddenly glistened with the sheen of dark scales. Noressa saw her limbs faintly through the saurian image that now overlay her own. She welcomed into herself the vital presence accompanying the scaled form. Using hands tipped with great horned claws, Noressa shredded her bonds, both physical and arcane. Her anger drove her forward to rout every tendril of contact. Her power was a blue shield, forcing the Other back upon itself. Wielding her newfound might, Noressa pressed the entity back until it fled completely, leaving only the wailing echo of its hate. Noressa pursued, her mind sweeping the night until she could reach no farther. Only then did she curb the flow of power.

Noressa brought her mind back to the cottage, to her body. Hands before her face, she marveled at the vision of smooth, black scales over her skin. With gratitude, she touched the mind of the creature she had summoned before to guard her sleep. She was answered by a harmony like that which her mindtouch had known moments before in the lives of the forest. That harmony gave her power a foundation it had lacked. Could she but tap that foundation at will, her power would flow steadily, ever at her command.

But even as she made that discovery, she lost it. With the terror vanquished, the need gone, her new strength, too, was fading. Noressa clung to her remaining power. There was one other thing to be done.

Noressa was aware of her surroundings. Of Bydawine beside her, questioning. In the doorway of the sleeping room, Khelcri stood with sword drawn. Soreen and Grantha peered from behind him. But there was no time to appease the fear in their eyes.

Noressa disregarded them all, moving to the cot where Medwyn had raised himself and sat swaying on its edge. Moonlight on his face showed the strain of his exertion in having risen. He put out a trembling hand. "Child, what has happened to you?"

Noressa smiled, gently closing her clawed hands over his. She closed her eyes and let flow the energy still within her. Then she went down deeper, drawing more power from the earth, feeling as if her bare feet were rooted into the dirt floor of the cottage. Through the guardian, into herself, and down her arms, the strength moved out into Medwyn. The trembling left his hands, his grip tightened in hers, and he drew a steady breath. When it was done, her power again began to fade.

Noressa opened her eyes and returned Medwyn's smile. He sat easily on the bedside. The pain was gone from his face. Noressa murmured words of thanks and release, and relinquished her hold on the guardian. It withdrew quickly, the image of its presence paling from her skin.

Once more alone in her own mind, exhaustion rushed to claim her. She sank to her knees and felt Bydawine's strong arms come around her. Noressa was content to let his embrace lead her into a black gulf of serenity.

* * * *

Felaya whimpered. It was all her body could do as yet. She lay curled on the stone floor of her chamber, nursing the soul wounds she had sustained in the battle. Her hatred crackled the air; her whimpering tore at her ears with the stridency of her rage. Twice beaten by the daughter of Breann!

Never again, Felaya vowed.

Yes, the child held more power than her mother, but more important, Felaya had seen her greatest weakness.

Now she could wait and gather her strength while she eased her wounds with this sweet balm.

CHAPTER 14

Bydawine jerked himself awake. He started up from the rumpled straw sack that had been Noressa's pallet. There was a moment of self-anger for having dozed, but he shook it off when he saw Noressa lying quietly on the cot before him. He placed a hand on her brow, and a tiny smile eased across her lips.

"Have no fear, young Bydawine; she is well."

Bydawine spun toward the speaker, who stood silhouetted against the flames of the hearth. It was Medwyn. The elder moved to stand beside the bed.

Bydawine chilled, remembering Noressa's screams and wild writhings. Now here was Medwyn, whole and sound as a result of Noressa's magic, while she occupied his sickbed. Bydawine fought his anger.

"After what happened last night, you can say she is well?"

Medwyn nodded. "Last night was not an illness, but an attack of sorcery." He raised a hand, as if testing a breeze. "Great powers struggled here, with Noressa emerging the victor. However, much energy was expended." Medwyn dropped his hand, smiling down at Noressa. "She only sleeps. Her attacker also will need to replenish itself. I doubt we shall be troubled for some time."

From the bedchamber came the murmur of voices and the sounds of someone stirring. Presently Khelcri emerged. Good morrows were exchanged between the three men, and Kelcri asked after Noressa.

"She is well," Medwyn answered, "but she will sleep a long while."

Bydawine would have spoken differently, but Khelcri appeared satisfied with Medwyn's answer and asked after the elder's health.

"I am well."

"Good. The village elders wish to speak with you," Khelcri said. He looked at Noressa. "They will have many questions."

Medwyn bowed his head. "I await the meeting with pleasure."

Soreen and her daughter joined them.

"You will not go until after the morning meal." As Khelcri began to obect, she gave him a stern look. "The elders have waited through the night; their questions will keep until our guests have breakfasted."

Noressa turned in her bed, clutching the blanket. Her movement dislodged the bundled staff. Fully a third of the wand protruded from its hiding place. In the brilliance of its unveiling, Bydawine stood dumb, awaiting the astonished outcry from the others. But Khelcri only picked it up, peering at the thing in the weak light of the cookfire.

"Ah, my staff." Medwyn strode forward and took the blazing wand. "One's bed is an odd place to keep such a thing, but it is an old friend."

Bydawine knew then why the magician had never shown a desire to conceal his staff. The others couldn't see the light! Even Noressa, with all her Talents, hadn't seen it. An unaccustomed pride filled him.

Bydawine glanced up to find Medwyn watching him thoughtfully, the staff held lightly in one hand. Bydawine said nothing and wouldn't look at the staff. He brought a stool to the bedside and resumed his watch over Noressa until Soreen called him to breakfast.

Tensions through the meal were not as high as Bydawine expected. The family seemed to have accepted the midnight invasion of their home by wild sorceries. He threw a suspicious glance toward Medwyn, but said nothing.

After the meal, Khelcri and Medwyn departed. Bydawine returned to Noressa's bedside.

When the table was cleared, Soreen came to stand beside the cot. Grantha peeked from behind her mother's skirt. The worry in Soreen's eyes prompted Bydawine to assure her that Noressa was well.

Soreen nodded. "The elder has explained it." She touched Grantha's hair in a soothing gesture and said, "The next cottage stands empty. I go to prepare it for the elder and yourself."

Bydawine shook his head. "You are kind, mistress, but such preparations aren't needed. A few days, at most, will see us returned to Dromund."

Soreen looked confused. "To Dromund? But the elder said—" She stopped when Bydawine stiffened.

"What did the magician tell you?"

The woman was suddenly distant. "It is of no importance. Our guests must not remain on the floor, even for a few days, when there are beds at hand." Then she left the cottage, the child trailing close behind.

The day passed slowly. Soreen came twice asking after Noressa, and finding no change, returned to her work. Bydawine waited for Medwyn, honing his anger to a fine edge, but the magician didn't return until long after Soreen had begun preparing the evening meal. When Medwyn did return, Bydawine confronted him as he entered the cottage.

"Noressa sleeps still, and I would speak with you. Privately."

"Good." Soreen's words cut in before Medwyn could answer. "You may speak outside and give me the chance to tend the lady Noressa." Both men looked at her in surprise. "She is in need of a woman's care," Soreen said and waved them from the cottage.

Outside, Bydawine motioned for Medwyn to follow. Then he let his anger carry him deep into the forest before he turned to face the magician.

"You told the woman Soreen that we are to remain in Sidra. She has prepared a cottage for our use!"

Medwyn leaned on his staff and nodded. "Mistress Soreen is a kindly woman."

Bydawine glared at him. "You haven't the right to say what we are to do or where we are to stay! When Noressa has regained her strength, we must return to Dromund and raise an army for her."

"I see." Enlightenment filled Medwyn's face. "It is you who will make Noressa's decisions for her. She has agreed to this course of action?"

Bydawine hesitated, disconcerted by Medwyn's sarcasm.

Then his defiance returned. "She did not gainsay me when I spoke before the elders last night."

"No, she would not—not before the others. But it was her wish to remain in Sidra, that much I remember. It may even be that she cannot leave. There are powers at work that you do not understand, my young friend."

Bydawine scowled.

Medwyn smiled. "You object to being addressed so? But that is how I view our alliance. One day your intolerance of me will be replaced with understanding. Then we shall be of great importance to one another."

Medwyn straightened, moving the staff from his right hand to his left, the movement almost a caress of the shining wood. Bydawine's gaze followed the staff. He shook off the urge to mimic the elder's action, telling himself he didn't really want to touch that smooth wood. Then Medwyn's last words made themselves understood, and he drew away with an angry denial on his lips.

But Medwyn put out his hand and Bydawine couldn't move. The bantering was gone from the magician's voice. "Stay but a moment, Bydawine. I see the matter offends you, so I will say what I must and then speak no more of it." He sighed. "It matters little that you regard me not as your friend, but you are of great importance to Noressa. I have seen her fondness for you. And the time shall come when she will have need of your strength and counsel. That decision will come soon enough. Do not let your anger with me turn you from her." Medwyn lowered his hand and made his way back toward the village.

Bydawine stared after him a long while, the magician's words echoing in his head.

When Bydawine returned to the cottage, Medwyn stood beside the cot. Soreen was tucking the blanket over Noressa, much as she might have done for her daughter. She gathered an empty bowl and cup from the floor, then smiled encouragement at Bydawine as he moved to take her place on the stool.

"The lady has eaten and should sleep well now."

Bydawine leaned close to Noressa, whispering her name. She opened her eyes and smiled. He took comfort in knowing that his was the last face she saw before she slept again.

* * * * *

Bydawine was up before dawn the next morning. Dressed and waiting, he paced the tiny cottage he had shared with Medwyn. Medwyn's empty bed gave mute evidence that the mage had risen even earlier. He had not heard the elder leave. Now Bydawine waited, watching through the open door for Medwyn's return and the wakening of Khelcri's household. When there was, at last, activity in the next cottage, Bydawine hurried over.

Khelcri answered his knock. "Good morrow, master Bydawine. Enter and be welcome."

Bydawine returned the greeting absently and looked toward Noressa's bed. It was empty. Khelcri watched him with a knowing smile and pointed silently to the bedchamber.

The curtain was drawn, but Bydawine heard the murmur of female voices. Soon Grantha scurried out and ran laughing to her father. Soreen and Noressa followed, giggling like children. Soreen nodded greetings. Noressa, dressed in tunic and skirt, spun quickly in the center of the room.

"Bydawine, do you know me?" she laughed. "I am Noressa in the guise of woman. Soreen was kind enough to loan me these clothes." She winked at him. "But I have kept the other things as well. I may yet decide to resume my travels as a free-riding huntsman."

Bydawine couldn't say what he felt. He was relieved and pleased by her high spirits, but there was regret, too. Now he must share her company with the others.

"I am pleased to see you well recovered, Noressa. I had worried that you were injured."

She laughed and knelt before him. "Poor Bydawine, I have given you nothing but worry since our first meeting." Her smile faded to seriousness and she squeezed his hand. "I feel as though I have been absent a long while. It is good to come back to old friends."

Bydawine felt his cheeks grow warm and hoped Noressa couldn't hear his heart pounding. He was conscious of the others watching them and longed for a few moments' privacy. But before he could speak, Noressa looked past him, delighted.

"Medwyn!" She moved across the room to the magician, who was just entering.

In silence, Bydawine strode from the cottage.

That day Bydawine spent with Bohsra. And many days thereafter. His military experience and knowledge of Tylek's recent activities were welcomed in the rebel council.

In reports from the various rebel camps, Bydawine followed Tylek's return to Sidra and progress toward Castle Ac'talzea. Runners brought confirmation that the rebirth of the tohl and the general blooming of the land was spread throughout the country. And he couldn't contain his excitement at reports of an army gathering across the Bourne at Stagget's Keep. He waited eagerly for the reinforcement of his uncle's allies.

He worked hard at being useful. And he worked hard to ignore the strange emotions that disturbed his sleep and intruded into his waking thoughts. Many days his activities were such that he saw little of Noressa. Still, he couldn't help but be aware of her presence.

Before dawn each day, he feigned sleep as Medwyn rose and left their cottage to meet Noressa. Together, mage and apprentice set off into the greening forest under the cloak of Medwyn's concealment spell, and Bydawine watched until the silver light of the staff disappeared into the woodland. When Noressa returned in the late mornings, he might see her with the other women, gathering the new roots and herbs that now flavored their meals. Fish and small game were plentiful now, and he might hear her exclaiming over some hunter's good fortune. Evenings Bydawine returned to the cottage to partake of the meal Noressa prepared for them. She joined them as they ate, and she kept them informed of the village and its activities. Bydawine watched the animation in her face and saw the love that was growing in her for the people of the village and the land.

Nearly half a cycle passed in this way. On a warm evening, Bydawine sat staring into his food, while Noressa talked of her day. I am losing what little I had of her to this half-dead country, Bydawine thought glumly. The thought soured his appetite and he could not finish his food.

Bydawine slept little that night. He was up before Medwyn, going to meet Noressa at Khelcri's door. Before she could voice her surprise, he took her hand and began leading her into the trees behind the village.

"Come walk with me, Noressa. There is much we must settle."

She hung back. "I must wait for Medwyn. He will wonder what has become of me."

"No," Bydawine lied, quickly before his courage failed him. "I told him I wished to speak with you, and he agreed to forego this morning's lesson." She looked puzzled but followed without further argument. Bydawine led her away, his pleasure at her trust tainted by guilt.

Dawn was only a few moments old when they came to a small clearing. Sunlight filtered through the canopy of leaves playing games with shadows. The air was tinged green, and spots of brightness dappled the forest floor. Tendrils of mist, like disconsolate wraithes, twined about their feet.

Noressa danced into the clearing, long braids flying, shawl snapping in her wake. Bydawine leaned against the bole of a fallen quenner tree and watched, smiling in spite of himself. Her gaiety was irresistible.

Noressa settled onto the tree trunk beside him, modestly smoothing the long brown skirt to her ankles. She sighed, a long exhalation that ended in a humming sound of pleasure, and sat bumping her heels against the tree. "I have never felt so happy . . . so alive and full."

Bydawine nodded. "No doubt your long sleep was refreshing."

Her expression sobered. "Yes, I was . . . tired." Then she brightened, and her smile woke a sharp longing in him. "Are you not recovered from my long sleep, Bydawine? Soreen tells me you sat by my bed for two nights and a day. Each time I woke, you were there."

Bydawine shrugged. "I slept. And you only woke once, when Soreen made you eat."

"But I felt you with me often. Could I have only dreamed that?"

A strange ache tightened his chest, and he dared not answer the puzzlement in her eyes. Instead, he hoisted himself onto the tree and struggled to quell his wash of emotions.

Noressa was still the open, innocent girl he had led from his bedchamber in the keep. But she was also different. She had changed in her battle with the unseen adversary. She was stronger, more sure of herself. And that independence frightened him.

He was terrified when she collapsed in his arms after healing Medwyn. But this new feeling was the fear of a loss yet to come.

But how can I lose what was never mine? he wondered, watching her curl the end of one braid around the end of her finger.

He signed in confusion, then asked, "Can you speak of it? Of what happened? Medwyn explained something of it, but—" his voice fell to a whisper—"it has been long since we talked."

She stared into the forest a long while. Finally she told him, first of the attack on the riverbank, then the battle in the cottage. Through her words, Bydawine lived her terror and near destruction and, at last, her triumph. He began to understand the change in her.

When the telling was done, they sat together in silence. It was a long while before Bydawine realized that at some time Noressa's hand had come into his and was there still.

Her touch evoked a sudden longing that angered him. He dropped her hand and pushed himself from the log, then paced to and fro, shaking the stiffness from his legs. Hard, bright shafts of sunlight told him it was long into the morning. "We should start back. Medwyn will be waiting to speak with you."

Noressa slipped from the tree and they began to walk. Bydawine was trying to find an easy way to broach the subject of returning to Dromund when Noressa spoke.

"You know that Bohsra has spoken to Medwyn concerning the royal child they took into hiding?"

He nodded.

"I had expected to be put to the test and declared either queen or fraud, but no one yet has spoken of it." She hesitated. "I think Medwyn has put an enchantment on them. They speak of it among themselves, but never to me. Medwyn says it is for the best, that we have much to learn, you and I. But I am still Noressa, lady of an empty title."

Bydawine was surprised at Medwyn's reference to him, but remembered their talk in the forest. The memory made him hesitate before his next words, but he couldn't keep silent.

"Perhaps he is right. Now we may return to Dromund and my uncle's forces. We shall rouse the whole land, and when next you see Sidra, it will be from the head of an army. No one will doubt you are queen then."

Her answer was so long in coming, he began to think she agreed. Then her words gave substance to his foreboding of loss.

"I can never leave Sidra, Bydawine. Not while there is so much undone." She raised a hand to stay his protest. "Please, Bydawine, hear me. I was told to follow my dream, but I tried to run away from it. It pursued and found me. I tried to ignore the summoning only long enough to help you, and we are both thrust headlong into this war."

She paused, but the look of determination in her face kept him silent.

"In my short time here, I have found a place that my heart says is home, and I have touched a power beyond any I ever imagined. My destiny lies here. Who can say what would befall me if I tried to escape it again?"

Bydawine didn't answer until they reached the forest edge and saw the village. Then he was careful to keep his words devoid of emotion. "Bohsra's men report that Tylek crossed the Bourne two days behind us, so my home is free. They also tell of an army massing at Stagget's Keep. That will be our allies from Tarragon. I should return to Dromund. Perhaps I may still convince them to support you."

Noresssa knelt before him, a sadness darkening her eyes. She clasped his hands tight. "Go if you must, Bydawine. Our seven-day pact is long finished, and I am no longer bound to ride with you. But you are my greatest friend, and were it in my power, I would bind you so that I might never be without you beside me."

Then she was up and gone, hurrying to meet the white-haired magician coming toward them. Bydawine watched her go, knowing it was very likely that he would never see Dromund again.

CHAPTER 15

The remainder of Bydawine's day was a vague recollection of faces and words. He had some memory of being with Bohsra and hearing the runners' reports, but all was blurred by moods of breathless elation, followed by silent despair.

He savored the memory of the morning walk. He relived, over and over, the touch of Noressa's hand in his and her sadness when he said he would leave.

Until then, he was determined to return to Dromund and the barren but comfortable life in his uncle's employ. He might have been able to leave the matters of magic and monarchy to those for whom such matters were important. Perhaps distance could mitigate the possessive anger that scrabbled always at the edge of his thoughts.

But he had waited too long.

Noressa did not want him to go. She had said as much. And there was Medwyn's prediction that she would need his strength and counsel. That didn't strike him as a likely future. Already she had rejected his advice to return to the safety of Dromund. And as for strength, even the boy Jatrae could defend her better than he in battle.

Of course, he could always entertain. Noressa might stand in need of a jester to dance and sing and confound her with riddles, as Pashet had been wont to have him do. But he knew at once what Noressa's reception of such behavior would be even as his own pride vetoed the idea.

Then what was he to offer?

The day passed, and Bydawine managed to mutter unrecalled answers to Bohsra's questions. He stared unseeing at maps and half listened to plans made. Finally he made some excuse and fled to the solitude of the forest until night sent him back to the village.

He stood an unremembered time just watching his cottage and Khelcri's. He was gathering his courage to face Noressa. Surely she would be angry with him for this morning's lie. He had no doubt that Medwyn had told her of the deception. Might she even be angry enough to regret her words of friendship?

The darkness was suddenly brightened as Medwyn, staff in hand, moved across the village common with Noressa beside him. They paused to speak with Brameth and Jatrae. Brameth nodded a solemn greeting. Jatrae bowed in profuse homage, then stepped close to Noressa, whispering in her ear. She laughed, and the sound, light and cheerful, touched a chord of envy in Bydawine.

Bydawine watched the four, bathed in the silver light of the staff, and his answer came to him. Magic was his offering to Noressa.

He tried to deny the thrill of that thought. He had little experience with magicians, save the occasional dream-caster his uncle consulted. But the idea would not be argued away.

A tiny part of him prodded at his mind. What else had he to offer? Not his military advice—for that she had Bohsra and the others of the village council. His armies, mercenary and only half loyal? Did she not have a country of warriors awaiting her return?

But *he* had seen the power of the staff. *He* had felt its strength. That was something not even Noressa's amulet had shown her. And if her battle was to be one of sorceries, would she not stand better for having two magicians at her side?

Bydawine moved his hand against the tree trunk nearest him. It recalled his first touch of Medwyn's staff. After the battle in the glade, he had meant only to hide the silver light by wrapping the wand in a dead man's cloak. But there was a strangeness to the smooth, gnarled wood, a warmth and a faint stirring of—what? Recognition? Welcome? From that carved stick of wood, Bydawine still held an impression of knowledge. It had responded as if alive and opened itself to him.

He felt the wand's silver gleam drawing him. He wondered what might happen if he called to it. The staff was willing. If he wished it hard enough, perhaps . . .

Medwyn's head snapped up, and he gripped the staff in both hands. Bydawine felt a mental slap of resistance and stood helpless before the wave of anger that followed. Medwyn stared in his direction with a sureness that told Bydawine there was no darkness that could hide him.

Seeing Medwyn's agitation, Brameth and Jatrae drew weapons and would have raised the alarm. But Medwyn spoke quietly, and the men replaced their arms and slipped away across the common. For a moment longer, Medwyn held Bydawine fixed in the darkness. Then the mage turned away, escorting Noressa to his cottage, silencing her questions with a shake of his head.

Bydawine shivered. Fear, awe, disbelief came in waves over him. He had almost taken Medwyn's staff! Then fear crowded out all else, and he wondered at the consequences that might be forthcoming. No magician, however benign, would take gently to having his most valuable tool snatched from him. He imagined Brameth and Jatrae circling through the darkness toward him. At any moment, they would leap from the shadows and drag him before the enraged elder. Run! his mind screamed.

But he waited.

And none came searching for him. Nor did any punishing sorceries manifest themselves.

For a long while, Bydawine stood wondering at this. He had nearly stolen Medwyn's magic. Did the mage dismiss his ability to do so again? Bydawine stared into the night sky. The stars in the Sorcerer's Girdle glittered brighter than any others. Perhaps Medwyn was giving him challenge. The mage certainly knew of his distrust. Now, Bydawine thought, we both know I hold a measure of Talent as well. But I am not foolish enough to come against you with only raw ability. I, too, will learn the secrets of this magic. And who better to teach me than you, Medwyn? He smiled, watching the glimmer of stars in the Girdle. "I accept your challenge, Medwyn. And tomorrow you shall teach two pupils."

Bydawine hurried to the cottage, his decision giving him the courage to face whatever awaited him there. Noressa showed no sign that she knew of the morning's deception. She greeted him with relief.

"At last you return, Bydawine! Brameth said you left them early today, and no one has seen you since." She stopped uncertainly, and he saw something of the morning's sadness in her face. "I thought you might have gone without giving farewell."

"I have decided to remain in Sidra." He basked in her immediate delight. "I may yet be of some use to Bohsra."

Noressa nodded happily. "Indeed, to us all. But come and sit down. We have waited the meal for you, and everything is hot."

Bydawine took his seat at the table, across from Medwyn. He faced the magician with defiance, prepared for his anger. But there was no reproach in Medwyn's face—only a spark of amusement and that fatherly smile.

Then Noressa bustled around them, setting out plates of boiled shabas and juicy chunks of roast yarja. Bydawine found that he had a hearty appetite. And he listened with interest to Noressa's account of her day in the village life, for now he, too, was part of that life.

* * * * *

Bydawine lay silent in his bed, eyes closed, breath steady, and listened to Medwyn's quiet movements. The light of the staff brightened and faded against his eyelids as Medwyn passed his cot. Then the mage was gone, pulling the door shut without a sound, and darkness claimed the room.

Bydawine jumped from the bed, hurrying into his clothes. He stole from the cottage and crouched before the door in the early morning coolness.

Medwyn waited at the door to Khelcri's cottage. Bydawine was careful to keep far back from the light of the staff. It wouldn't do to jeopardize his plan at the outset by being careless. Soon Noressa joined Medwyn, carrying a large leather sack over one shoulder. She fell in step beside the magician as they crossed the common. At the forest edge, Medwyn laid a hand upon her arm and they vanished. Only the light of the staff marked their continued progress into the wood.

Bydawine resisted the urge to follow. He knew the glade that was their destination and set out on the route he had planned the night before. Twice he lost his way and had to retrace his steps, his anger at the lost time almost preventing him from finding his landmarks. But as the faint morning light brightened through the treetops, the way became easier.

The edge of the sun was already visible over the forest top when Bydawine reached the glade. A rough oval, with a growth of tender new grass, most of the area was encircled by a thick stand of trees and thorny underbrush. A barrier of black stone spires, some towering over the highest tree, thrust from the earth. A wind-twisted osfo grew at the base of the rocks, its roots insinuated into and around many of the stones. A few of the glossy spires were shattered and lay in a jumbled heap spilling into the glade. Poised as in an attitude of grief, several of the osfo's branches reached into the glade and sprinkled the wreckage with their sweet-scented blossoms.

Bydawine's goal was the largest of these boughs. A rope set the night before let him climb quickly to his prepared spot. He nestled behind the screen of twigs and wild greltberry. His place was secure but not comfortable, and he wished he could have simply asked to join the lessons. But he felt sure Medwyn would have refused.

Well enough to teach a queen, but a subservient dwarf is beneath consideration. His own thoughts mocked him.

At that moment, Medwyn and Noressa appeared in the glade below. He held his breath, awaiting discovery. In the strong morning light, he hadn't noticed the slim line of the staff's light heralding their approach. But each set about his or her own tasks, not even glancing up. Bydawine dared breathe again.

Bydawine watched the magician set concealment and warding spells around the glade. He remembered the first time he had followed Medwyn and Noressa, thinking it an easy thing to hide and observe the lesson. He had approached the glade with reckless abandon. It was only after he regained his senses, wandering in the forest, that he realized a warding was in effect.

A morbid curiosity made him wonder what would have happened if only half of his hiding place had been included inside the warding spell. Perhaps being halved by a warding spell would do him no harm. The osfo showed no sign of suffering when only a few of its branches were included in the spell. Still, Bydawine risked discovery to move a handbreath closer to the end of the branch.

Below, Medwyn was inspecting Noressa's work as she set out the contents of the leather bag she had brought. Her long-fingered hands were quick and graceful, and Bydawine recalled how only yesterday they rested warm in his. Then Medwyn smiled his approval of Noressa's efforts, and Bydawine was suddenly angry.

What right had Medwyn to take so fatherly an attitude toward Noressa? She was, after all, his queen, not a child. She was a woman, grown and competent, with no need of strangers to tell her how things must be done.

Bydawine's anger turned back on him, and he saw the true cause of that emotion. His sense of protection toward Noressa was now a jealousy that begrudged her the most innocent of relationships. His concern was becoming a thing so deep, he refused to name it. She had changed something in him, in his concept of himself. He no longer accepted the prospect of a lonely future in some obscure keep. He, too, was grown and competent, with a man's need for power and independence. Now he was in a position to obtain that power.

The idea was thrilling, frightening. Bydawine squeezed his eyes shut and inhaled deeply of the osfo's sweet smell. But he was reminded of the strings of osfo blossoms Noressa and Soreen gathered and hung to dry before their doors. He frowned, thinking of the camaraderie growing between the two women, and pushed back another stab of jealousy. It was good for Noressa to have the friendship of another woman, even if it meant she had less time for him.

But his jealousy whispered, She always has time for Brameth. Oh, what gentle glances pass between them. And does she not blush so prettily when they sit talking before the fire?

That is no affair of mine! Bydawine argued with himself. I, too, am busy with my duties and do not have time for such pleasantries.

But his resentment belied his indifference. He sent Noressa an angry glance and was dismayed to find the lesson had already begun.

In his hands, Medwyn held a larger version of Noressa's

copybook. On its open pages glittered exotic symbols that seemed not so much drawn as engraved upon the thick parchment. Bydawine watched with avid amazement. Gone were all arguments and self-doubts. There was no other world outside the perimeters of the tiny glade as he surrendered himself to the enchantment of sorcery.

CHAPTER 16

Get out! *Get out!*

The *knowing* sent Noressa bolting from her bed. Scraps of dream, like shreds of a burial cloth, clung to her. She stumbled across the room, pushing away images of men and women staring, sounds of her own voice begging assistance, and the thunder of approaching riders. She leaned against the doorframe of the family sleeping chamber and rapped hard on the wood.

"Khelcri! Soreen! Wake up, quickly."

Even as she turned away, there sounded the hiss of a sword being drawn and quick footfalls. Khelcri's voice sounded harshly from the door.

"What has happened?"

"We must leave at once," Noressa answered over her shoulder. She bent to light a candle from the embers in the grate. "You must wake the village."

"Why? What is the danger?" He moved into the room, looking perplexed, his sword still at the ready. He motioned for Soreen to remain in the bedchamber.

"I do not know." Noressa stared at the trembling hand which held the candle. Was it really her own? It obeyed her wish to set the light on the table. "I cannot say what the danger is, only that it is very near. Tell the people to carry whatever they can and flee into the forest."

Khelcri lowered his blade, sympathy in his eyes.

"It would seem, lady, that fear has menaced your dreams this night. Not uncommon in these times, but I cannot alarm the village for a nightmare."

"It is no dream!" Anger made Noressa's voice strident. "The warning is here." She brought her fingertips to her temples. "The danger is very near!" Never had the *knowing* filled her with such terror. She pressed her hands to her ears to shut out the noise of the outside world. But that left her alone with the silent clamor in her mind. She clenched her fists hard against her mouth to keep from screaming and stood helpless, hot tears spilling down her face.

Then came a pounding at the door and shouts from a muffled but familiar voice. Noressa ran to unbar the door and flung it wide against Khelcri's cry of warning. Medwyn and Bydawine entered together. Bydawine took her hand instantly.

"What is it? What has happened?"

Noressa let herself be drawn to her knees. "Bydawine, tell them it is no dream." His strong grip steadied her. "Make them believe we must leave here at once!"

Running footsteps approached, and the village sentry burst through the doorway, sword in hand. "What has happened? What is all the shouting?" Behind him, fair-haired Tel from the next cottage peered over his shoulder. From across the village common, there was more shouting.

Khelcri sighed and laid his sword on the table. He rubbed both hands over his face. "There is no danger, Coris. The lady Noressa has had a nightmare."

Noressa's anger swelled, sending her to her feet. Bydawine, too, moved to confront Khelcri, and Noressa was startled by a tone of menace she had never heard in the dwarf's voice. "If Noressa reports danger, you had best heed her warnings."

Khelcri stiffened, suspicion flaring in his dark eyes. "You may speak true." His hand rested on the hilt of his sword. "It strikes me odd, though, that the lady would know of any peril before our runners and sentries."

The two men glared at one another. Anger glittered in their eyes, and their shadows jumped crazily with the guttering of the candle flame. Soreen spoke from the gloom of the bedchamber, her voice shattering the sudden tension. "Our greatest peril now would be to fight amongst ourselves." She moved into the dim light of the candle and handed Khelcri his scabbard. She set about lighting other candles, and her words, brisk and competent, loosened the knot of fear in Noressa's throat. "It is well known that the lady is a pupil of magic. It would not be unseemly if she were to possess the sight as well, a thing not unknown even among our *own* people." Soreen gave her husband a stern look before turning to Medwyn.

"Perhaps, elder, you would know more of this."

Medwyn shook his head. "I know only that Master Bydawine woke me saying the lady Noressa had need of us."

"But it is you who need her!" Bydawine's angry words cut through the murmur of the crowd now gathered outside the cottage. "If you would preserve yourselves and your families, you must obey her!"

Again Noressa heard that strange quality in his voice, a haughty belligerence she hadn't suspected in him. Yet her attention was not for him, but for the man who stood watching her from the door. Bohsra was silent, regarding her with a severity of expression that made her tremble as much as the *knowing*. She swallowed hard and returned his look with a composure she did not feel.

"And what is it the lady would have us do?" Bohsra's question brought silence to the room.

Noressa centered on the *knowing* throbbing in her head. The unreasoning terror was fading, leaving only a hard certainty of what must be done. Her words came in a rush, calm nonetheless.

"The people must take all they can carry—food, clothing, tools, even their animals—and go into the forest."

Silence held like a brittle glaze while precious moments passed. Then Bohsra gave a curt nod and stepped from the cottage. Noressa heard him calling orders, and the crowd thinned from the doorway. She let go a breath of amazement. He had taken her word without question!

"You have done well. Bohsra is not an easy man to persuade." Noressa heard the warmth in Soreen's praise as the other woman stepped beside her.

"Thank you, Soreen, for your support. But how did you know to trust me?"

Soreen shrugged. "I didn't. But an enemy has come to you once before in this house. Perhaps you sense its return."

Medwyn came near them. He gently brushed a strand of hair from Noressa's cheek and gave Soreen a sidelong smile. "Perhaps, too, Mistress Soreen, you hoped for a new Shay?" His words were without rebuke, but Soreen blushed.

Bydawine and Noressa shared a confused look. Bydawine demanded of the magician, "Who is this 'Shay?' "

Medwyn smiled. "She is a sighted one. A healer and reader of omens. The Nandil Shay is sister to the earth."

Soreen was repentant. "Forgive me, Noressa. Khelcri's granddam was such a one, a powerful Shay. It is said she contrived the twining of Khelcri and Culric." She knotted her hands and sighed. "So much has changed since you came. I hoped—" She looked to Khelcri for assistance.

Khelcri stepped into their midst. His sword, now snug in its scabbard, swung on his waist by a thick leather belt.

"So much has changed since you came, we had hoped the prophecy was now fulfilled."

"What prophecy?" Bydawine and Noressa spoke together. Medwyn paled.

Soreen drew breath to answer, but Medwyn spoke first, in his eyes an old pain.

" 'When the dying land greens, and Shay does lead the soldiers of rebellion, then will the warriors of the Chidd join with the Army of Stone. And the crown of Ac'talzea shall rise on wings of night to smite the conqueror.' "

A moment's silence held them, then Bydawine spun to face Medwyn.

"You knew of this thing and said nothing? What was your plan, to sacrifice Noressa for the sake of your magician's gibberish?"

Anger sparked in Medwyn's eyes, and his words were cold. "Curb yourself, young one, for you speak of things you do not understand. This promise is one that came to me—and to Salet—in a dream some days after leaving our queen. We pondered it these many years and could not discover its meaning."

"Yes, yes!" Soreen agreed excitedly. "It came as dream and vision to all the Shay the night our queen died." She looked at Noressa. "Can you not see our hope? You are here and the earth grows full and green. You bring the touch of healing and foretell our dangers. These are the arts of Nandil Shay, and now even the army follows your word. The promise is being fulfilled. And when all these things are done, the crown shall be returned to the throne and Sidra will be free!"

As Soreen spoke, an understanding came into her eyes. "You . . ." She looked to Khelcri; together they stared at Noressa.

Now they know me, Noressa thought. Then Bydawine's angry voice cut in.

"And how are these things to be done? Warriors of Chidd and Armies of Stone, indeed! Is there some magic to bend the will of vipers and the rocks of the earth to fight for our cause? If so, why have you not gathered your Shay and gone against the mistress?"

"Because the sighted ones are no more in Sidra." Khelcri's voice was low, his tone warning. "Their power is in the reading of portents, in teaching, and the giving of comfort and life. They had no strength against those fiends that came for them by night." Noressa shivered at his mention of night fiends. Khelcri noticed and gentled his voice. "The Shay were a strength to our people. Another would have been welcome."

Noressa read the apology in his eyes and let her smile carry her understanding.

Khelcri turned and embraced Soreen; he kissed her tenderly. "I must go with Bohsra. You can do what is needed here?"

She nodded. Beside them, Grantha stood clutching her father's long boots. Khelcri bent and gathered her in his arms. Grantha said nothing, only squeezed his neck tightly with one arm. Then she thrust his boots at him and whirled to bury her face in Soreen's skirt.

Bydawine tugged at Noressa's sleeve and said, "You will stay with Soreen. Medwyn and I will take what we can from our cottage."

His words were gentler now, but the tone of command was clear. Noressa stared in silence as Bydawine motioned for Medwyn to follow and left the cottage.

A moment later, Khelcri, too, was gone. Together, Noressa and Soreen set to the task of bundling up their lives.

A short time later, Noressa stood at the edge of the village and watched the last two wagons lumber into the forest. Her few belongings, and those of Soreen, were lumps of shadow lost among the wagon's load of other such shadows. Noressa wished she could have gone with the other women. But the danger was coming for her. It would have been senseless to send the others to safety, then bring the danger into their midst.

She gripped her bow tightly and shifted the weight of her

quiver to a more comfortable position on her shoulder. With the threat of this new danger, she had exchanged the modesty of her cottage-wife apparel for the comfort of her hunter's clothes and taken up her old weapons. She hadn't used them since beginning her lessons with Medwyn, and they felt awkward now. The mage had warned this might happen, saying that magic was a personal and more natural defense. But while it might be magic that pursued her, she preferred physical defenses in which she was proficient.

Her gaze fixed on a single cottage, where a faint yellow glow proclaimed activity still within. Then the light was extinguished, and a figure, silhouetted by the ember pot it carried, slipped away into the woodland.

Now the world was all black. Diml had not ridden the sky, and night was in its darkest time just before dawn. Noressa shivered and pulled her cloak tight against the desolation that gripped her. She tried to shake it away, thinking it a projection of her own fears. Her fist clenched on her bow and she admonished herself. Courage, girl, you do not face this thing alone. The men of Drael stand within the forest shadows, weapons ready in your defense. The fear mocked her, growing as it did so. What weapon can stand against the power that comes for you?

A noise and the sense of an approaching presence sent her heart leaping. She whirled, reaching for the longknife at her belt, and flattened herself against a tree. A familiar voice stilled her.

"Nay, peace, my lady. 'Tis I, Jatrae, come to bring you away." He bowed as deeply as ever, but his tone was somber.

Noressa suddenly understood the fear behind her and slumped back against the tree. "You must warn everyone," she whispered. "They send a spell of terror to disarm us. Stay back from the village until the battle is joined."

"Who sends this magic, my lady?"

Noressa felt foolish that she could not answer his question. She was silent while he led her deeper into the trees.

He brought her to a wide place between two young quenners. Filtered starlight let her recognize Medwyn, Bydawine, and Brameth standing with Bohsra. They were in whispered conference with a man she did not know. She waited while

Jatrae gave Brameth a hushed report. Then Jatrae bowed to her and was gone.

Medwyn beckoned her forward, and she went to stand between him and Brameth. The rebel was close enough that she could feel his body warmth. She told herself that the flutter inside that made her catch her breath was due to the approaching danger. Then Bydawine spoke, his words startling in the darkness.

"The village is empty, Noressa. What would you have us do now?"

Brameth retreated a pace, allowing Bydawine to move between them. Noressa was both relieved and dismayed at his intrusion. But Bohsra had finished speaking with the stranger, and all attention was on her. She stared through the brush toward the empty village and let the *knowing* fill her mind with its dull ache.

"We wait. That is all I know."

The wait was not long. Medwyn sensed it first, stiffening into an attitude of displeasure. "It comes." His words were cold. A moment after, Noressa felt it also. It was a tingling in the air like the vibration of a single high note held so long it set her teeth on edge. Magic.

They burst forth as if from nothing, a thundering, bellowing pack on the far side of the village, soldiers in full battle dress. They rode their mounts through the fields of tender zalia sprouts. Wide kifera pads trampled the hills of new-planted shabas. The riders, screaming their frenzy, used swords, lances, even torches in toppling the arbors that would have held the fragile lirsa vines. As a shrieking river of terror, they poured into the village. Filling the open common with a ring of protection three men deep, they encircled their red-bearded leader and his black-robed companion.

"Jaaben!" Noressa tasted her fear in the word.

"And Tylek!" She heard Brameth's angry growl.

Medwyn's voice came sharp, silencing the rebel's promise of foul destruction. "It is not Tylek, only a High Adept."

They were all silent as Jaaben stood in his footstraps and shouted challenge to the empty hamlet.

"Awake, you treacherous peasants, and send out this girl you would name queen. Give us the ursurper to the throne and we shall deal gently with you!"

Noressa heard Bohsra's sharp intake of breath. She took a quick glance at his face, noticing his amazement. Then she returned her attention to the spectacle ahead. Even as Jaaben spoke of leniency, his men were storming the cottages. The first soldier to emerge with news of the abandonment was met with harsh disbelief.

"Impossible!" Jaaben bellowed. "You have not searched well enough. Search again!"

Moments later, an officer stepped from Tel's cottage. "The village is empty; all are fled. And seemingly they knew of our coming, for they have taken all, down to the last cooking pot."

Jaaben turned his fury on the man beside him. "This is your doing, magician! You were to conceal us. What kind of magic do you practice that allows an entire village to pack itself away into the night? When my brother hears of this failure, he will tear out your heart and feed it to his hounds!"

While Noressa easily heard Jaaben's furious berating, the Adept's quiet reply was inaudible. Its effect, however, was not to be mistaken. Jaaben drew back as though stung and glared his hatred. Then he turned his rage on his men and beast. He reared the kifera, pulling the hapless animal in a tight circle. He brought it down to all fours and spurred it with cruel jabs, charging the ring of soldiers, jerking to a plunging halt an instant before trampling the nearest man. Chest heaving, Jaaben sat his sweat-soaked mount, and all was quiet save the gentle hiss and crackle of torchflame. At last Jaaben drew a great breath and roared, "Burn it! Burn it all!"

Torches, a dozen and more, arced high into the paling night sky, orange stars of destruction plummeting into the season's dry tinder that was the village of Drael. In the same moment, an answering volley of destruction sped through the night. Slender shafts of death from the bowmen of Drael caught the soldiers unaware. Many fell, if not dead, then at least grievously wounded.

One of Noressa's arrows was among that first flight. Its target was Jaaben's throat. But at the last instant, he turned slightly and the shaft clattered across the top of his breastplate.

At once the battle was joined hand to hand, and Noressa

lost track of Jaaben in the surge of fighting. The villagers, outnumbered though they were, took a grave toll of Jaaben's men. Unencumbered by heavy armor, they slipped in to slash at exposed areas between armor parts and bucklings, then slipped away just as quickly. Noressa continued with her arrows. The next two found their marks in enemy flesh, while the fourth sank into the belly of an unlucky kifera. Bohsra moved away, shouting orders, and Brameth was a maddened zealot of death. It seemed the villagers would put the soldiers to rout before the battle was truly begun.

Until the men of Drael began to stumble and turn in confusion to strike at nothing. Or even a compatriot.

Noressa, too, was bewildered. She moved to face the creeping form of a soldier on the edge of her vision and found nothing. She whirled to face another behind her, only to hear his mocking laughter from another direction. She leaned against a tree and listened hard for something beyond the scream and clang of the fighting. The *knowing* pricked hard at her, and she heard again the angry buzz of magic in the air.

"Sorcery!" she shouted to any who might be able to hear and understand. "We are enchanted!" Then she saw Medwyn striding into the thickest part of the battle. He was unarmed and alone, making for the pale-skinned magician sitting his kifera in the center of the common. Combatants stepped, unknown, from his path and closed behind as he passed. They created a circle of emptiness around him like the void that surrounded the mounted sorcerer.

Screaming his name, Noressa flung herself after Medwyn. She ignored the hands that clutched at her, the voice that frantically called her back. She cast aside bow and quiver to draw her long-bladed hunting knife as she surged forward. But entering the fight was no easy matter.

The ring of burning cottages sent up a wall of heat and smoke as impenetrable as any wall of stone. Each breath was an agony. The morning breeze whipped smoke into her face, and she was blind, unable to tell friend from enemy in the press of bodies. She stumbled back, then bent low and plunged headfirst into the turmoil. The smoke shifted again, and from the haze charged the armor-clad figure of a soldier, his sword coated with a dark wetness.

Noressa threw herself to one side, hoping to take advantage of his momentary surprise. But he was too quick. He blocked her path with his sword, and with his free arm, he crushed her to him. Noressa struggled, but he pinned her hard against his breastplate, and the tip of his scabbard pressed hard into her ribs, making breathing painful. He dragged her through the fray, bellowing in triumph.

"Victory! We have victory!"

Noressa still held the hunting knife in her right hand, but its length worked against her. Squeezed in the crook of his huge arm, she could make only short, jabbing strokes that glanced off his backplate.

He dragged her on. His arm was hard across the small of her back, his hand gripping her left arm just above the elbow. The pressure of his mailed hand sent a lance of pain up through her shoulder, but she was able to move her arm below the elbow. Noressa closed her eyes against the pain and smoke and moved her left arm in a half embrace around his waist, searching for what she knew must be there. When her fingers closed about the hilt of his short dagger, she spared no time for exultation. Noressa jerked the blade from its sheath and trailed the knife tip across the wide leather belt until it slipped into the narrow space between belt and breastplate.

Then she shoved.

Her captor's cry of victory ended with a grunt, and they crashed to the ground. The air was cooler there, cleaner, and Noressa gulped it in as she rolled away from the soldier and his surprised, slack face. She lay huddled as one of the dead, tempted to remain where breathing was easier. But she forced herself up before the rush of feet and kifera pads crushed her.

She had lost both dagger and hunting knife and stood deep within the throng of enemy soldiers. The cottages had burned quickly, most reduced to smoldering heaps that sent columns of gray smoke billowing over her head. The smoke was now more a menace to the mounted warriors than those afoot. Her brief capture had succeeded in bringing her closer to Medwyn, but now she was unarmed. And Medwyn was still out of reach, beyond the shifting ring of fighters.

Noressa caught sight of Medwyn and his magical foe and was transfixed watching the two. Jaaben's High Adept raised a black-gloved hand. His fingers pulled green-red tongues of flame from the air to form a seething incandescence, which he hurled down on Medwyn. Noressa screamed and lunged forward. She didn't see the approaching kifera until it blocked her path, a wide, furry wall of flesh. A powerful arm encircled her waist and lifted her high onto the front of the riding pad. A familiar voice growled in her ear.

"Well met, young Noren! Welcome again to our brave company!" Fear wrenched Noressa's heart at Jaaben's gloating, and she struggled in panic. Jaaben squeezed tighter and chuckled. "Had we known the truth about you before, we would have made you most welcome. Pretty boys are nice, but we shall enjoy your true self even more!" His lips were hot on her neck, his hand taking wild liberties beneath her cloak.

Fury burned with her shame. Below that seethed another, more dangerous heat that threatened to melt her from within. She sent part of her mind plunging toward that heat as she turned her head to Jaaben and spat her anger. "Release me, you harlot's mongrel, or I shall destroy you where you sit!"

Jaaben laughed and raised his voice to his men. "Retreat! Retreat! We are victorious!"

Noressa gave herself over to her fury and time became a jumble. The amulet burned at her throat. She was suffused with strength; it flooded her until her skin prickled with it. She was all-powerful, and nothing could stop her!

But at the moment her vengeance was about to burst forth, she felt Jaaben being torn from her. His grasp nearly dragged her from the kifera, and she had a glimpse of him tumbling, openmouthed, to the battle-churned earth. The terrified kifera reared, and she slipped from its back, to be caught once again in powerful arms.

Noressa squirmed to face this new attacker, but all strength drained from her when she looked up into Brameth's yellow eyes. For an instant, she pressed herself into his embrace and the world faded, leaving them alone in eternity.

Then, with a blue-white flash, the world slammed in around them. The air felt thin, Noressa dizzied. Behind her, a sharp, high wail rose and was abruptly cut off. Soldiers broke and ran. The triumphant villagers pursued, and Noressa was chilled by the battle lust in Brameth's face; she read his desire to follow. He glanced down at her and the look faded. He drew a deep breath, his chest swelling against her, and his hands moved gently across her shoulders.

Noressa could have stayed forever in his arms, being warmed by the promise in his eyes. But he loosened his hold and stepped back, then retrieved his battle-axe from the ground. When he straightened, his face and voice were politely neutral.

"Are you unharmed, my lady?"

She blinked, trying to comprehend the sudden distance between them, making mental assessment of herself. She would be bruised and sore come the morrow, but there were no bones broken and the blood soaking her tunic was not her own. She nodded in answer.

It was all she had time to do before they were accosted by a combat-fevered Bydawine stomping toward them. A long knife in one hand glinted back the first rays of morning. His curses singed the air.

"I had him! Nearly within my grasp, and the butcher escaped me. Jaaben the Invincible, hah!"

He paused for breath, and full recognition of them came into his eyes. He glared from one to another. "So," he addressed Brameth, "you found her." Brameth had no time to answer, for Bydawine turned to Noressa, and she was taken aback by the sarcasm in his words.

"Are you well, my lady? Are you unharmed?" She nodded. "Good!" Bydawine dashed the knife to the ground in disgust. "Then please explain which demon possessed you to throw yourself into battle, unarmed and without escort? Are you brain-hindered? Or do you simply think yourself immortal?"

His anger pounded at her, and she tried to protest. "I only went to assist Medwyn." At once, the memory of the magician's peril returned. She whirled, searching the burned-out village for him. "Medwyn! What has become of him?"

The mage's own voice answered: "Naught but the bringing down of some haughty student."

Medwyn picked his way over the tangled legs of a fallen soldier, leaning heavily on his staff. He stopped to catch his breath, fatigue lining his face. Noressa hurried to give him her arm. A quick glance about for Jaaben's sorcerer showed only a blackened hole where he had stood.

Noressa asked, "What has become of the young wizard?"

Bydawine answered, almost shouting. "He is destroyed, as you would have seen, had you kept your wits about you. Did you not see the elder move unharmed through the battle? Did you think he hadn't the power to overcome an upstart such as that one?"

Noressa could stand no more. Her own anger burst out. "Silence!" She planted herself squarely before the glowering dwarf. "How dare you upbraid me so? I thought only to lend assistance. Not like you, who have become a surly, mean-tempered fellow. I am surprised you joined the fighting at all. You are much better at skulking about, frightening the children and showing disrespect to the elders."

Medwyn stepped between them and laid a firm hand on Noressa's shoulder. "Gently, gently. I will not have my pupils fighting between themselves." ——

Noressa stared; Bydawine paled.

"But—but, I am your only pupil," Noressa stammered.

Medwyn shook his head. "Not since a full cycle and more. Bydawine progresses well, but I feel it is time he came down from his tree and joined directly in the lessons."

"From his tree?" Noressa was outraged. "Do you mean to say he was spying? He has been stealing our magic?"

"He has taken nothing that I have not allowed," Medwyn answered, a grim look passing between him and the dwarf. Then he smiled. "You should speak kindly to young Bydawine, for it was his magic that brought you out of Jaaben's grasp."

Noressa's anger fell away, replaced by a touch of wonder. She gaped at Bydawine. Warrior, adviser, orator—and now magician. Was there nothing this tiny man could not be? Then Medwyn's words demanded her attention.

"Now let us put this matter aside, for there are others who require our attention."

It was then that Noressa became truly aware of the carnage around her. As a child, she had listened to the minstrel's rousing war songs. She had shivered in childish delight as the elders recounted old battles. With her quenner-wood sword, she subdued groves of jerjal warriors; her prowess brought down the trembling clans of melosa weed. Now her youthful fantasies of battle and adventure were being fulfilled, but there was no satisfaction in it. Dawn came, painting the village as a ring of smoldering ash heaps circling a death field. Smoke carried up the stench of sweat and blood. In the hazy morning, pain-filled moans from the wounded clashed with the silence of the dead. The sight of each sprawled body showed Noressa a life she had shattered. These lives and how many more? she wondered. Mothers, wives, children—who waits upon the return of these fallen?

Guilt stabbed at her like the splinters of a shattered icicle. This morning she had taken human life. She had caused much death. That made her *chen serit*, the war bearer. Would her people count her worth the cost?

The onus of her situation pressed on her, and she wanted to flee. But she recognized that no distance would be great enough to let her escape this pain. Better to let its impetus send her forward in a rebuilding of life. Noressa drew a deep breath.

"So be it," she spoke, unaware of her seeming deference to Medwyn's behest. "Bring me balm and bandages." Noressa moved to the nearest injured, not caring whether he were friend or foe.

CHAPTER 17

For Noressa, the morning passed in a hazy succession of men beneath her hands. Different faces, different wounds, but always the same pain. Yet her mind was not on the activities she performed. Her thoughts wandered searching for . . . something. There was more she should be doing, but just what refused to come clear. Her hands worked without direction from her, cleansing and binding, and her lips mouthed gentle reassurances.

The injured were separated into two groups, allies and enemies. The women were recalled from the forest to care for their men. Temporary shelters were being erected, and cookfires appeared across the trampled square as women set up housekeeping. Children scurried about, bringing wood and carrying water.

Noressa soon realized the number of wounded exceeded the full number of men usually living in the village. Several of the men she had tended were unknown to her, as were many of the women working around her. But these things she noticed vaguely, the bustle and commotion falling as a dull clamor on her ears. The only clear sounds were those of grief from women whose households had been touched by death.

Such sounds coming from nearby drew her attention.

An old woman, assisted by a girl who might have been a daughter, worked feverishly on the wounds of a young man— a boy, really, Noressa thought. He didn't look to be even as old as she. Suddenly the old woman ceased her ministrations and stared hard into the boy's face, one gnarled hand over his chest. She sighed and shook her head. Then she brought forth a small cloth and veiled his face. "He died with honor," the woman said to the girl beside her. "Tonight Diml's consort will be swelled by one more."

But her words held no comfort for the girl, who lay prostrate over the body, sobbing. The old woman gathered the girl in her arms, rocking, murmuring as if soothing a babe. Noressa glimpsed the shadows of many such sorrows in the old woman's faraway stare.

Noressa listened to the girl's muffled sobs. Brother? she wondered. Or even husband? She turned away, flinching, as yet another shard of guilt stabbed deeper.

A moan of pain brought her attention back to the man she was tending. In her distraction of watching the two women, she had gripped too tightly on his leg wound and started the bleeding afresh. She quickly stanched the flow and bound the gash, then moved away, searching for another patient.

She stepped carefully between men, seeing that all had been tended, either bandaged or veiled. As she stood wondering what to do next, she caught sight of Bohsra striding across the square. He was accompanied by several men she didn't recognize. The elder moved in among the soldiers, questioning. His attitude was hard and unyielding as he confronted each man. Noressa watched with growing apprehension, knowing that her own confrontation with him was not far off. When Bohsra left the group, his expression was grim but satisfied. He passed near her and their eyes met. Noressa dropped her gaze first, shivering at the anger in his look. She heard her name called and stumbled toward the voice, grateful for the interruption.

Seated at a cooking fire, Heska beckoned her over. She handed Noressa a mug of hot broth and motioned for her to sit. "Come rest awhile," Heska urged. "You have worked overlong, and there will be more when the others return."

Others? Noressa remembered the villagers who had pursued the fleeing soldiers. She settled herself to the ground, careful that she didn't spill any of her drink. The broth was thin but hot and spicy. She sipped it gratefully and wondered how Medwyn and Bydawine fared. Their presence had been commanded by Bohsra at battle's end, and she hadn't seen them since. She let that worry fall, telling herself she would have known somehow if anything were wrong. She sipped her drink again and let its warmth bring her some measure of comfort.

She sat with Heska a long while as the woman tended her

cooking pot with one hand and soothed her restless babe with the other. The woman gave freely of her broth to any who stopped at her fire with empty bowl or mug. Watching one woman depart, balancing two bowls of the steaming liquid, Noressa asked, "Who is she? I haven't seen her before."

"She is Natha, from Creen, the village to the south." Heska shook her head in pity. "She has lost two brothers this night and has no word yet of her husband." Heska turned to Noressa with something of a smile. "I am more fortunate. My man was not sorely injured, the powers be thanked. He works even now." She pointed with her cooking spoon to a group of men lashing the final supports for a three-sided shelter. Of the four, she recognized only Heska's man, Tel.

"So many strangers," Noressa said. "How did they come to be here for our battle?"

Heska gave her a strange look, but a shout from behind prevented her reply.

From the west, the jubilant villagers returned. Most walked, some leaned for support on a comrade, but a few were carried in makeshift litters. Noressa hurried to kneel beside the closest stretcher and was assessing the man's injuries when a frantic plucking came at her sleeve.

Jatrae bent over her, a desperate urgency in his face. "My lady, you must come at once! Khelcri is sore wounded!"

Khelcri! This was too close to home. Noressa shook her head against the pain Jatrae's words brought. The tears she had held back all morning came in a blinding rush. Jatrae gripped her arm, panic a rising note in his voice. "This man has only broken limbs. You must come with me! My brother dies!"

Noressa swiped tears from her face. "Then what good am I to Khelcri? I have no sway over death."

"But you must!" Jatrae insisted, pulling her to her feet. "Soreen says that you are Shay."

His words brought sudden attention from those around them. Noressa saw hope, disbelief, even fear, and she fought her own rising panic as Jatrae tugged her along.

When they reached Khelcri, Soreen was huddled over him, her fingers twitching ineffectually at the blood-soaked rags beneath his tunic. Grantha stood clasping and unclasping her tiny hands. Her wide topaz eyes never left her father's white face.

Noressa bent and slowly peeled back the makeshift bandage to reveal a knife wound to the chest. The cut was small, but Khelcri's gurgling breath told her its thrust had gone deep. "I can do nothing for him." She straightened, hearing the death knell in her words.

"Are you certain?" The question was Medwyn's. He stood behind her, one hand on her shoulder. Noressa turned and clung to him.

"Medwyn, Khelcri is dying and they think I can heal him."

"And can you?" The magician's arm was strong around her shoulders, comforting. "Have you ever done such before?"

"No," she whispered, while visions of her own scaled and taloned hands reaching for Medwyn's came unbidden to her mind. And she knew what it was her mind had searched for all morning. She thrilled to the memory of that power even as she denied it. "I cannot summon such energy again."

Medwyn looked away over the treetops. "Then he will die."

She could read no expression in the magician's face, no inflection to his words. Still, she felt the accusation and exploded in angry rebellion.

"Why me? Why must I always be the one to give? However much I do, more is demanded!"

She pulled away from him, fully intending to leave the village and all it held. Let someone else carry the responsibility. She would renounce her birthright, abandon the magic that Medwyn offered. Why spend her time on these people when she had a summoning to answer and her own peace to find?

Noressa turned to go and met Soreen's anguished gaze. The woman did not speak, but the silent pleading of her tears shattered Noressa's anger. Abruptly she sat and began unlacing her boots.

When she was barefoot, Noressa dug her toes into the cool earth. Soil filled the spaces between her toes and dust covered her ankles. Reaching deep, she summoned the red-eyed lizard. Only when it began to stir did she realize that it was not protection she required but a different kind of succor, and she released it. She wouldn't need a guide to find what she wanted this time.

Noressa turned down another mind path and felt herself

moving outward. She flowed from herself into the open breath of the world. She was aware of her body on the ground, hands and feet pressed to the dirt; her lips chanted commands that came as old, old memories through the haze of pain clinging around her. Her mind sped away into the woodland in all directions to merge with the vitalities there. She settled into the essence of the giant quenners and thick-leaved swayle brush. She mingled with the soft kiman grass and let herself be drawn down until she curled and twisted among the roots, drawing, as they did, her energy from the earth.

Feelings, almost sensual in their permeation, tingled through her toes and fingers, spreading up into her limbs. Noressa shifted her mind to focus on the source, and power flooded through her. Weariness fled. Pain vanished. Raw, unchanneled *life* beat in her, and her entire being pulsed with its rhythms.

Noressa crawled to Khelcri. She sensed the slow ebbing of his life even before she touched him. Gently she laid her hands on his chest, on his wound. She gathered the fading energy and directed it back into his body, augmenting it with the wildness surging in her.

She smiled as his wet gasping quieted to an easy breathing. His heart found its rhythm and color flushed his blue lips. Beneath her fingers, his skin rippled, the edges of the knife cut pulled together and knit. When his life complement was filled, she drew away.

Then hands were on her; she was pulled to her feet and led to face another fading life. That done, she moved to another, and still another. Beneath her fingers, shattered bones rejoined, mangled organs became smooth, and eyes regained their vision. She marshaled lost energies, drew new strength from the earth, and directed it back to those still living. At one point, she was led to a body lying still and cold. Noressa touched, then drew back from, the empty shell that had been a man. She ignored the wail of protest that followed and moved on. Death was a natural balance to life and one she could not change.

At last it was done. Hands no longer tugged her in one direction or another. Her feet scuffed into the earth, she stood immersed in strength.

A voice called to her, a familiar and cherished sound, yet she fought its summons. There was yet one left unwhole, incomplete. Her mind circled, searching out the imbalance. The voice came again, demanding. She had strength but no purpose. The voice offered direction, and she followed. She spiraled down, being led to the last incomplete form, and found, at last, her own body vibrant with power but empty of control. She plummeted into herself.

Noressa was suddenly aware of her mind's isolation. A babble of excited voices assaulted her; she choked on the sweet scent of woodsmoke. Bereft of strength, she fell to her knees. Only Bydawine prevented her complete collapse. He held her up, his voice a consoling gibberish in her ear.

Again she was grasped by many hands. Lifted, wrapped in a warm blanket, she was carried to a soft place. Women surrounded her, known and unknown. She was touched again and again. A gentle stroke to hair or cheek; a quick pressure on her hand. Someone spread more blankets over her, and there were words of gratitude and devotion.

Standing apart, Medwyn watched her, pride shining in his eyes. Noressa struggled to sit upright. She longed to tell him of the wonders she had found. She would tell him of broad channels of power coring through the earth. She would speak of energies that sizzled and hummed through the air. Of forces that migrated between earth and sky, belonging to neither plane, yet bound to both. These mysteries and more she would have shared with him if only she could rise. But her body refused.

She sank back into her cloth nest and gave herself up to the ministries of her various nurses.

CHAPTER 18

 oressa opened her eyes to warmth and shadows. Bundled beneath a mountain of blankets, she could scarcely move—not that she minded. She was enjoying the lazy sensations of waking to such comfort. She yawned and stretched and would have burrowed back under the quiltings, but a voice roused her.

Soreen was beside her, smoothing and patting the coverlets, asking a hundred questions. "Are you rested? Would you rise, or do you wish to sleep longer? Are you hungry?"

The last question brought an eager response from Noressa's belly and wakened her fully. She nodded as the aroma of roasting meat sorted itself from the jumble of perceptions crowding her newly wakened senses. "I am very hungry."

"Good!" Soreen beamed and spoke to the man who peered, grinning, over her shoulder. "Go tell the elders she is wakened, but they must wait until she has eaten."

Khelcri's crooked grin widened and he slipped away.

Khelcri!

Remembrance of all that had passed swept over her, and Noressa sat straight up. "Soreen, the battle! The wounded!"

Soreen clucked and patted Noressa's hand. "Do not trouble yourself over that. It is done and well past."

"Well past . . . Have I slept overlong again?" Noressa wondered if she would always lose precious days from her life each time she performed a healing.

"Only since this morning," Soreen answered.

Noressa looked around the tiny room, finally recognizing it as one of the slant-roofed, three-sided shelters put up after the battle. Grantha was huddled in the shadows of the far corner, watching her. Through the blankets draped across the open end, Noressa caught the flicker of a cookfire, and the solid darkness beyond that proclaimed itself night.

Soreen moved to speak with someone beyond the curtain, then returned and laid out a set of fresh clothes. She chattered all the while of people whose names Noressa did not recognize and places she did not know. Only once did Soreen speak a familiar word, "Creen," and Noressa had a memory of Heska's soup and strange women. Noressa slid back into the warmth of her quilts and let Soreen's friendly prattle wash over her. In a few moments, a platter of sliced meat with bread and baked shabas was delivered, enough to feed three people. Along with it came a basin and pitcher of hot water, wash linens, and two pats of sweet-scented nefa soap. Soreen gathered Grantha from the corner and carried her outside, pausing to glance back over her shoulder. "If you have need of anything else, call and I will hear you."

Noressa washed and dressed quickly. Then she cleaned every bite from the platter, wondering how being filled with such power could be so draining. As she ate, she remembered Soreen's surprised recognition of her, and Bohsra's shock when Jaaben demanded the heir to the throne. She was especially mindful of Bohsra's hard look after the battle. She hadn't been completely honest with these people, and men had died, unknowing, in her cause. Now she must face their anger.

She stood, shaking the folds of her borrowed skirt, trying to shake away fears as well. Reluctantly she moved to the curtain and, with a quick breath, stepped from the shelter.

A press of smiling, jubilant women surged forward, jostling Noressa from one to another as each tried to be near her. Each exclaimed words of thanks and vows of unswerving loyalty. Astonished, Noressa let herself be swept along on the tide of their momentum to the bonfire in the center of the square. A way opened through the crowd of men ringing the fire, and she was seated on a log between Medwyn and Bydawine. Soreen appeared from the crowd and laid a thick shawl across Noressa's shoulders and remained nearby. Bydawine wore his characteristic scowl. To her left, Medwyn smiled briefly at her and returned his attention to the semicircle of men facing them.

The Council of Elders. At her appearance, they whispered among themselves, their wrinkled faces lit with firelight and hope.

Medwyn leaned close and patted her hand. "Jaaben has dispelled my magic, but you are strong enough now to face your people. Do not be afraid."

Before she could answer, someone spoke from the crowd. "All are present. This council begins."

Bohsra rose from his place among the council and stepped forward. His gaze moved out to the crowd around them. Noressa, following his look, frowned. There were many strangers. The number of the assembly was almost three times the size of their village, Drael, and there was a disturbing familiarity to some of the new faces, though Noressa was certain she knew none of them. Bohsra's words pulled her attention back to him.

"I bid welcome to our neighbors of Creen and Tath. We give our thanks for your brave assistance in this day's battle. And we grieve with those whose families have been touched by death." His gaze raked over Noressa. Some unexpressed thought flared behind that hard look, and he went on. "In times past, we would have asked for the blessings of the great powers to ease the suffering of our wounded. But it seems our prayers are answered before they are spoken." His scrutiny returned to Noressa. "And we are gathered to find out how this is so."

Bydawine sprang from his place. "Do you expect the lady Noressa to know the will of the gods? How can—"

Bohsra cut him off with a sweep of his hand. "I believe there is much we can learn from the lady. And this time we shall hear the answers from her own lips."

Bydawine opened his mouth to argue more, but Noressa leaned forward and pulled him back beside her. She whispered, "Let it pass, Bydawine. The time has come for full honesty."

Bydawine sat. Bohsra beckoned to a man standing behind the row of council elders. It was the stranger who had stood with them in the forest awaiting Jaaben's arrival. He was not of Drael, but Noressa had a picture of him against a dark cottage amidst the tumult of many voices. She shook away the vision as Bohsra spoke to him and pointed at Noressa.

"Krelser of Tath, do you know this lady?"

The man nodded. "Yes. Last night a woman appeared in

our village calling us to arms. She bade us hurry to the aid of Drael, then was gone like mist in the wind." He, too, pointed at Noressa. "This is she!"

Agreement swept the crowd; many of the strangers nodded. A second man and a woman were called forward, this time from the village of Creen. They recounted a similar story, and again Noressa was named the spectral visitor. Excitement was high; even the old men of the council muttered enthusiastically among themselves. All were pleased with the proceedings—all save Bohsra.

He stood cold, aloof, and when he stepped close to her, Noressa couldn't suppress a shiver of fear. She was confused by what she had heard, confused by vague images of these same people crowded round her in darkness while she begged for their aid. She had thought those visions only dreams, her cry for help the stuff of a nightmare. But these people were saying she had truly lived her night plays, and they were pleased with her for it. Bohsra's anger now was unexpected, another thread in her mind's tangled disorder.

He stood glaring down at her. The crowd gradually quieted, sensing his displeasure.

"What are you?" Bohsra's words were sharp, more of a challenge than a request for information. "You who slip into our midst disguised as one persecuted by our enemy, then pull that very evil down on our heads!" His arm swept outward, the gesture encompassing the ruined village and its homeless citizens.

Noressa held herself rigid, uncertain how to answer. She knew what was in each of their minds regarding the significance of her presence. But what was Bohsra's anger? The others accepted her without question. Why did he alone oppose her?

Then steadying hands were on her shoulders, the protective warmth of a body pressed close behind, and Soreen's voice sounded over her head.

"She is Nandil Shay." A concurring murmur riffled through the women. Soreen continued. "She has brought life back to our land. You have hunted the fat yarja and eaten sweet new vegetables, yourself, elder. And you watched her heal our dying this very day. Why do you not see her as she is, the new

Shay and harbinger of life to our people?"

"Because I do not understand what I see." Backlit by fire-light, he was a figure of looming darkness. Anger strained his words. "Who is this spell-caster child with a face that only now do I recognize as that of my dead queen? A child traveling with a magician whose name awakens hopeful memories in me that cannot be remembered. What magic is this?"

"The magic is mine." Medwyn's voice came quiet and deep over the crackle of the flames. "A simple protection."

Even Soreen was surprised. "You felt she needed protection from us?"

"From your expectations," Medwyn answered. "From duties placed on her that required too much too soon. No doubt you would have welcomed her and crowned her queen the first day had you known her true identity." Soreen nodded. "And be-lieving her mere presence a fulfillment of promise, you would have expected an immediate victory over the mistress."

"That is why we have watched for her." Bohsra's words were flat.

Medwyn shook his head. "But she has not the strength nor knowledge yet for such a battle. My spell was to gain time for her to study her Talents."

At Medwyn's reply, Bohsra's lips pulled into a thin, ironic smirk. Suddenly Noressa knew the reason for his anger.

Yes, I see your fears now, good Bohsra. You see your cham-pion come at last, but she has no power. The deliverer is only a girl-child who must be coddled and protected while your peo-ple continue to die in her name. She forced down a bitter laugh. And you may be right in your anger, she thought, men-tally counting off what few spells she had mastered so far. Cer-tainly none of them were great enough to challenge a practiced sorceress.

Noressa lifted her chin, letting a tight smile play across her lips. Her eyes met Bohsra's. The smile said, *Yes, I understand, but there is naught I can do for it.* She swallowed her bitter-ness and went to stand before the fire. She spoke, loud enough for all to hear.

"Bohsra is right to question what he does not understand. I admit I have kept much from you, but now I will tell you who I am and what I have done."

Firelight glinted on Bohsra's silver hair as he nodded. "Speak, then."

Noressa told them of her childhood on the mountain, of her parents' deaths, and the terrible pull of the summoning. She spoke of Edell, the amulet, and the fiends. The illusions of the amulet she confessed in her account of the escape from Wigram Keep and her first meeting with Medwyn. Long into the night she talked. The fire burned low and was built up again. Mothers rocked sleepy children, and rations of bread and meat were passed among all. Pulling blankets and shawls around themselves, her listeners settled themselves to the ground, for none would leave before they heard all.

When she had done, Noressa stood before the council.

"I believe myself to be this heir you have awaited, but I have never sought such honors and will gladly set them aside to any other you name. If you hold me to this duty, then I vow to wield whatever power is mine in defense of this land. If you do not accept me"—she looked to Bohsra—"I will count myself free to pursue my own quest."

With a single voice, the crowd proclaimed her queen. Oaths of love, honor, and loyalty filled the darkness. Medwyn, looking proud, and Bydawine, smugly satisfied, came to stand beside her.

Noressa basked in the fervor of her people and, for a time, forgot even the sharp-edged urgency of the summoning.

CHAPTER 19

Jaaben's rout was being called "The Battle of Heroes." A new queen and a new confidence had come to the land of Sidra. Since the battle, there had been no further attacks of sorcery. Throughout the countryside, even the patrols of human soldiers from the mistress's army were staying tight in their keeps and fortified places. Travelers moved freely between villages. Forges of the metalsmiths glowed day and night as arms were made and mended openly, in defiance of the years'-long ban against weapons manufacture. A few tired souls entertained quiet dreams that Felaya's domination was through, but inside they knew the truth. Nothing would be resolved until the true heir sat upon the throne of Ac'talzea and the power of the mistress was broken. Medwyn warned against complacency, saying the interlude was only a temporary withdrawal while the mistress gathered her strength for a decisive attack.

Still, something was changed. The pall of gloom that had tainted every thought, grayed every color, was gone. Life was bright and clear and worth challenging.

The men of Creen and Tath remained a halfcycle to assist in rebuilding the cottages of Drael. By the end of the halfcycle, the homes were complete.

Fields trampled by invading kifera were plowed again and reseeded. By the fullcycle, sprouts made a carpet of bright green against the black earth. In the woodlands, herds of yarja gathered, mornings and evenings, to suck noisily at the riverside. Flocks of garish yellow and black dessos filled the trees along the bank, squawking their impatience at the intrusion of the herds. But the birds eagerly set upon the bugs and mudworms churned up by the yarja's sharp hooves. Everywhere the land burgeoned with life, and an answering vitality rose in the people.

Noressa set aside her anger with Bydawine for having "stolen" magic lessons from Medwyn. She found a new pleasure in his company as they studied under the elder magician's strict tutorship. In an unspoken rivalry to outperform the other, each found his greatest skills lay in very different directions. While Noressa was content to learn only simple philters and formulae, Bydawine excelled in the physical sciences, alchemy above all. Even Medwyn was surprised at Bydawine's prowess. Noressa, in turn, found she was truly "sister to the earth." She learned quickly to tap and channel the powers flowing through the body of the world without losing self-control.

But her greatest fascination was the mindspeak. With it, simple minds could be coaxed, directed; she used it often in drawing small animals and birds to entertain the children. And it was the mindspeak that bound her to Medwyn and Bydawine. The depth of that link between her and Bydawine was a puzzle. He seemed a part of her, reading her moods and often coming to her aid on some problem before she realized she had called to him. And all the while, she struggled against the call of the summoning.

The days rounded to a fullcycle and more. Diml had waned to dark and begun to swell again before that summoning shattered the delicate peace of the village.

Perhaps it was the lingering heat of the long summer day. Or it could be that Noressa finally tired of being the village's coddled treasure. Except for her daily trip to the hidden glade for Medwyn's instructions, she was no longer allowed to wander the forest. The many household tasks that had filled her mind and busied her hands were now considered unseemly for one of her station.

On the evening she threw down her ultimatum, Noressa held youngling court as she did every evening. She sat before her cottage on the edge of the common. The village children were gathered, enraptured by the illusions she conjured to play out the stories she told.

The children huddled together in fascination, watching the miniature vision of the disobedient innkeeper's daughter fleeing the hideous hizzledrig. The hizzledrig had no form; its mass was a seething of half-formed shapes. Clawed limbs and fanged heads grew and were absorbed back into itself as it pursued the hapless maiden, until at last the girl recognized her own fears and shortcomings in the monster and, facing down her terrors, tamed the beast.

The children shivered and sighed with the maid, cheered her on to victory, and then, when it was done, laughed and clapped and begged for another story.

But Noressa, fighting a monster of her own in the ache that pounded deep behind her eyes, refused. She leaned toward a boy whose unruly hair seemed always to hang in his face. "Did you find a treasure today?" she whispered.

The boy nodded, grinning, and handed her the shell of a jerjal nut. The red shell was packed with moss, mud, and tiny pebbles. Noressa looked it over, then tossed it high into the air. On its downward plunge, the thing burst into multihued spangles of light that resolved themselves into tiny human shapes that scattered on shimmering wings across the common. Shrieking their delight, the children scattered after them into the deepening twilight.

Only Jatrae remained, frowning. He had stood at the edge of the gathered children, watching the story unfold. Now he looked at Noressa with concern.

"Are you not well, lady? You look fatigued, and you send away the younglings with but one story."

"I am tired, as you say, and my head pains me somewhat."

"Shall I bring the elder? Perhaps he will have a draft to soothe—"

"No! I have potions enough of my own without another's meddling!" she snapped as another pain throbbed between her eyes. Noressa regretted her anger immediately, seeing the young man's face pale. "Forgive me, Jatrae. I am not angry with you, only in need of rest. I will take myself to bed early this night."

She ground her teeth hard to hold back the other words she wanted to shout: Rest, that is what I need! But there will be none in my bed, nor anywhere, so long as I fight the summoning. From the moment she had accepted her place as queen and set aside her search for the summoning, it had never ceased tormenting her.

She let him assist her up, then clucked her tongue in irritation. Stumping across the common toward her was Bydawine, his stocky figure unmistakable even in the falling darkness. Medwyn's taller form followed a short distance behind. In less than three cycles, she had come to regard Bydawine as her greatest friend. His companionship filled a loneliness of which she hadn't even been aware until they began their adventures together. But there were times when she worried that the strange bond between them was slowly stealing away even the privacy of her own thoughts. She had hoped to make it to bed without too many questions, but now . . . With a sigh, she sat down again.

"What is it? What is wrong?" Bydawine demanded to know, even before he was completely stopped.

Jatrae and Noressa spoke together, their words stumbling over each other. They stopped, and Jatrae deferred to her.

"It is nothing, Bydawine, only that I am weary and would retire early."

Bydawine's expression made it clear that he didn't believe her. He looked with suspicion at Jatrae. "Have the children been at you again? You shouldn't encourage them, Noressa. You have enough to do without that. Sometimes it seems you have more children than dust hanging on your ankles."

Noressa felt anger warm her cheeks. As always, Bydawine seemed to know that she was troubled and had come to her aid. But since becoming Medwyn's pupil, he often displayed a streak of arrogance. This confused and annoyed her, for she was especially fond of this strange little man. But tonight she would not stand for his bullying. She opened her mouth, but Jatrae stepped forward.

"The fault is mine. The lady storied the children with the hizzledrig, then sent them away. I could see the lady was tired, but I pressed her further about the hizzledrig. I had the notion that if she could fashion a small monster for the children, perhaps she might form a *ne-alit* to be sent before us in battle. It was foolish, and you should be angry with me, Counselor Bydawine, not the lady."

With a practiced flick of his wrist, Medwyn gestured, and flames licked up from the torches set around the common. In the wavering orange light, Noressa saw Bydawine's face. The dwarf was scowling up at Jatrae, but his eyes held a gleam of interest. Bydawine turned to Medwyn.

"Mayhaps the boy has stumbled onto a good thought. How would it be if Noressa were to send a *ne-alit* to confuse our enemies? Is there much to the construction of such a thing?"

Jatrae gave a grunt of surprise. "I have already said it was a fool's idea. Certainly you wouldn't expect the lady to embrace such a wickedness!"

The concern in Jatrae's words was loud enough to draw the attention of Coris and Tel. The two were leaving Tel's cottage to prepare for their night's watch, but they turned and came to stand with Jatrae. Noressa fidgeted on her bench, wondering how to gracefully excuse herself from this growing entourage.

Medwyn raised a questioning brow, then asked, "What is a *ne-alit*, in your mind, that it is so wicked?"

Jatrae shuffled his feet, exchanging a quick glance with Tel and Coris. "It is an evil thing—a blank soul sent to destroy."

Medwyn shook his head. "Not a soul. A *ne-alit* has no life. It is a very strong shadow magic, a picture of things that are not. What are these illusions Noressa spins for the young ones if not a form of shadow magic?"

"But the shadow magic is an evil thing," Jatrae insisted, looking worried. "The elders say it was such that killed our Shay, sucking the breath out of them as they slept. Do you say the lady Noressa should practice these dark works?"

"Magic is only a tool," Medwyn answered. "If a man uses a stick to beat his neighbor, you wouldn't say the wood was evil. A *ne-alit* differs from simple illusion only in its purpose and strength of detail. Depending on the ability of the spell-caster, a shadow magic may be seen, heard—even touched. But there will always be some flaw. Find that weakness and you will destroy any *ne-alit*'s power."

Noressa stifled a groan at the impromptu lesson. She turned her face away from them all, wanting no more talk of magic. Too often in the past days, her incantations had gone awry, her concentration broken by the summoning. Too many nights she had awakened, sweat-soaked and trembling, with the sudden call aching through her skull. Then a familiar voice intruded upon her thoughts. She turned to stare at Bydawine as he planned aloud.

"This is good. A *ne-alit* will be a strong weapon in our defense against Felaya. Noressa should begin her studies of this tomorrow. She is the illusionist amongst us. I think she is best suited to the skill. And I think also—"

Noressa made a sound of disgust. "Oh, cease your prattle, Bydawine!" Now everyone was staring at her. "You think too much. And you think too much for me! Am I not even allowed my own mind now that I am queen? I may have made a great mistake accepting this position. I had hoped by revealing myself completely, I would be able to move freely among my people to accomplish what needs doing. But now every decision is made for me, and I am more a prisoner than if I were shackled. It cannot go on. I have put aside my *aramil* too long."

There was a gasp of surprise all around, and a long silence. Then Medwyn touched her hand. "You did not tell us you had vowed a lifejourney, child."

Noressa hung her head, pulling at the long braid looped over her shoulder. "It is not the custom to bandy about such a personal thing. And when I vowed to answer the summons, I had no other goal. The summoning has always led me eastward. Felaya is eastward. Once I began the struggle for my birthright, it seemed the natural thing to combine one with another, for either could mean my death." She drew herself up, looking eastward, into the darkness past the torchlight. "I cannot deny the summoning any longer. It punishes me every moment I delay. Even my royal oaths cannot hold me back from it."

Medwyn cautioned her sternly. "Be careful what you say, child. Many lives depend on your words."

"It cannot be helped," she whispered. "I must complete my *aramil* before all else. I will gladly accept all assistance, but failing that, I pray only for understanding. For if it means I must renounce hearth and clan and all other vows, then I will do that also."

*   *   *   *   *

Dawn was not yet a gray promise to the east. Noressa stood with the rest of the village as Bydawine and his party prepared to leave.

Last night, when she had threatened to renounce all if she

were not allowed to complete her *aramil*, the council had been hastily convened. After much argument, it was decided she would be allowed to travel eastward, but only after Bydawine returned from Dromund with either his uncle's army or a formal denial of assistance. Until then, Noressa was to be hidden in a secret place.

Now she waited with Bydawine as the last of the provisions were loaded on the kifera. She knelt beside the dwarf and touched his hand.

"Will you be away long?" she asked, already knowing his answer.

"Only as long as I must."

"But why must you go? There is yet time to let Brameth carry a letter. Your uncle will recognize the mark of your hand and the seal of your ring."

"You know why I must go." His tone was that of someone explaining a serious thought to a child. "My uncle would not believe such a letter, seal or no. There are too many ways in which it might be a deception." He frowned. "I cannot say why he has delayed crossing unless he feared losing men in the spring flood. But the river has been calm a full cycle now, and I can only believe further troubles hold him. For these reasons, I must go to him personally."

"I am the queen," she murmured without spirit. "I could command you to remain."

"And I would stay. But that would accomplish nothing."

At that moment, Brameth signaled that all was ready. Bydawine hesitated, a softness in his face as he looked at Noressa. Then he straightened his shoulders and frowned.

"It is not seemly for a queen to kneel before her subjects."

Noressa shrugged. "I am an unseemly queen." She leaned forward and embraced him. "Be watchful, dear friend," she whispered. "I sense ill-bodings for this venture."

She rose and went to stand with Medwyn, where she remained long after the last kifera had vanished into the darkness.

CHAPTER 20

The journey from Drael to the river Bourne was accomplished in just under two days. With no injured to slow them, as Medwyn had in their journey to the village, they made excellent time. Still, Bydawine chafed at how long they were in reaching the river.

Eventually he stood with Brameth and Culric on the bank, watching the swift current. The muddied crest of the spring flood had subsided to less than half that of the torrent which had almost swallowed him, though its speed was still dangerous. At the water's edge, twelve men struggled with the wooden barge that would soon be launched into the river. With the water tugging at the bow, the men paused, and Bydawine passed them the cloth bundle he carried.

The cloth was unfurled and attached to the single tall wooden spar at the front of the craft. Bydawine felt a swell of pride as the green and white pennant snapped in the late afternoon breeze. In the center of the two-colored field, the women of Drael had stitched a yellow crown resting on a wreath of qwizel vines. The vines stood for strength and loyalty. And no other standard of Dromund, save the king's, could boast a crown on its field, for no other lordholder could trace his lineage to the throne. With his family crest dancing above him, Bydawine led Brameth onto the barge.

The five other men picked to accompany them came aboard, and the barge was launched. They were quickly pulled into the current, and Bydawine clung to the railing while the others began poling for the opposite shore. On that other shore, the soldiers of Dromund followed the progress of the barge, urging their kifera along the sandy bank. The launch had taken place a full measure above Stagget's Keep. Brameth had estimated it would take that distance to make the crossing before the current carried them over White Mist Falls, only half a measure below the castle. Stagget, too, had anticipated such a move, and his men stationed along the bank had kept Bydawine and his group under watch their whole journey upstream.

Bydawine choked on a spray of water that caught him off guard and began to wonder if Brameth had miscalculated. Already the battlements of Stagget's Keep had appeared, and the barge still rushed along in the center of the river. The water had become too deep for poling, and now only the steersman had any control over the barge. Bydawine tossed his head to clear the water from his eyes, not daring to let go the rail as the craft lurched and dove in the savage current. He was soaked from the spray thrown up over the bow and was finding it difficult to maintain his footing on the water-slick logs. He closed his eyes against the sight of the churning water speeding along beneath him, but that only increased the queasiness in his belly. He opened his eyes again.

Brameth was shouting orders above the roar of the current. The big man moved to take over the rudder, and Bydawine glanced up to see the sun-washed walls of the keep slide by. So quickly? Fear clenched his insides as a new sound forced itself upon his awareness. It was the deep rolling sound of faraway thunder, though Bydawine knew there was no storm brewing. He looked ahead, already visualizing the mist-shrouded falls that waited around the bend of the river.

Bydawine felt the off-balance tug of the current as the barge sped into the turn of the river. The barge listed outward toward the Dromund shore. Brameth strained against the rudder and shouted. Together, the men on the port side rushed to the opposite side of the craft. Bydawine understood the intended plan, but instead of the displaced weight sending them out of the current, it only threatened to capsize them as the swirling water dropped them into a trough. The men hurried back to their former places, trying to stabilize the barge, and the river swept them around the bend.

A thunderous roar filled Bydawine's ears, and white froth foamed high into the air. He shivered with the chill certainty of death close at hand. The falls loomed nearer, and he wished for wings to lift them from this death trap. Then he cursed his own stupidity.

"Fool!" he shouted to himself. "Not only birds can fly!"

Bracing against the rail, Bydawine began a levitation chant. Drawing all the power he could summon, he channeled it into the spell. But he did not will the barge to rise; instead, Bydawine pushed mentally against the water, sending them skimming sideways in the current. A shout went up from the men when they saw the shore drawing nearer. They set their poles in the water and Bydawine pushed again. Two men shouted that their poles had found purchase on the river bottom. Bydawine scarcely heard them over the booming of the falls as the barge was swallowed by the swirling vapor. He pushed a last time, trusting in luck that it was in the right direction.

He fell to his knees as the barge slowed suddenly, grinding through a rocky shallow. Then it pulled free and sped forward a moment before slamming into a jumble of boulders appearing from the mist. Bydawine was flung full length and felt more than heard the wood splinter beneath him. He was engulfed by a cold wave sluicing over him and found himself crawling underwater over sand and rocks, away from the pull of the current. Finally his face broke the surface of the water, and he staggered ashore.

He collapsed against a pile of rocks, filling his lungs with cool air. Nearby, another man lay gasping. Other shadowy figures emerged from the direction of the water, and Brameth's voice sounded eerily from the mist, calling to each of his companions. When all had answered, Bydawine breathed easier. His panic had made him forget his own capabilities and nearly killed them all. As it was, they had lost the barge and, more important, the pennant. He hoped the men of Dromund had been able to see and recognize the crest. It might be the only thing between them and execution on sight.

Culric lay beside him, and of a sudden he rose to his feet, nearly trampling Bydawine in the mist. His sword was half drawn and he hissed for silence. "Sssst! Listen!"

Bydawine strained but heard nothing save the Bourne rushing to hurl itself into the gorge below. When at last he heard the jingle of harness and the scrape of metal-booted feet over the shore rocks, it was too late.

A line of riders emerged from the mist, swords drawn, their

war-trained kifera forming a living, steel-clad barrier. Archers stepped through the line and took stance, bows nocked and ready. A voice from one of the riders commanded, "Drop your weapons and kneel. You are prisoners of Brazel Drut, Lord High Ruler of Tarragon."

* * * * *

The march from the river to the keep was a humiliation. Bydawine identified himself at once to the *j'hen*, leader of the Tarragon soldiers, stating name, lineage, and rank in his uncle's army. But the captain of the troops responded only by herding them away from the river and back toward the castle.

Of course, their crossing was known by all at the keep. Many soldiers rode out to meet them until the *j'hen's* original *quar* of twenty-five men swelled to well over a hundred. In the light of the rider's torches, Bydawine could distinguish the insignia of several other clans and at least two more lordholder crests. And he recognized many faces among the soldiers. But if they knew him, they gave no sign of it.

Inside the keep, they were taken immediately to the council hall. The room, larger than the council chamber at Wigram, was furnished in much the same manner. The lordholders' table was set across the far end of the room. Below, two officers' tables were set lengthwise to it. The smoky torches sent a haze drifting over the stone-walled room, setting an ominous tone for the sight that greeted Bydawine's eyes.

On the wall above the lordholders' table were the crests of the lords in residence. Hanging were the expected trio of standards—his uncle's crown and wreath, Stagget's red and black field centered with a blooded dakwi, and Lord Drut's sword and heart on a sea-blue pennant. But in prominence above them all hung the pure white silk emblazoned with scarlet scroll and mace of Lord Kreth, holder to the province of Idbi Rans. He was also High Counselor to the king, residing more in the royal house than at his own keep. That he should have left the king's side to be here was disquieting.

But what sent Bydawine's hopes plunging was the sight of his cousin, Norwick the Younger, seated among the lordholders rather than in his usual place at the officers' table.

Only one reason could account for such a placement.

Uncle is dead.

Grief battled despair. Bydawine loved his uncle, and he had counted on his uncle's trust and sympathies for the military backing he needed. Though he believed his cousin would side with him, Norwick was young and inexperienced in his new role as lord, and his voice would carry little weight in the vote to come.

Behind him, Bydawine felt the menace of the armed soldiers; ahead, he faced the strange antagonism of those he had always known as allies and friends. Only Norwick's face gave any sign of welcome, though he, too, remained silent and unacknowledging.

Then there was the *other*, a searching touch of magic. It swirled about him, seeking, probing, a touch so delicate Bydawine knew that had he been untrained in such matters, he would never have noticed the contact. He tried to block his mind against the intrusion, but the unseen magician was too strong, too well schooled in his craft. Bydawine was forced to endure the silent examination.

When the probing withdrew, he nearly stumbled forward, he had resisted so hard. Culric laid a steadying hand on his shoulder, and when Bydawine again looked toward the lord's table, an elder stood beside Lord Kreth's chair.

He was short and thin and wore the gray robes of a sorcerer. Stroking his fulsome white beard in a manner that bespoke years of habit, the mage spoke. "There is no magic loose here, my lords. These men come in their true selves. But there is knowledge in this one." The mage pointed to Bydawine. "His power is strong, though untried."

Tension in the room eased. "Thank you, Azber," Lord Kreth replied, lacing his hands on the table and leaning forward to examine the group with more interest.

Lord Stagget harrumphed his pleasure with the elder's proclamation and leaned his burly frame back in his chair, his bushy red brows relaxing their worried furrowing. Norwick's face creased into an open grin, and he slapped the tabletop in pleasure.

"Ah, cousin, forgive these sour faces. We meant only to be certain that you were not another example of Tylek's magic sent to plague us. But well met and welcome! We had nearly given you up for dead." Norwick rose and made as if to come around the table.

"Hold, young lord!" Brazel Drut, of all the lords, was the only one who did not appear satisfied with Azber's pronouncement. Now he stayed Norwick with a brusque command and glared down on the travelers. "This may indeed be your cousin, but he returns in suspicious circumstances and in strange company. It is best that we proceed slowly."

Norwick hesitated, then sat again, his face set in defiance. "Do not proceed too slowly, Lord Drut, for I would welcome my cousin properly."

Lord Stagget grunted in agreement. "That is only right, young Norwick. Our guests should be made comfortable." He motioned to the steward in attendance at his side. In moments, an army of servants brought table and benches, and the company of travelers were seated. Before Drut's glowering, a stream of young servants brought dish after dish of hearty country fare.

Wonder vied with suspicion on the faces of the Sidrians. Bydawine knew that, save for Brameth and Coris, none were old enough to remember the luxury of such dishes as were set before them. Even Bydawine found himself surprised by the seeming extravagance after his recent struggle in Sidra just to keep a bit of meat in the vegetable pot.

So they feasted on crisp spring vegetables and roast dakwi basted with tart grelt berry sauce and *diitha*, flaky layered bread covered by a sweet, hard glaze. On these and many other dishes, the men of Drael indulged, though Bydawine was pleased to notice that they took little of the red wine and mulled targ. And while they ate, Bydawine told the court of his adventures in Sidra.

There was some laughter, derision for Jaaben when Bydawine spoke of their escape from the castle, and awed murmurs at Noressa's nighttime battle with the scarlet entity. He spoke of the mysterious Token of Dragonsblood, of skirmishes with Jaaben's men, the sudden greening of the land, and Noressa's confirmation as queen. And he spoke of the Sidrian people— of their courage, forbearance, and loyalty in the midst of their deprivation.

The court listened. Lords and soldiers, officers and servants, all heard the tale of marvels. When Bydawine finished, there was silence and not a few tears.

Bydawine waited, his meal almost untouched before him. The men of Drael, too, sat unmoving, their appetites lost in the power of his oratory. Bydawine looked from lord to lord. Of Norwick's sympathies there was no doubt. The young lord met Bydawine's gaze, wonder and admiration in his smile. Stagget remained as he had through much of the tale, head resting in one huge hand, eyes averted. Lord Kreth, pale and withdrawn, stared into the depths of the torch smoke. So it was Lord Drut who spoke first. Brazel Drut, who through the entire meal sat with arms crossed, glowering in open hostility. Now his words cut cold and sharp through the smoke and silence.

"An entertaining story, Master Bydawine. But of what importance is it?"

Norwick's excited voice sounded through the hall, stemming the rush of angry words that would have spewed from Bydawine. "It is clear, Lord Drut, of what importance. Now we know that this is the time for which we have awaited. We must attack! Here sits this fine company, envoy of Sidra, come to ask our aid in crushing this tyrant. Is that not why you have returned, cousin?"

Bydawine nodded.

Norwick rushed on. "To delay further would be to accept the shame Tylek has given us. It would be to accept defeat. This is the time to avenge ourselves! We can only seize this chance now!"

Norwick stood before the company, face flushed, eyes sparking with excitement. His hair lay against his shoulders, seemingly a burnished golden hood in the smoky light. He stood tall, his body taut with restrained passion. A murmur swept the room, along with restless movement, the clink of arms. And beneath, a tone of approval.

Bydawine gazed upon his cousin with awe, and a fleeting image impressed itself into his mind—an image of glory, power, and despair. Norwick shimmered before him in a blue-gold haze, and Bydawine couldn't restrain the whispered prophecy that fell from his lips. "Behold a future king."

But as before, it was Lord Drut who shattered the delicate mood with his cold words. "Yes, I thought as much. A sad tale of oppression, and we are expected to rush headlong to the rescue in a valorous passion. You are young and too easily impressed, Lord Norwick." Brazel Drut waved a hand in Norwick's direction, a gesture of dismissal, and leaned back in his chair. "We must examine this situation carefully. We must be certain of the consequences."

Bydawine's anger burst out. "Consequences! I will give you consequences!" He scrambled down from the bench to stand, indignant, before the high table. "Death is what will come of it. Either the queen or the usurper. If Felaya triumphs, then your own deaths will be close at hand." Bydawine knew he spoke dangerously, but he didn't care. He must convince these men of Noressa's importance in Sidra's survival. "Think on the history of this conflict, my lords. Felaya murdered her own sister to achieve the power of the amulet. She has held a country in thrall for an entire generation while she searched for the child she believed could yield her this power. And now she has sent invaders to Dromund."

Bydawine paused for a breath and rushed on. "If Sidra falls and the mistress obtains this amulet, then our destruction is not far behind, for her ambitions will not be content with a single crown only."

Again the mutter of soldiers among themselves, anxiety and confusion sharp in their whispers. The smallest flutter of hope stirred in Bydawine. He turned to the one man whose word would be law.

"Lord Kreth, it is known that in this war with the mistress, Brydon appealed to our own king for aid and was refused."

"Not refused," Lord Drut interrupted. "The council had not yet reached a decision on the request when the war was ended."

"The council," Bydawine snapped, "deliberated the appeal for more than three cycles! And it is further known that Lord Kreth is the only one who spoke in favor of Sidra."

It was then that Lord Stagget roused himself from what Bydawine had assumed to be a drunken stupor. Stagget raised his head to stare unseeing at the gathering before him, and Bydawine was shocked at the sorrow etched into the old warrior's face, the anguish in his voice. "True. The lad speaks true. We dissembled amongst ourselves, speaking of armory stores and troop strengths and—" he turned to Lord Drut, eyes in a thin-slitted glare—"and *consequences*." Then the emotion drained from him and he slumped once more in his chair. "We knew of the sorcery that had invaded Sidra, and we feared it. We trembled like children at night shadows. And when it was ended, we sent ourselves home to our hearthfires and our sweet, plump women, saying, 'Now it is past and done, and the queen's own sister sits as regent for the child. All is well.' " Stagget's head rested once more in his hand. "We dishonored ourselves before an ally, and now our children pay the reckoning of our cowardice."

Bydawine stood shocked beyond words, for there was no mistaking the glitter of tears that slipped down Stagget's face to lose themselves in his mass of red beard.

"You berate yourself overmuch, my good Lord Stagget." Brazel Drut's superior tone broke the ensuing silence. "A short occupation, a few treasures stolen, yes. But no great damage done."

Norwick stared at Lord Drut, disbelief and anger in his face. But it was Stagget's howl of rage that reverberated to the heights of the stone-walled chamber.

"No great damage?" Stagget sprang from his seat, one white-knuckled hand hurling his chair aside. "Is it your practice, then, to send out the daughters of your house to pleasure your enemy's men?" Stagget would have advanced on Lord Drut, but Norwick held him back. The men of Tarragon pressed close behind Bydawine and his companions, while men of both clans rose, weapons half drawn, each ready to leap to the defense of his lord. But Stagget held, fists clenched before him, body trembling with an ire so terrible he could scarcely choke out his words.

"Have you not seen my Oray, who sits daily in the garden, babbling to the winds and plucking threads from her gown? Do you know nothing of Lirsa, my sweet Lirsa, who screams with terror at the approach of any man—even her own father?"

Stagget shook free of Norwick's grasp, and Bydawine watched grief battle rage until the anger won out. But it was a cold fury, and the lordholder's words came hard and measured. "Is it no great damage that a lord should die in his own dungeons and his son become holder to a keep of ashes and rubble? Or that we cannot sleep safe in our own beds, nor welcome the kinsman of our ally without arms and sorcery? See the truth, Brazel Drut, for it can no longer be hidden. The war was never ended; it has only smoldered these many years. Now it flames high again and threatens to consume Dromund as well. Again Sidra begs our aid, and we dare not let this summons go unanswered."

Stagget swung to face the men of Sidra. "I will live no more with the blot of dishonor upon my brow. You will have your army! My army. To the last dagger and half-trained swordsman, I, Stagget Dakwikiller, pledge you my support!"

Joy swept over Bydawine at the man's bellowed promise.

"And mine!" Young Norwick shouted to make himself heard over the tumult of cheers as the men of Wigram and Stagget Keeps roared their approval.

The men of Sidra rejoiced, pledging unheard toasts with great gulps of wine. Stagget clasped wrists in a fierce acceptance of Norwick's alliance. Only the men of Tarragon were restrained as their lord shouted for silence. At last order was restored, and Lord Drut faced Stagget with his own anger.

"What you speak is treason! Lesser men have been hanged for such talk, Stagget. Your fealty is to your own king. This council has made no decision, and you will make no move until that decision is made."

"Is it not in the service of our king to defend our land from invasion?" Stagget answered. "Would you not rather we carried the battle to our enemy than wait until our homeland has become a torn and trampled battlefield? No, I have given my pledge before this company, and I will not take it back."

"To what have you pledged yourself?" the lord of Tarragon demanded. "To a motley band of self-proclaimed rebels? To some unseen child queen who may be nothing more than the wild fantasy of a dwarf? Only the king may make such alliances."

Norwick stepped between the two older lords. "Then let us hear from the king's man. What say you, Lord Kreth? Shall we stand by our ally or no?"

There was a breathless silence. Bydawine found his gaze locked with that of Lord Kreth, trying to discern any hope in those faded blue eyes. At that moment, Bydawine wished desperately for Noressa's talent of mindspeak. If Lord Kreth could but know her fragile beauty or her joy of life, if he could but sense her vulnerability, Bydawine knew what answer would be given. But he could only stand impotent with his ache of longing before Lord Kreth's unreadable stare.

When the king's man spoke, his words were as soft and faded as his eyes. But they carried the finality of the executioner's axe. "The night grows late and the morrow approaches. Let us speak of it then." He rose and, leaning heavily upon his magician's arm, shuffled from the hall.

CHAPTER 21

Bydawine paced like a caged cle-er in the richly appointed bedchamber that was his prison. Diml's light was a silver ribbon through the narrow window he had thrown open. The silken coverlet on the massive bed was unruffled, for he had not slept since being brought to the room. A serving stand, carved from a single piece of quenner wood, held platters of fruit, wine, meats, and sweetbreads, all untouched. The fire was all but dead in the grate.

Again Bydawine stomped across the room, but his pacing did nothing to dispel his outrage. He was betrayed!

Not completely, he reminded himself. Norwick had supported him, and Stagget. It was Lord Drut who openly opposed him. And Kreth who refused him with silence. Not only had he been refused aid, but now he was also a prisoner of his own allies and of a certainty would not be allowed to return to Sidra.

Bydawine paused before the window that faced out over the courtyard. From his position, he could only stare up into the black and silver night. Morning wasn't far off and the stars were dimming, compounding his sense of injustice as even their feeble light was fading.

The night wind carried the jangle of traces from some restless beast on the grounds. The sound reminded Bydawine of chains, and he wondered if Brameth and the others were as comfortably imprisoned as he. They would be buried in the deepest dungeon if Lord Drut had his way. Bydawine hoped Brameth had done nothing rash to give Drut authority to order such treatment. Though Brameth had quietly let himself be led away, Bydawine remembered the determination smoldering in those golden eyes.

"I'm sorry, my friend," Bydawine whispered to the stars.

Brameth's face faded. He thought of Noressa as he had last seen her—resigned and without spirit.

Deep inside, the memory of her quick farewell embrace warmed him, and he shook his head, thinking of the changes in her.

She had grown thin since being proclaimed queen. Worry had set a permanent frown on her brow. He sighed, knowing she would have left the village by now, moving to whatever hiding place Bohsra had deemed safe.

"I cannot fail her! Am I not kinsman to the lord of Wigram? Do I not have legitimate right to demand satisfaction for the wrongs I have suffered? Am I not a magician with power of my own? I will not be held down by old men frightened of their own shadows!"

His mind was a fury of ideas, escape the core of each thought. He had almost decided on a daring plan when there came the sound of scuffling in the hall and a muffled cry. Then the door swung open to admit a grinning Brameth, carrying the limp form of a soldier. Behind him followed the other men of Drael, pulling a second unconscious guard. Culric unceremoniously dropped the arm of the guard he carried. With a grin in Bydawine's direction, he set about lighting candles from the embers on the hearth.

Astonished, Bydawine made no move as the last man to enter, young Norwick, rushed to greet him.

Bydawine was swept from his feet and embraced like a child. He suffered the indignity joyously. When returned to his own feet, he clasped Norwick's wrist and did not let go.

"Well met, cousin! I hadn't expected to see you again until the council reconvened."

Norwick knelt before Bydawine, his grip returning the eager salutation. "And I hadn't expected to see you again at all, Bydawine. I was all but certain my father's dungeon would be my tomb. And I had no doubt your sharp tongue would have had you executed long before Pashet's men found their quarry. I was pleased to learn you had escaped and wondered often what befell you. Imagine my wonderment yesterday to hear that a band of Sidrians was crossing the Bourne, flying the banner of Wigram Keep! However, when the council reconvenes, Bydawine, you and I shall not be in attendance."

Norwick smiled, and Bydawine saw in his eyes the gleam of mischief that in their youth had promised high adventure. Such adventures were usually followed by an equally high censure from their elders.

"Not attend?" Bydawine would have protested, but Coris chuckled and knelt beside them, turning his face to reveal a large swelling beneath his left eye.

"Hear him out, Master Bydawine. He came to us alone and unarmed, and we thought him easy prey. But once he had our attention"—Coris touched the swelling gently—"we realized he was more valuable as friend than hostage."

Brameth stepped to the window and peered down into the courtyard. When he turned back to the room, he was grinning. His look of anticipation matched Norwick's spark of mischief. "It seems that your Lord Staget will keep his promise of aid, Master Bydawine. But we may be forced to convince Lord Drut's men to allow us leave to return home."

Norwick nodded. "Yes, Lord Drut was ever a contentious ally." He moved to sit on the edge of the bed, pulling Bydawine up beside him. "But Father knew well how to handle him, and I will follow his example."

Bydawine raised a brow in surprise. "Then you will tell Brazel Drut that he is a fool and take your own path?"

Norwick shrugged. "Perhaps I may not speak as bluntly, but I will not remain silent. Father would not have."

Norwick's voice broke, and Bydawine laid a hand on his shoulder. "I, too, grieve for your father. I trust his death was a noble one. Quickly, in battle?"

Norwick shook his head. "There's little nobility to starving in your own dungeon." He sighed. "I sorrow at my father's death, but my deepest grief sits now with Stagget. I know that my father lies at peace in the knowledge that I shall avenge him. But Stagget must live each day knowing that no vengeance, however great, will erase his daughters' pain."

Nor your own, cousin? The question slipped through Bydawine's mind, but he did not give it voice. It was this same young man who, not so many cycles past, had stalked the halls of Wigram Keep behind a facade of studied indifference, awaiting the *yazel*'s return. And it was this young warrior who drank the most and sang the loudest when the marriage broker returned with Oray's acceptance and Stagget's approval of the offered betrothal. Bydawine considered what a useless burden life would become if Noressa were ever taken from him. He dropped his hand to the other's wrist and squeezed, willing strength and comfort to his cousin.

Norwick breathed deeply and squared his shoulders. He forced a smile. "But that is why I have come, Bydawine. Stagget will have his revenge and none will gainsay it. He knows that to wait for the council is useless, so we leave at once for Sidra."

Bydawine stared. "Now?"

"This very moment," Norwick assured him. "We have been ready these many weeks. There are barges built and measures of ferry line. Our men are sick to death of drills and polished weapons and mock swordplay. Naught but the final decision to go has kept us here, and you have made that decision for us, cousin."

"But Lord Drut—" Bydawine protested. "He will not permit us to leave. And what of Lord Kreth and his magician?"

Norwick shrugged. "A portion of my army and Stagget's will stand against Lord Drut while the rest cross. As for Azber . . ." He shrugged again. "We must leave that to you, cousin, for we have no other magician."

Norwick stood, readiness in his stance. Bydawine merely sat, his gaze switching alternately from the men before him to the unconscious guards on the floor.

I cannot match this magician. He will destroy me. The knowledge was a cold certainty in him. But he wouldn't let the others know about his fear. He might prevail long enough to allow Brameth and the others to return to Sidra. He kept his seat on the bed and held Norwick with a stern look.

"Cousin, are you certain this is the path you would choose? To go against your comrades and the king's man is treason, and once past, it cannot be undone." Bydawine gestured at the room and to the window, where night's blackness had paled to murky gray. "If you leave now, you will never return."

Norwick fingered the green and white sash tied at his waist, the badge of his new rank as lordholder. "It will be difficult to leave all that is loved and familiar. My name—and yours, cousin—will be stricken from the rolls of the land. We shall be as hated and feared as a chidd in the cradle. But we have each taken a vow, knowing this might be the outcome." His words were solemn, his lips curling up in a bitter humor. "So I say, let us bear our disgrace with honor, eh, cousin? Let us travel as free soldiers under a new banner, a white serpent on a green field. We will begin a new life in a new land as warriors of the chidd."

The men of Drael murmured in excitement. All doubt fled, and Bydawine sprang from the bed to clasp Norwick's wrist.

"A new life, cousin! And one that is well omened!"

Candles were quickly extinguished, and Norwick led them from the room down the great stair. Moving along the steps, Bydawine tried to shrug off the feeling of some impending act. The air felt thick, as though a fine powder were sifting down, but all was clear around him.

"Where are the guards?" he whispered to Norwick. "We should have encountered more patrols by now." But it was obvious the young lord knew no more than he.

It seemed they would pass unmolested through the eerie silence of the keep, but coming upon the landing at the second level, they beheld two men staring down into the courtyard from an open window.

Heart drumming painfully, Bydawine recognized the gray robes and bald head of the elder, Azber. He was certain his moment of confrontation had come when Azber turned to observe them in cool appraisal. Yet the magician remained silent and, after a long moment, turned back to the window.

Beside the magician, swathed in the scarlet robe of his office, Lord Kreth gazed into the emptiness of the brightening sky. When Kreth slowly faced their group, Bydawine felt the men of Drael tense around him. He knew they were calculating their chances of quietly overcoming the pair, and Bydawine already knew the futility of such a move.

It was Norwick who initiated the first action. Motioning the others to remain, he stepped forward and greeted the king's man. "Good morrow, Lord Kreth. Considering last eve's late hours, I hadn't expected you to rise so early."

A thin smile fluttered at Kreth's lips. "There was a time, Lord Norwick, when I was but your age, that such hours were common to me. And your father." Lord Kreth let his gaze wander again to the sky. "You are much like him, Norwick. A handsome youth abounding with energy and devotion to duty."

"True, Lord Kreth, I have my devotion, but it is sometimes difficult to be certain of my duty. Is it to vows given in good faith in times past? Or to what a man believes is right, though that belief may turn him against all he holds dear?"

"A difficult question. And the answer is none easier. Ponder the traveler who stands at the fork and must choose a path. Both are correct, yet either will be wrong."

"And how will he choose?" Norwick asked.

Lord Kreth turned from the window, shaking his head. "It is a decision each traveler must make alone." Kreth moved past Norwick, once more leaning on Azber's arm, and began to climb the stairs. The men of Drael stepped back, and Kreth, looking neither to left nor right, passed through the gauntlet of Sidrian prisoners.

Bydawine watched them disappear up the stairs and listened to the eerie silence washing down around them. Suddenly comprehension flooded his mind. He hurried down the remaining stairs, eager to verify his suspicion. He laughed aloud at the sight that met them at the bottom of the great stair.

Slumped against walls and furnishings, sprawled in hallways and across thresholds, the men of Brazel Drut slept in quiet repose. In the council hall, Lord Stagget came to meet them, embracing both Norwick and Bydawine and touching wrists with each man of Sidra. He returned their arms and possessions taken from them at the river but could not explain the slumber of the Tarragon men.

"It is the same throughout the keep," he told them. "All of the Tarragon clan is in the same state." He raised a questioning brow at Bydawine, who shook his head.

"It is not my magic, lord. I have not the power. This is the elder's handiwork. Only those who would oppose us are touched by the enchanting."

Norwick glanced upward and smiled. "Lord Kreth has chosen his path."

* * * * *

The day passed quickly. After the first wild crossing, when a small barge was sent to establish a ferry line, all went smoothly. Two more lines were set up, and the three barges crossed again and again with troops, mounts, and supplies. It was nearing evening when Bydawine prepared for the final return to Sidra. Mounted on a war-trained Dromund kifera, he went in search of Norwick. He found his cousin on the farthest ferry ramp, speaking earnestly with Stagget.

"Bydawine." Norwick waved him closer. "It has been decided that Lord Stagget will remain in Dromund. Perhaps together he and Lord Kreth may yet convince the king of our loyalty."

Bydawine was both eager to begin the crossing and loath to leave his home again. But he nodded and managed a proper response as Stagget bid him a safe journey. Then the last items were loaded and they began the final crossing.

Once landed, Bydawine sat his mount and supervised the last of the army's kifera and camp followers being unloaded onto Sidrian land. Across the river, Stagget raised an arm in a last farewell. With Norwick and Brameth beside him, Bydawine responded in kind. Afterward, he rode his beast through the milling army in silence, turning once for a last glimpse at the life he had relinquished. Then he looked only eastward, to his new, self-chosen future.

CHAPTER 22

I t was sometime after dark when Bydawine and the rear portion of the army caught up with the forward group. They made camp only two measures from the river, but it was far enough that the army would not be caught against the river should they be attacked during the night.

When Bydawine and Norwick finally sat down to a hot meal, Bydawine's exhaustion overcame his excitement and he couldn't eat. He had been two days and a night without sleep, and when Norwick offered to share his tent, Bydawine accepted at once, curling himself into the first bedroll he stumbled over.

It seemed but an instant later that someone shook him. Bydawine groaned and tried to roll away. He pulled the warm blankets farther over his head and muttered an obscenity. Shaken again, he reached an arm to flail at the bothersome intruder. That only gave his adversary an opening, and Bydawine felt his blankets jerked away. At last the urgent words being repeated in his ear cut through his sleep fog.

"Wake, Bydawine, wake! A runner comes with news of your queen!"

"What? Noressa? Here?" Bydawine squinted up, recognizing Norwick in the light of an oil lamp.

"No, cousin. A runner. And he brings ill tidings."

Bydawine was out of his bedroll and into his boots before his eyes were accustomed to the lamplight. It was still dark as he hurried behind Norwick to a ring of men gathered at a cookfire.

Kneeling on the ground, a young man trembled. His breath came in ragged gasps. Clearly he had run beyond his endurance. In the unclear light, the man's features were vague, undefined, but there was nothing vague about the distress of the men around him.

"What is it?" Bydawine demanded. "What has happened?"

Jatrae, standing with Culric, stared at Bydawine, despair filling his eyes. "The lady Noressa has been taken. The mistress has her!"

"Impossible! How could she have known where Noressa was hiding?"

"She never left the village," Brameth said, both hands clenched on the thick handle of his battle-axe.

"Is this true?" Bydawine demanded of the runner.

The man paused in his gulping from a bowl of water. He hung his head, his hands shaking so that the water spilled over the sides of the bowl, splashing onto the earth like great tears. "It is true." His voice was low and harsh. "You were not long gone, and we were preparing to depart, when they came upon us. From nowhere, as in the Battle of Heroes. We had no defense. I was dispatched at once to warn you."

Bydawine's mind raced with questions. How could he not have known such a thing? Surely Noressa would have called to him in the mindspeak. Had she no intimation of the coming danger as before? And what of Medwyn?

Something was wrong. Bydawine couldn't accept the totality of his sudden fear. He pressed close to the runner. "It took our party of twenty men only two days to reach the river. Since then we have spent a night and a day in Dromund and ferried an entire army across the river. If you left so soon after us, why has it taken you three and a half days to reach us?"

The man cowered away, one arm raised before his face as if expecting to be struck. "There is terrible magic abroad. I could trust no one and spent much time hiding from those I might have called friend. Nothing is what it seems."

"And what of the queen's magician?" Bydawine demanded. "Where is Medwyn?"

Still hiding behind his arm, the boy's words were muffled but unmistakable. "Dead . . . bested by Tylek."

Something cold and sour twisted inside Bydawine. He looked to Brameth. "We must leave at once. A small group of your best men."

Brameth nodded. "They'll make for Castle Ac'talzea. The

witch's power is strongest there."

Bydawine turned to Norwick. "I'll go with Brameth. Our small band will travel quickly. The mistress will have a large contingent to protect her, and that will slow them. We should overtake them in two days at most. Our band will hold them until you and the army can arrive. Jatrae will lead you."

He didn't wait to hear either his cousin's reply or Jatrae's protest at being left behind. Their group was gone before full morning.

Brameth led them. He chose paths that allowed them to move at a steady trot while maintaining some secrecy of their passing. As he guided his kifera behind Brameth's, Bydawine's thought sped ahead of them.

Tylek and Felaya, together. The war was finally begun, but it was Felaya who had struck first, catching them unprepared. Now they must intercept Felaya before she reached the castle. Once behind its protecting walls, she and Noressa would be forever out of reach.

But she will not harm Noressa before then, Bydawine told himself, or she would have done it already.

They made good progress during the morning. Near midday, they met a hunter, who assured them that the mistress had passed through the area only a few measures east the day before. Hearing that, Bydawine argued for more speed and urged that they cut across country. Brameth refused.

"That would only add distance. We know where they go. We are not trying to catch them. We must cut ahead and prevent them from reaching the keep."

Bydawine had to be content with the other man's logic. Brameth knew the land better than he. But that didn't stop his worry, and he followed blindly, thinking dark thoughts of Medwyn dead and Noressa alone among her enemies. Every little while, he reached out in the mindspeak, but there was never a reply.

It is only the great distance between us, he consoled himself. Only the distance. His fear would accept no other consideration.

Not until late afternoon did they recognize the first trap.

Just before entering a small stand of trees, Brameth reigned his mount. He pointed to a clump of nius fern growing thick at the base of an osfo. "We have passed this place before. More than once." When Bydawine looked askance, Brameth motioned ahead to a small thicket of young quenners. "Beyond the trees are swayle brush. After will come a clear space, then tohl and needleflower."

They rode forward, and when the swayle brush gave way to the flower patch, Bydawine swore under his breath. Now that the aberration had been pointed out to him, he could feel the delicate hint of magic around them. It was an excellent trap. And preoccupied with his own toughts, he would have retraveled the circle again and again without noticing it.

The spell was a simple one, an enchantment of misdirection, and one that he banished easily. But the simplicity of removing it did nothing to ease his anger at having been fooled. It was clear he must forego his self-pity and stay alert, for there would be other such traps. Already his incompetence had gained Felaya valuable time.

Yet there was some small reward in the incident. Brameth was also clearly angry with himself for having been fooled. For the rest of the day, they rode hard, sacrificing stealth for speed. They came upon one other misdirection, and Bydawine led them through it easily. They stopped after dark, only for the sake of their mounts, and made a cold camp.

Sitting in the silent company of the others, Bydawine forced himself to eat his ration of bread and dried meat. He had no appetite, but he knew he couldn't afford to be weak with hunger when they caught Felaya. He forced himself to take heart in the sweetness of the osfo's blossom and the natural beauty around him. Noressa had negated Felaya's spell of slow death over Sidra and brought life back to the countryside. So long as the land bloomed, he was certain Noressa still lived.

With the first hint of dawn, he was the first to wake. Within moments, their group was again under way.

They traveled nearly the full day without incident. The sun was still a handspan above the horizon when they came upon a battlefield. It was a small glade, trampled and littered with bodies. Leather-clad rebel fighters embraced the armored bodies of soldiers, comrades in death. Trees were blasted, and deep, smoking holes were gouged into the earth by wizard's fire. They were cut so recently, the hair rose on Bydawine's arms and he tasted the metallic sharpness of the magic.

Brameth stared down at the bodies, and Bydawine saw eagerness blaze in his eyes. "The insignia of Eksorm! Our fighters held Tylek's own men here!"

Bydawine rose in his stirrups, every fiber of him responding to the residue of magic and death. "Noressa must have fought with them! Who else could even hope to match Tylek's power?"

Brameth raised a hand for silence then and stared deep into the trees, listening. They all listened. From far away came a sound, not of forest life, but of life all the same. Culric's sharp ears defined it first.

"It is Kaer's Ballad of Victory! Our men! And they come this way!"

No mount was spared as their group raced to meet the band of victors. They burst upon the singing rebels amidst the trees, and a shout of welcome went up from both groups. Bydawine scrubbed with ashamed relief at the stinging that blurred his eyes when he saw Noressa. Riding on the shoulders of the rebel throng, she brandished a bloodied sword and raised her voice in the victory song.

Bydawine sidled his kifera among the crowd to come near her bearers. "Noressa, the powers be thanked, you are well. I had nearly given up hope."

But she seemed not to hear him, her gaze held on the riders still ahead of her. Only when Bydawine leaned far out to pluck at her sleeve did she turn to him, beaming a smile that included him with half the crowd. Then her attention reverted to the men dismounting ahead. She signaled to be released and dropped lightly to the ground. With a cry of joy, she hurried to the front of the mob. Bydawine watched, embarrassed and confused, as she flung herself into the embrace of an astonished Brameth.

A shout of approval went up from the host of rebel fighters. The band of riders was enveloped in an exchange of happy greetings. Noressa clung to Brameth with an ardor Bydawine had never seen. She clasped her arms about his waist and buried her face against his chest, her body shaking with sobs.

Bydawine could only stare. He had never suspected the depth of the attraction between the two. Nor had Brameth, apparently, from the surprise that was written on his face. He held her with uncertainty, his large hands resting lightly on her shoulders.

Perhaps she is merely glad to be free of Tylek and the mistress, Bydawine tried to convince himself. He rode closer to hear what was said as Noressa quelled her tears and raised her face to Brameth. But Noressa expressed herself without words.

She reached up and pulled Brameth's face down to hers for a kiss that was long and deep.

Bydawine felt his face grow hot. Color drained from his sight. An angry buzz sounded in his ears, and he was suddenly swallowing hard against feelings that were both sour and dangerous. He would have whipped his mount away to escape that scene, but he was held in place by the throng of men. Another shout of approval went up from the crowd. Noressa stepped back, blushing as if only now realizing she and Brameth were not alone. Bydawine turned his face from the sight.

At last there was a quieting of the men's exuberance, and Bydawine forced himself to look at Noressa again. She clung to Brameth's arm, signaling for silence and smiling at them all.

"I cannot tell you of my joy at being once more among my friends. I thank you all for your courage."

Over Noressa's head, Brameth met Bydawine's gaze. The bewilderment in the warrior's eyes helped to blunt the sharp edge of Bydawine's sudden anger. A cheer went up from the men at Noressa's words, but she waved it down.

"Now we must care for the wounded and divide our spoils."

Spoils? Bydawine expected wounded in a battle against such adversaries as Tylek and Felaya. But what spoils could there be?

He followed as Noressa led the way toward the rear of the column. He couldn't help watching the gentle sway of her body, the graceful way she moved through the dappled light of the forest. A chance ray of sunlight picked out the blue-black glint in the dark hair that hung loose to her waist. Shadows pressed close, seeming to blur her form's outline. But when she turned her head and smiled in his direction, there was nothing unclear about her. Then she stopped and greeted the injured who hobbled along or were carried in a line of wagons.

Pulled by sleek, spirited draft beasts, the wagons were of fine construction and loaded with goods enough to supply three villages. In murmurs and half-sentences, Bydawine caught snatches of conversation between his riders and the conquering rebels.

" . . . men from every village . . ."

" . . . tracking was easy; we followed Jaaben's stink."

" . . . Lady Noressa, who turned the battle in our favor. Greater magic than the mistress!"

Bydawine felt no answering joy in his men's laughter at the stories of soldiers turning tail once they were abandoned by Tylek and Felaya.

He listened to these things and watched Brameth attempt to disengage his arm from Noressa. At her look of displeasure, Brameth bowed slightly and waved a hand at the caravan.

"I must see that a suitable place is found to make camp. We will need space for the tents and water for the beasts."

Noressa wrinkled her nose and reclaimed his arm. "Then let someone else go. I need you here. What if Tylek's men should return?"

"You will be protected, my lady," Brameth assured her. "Your men will fight for you again, should the need arise. He looked toward Bydawine, eyes pleading. "And surely you are anxious to speak with Counselor Bydawine. Let him tell you of his army, and I shall return shortly."

The pouting left her face, and Noressa looked at Bydawine with genuine interest. "You were successful in raising an army in Dromund." It was more statement than question.

"Yes." Bydawine couldn't understand his discomfort now that he had her attention. "That is why we returned so quickly. They follow even now. When we heard of your abduction, our group came ahead to slow Felaya until they could arrive. A man will be sent to guide them here, and they should arrive before the morrow's eve."

"That will be time enough," she murmured, looking thoughtful. She smiled at Brameth. "I see you are right in this. Let us make camp soon, for there is much to be done."

Brameth tried to hide his relief. He bowed once more and sent Bydawine a questioning look as he moved away into the crowd. But Bydawine had no answers, only more questions that he was hesitant to speak. Now he watched with reluctance as Brameth left. He was uncomfortable with this victorious Noressa. Still, his nagging curiosity forced him to draw her attention. "Noressa, I must ask—"

She turned from watching Brameth's departure, the vague smile on her lips again. "I know you will have many questions, Bydawine, but let them wait until another time. I am too weary now."

She turned and made her way to a nearby wagon. Wrapping herself in an embroidered coverlet, she settled back on the wagon seat, eyes closed. Bydawine let her go and tried to understand his relief at her snubbing.

Brameth was not long in returning, and Noressa immediately commanded that he ride beside her wagon. She made no effort to hide her displeasure that he took every opportunity to move back and forth along the column to be sure all was well. Bydawine rode behind their wagon, close enough that he might watch Noressa, but far enough that he couldn't hear what passed between her and Brameth.

In time, they came to the campsite, a small meadow with a brook laughing through it. Once arrived, Brameth rode off to personally supervise the raising of the tents and shelters carried in the wagons. When Brameth left, Bydawine took himself to the edge of the meadow. He sat alone while the men scurried about erecting the camp. Evening shadows covered three-fourths of the clearing. Fading sunlight was still warm on the opposite side of the meadow, but on his edge of the glade, night was already falling. In the darkened forest behind him, a single nightpeeper began its staccato trill. It was that short interval of twilight when the last of the day creatures secreted themselves and the night creatures were not yet emerged: the time of change. It was usually a time Bydawine enjoyed, but this night he felt strained, his perspective disjointed. He fretted over a dozen prickly wonderings, but couldn't settle on a single thought.

His solitude was broken when Culric drew up beside him. After a short silence, Culric waved at the forest around them. "Sentries have been posted, though I don't fear the return of any of Tylek's men." Bydawine nodded. He could sense the other's tension. When Culric spoke again, Bydawine knew the man chose his words carefully.

"The lady Noressa must have suffered a mighty ordeal in her capture. She seems—" he hesitated—"most joyful to be among us again."

So! It was not only his jealousy. Others noticed a strangeness in her. A memory plucked at him, unable to voice itself through his fatigue. When he spoke, Bydawine didn't know whether his words were excuse or argument to Culric's. "The lady has been through many ordeals this past cycle."

Culric nodded, and silence held between them until he murmured an excuse and departed. Bydawine remained at the meadow's edge until night had completely fallen. The darkness was a comfortable mantle. Swathed in its softness, unseen by any, there was no need to act. He couldn't even remember clearly what action he had intended; it was easier to let the gentle pressure of the night push the worry from his mind. He sat in the darkness and watched the camp settle itself for the night.

The tents of Felaya's routed entourage crowded the field like a herd of great humpbacked beasts. The glory of their tumultuous colors—scarlet, azure, verdant greens, even cloth-of-gold—was dissolved in the darkness. Only where the leaping flames of a cookfire, or dim lamplight from within, illuminated some small patch of cloth was their opulence revealed.

Centered in the gathering of cloth castles, one stood apart from the others. Larger and crowned with a ring of pennants that snapped unseen in the night breeze, that tent sat alone on an island of darkness. There was no cookfire before it, and only the dim light of a single oil lamp inside gave the red-and-gold-striped tent any form at all. And it was to this tent that Bydawine's gaze was drawn and held, to this tent that he himself was drawn, his mount carrying him past the first few fires before he was aware that he had urged it forward.

The smells of roasting meat and hot journey bread wafted around him. Someone called out, bidding him join their feast. Only the sudden cessation of movement pulled his attention from the center tent. Bydawine looked down to find Coris holding his kifera's bridle, Culric beside him.

"Master Bydawine, come dine with us," Culric invited.

Bydawine hesitated. His gaze moved from the men beside him to the tent that beckoned ahead, the place where *she* waited. He was drawn, yet he did not want to go.

A touch at his boot brought his attention back to Culric, and Bydawine managed a tight smile. "Perhaps I will join you. There is much I would speak of to Brameth. He shares your fire this night?" There were uneasy glances and a shuffling of boots; Coris dropped hold of the bridle. "He does not, then?" Bydawine heard the strain in his own voice.

"He does, yes. But—" Bydawine watched Culric draw a quick breath, head the quick, monotone words. "The lady called him to her tent, and he has not returned."

Yes. Bydawine did remember seeing Brameth enter the main tent shortly before dark, but he hadn't seen the rebel leader exit. Jealousy seared through his belly. Without a word, he kicked his mount forward.

Pulling up before the entrance to the center tent, he was met by two rebel fighters, both unknown to him. "Inform the lady Noressa that I would speak with her—and with Brameth."

The men smiled politely, but neither moved to relay his message. The taller of them spread his hands in a sign of helplessness. "I am sorry, *dajon*, but Master Brameth has long since departed and the lady has retired."

Bydawine felt his anger seething toward a dangerous new level. He hadn't mistaken the tone of mockery in the man's use of the respectful title *dajon*, nor their obvious deceit. For an instant, his old attitudes writhed at the edge of his mind, the old embarrassment at his misshapen body, the remembered pain of whispered asides and averted glances as he passed.

Then he caught hold of his anger and held it as an invisible shield. These mannerless whelps are no better than I! He could force his way in, cause an uproar that would bring Noressa out to him. But he hesitated. There was more than one way to handle such matters.

Nodding to the men as if in acceptance, Bydawine turned and rode back the way he had come. At the edge of the camp, he dismounted and worked his way around the camp until he stood at the rear of Noressa's tent. He crept forward carefully, lest he meet another guard in the dark, but there was no one. Only the night sounds and the murmur of nearby voices.

The voices came from the tent before him, one a woman's soft laugh, and the other a deep rolling sound that Bydawine recognized too well. Lamplight cast silhouettes on the cloth wall, one small and slim, the other tall. He watched the smaller of the shadows move forward until the two merged for a long, silent moment. Then the smaller form stepped away and, reaching upward, extinguished the lamp.

For a while, Bydawine stood in the darkness, his mind reeling with thoughts he dared not visualize. Then his anger burst hard upon him, and he was running, stumbling blindly through the camp and out into the shielding maze of forest.

* * * * *

It was nearly dawn when Bydawine returned to the camp. Stumbling into the nearest tent, he collapsed into an empty sleeping roll. It was full day when the sounds of shouting and the thunder of many kifera pads woke him.

He staggered into glaring daylight and found himself surrounded by his army. Norwick rushed to him, concern clouding his face.

"Cousin, what has happened? Have you lost the trail? Are your men not well?"

Blinking to adjust his eyes to the light, Bydawine peered around the empty meadow. Everything was gone. No tents, no wagons, no rebel compatriots.

And no sign of Noressa.

Most of his men still sprawled in a half-stupor amongst their bedrolls. A whisper of magic faded, his men began to rouse, and Bydawine shook off the final dregs of the sleep spell that had been shattered by Norwick's noisy arrival. Brameth staggered up to stand beside him.

"Were you bewitched as well?" Norwick's words tugged at Bydawine's mind. When Bydawine did nothing but stare, his cousin nodded, saying, "It must be so." He laid a steadying hand on Bydawine's shoulder. "The runner who brought the news of your queen was *ne-alit*. He spilled the wine we gave him; his meal was found uneaten. Two of my officers came upon him by surprise, and one claimed he had no mouth. The other says the man was blind."

"Of course!" Understanding dawned in Bydawine. "No matter what the skill of the conjurer, there will always be something not quite right. And none of us ever saw his face!" He smiled. "That must be what happened to us as well. Surely last night's apparition was none other than Felaya herself." He looked at the empty field again. "But what was to be gained from it? None of our mounts or supplies are gone." Joy thrilled his heart. "If it was all shadow magic, then Noressa is safe and well. And she did not—" He took a huge breath, holding back his words of excitement, but his mind shouted his jubilation! Noressa is not the seductress he had seen last night!

Beside him, Brameth groaned and dropped to his knees. He hid his face in his hands. Bydawine stepped toward him, but the rebel drew away. When Brameth at last raised his head, Bydawine caught his breath at the anguish in the giant's face.

"The lady Noressa is lost." Brameth's voice was a harsh whisper. "I—we—" He gestured to where the main tent had stood.

"Truly, I believed her to be the lady Noressa. She spoke of having been given a potion that robbed her of many memories. She begged me to help her recapture those memories. We . . . talked late into the night."

Coldness swept Bydawine. "You told Felaya where Noressa is hidden."

Brameth hung his head, and all the sun's brightness could not pierce the darkness in Bydawine's heart.

* * * * *

Triumph! Felaya exulted in her victory even as exhaustion threatened to overwhelm her. To use that much magic, especially the quick transport back to the keep, would cost her much in personal strength. She would be weak for days and dependent on Tylek's power and those spells already in place. But the price was well paid. The illusion had worked perfectly. By tomorrow, Noressa would be here and under her control.

Felaya gorged on the wine and foods spread before her, but she savored her success more than any delicacy. Then she stumbled to her bed. As the maid undressed her and began rubbing warm oil into her skin, Felaya thought of another's touch.

Brameth.

She remembered his gentleness as he caressed her, his battle to curb his great strength as their fervor grew, the explosion of his love as they became one.

That he loved Noressa was without doubt. But she, Felaya, had stolen the first taste of that love. The memory of that theft was a lingering sweetness on her tongue.

CHAPTER 23

Noressa cast a longing glance through the open cottage door. Half a measure down the hillside came the bright reflections of afternoon sun as the waters of the narrow Leal River flowed down toward the Tarel Valley. She was restless, and she envied the water its freedom.

Noressa sighed, curling her toes in the silky fur of her daxet-skin slippers. Soreen paused in her stirring of the rich fish stew to send her a concerned glance. "You are well, Noressa?"

"No. I mean, yes, I am well. I am so well that I sicken from it!" There. Her peevishness had slipped out again, and Noressa regretted it at once, seeing the hurt that flashed across Soreen's face. "Forgive me, Soreen, I grow impatient again. Here, let me tend the stew while you prepare the rest of the meal." She took the wooden ladle from the other woman and stirred deep in the pot. Soreen stepped away, understanding in her eyes.

Noressa settled before the fire. Letting the swirl of her stirring smooth away some of her anxiety, she glanced around the cottage. This one was much like the other in Drael, save that the thatch and timber roof and walls abutted a cliff of hard, red dirt. Thus, while appearing as a small single chamber on the outside, the cottage actually boasted three additional rooms carved from the cliffside. This afforded her the privacy of her own room, which she had lacked in Drael. Soreen and her family occupied one of the remaining two rooms, and Medwyn the third. This gave their household the feel of a true family.

Family. The word brought a quick picture of her mother, Rina, humming as she worked a batch of bread dough, and her father emerging from the forest, a string of daxets or a brace of meirmeks swinging from one hand. And the many questions she carried of her true parents came spilling in once more. The loneliness and fear came, too.

I have been blessed with two families and lost both. Now I have had the great fortune to acquire a third. Shall I lose this one as well? No, she scolded herself. Such thoughts are self-defeating! But her mood was difficult to break.

The six days since Bydawine's departure had seemed to crawl. Only the half-day journey from Drael to this tiny village had been worthwhile. Then her relief at finally moving in a positive action gave way too soon to the frustration of boredom and inactivity in her new prison.

Prison? Is that a way to think of the protection and fealty your people give you? But the sense of confinement would not be shaken. If she walked out-of-doors, she was accompanied by either Heska or Soreen and at least a hand's count of soldiers. Indoors, she was treated as though she had already assumed the throne. Soreen and Heska waited on her every need. Only grudgingly was she allowed to help with simple tasks such as sweeping the cottage floor or cleaning vegetables.

Noressa wanted to scream and stamp her feet. Why couldn't they see that because of all that was on her mind, she needed some activity to make her forget? But she couldn't speak of it without raving, and she wouldn't allow herself to become hysterical. So she held her tongue and spent much of her time alone in her room.

Often she reviewed the sorceries Medwyn had taught her. But as often, she sat quietly, searching out the source of a strange power that teased at her. This was something new. It was unlike the painful intrusion of the Other or the familiar mindspeak of Medwyn and Bydawine. This was a thing she knew to be a definite part of herself. It was a force more potent than the simple alchemies or levitations Medwyn had shown her.

She stared unseeing into the stew, the whorls and eddies of the creamy mixture matching the vague thoughts curling through her mind when she tried to lay hold of this new thing. It was of such a strangeness and wonder that she had kept the secret of it, not even confiding its presence to Medwyn.

Soreen brushed by, her passage bringing Noressa back to the job at hand. Noressa leaned forward to inspect the stew. Satisfied with its consistency, she swung the pot on the long metal arm far enough from the fire that it would stay hot without becoming scorched. That done, she found herself again with nothing to do, and her troubles pressed themselves to her.

The day before, a runner had brought word that Bydawine had returned from Dromund with an army and was on his way to her. There were rumors that his army brought wagonloads of exotic foods and weapons of fine, hardened steel. Bohsra himself had set off downriver that morning to supervise the portage of troops and supplies.

"Return quickly, Bydawine. I am anxious to be done with this waiting." Her words were whispered to no one in particular, yet she glanced about, fearful that some capricious spirit might hear and cause Bydawine to suddenly appear. She *was* anxious for his return. But she knew that whatever plans she had made to complete her *aramil* first, nothing would be accomplished until she came against Felaya. Her self-doubt increased the nearer she came to facing her aunt.

Would the strength of her newly acquired sorcery be a match for Felaya's experience? How many of the people she had come to love would die because of her inept blunderings in magic? But a fear worse than that of her own death was the possibility that she might never unravel the mystery of the summoning.

Her mind brushed that thought, and the summoning wrenched at her. Noressa clapped her hands to her head against the sudden pain. Never before had there been such a desperation in the call. The pain cut through her mind like a knife.

Soreen's frantic voice penetrated through her agony, and Noressa heard the sound of her own crying. She clung to Soreen, fighting to push away the pain, but the summons came keening into her mind, and Noressa scarcely heard Soreen shrilling for Medwyn before all went black.

* * * * *

She woke to cool darkness. The smell of earth and the scratchy coverlet told her she was in her bed in the tiny room hollowed out of the cliff.

Someone sat on the edge of her cot, and at her first movement, a hand stroked her brow. The skin was warm, the touch soothing. She recognized Medwyn's outline in the pale light shining around the curtain hanging in the doorway.

Noressa closed her eyes and let his gentle touch ease her into dreamy peacefulness. She was tired beyond exhaustion. The summoning seemed to have burned itself out in that final blaze of pain, and her mind was blessedly empty.

She realized where her thoughts had drifted and started up in terror. Medwyn firmly pressed her back to the cot, his voice low and compelling, urging her to rest.

The summoning. She tried, but could think of nothing else and lay stiff, waiting for her agony to begin once more. But after long moments, the only pain was that of a cramp in her leg. She relaxed.

"Tell me what has happened," Medwyn said, removing his hands from her shoulders.

Not sure of how much she could say, Noressa spoke. Slowly, fearful that the hysteria would overtake her again, she told him of the summoning's painful compulsion, and of her fears that she was not fit to rule or sit at the head of an army. She told him of being afraid that her magic would bring more destruction than healing to those she loved. "I am only a child, Medwyn. I know more of games and stories than of battles and potions." He made no reply, letting her talk out all her demons of self-doubt.

When she had done, Noressa let herself lie in the darkness, savoring her relief that the story was told and no horrors had seized her. She felt Medwyn move from the bedside, heard him settle on the stool next to her cot.

"Until now, I hadn't realized this call was of such importance to you."

"It was the reason I began my journey in the first place," Noressa answered, sitting up. "Not because Edell brought the amulet. Had it not brought me in the direction I wanted to go, I would have buried it with her. From the beginning, I have wanted only to find the place where I belong. But until I answer the summoning, I will never know peace."

She strained to see him, but could only make out a faint shape in the light gleaming through the blanketed doorway.

Still, she knew how he would look, sitting very straight on the stool, arms crossed, the fingers of his left hand drumming his upper right arm. His face would be grave, a distant, inward look to his eyes, the left corner of his mouth turned down.

He was so like her father, stern and unyielding in matters he thought important, but generous in giving deserved praise, or patient in matters that would have sent most fathers searching for a whipping stick.

Medwyn was quiet a long while, then sighed. "I do not know how we shall explain this to Bohsra."

Noressa shivered. "Nor do I. But it must be done." She balked at facing his anger again so soon. His resistance to even letting Bydawine go for reinforcements had been almost impossible to overcome. What would he say now? But Noressa knew that answer and shivered again. "Perhaps it would be best if I left and said nothing."

"Mmm." The sound carried its own picture. Noressa imagined Medwyn's brows arched in that expression of judicious questioning. Had she examined alternative paths? Was time given to consider the effects of her proposal on others who would be a part of it?

No, her mind answered. And no again. She was acting purely on impulse, as Bydawine would have quickly pointed out.

And what of Bydawine? she asked herself. What would he say when he returned to this stinger's nest with an army, only to find her gone and no war to fight?

"But it is not as though I am abandoning my throne," she protested aloud. "I am merely setting it aside for a time. And the people will need a defense until then, so an army will not stand idle waiting for me."

Yes, Bydawine would be angry. And he would not understand. But she had no doubt he would support her. That idea comforted her more than thoughts of any army or magic power.

She let herself lie down again, as Medwyn's touch on her shoulder urged her back down on the cot. His words were soft in the darkness. "Rest now, and we will speak of it later." His fingers brushed lightly across her forehead.

When she woke later, Noressa couldn't remember having

gone to sleep, but she felt stronger, once more in control of herself.

Medwyn still occupied the low stool beside the bed. When she was fully awake, he patted her hand and rose. "It is good that you were able to rest. I will send Mistress Soreen to attend you."

He departed, and a moment later Soreen entered, bearing a single candle. "The elder says you are improved. Shall I bring you some food?"

Noressa was sitting up, searching in the dark for her long boots. In the sudden light, she found them and pulled them on, pleased to see that her fingers didn't fumble over the lacings. She hesitated, then shook her head. She was hungry, but she had no desire for food. It was company she wanted. "Thank you, but, no. I would rather just sit with friends now." She looked up and was rewarded by a lessening of the worry in Soreen's eyes.

Boots done, Noressa stood. "Has Bohsra returned?"

"Not yet. But he is expected soon."

Noressa didn't look forward to their coming confrontation, but she was sure now of what must be done and would let nothing stop her. In silence, she preceded Soreen into the main room.

Doors and windows were closed and barred, marking the hour at some time past dusk. Khelcri was deep in conversation with Medwyn before the fire. He looked her way as she entered, and his expression told her that Medwyn had already informed him of her decision. Concern and surprise were in his face, but no reproach.

Does he trust me so much that he will accept anything I do? And what of the others? Noressa wondered. She took a deep, quick breath, trying to ease the sudden tightness in her chest, and looked away from Khelcri. Such loyalty was only one of the many responsibilities pressing on her. I will bring much pain to these people.

Khelcri rose, offering her his place on the bench before the fire, but Noressa declined, settling herself on a stool in a corner. She rested against the rough wall timber behind, closed her eyes, and let her mind drift. Soon she heard the dry shuffle of small feet across the packed dirt floor and felt the presence of someone nearby. She opened her eyes.

Grantha stood beside her, studiously chewing the end of a tawny curl, watching her with wide topaz eyes. Noressa held out her arms and the child scrambled into her lap.

Noressa hugged Grantha close and thought briefly of the others who would not share tonight's game. She missed the nightly crowd of children who gathered to be awed by the marvels she conjured. Noressa enjoyed the evenings as much as the little ones, and she found it a pleasant way to practice design and control of her illusion weaving. But, unlike Drael, there were few children in this exile. And none were allowed out after darkfall. For this little while, then, she would perform only for Grantha. The touch of loneliness that had crept into her heart more and more she thrust away, along with the demands and cares of her many problems. For the next short while, she and Grantha would spend their time in seeking only pleasure.

Noressa hugged Grantha once more. The girl nestled close and smiled, waiting to begin their game. Noressa whispered, "Did you find any magic today?"

Grantha responded with a solemn nod and reached into the pocket of her skirt. With great ceremony, she placed the retrieved object into Noressa's hand. Together they stared at the tiny gray pebble Noressa held.

"What kind of magic does it hold?" Noressa asked.

Grantha shrugged, never looking away from the stone.

"Well," Noressa began, "if you do not know, how—"

She stopped in mock surprise. The stone was pulsing with a pale, gray-blue glow. The color brightened and the stone jerked. It grew until it filled Noressa's hand. A loud crack sounded and the rock split in half. Shafts of vivid blue light streamed upward, and the stone crumbled to ash. The column of brilliance struck the thatched ceiling and spread. Gray, blue, black, pristine white, it roiled and foamed above them until it covered the entire room. Noressa felt Grantha shiver with delighted terror as miniature lightning crackled only a few feet overhead and distant thunder rumbled somewhere in the cloud's heart. Then the cloud rent itself and sent down a rain of stars.

Silver, red-gold, green, a thousand colors in tiny spangles of brightness blazed down. They skittered across the wide board table, caromed off shelves and pottery, and layered into sparkling mantles on the heads and shoulders of those who sat beneath the deluge.

Grantha sprang down to dance among the piling drifts glimmering on the floor. She snatched up handfuls of the brilliant spangles and hurled them back into the cloud. Her parents watched, joining her laughter, and Medwyn waited patiently for the display to end. Noressa let herself catch Grantha's excitement and for a few moments forgot all that awaited her outside the cottage walls.

Grantha whirled and spun, capering through the rising mounds of rainbow sparks until she dizzied herself and she sat down abruptly on the floor. She watched in wistful silence as the pearl-sheened cloud ceased its rain and drew in on itself until it was gone. The fallen stars faded.

Medwyn and Khelcri resumed their talk. Soreen took up her mending basket and drew a candle nearer her. But Noressa waited, the sidelong glances and restless sighs of the child telling her that their game was not yet ended.

She smiled encouragement until Grantha came to stand at her knee, left hand clutching a second treasure. Noressa accepted the prize, a twig only half a finger in length. Noressa examined it critically, hefted its tiny weight between thumb and forefinger, and shook her head. "I sense no magic here, Grantha." She turned and placed the twig into a knothole of the wall timber behind her.

Grantha dropped her head in disappointment and stood peeking at Noressa from beneath her tumble of curls. Then she was smiling and pointing. Noressa turned, trying to hide her own smile, already knowing what she would find.

Where she had placed the twig, a limb the thickness of her arm jutted from the wall above her head. Its length was dotted with green buds that swelled and burst, sending out a mass of curling tendrils. Each vine weaved through the air, seeking support. Falling to the floor or back onto the wall and taking hold, they grew, sending out new shoots and runners in all directions. Several of the fallen vines writhed across the hard dirt floor to twine themselves around Grantha's ankle. She squealed and scurried to the safety of Noressa's lap. Moments later they were encompassed within a bower of withy vines and saplings.

In rapid succession, new buds appeared, swelled, and burst into flower, filling the room with a sweet frangrance and a riotous jumble of color. The blooms withered and fell, leaving only a heady perfume to mark their passage. Then the fruit began its own pageantry.

Fruits of every kind. Small red lirsa beans, hard green jerjal nuts, even the tangy, thick-skinned korba melons grew long and yellow and ripened before them.

The bower was festooned as a sensory temptation Grantha could not resist. She plucked a grelt berry and popped it into her mouth. Her look of disappointment when she found nothing on her tongue gave Noressa a twinge of guilt. Noressa dropped a kiss on the child's curls and squeezed her tight. "You must remember, Grantha, that my magic cannot make real things. These are only dreams and wishes."

"Only dreams and wishes. We are not real!" The words echoed high and faint in Noressa's ear, and she turned with Grantha to stare, delighted, at the tiny face peering from the tangled vines. The creature's nose, large and hooked, preceded the rest of its face by at least twice its natural length. Bright black eyes twinkled, and a double-pointed beard quivered in time to its cackling laugh.

Noressa looked to Medwyn in amusement, wondering what had tempted him to join their game. But Medwyn was still deep in conversation with Khelcri. She turned back to the little man. Surely this must be the old wizard's magic, for she knew it was not hers.

"Hee! Hee! Only dreams." The tiny man wriggled from his leafy hole and scrambled down the nearest vine. Coming within a handspan of the floor, he sprang outward, then tumbled and twisted in midair to land on his feet, spin once, and bend the knee before them. All the while he caroled a haunting tune that made no sense but was strangely compelling.

Grantha clapped her approval. The sprite gloried in her favor, eyes closed, head tilted to one side. Then he was on his feet again, hands clasped to his heart, gazing longingly at Grantha.

"Oh, beautiful child, worthy child, would that I might

whisk thee away, as well, and teach thee the joys of power and domination. But alas, I am come for another and must fulfill my charge."

His words struck a chill in Noressa. She tightened her grip on Grantha and looked to Medwyn in confusion. Surely he couldn't have meant such a strange speech. Medwyn was watching her with a similar puzzlement. But the creature was speaking again, and his singsong voice demanded her attention. His words were frightening, but their sound was soothing, with rhythms of the song he had been singing moments before. They enveloped her in a cloud of lassitude that numbed the edge of her mind.

"I am dreams, wishes, thoughts. Made of shadows, wants, and naught. Of substance I am bereft, though I come to bear my master a gift." He advanced slowly. Hand outstretched in invitation, he beckoned to Noressa. "Come, sweet girl, pretty girl, enter my master's world."

Noressa felt herself leaning to meet his bright gaze. His eyes were wide and dark, drawing her in. His brassy smile was a challenge she dare not resist. Her world narrowed to a scarlet sphere, a place of flames and song, her only focus the gleaming eyes of the little man. His warbling chant twined through her mind, every note a thrumming silver thread cast round a single thought until her mind was numb and her whole being trembled in time to the haunting sound. This was *power*. Deep within her, it awoke an answering resonance.

As from a distant world, Medwyn's shout of warning came muzzled, incoherent. Like rain against a glass bead, his voice touched and flowed away from the thin crystalline halo the sprite's song cast round her. The tiny man's smile taunted, tempted. And his hand still beckoned.

A faint, familiar voice slipped beneath Medwyn's roar. "Come back! Go not!" Her own—or was it? A small part of her turned away, straining against a single silver note, but the effort was too much. She wondered if she possessed strength enough to resist the sensual caress of the magic imprisoning her, found she did not wish to resist. Noressa felt herself slipping away, a languid ease drawing her down into the heart of the fireball.

Shards of pain exploded through her. She fell to her knees

as the silver threads of song hardened and shattered, catapulting her back into her world, back to the panic of suffocation and a child's piercing scream of terror.

It was Grantha's screams that had brought her back. The child, forgotten in the moment of spellbinding, held Noressa in a death grip about the neck. Her shrieking sounded directly in Noressa's ear. Around them, a circle of flames leapt to the cottage roof, fanning out to cover the entire room. But the dry thatch did not burn, and the flames gave no heat, only an angry, impotent crackle.

Medwyn's voice came from outside the flame, fearful, demanding, enraged. "Refuse him, Noressa! Refuse him! You must not accept him! Refuse! Refuse!"

The sprite still waited, anger in his face now, and demanded her surrender with his song. But Noressa closed her eyes to him, her thoughts refusing him while her hands fumbled to pull Grantha's arms from her neck. At last she loosened the child's grip and drew a shuddering breath. With her first exhalation, she banished the fiend. "Begone, creature of magic! I will not have thee!"

She caught a glimpse of terror in the sprite's face. Then a rush of frigid wind whipped through her as the blazing circle condensed, sucking into a single tight spiral of flame that centered on the creature. There came a flare of fire within fire, a wild shriek, and the whirlwind swirled upward and was gone.

Noressa collapsed to the floor, her mind empty, her body paralyzed. The hard-packed dirt was a cold surprise against her cheek. She felt as if the nonexistent heat of the flames had been trapped within her body, and she closed her eyes, letting the cool dirt pull it from her.

She lay so, unable to move but aware of all that went on about her. She heard Medwyn questioning as he knelt beside her, but could not respond beyond opening her eyes. Khelcri's roar for guards and troops pounded through her, and she watched a terrified Soreen attempt to calm her equally terrified child.

Her helplessness lasted only a few moments. Then strength began flowing back into her limbs in a stinging rush. With Medwyn's help, she was able to sit upright. He held her chin in his hand, forcing her to meet his gaze. A flicker of relief passed over his face when she tried to smile and managed to whisper his name. Then his face closed; tight, hard lines made a mask of the gentle face she had come to know.

"We have been found out." His words were as flat as water-worn stones. And though she had known it from the moment the fiend's song had been shattered, his statement had a withering brand of finality to it.

A shouting that had grown louder around the cottage burst in upon them as the door was flung open and Bohsra entered, followed by a knot of armed men. Medwyn stepped over to meet him, keeping one hand on Noressa's shoulder. "The mistress has found us out and nearly succeeded in taking Noressa."

"No." Noressa shook her head, covering Medwyn's hand with her own. "It was not she, but some other—one I do not know." But the memory of it clenched at her stomach.

Medwyn nodded. "Tylek. I have known the touch of his power before. It was his calling fiend you fought, but he is so much a part of her that it can be said he does not exist. Only his treachery is a separate living thing." Noressa felt Medwyn's hand tremble beneath hers.

Fear? She wondered, and dread tightened the knot inside her. Did Medwyn see this Tylek as more of a danger than Felaya? But when she looked into his face, it wasn't fear she saw, or even anger. His eyes blazed with a fire she had never imagined the elder to possess: the fire of hatred.

She couldn't stop the shivering that seized her. Medwyn bowed his head, regret in his face, and Noressa knew his shame that he had let his pupil see this side of him. She looked away, somehow ashamed of herself for having seen it. But when Medwyn would have pulled his hand back, Noressa rose to stand beside him, slipping her hand into his and holding tight.

Medwyn's face softened, and she felt his answering pressure.

The moment of Medwyn's revelation had been brief and none had missed it, but nothing was said. Instead, Bohsra turned and spoke quietly to the man behind him. Three men nodded and worked their way through the rest of the soldiers to disappear into the torchlit night. Bohsra turned back to

Medwyn. "If we are discovered, then she will not wait. Her full attack will come tonight."

Medwyn agreed. "Had they been successful in taking Noressa, there would have been no fight. But now we are warned, and Felaya will waste little time before she comes to finish her task."

Boshra fingered the broadsword at his belt. "I have sent my captains to prepare the men. We shall be ready. And Master Bydawine and his army are even now being brought upriver from the Tarel Valley. They will be with us before morning."

Joy dissipated some of Noressa's fear. Bydawine here! Tonight! And Brameth!

Bohsra spoke to Khelcri. "Stay with your family. I will leave a quar of men to guard the cottage." Khelcri acknowledged him with a grateful nod as Bohsra left, ushering the rest of the crowd out before him.

An uneasy stillness settled over the village, where time and the night seemed to crawl. Noressa paced before the fire, and Medwyn, wrapped in his own thoughts, sat on the stool Noressa and Grantha had occupied. Soreen rocked Grantha into a troubled sleep from which the child woke several times, whimpering at some nightmare.

The twenty-five men Bohsra sent stood three deep before the cottage, and Khelcri had stepped outside to speak with them when the attack came.

Strangled screams of pain filled the darkness outside. Noressa rushed to fling the door open and stood aghast at the spectacle of drops of fire streaking down upon the village. A sharp hum of magic vibrated the air.

Medwyn pushed past her, incantations on his lips, and a wavering shield of blue appeared over the heads of the scrambling soldiers.

Noressa felt another beside her and found Soreen also staring out on the terrible scene. In one arm, she clutched a wailing Grantha; her other hand was clasped tight around a long-bladed knife. Fear and determination alternated in her face.

Noressa looked again to the shield above them, seeing it begin to fade. She wanted to go to Medwyn, to stand by his side, for she knew this spell and knew that her power could be joined with his to keep the shield strong. But she did not move. The *knowing* raged a warning within. She knew, as horrible as it seemed, that the firestorm was no real danger. The true threat came from another direction. The shouting outside reached a fever pitch as the shield faded away completely and the last of the firedrops found their targets. She heard Bohsra's voice calling encouragement to his men, and she was aware of the press of bodies trapping her within the cottage. But she paid them no heed. .

A familiar touch drew her mind outward toward the wooded stretch of land leading to the river. *Bydawine!* She called to him even as the ground beneath her began to tremble. His answering flash of mindspeak was a jumbled wash of rage and promise. She knew he was very near to reach her so strongly.

Then she felt the return of that cold flame summons of the wizard she had come to fear as much as Felaya. The trembling of the ground became a violent shaking, and Noressa staggered from the force. Soreen was thrown forward against the wall, where she clung to a timber. Medwyn and Khelcri were caught in the mob of soldiers outside. A grinding roar echoed from the mountain that formed the back wall of the cottage. Dust filtered down from the doorway crossbeam as Noressa spun to face the approaching danger behind her. She heard her cry mingled with Soreen's at the spray of rubble and dirt that exploded into the room.

A man, clothed in a black robe shot with silver and scarlet threads, stepped from the mountain. Power radiated in waves from his slender form. He smiled, cool and seductive, in a corona of flame. Too late, Noressa tried to throw up a shield against him, but a movement of his hand sent a swath of vermillion flame to enfold her, and she was frozen where she stood. She couldn't even cry out with her mind for assistance. She stared into bright black eyes and knew this was no demon, but the master himself.

Tylek beckoned, and she could only move toward him as the cold flames rushed in.

CHAPTER 24

At the river, Sidrian rebel forces united with Norwick's army in bloody battle against Tylek's soldiers.

Bydawine plunged through the human chaos, whipping his kifera forward with a short length of knotted rope. Moments before, he had stood, cramped and crowded, with the army on one of the barges bringing them upriver from the Tarel Valley. Forgotten now were both army and barges. There was only one goal in his mind—to reach Noressa. In his frenzy to reach the village, he whipped at mount or men, whichever was quickest at clearing the way. He clamped his jaw tight against the pain of the searing firedrops. He trembled to the magic resonating across the darkness at a silent, bone-shivering pitch. It brought the dry, sharp taste of fear to his tongue.

His fear was a jagged stabbing that hadn't subsided in the hours since the frantic touch of Noressa's mindspeak. That touch came slamming into his thoughts, not a direct call for help, more a muted sigh of despair. The magic she battled had reached through her mind to his, nearly dragging him down into some flame-encircled darkness. To drive that memory from him, he sent a vicious swing of his whip at a pair of men sporting Tylek's ebrot crest.

Ahead, in the village, a wavering shield of blue proclaimed an active magical defense. Too soon the shield faded, was gone. Cries of men, wounded and dying, clawed the edge of his awareness as Bydawine sent out a mind call. At once, he felt the wind's-breath touch of Noressa's mindspeak, but her call was a panicked clamor of warning and defiance. She fought an enemy who bore no face or name. He sent back his reply: *I know the danger. I will soon be with you.*

Her thoughts warned him of the peril. He felt her grappling

among her store of novice magic, searching for some defense against the sorceries raging toward her. The storm of firedrops ended, but now the ground trembled and rolled beneath his kifera. The beast staggered. Bydawine shifted his concentration to managing his mount. In that one instant, he felt Noressa's recognition of her attacker. Tylek! There was a flash of resistance, then resignation, and her mind whirled away in a scarlet haze.

Bydawine felt the link between them snap; his thoughts were thrust back at him. For long moments, he lay against his kifera's neck, trembling in terror.

Noressa was gone! Tylek had her! He knew this before the alarm was shouted through the village. He had felt her disappear into that cold flame of energy.

Bydawine straightened and pressed his mount forward. He must reach Medwyn. Together they must pursue the fiend that had swept Noressa from them.

He gained the edge of the village. The fighting was less intense here as Tylek's men, knowing their goal was accomplished, began pulling back. He moved forward, his attention on Medwyn, who stood with Khelcri before a well-guarded cottage. Not until a band of mounted soldiers were pressing close, cutting him off from the village, did his attention return to the actual fighting. Too late, he recognized the black-winged ebrot on helm and shield and a familiar hated face.

As the dome of a soldier's shield crashed down against his skull, Bydawine's last clear sight was of Jaaben's gloating smile.

* * * * *

He was alive, though that scarcely counted for much. At times, some small part of Bydawine's mind knew being alive was important. But at this moment, it didn't seem a worthwhile condition.

Images jumbled and careened through a gray-black fog. Shadows led his awareness through ever-growing mazes. His mind struggled to latch onto any single, solid thought.

At last he found a tiny anchor: pain. He concentrated on the welcome distraction, and slowly his world began to right itself. He couldn't find complete equilibrium, but the pain gave him a tangible reference point. After a time, other thoughts collected in tattered pieces to form a makeshift raft of coherence.

He was certain now that he lived, and certain, too, that his mental drunkenness was of magical origin. It was an effective hobble on his own magic, since he couldn't hold a complete thought longer than an instant. He found a rhythm of sorts in the throb of pain. Higher, lower, higher again.

There was a sense of moving, of being carried, then welcome stillness. His mind cleared, and a woman's voice drew his thoughts upward. He felt gentle pressure on his cheek and woke completely to find Noressa kneeling beside him.

It was her hand, fingers trembling, that stroked his cheek. Her eyes were black with worry. Strands of dark hair wisped about her face, giving her the look of a frightened child.

Bydawine was on his feet in an instant, one hand holding tight to the fingers that caressed him. His other hand smoothed back a lock of hair, then traced the firmness of her jaw. He touched her to convince himself that this was indeed Noressa and not another apparition. But he found more than just the touch of flesh. Noressa embraced him, and he felt a rush of feeling from her that made him giddy. It was deeper than any mindspeak they had shared, and the potency of it left him weak. She drew back, asking if he were well. The breathless sensation was gone so quickly, he wasn't sure what name to give it, wasn't even certain it had truly happened. But he knew this was Noressa.

He nodded that he was well, without bothering to check himself, and his own questions poured forth. "Are you uninjured, Noressa? Did they harm you? What happened?"

Noressa's face tightened. Her lips thinned, and she nodded toward something behind him. Bydawine became aware of what lay around them. He stood to his knees amidst a jumble of embroidered silk cushions. The high-ceilinged grandeur of strange council-room walls and the flash and shine of armor from a score of soldiers proved they were far removed from the river village. A rustle of cloth made him turn.

Descending from a throne of carved dark wood, a golden-haired woman approached. Her being radiated a sensual vital-

ity that drew, yet repelled, him. Her presence flowed around
him, smoothing the edge of his fear, placating his confusion
with unspoken comforts. It was *her* beauty reflected in the
polished armaments of the soldiers, her essence that warmed
the air. She smiled, and even the torchlight seemed to bright-
en.

"No one has been harmed, Master Bydawine, unless it is
yourself. Perhaps you did not fare well in the sorceries used to
bring you to the keep. I have heard that Jaaben was most ill-
mannered with his methods in persuading you to join us. Be
assured, I will speak to him personally of his behavior."

Her voice was soft, with a hint of laughter. Violet eyes held
their own amusement, and her hair was a rippling fall of gold
that reached to the stone floor. To every dream of womanhood, she was the reality: desire, beauty—and danger.

Bydawine tore his gaze from her to stare uncomprehending
at Noressa. Noressa breathed the name "Felaya," and his enchantment became terror. He tightened his hold on her hand
while his gaze searched for some escape.

Heavy wooden doors at the far end of the hall stood open.
Other than what might lie beyond thick drapes behind the
throne, these doors were the only way out. A line of soldiers
ranged along each wall. They stood at attention, their eyes
fixed on a distant, unseen point, lances and shields held in
courtly display with no sign of menace. But Bydawine's fears
were not allayed by the soldiers' seeming ignorance of them.
Perhaps a spell of misdirection would bring enough confusion
to allow them to escape from the hall. But would they have
time enough to find their way out of the keep, avoiding the
scorceries of both Felaya and Tylek?

However, there was no time to act. Felaya bent forward, her
hair a silken curtain falling across her arm as she took Bydawine's hand and drew him toward her. That mirthful voice
flowed over him once more.

"You are both fatigued and confused. Join me in a light
refreshment, and I will explain what I can."

Holding Bydawine with one hand, Noressa with the other,
she led them up three steps to the throne dais, seating them
on a padded bench. Servants appeared with trays of wines and
fruits. Platters of sweetmeats and roast fowl were paraded be-

fore them. Felaya supervised the servers until satisfied that her guests were comfortable, then took her place on the throne.

Bydawine touched Noressa's mind with a thought, a warning against the foods spread before them. He caught a flash of surprise on Felaya's face and wondered if she had intercepted his mindspeak—especially when she gave them a conciliatory smile and took a thin slice of meat for herself. Noressa and Bydawine picked at the delicacies on their platters but still did not eat.

After a time, Felaya rubbed the polished wood of the throne armrests and sighed. "Perhaps you are wise not to trust me too quickly. But soon I will no longer be forced to occupy this seat, and you will have others to fear." She smiled at the startled look that passed between Noressa and Bydawine. Again he felt her thinly veiled sensuality.

"You are surprised," Felaya said, looking to Noressa. "But is that not why you have come, to claim your place as ruler of your birthland?" Noressa nodded. "Then we are all in accord." Felaya leaned back with an air of contentment. "I have waited many years for you to return and free me of this obligation. Tomorrow, when you are rested, we will have time to speak at length. I shall begin teaching you what I can of the responsibilities of wearing a crown. Soon you will be mistress of Sidra."

Noressa shook her head, and Bydawine saw his own disbelief mirrored in her face. "How can you be sure that I am the true heir? Will you not put me to some test that I must prove my ancestry?"

Felaya flashed another of her room-brightening smiles. She put out a hand as though to touch Noressa's cheek, hesitated, and drew back. "No test is needed, child. Your face is enough to give me the truth. I look at you, and I look upon Breann once again." A sadness crept into her face. "And none but Breann's child could bear the Token of Dragonsblood. It was sealed to her heir with Breann's own death."

Noressa's hand moved to trace the medallion beneath her shirt. Bydawine watched Felaya's gaze follow. Was there a flicker of something dark behind those sad, violet eyes? He couldn't be certain, for she was speaking, the amusement once more in her face.

"I see that you do not trust my willingness to release the crown. From the stories I have heard of your treatment in Jaaben's hands, I understand this feeling. Surely you must know that had I been present, he would never have dared such liberties."

Two children, a boy and a girl, slipped from the curtains behind the throne, and Felaya turned to hear the maid's whispered words. The mistress nodded. The girl, perhaps twelve years old, stepped back to wait beside the boy. Felaya rose, motioning toward the servants.

"I know this day has been one of confusion and not a little fear for you both. You need rest and time to collect yourselves. There are hot baths and soft beds waiting. Tomorrow, Noressa, I will answer all your questions. And you will answer mine."

She gave them into the custody of the children. Bydawine felt her gaze upon them until they were beyond the drapes back of the throne.

Behind the curtain, stone walls on three sides formed a narrow hall. Here waiting servants stood, out of sight but instantly available to anyone on the dais. Two large wooden doors were set into the far wall. Between them, a narrow stair led upward. The girl led them up the steps to a short, wide hall.

The corridor was marked by three doors, one on either side and a third at the far end. Bydawine could see no other exit than the stairs they had just climbed.

The maidservant stopped beside the entrance on the left, pushed the heavy door open, and waited for Noressa to precede her. The boy continued down the hall toward the last door, beckoning for Bydawine to follow.

Bydawine stood, uncertain, until Noressa spread her hands in a gesture of weary surrender and stepped into the room. The maid quickly followed and pushed the door shut.

Once inside his own room, Bydawine was led through the apartment to an alcove paved in blue and gold tiles. A sunken bathing pool stood in the center of the room. The steam wafting from the pool and the fresh tang of soap and herbs made Bydawine realize just how long it had been since he had properly bathed. He was suddenly aware of the grit in every fold of skin, and of his own smell. He dismissed the boy, stripped, and eagerly immersed himself. He would have been happy to soak his aching body for hours in the scented water, but his worry for Noressa didn't let him linger.

He emerged from the bathing room wrapped in a thick white dressing gown, soft leather sandals slapping at his feet. The boy presented him with wine and led him to a table spread with yet another banquet. The child, only eight or nine, was a hand taller than Bydawine, yet not once had he allowed his eyes to meet his new master's glance. The boy stationed himself at the table, fork and plate at the ready.

"What will be your pleasure, lord? Meat or fruit?"

More worried than hungry, Bydawine declined to eat, but the child pressed him, cajoling and pleading. Finally his agitation at Bydawine's refusal to be served became so great that Bydawine accepted a plate simply to calm him.

After some hesitation, Bydawine ate. He consoled himself with the argument that Felaya would have killed them long before, were that her only intention. Clearly she wanted something further from them.

While he ate, Bydawine took in the confines of his latest prison. Effulgent splendor was the thought that came easiest to his mind. Not even his uncle's chambers had been so luxurious. Entering the apartment, they had passed through a room clearly designed for dancing and entertainment. The center of that room's polished floor lay open. Around the walls, couches and piles of cushions lay half hidden among screens of ferns and blooming plants. A tiny musician's stage was tucked into a far corner. In the sleeping chamber, where he sat eating, matched white sirre-skin rugs were a soft thickness beneath his sandals. A deep blue brocade canopy fell to the floor over the blue and white silks of the bed. Beaten gold ornamented table edges and door lintels, while marble and ivory benches piled with cushions offered cozy retreats before a blazing fire.

He wondered how Noressa fared and how they were to escape the castle. Certainly her apartment would be as wonderful as his own, but he hoped that such trappings wouldn't lull her into a false sense of trust for the mistress.

Thinking of Felaya brought a disquieting mixture of feelings. At once there came the familiar fear, an antagonism cutting so deep that a part of him shied from its intensity. Yet there was doubt. Could this woman truly possess nothing of goodness? He remembered her sadness in speaking of her sister's death, remembered also the manner in which her pale hand stroked a golden lock of her hair, the gentle curve of her full red lips. Bydawine caught his breath at the realization of where his memory led him. Guilt warmed his face, and he thought of Noressa.

He longed to talk with her and considered using the mindspeak, but he remembered Felaya's reaction to his earlier use of it. Had she truly known his communication, or was she only aware of the power used in its performance? Recognizing power was not as difficult as understanding it, he knew. Even now he could sense the flow of magic around them. He assumed there would be guard spells at the chamber door and possibly the stairway, as no one other than the children had accompanied them here. There didn't seem to be any magic directed toward him at the moment, but that still didn't solve his problem of how to reach Noressa.

A low growling reached him, and Bydawine recognized it as that of an empty belly.

"Boy, what is your name?"

The child jerked as if struck and his face paled. "Kej, my lord," he gasped and bowed quickly.

Bydawine remembered Noressa's accusation that his manner frightened the village children. He worked to gentle his next words. "You appear weary, Kej. Sit and rest yourself."

"Sit?" Kej stood rigid. He paled even more, till Bydawine feared the child would faint, and shook his head. "The mistress would not allow it."

"Am I not your lord now? Sit. And in the future, when I sit, you may also." From his couch, Bydawine tumbled a fat, white cushion to the floor. There was mistrust in Kej's eyes, but he sidled to the cushion and lowered himself into its softness. "If any question it, say your master will not have his servant above him."

Kej nodded, eyes wide. His belly rumbled again, and he looked away, hugging his knees to his chest.

"Now, eat," Bydawine commanded. "You will not serve me well if you drop from hunger."

Bydawine heard the gruffness returning to his voice but

cared little. Ignoring Kej's timid choice of delicacies, he picked at his own food. His thoughts were again turned to finding a way back to Noressa.

After a time, Bydawine walked to the room's single window and climbed up on the padded ledge. Kej abandoned his cushion to follow. Through the narrow window, Bydawine looked down into the yawning depths of a jagged crevasse.

The wall of the keep had been built precisely to the cliff's edge. To his left, he knew, lay Noressa's apartment. He looked in that direction in a faint hope that she, too, might have sought the solace of her window and he might catch a glimpse of her. To his consternation, the wall was a blank of stone. He stared at the unyielding rock, and an idea flared in his mind.

Carefully he walked the length of the room, counting in silence. He repeated the process on all sides of the room before moving into the dance chamber. He paced that room three times to be sure, then returned to the sleeping chamber, still trailed by the boy.

Smiling, Bydawine settled once more before the banquet table. If the ancient king of Sidra who had built the keep had been a man of strategy, then Bydawine felt sure he now possessed a way to reach Noressa unseen. Built as it was, against a precipice with only once source of access, the stairway from the throne room, the apartment grouping was nothing more than a dead-end trap, unless an alternate method of descent was provided. Three times his pacing in the dance chamber had come up five steps shorter than the sleeping room—not a noticeable difference to most observers, but enough that a narrow passageway might well be concealed behind the stone walls. And from its position, the passage would lead not only down, but also directly past Noressa's apartment.

With his mood brightened, Bydawine's appetite made a strong return. Now he needed no encouragement from the boy to enjoy his meal.

Toward morning, most of the candles still burned as Bydawine slipped from the bed. One or two guttered, nearly gone, but the majority still cast a good light. It was all he required.

He spared a glance at the boy huddled beneath a coverlet at the foot of the bed. He slept the hard sleep of one unused to too much wine. Bydawine regretted last night's ploy, knowing how badly the boy would feel when he woke. But it was either trick the boy into a drunken stupor or put him under a sleep spell, and Bydawine did not wish to draw attention by using magic unless absolutely needed.

Now he moved to the left side of the room, to that area within five steps of the outside wall adjoining the dance chamber. With so little space to cover and drawing on his experience in traveling the secret ways of Wigram Keep, it wasn't long before he found what he had suspected—the mechanism of a hidden passage. A bit of iron curved to appear as part of the ornamentation on a wall sconce was actually embedded in a loose stone. Bydawine nearly toppled backward as he balanced on a footstool to reach the sconce. But he held tight to the iron piece and pulled the stone out enough to swing open a narrow panel in the wall. He straightened, smiling with satisfaction at the correctness of his deductions. A simple eye for detail was a definite talent. But was it too simple? The unbidden question made him pause. Could it be that someone wanted him to enter this musty snake of darkness? Bydawine felt himself scowling, the pleasure gone from his minor triumph. No matter, he told himself; he must reach Noressa and there was no other path. He took up a candle and hurried through the opening.

From inside the passage, the entrance to Noressa's chamber was easy to find. A simple lever opened the panel, and Bydawine pushed into the room prepared to soothe the first cries of a frightened maidservant.

But silence was all that greeted him. The light of his candle showed him a bed of rose and white silks, but it was empty. The rest of the apartment was empty as well, save for a lone *kaara* bird in a tall, domed cage of iron. His heart beat a fearful counterpoint to his anger. Once again Noressa had been snatched away from him.

CHAPTER 25

Noressa woke with difficulty. Lethargy clung to her in tattered wisps. She felt heavy, and her mind wouldn't clear. Deep within, a familiar warning sounded, but she hadn't the energy to search out its meaning. Indolence shielded her from all thought, and she let herself drift in its comfort. Then a sound of movement nearby made her realize she was not alone. Noressa opened her eyes.

The maidservant, Yilla, stood at the bedside in the light of a single candle. She tugged at Noressa's blankets.

"Come, my lady, we are summoned."

Reluctantly Noressa sat up. "It is morning, then?"

"No. It is still some while before dawn. But the mistress has sent for you."

Noressa shivered. Now she was awake. She said nothing as Yilla wrapped her in a pale rose dressing gown, placed embroidered slippers on her feet, and led her from the apartment.

Moving down the stairs, across the alcove behind the throne, and out of the council hall, Noressa tried to shake the lingering disorientation of her wakening. What's wrong with me? she wondered as they hurried through the silent keep. She couldn't avoid the feeling that she was buried in some huge, ancient tomb. Only an occasional torch gave evidence that the living still held sway within the castle's walls.

Keep alert! she scolded herself. You are about to face your strongest enemy. But her befuddlement continued, and rubbing at her eyes until they hurt only made things worse. Jumping black starbursts swam before her, and she was forced to lean against the wall until they faded. All the while, Yilla pleaded in urgent whispers for her to continue. When at last they did, Noressa tried to memorize their route, but after several turns down similar stone corridors, she gave up. She was plagued by a sense of imbalance. Like a yarja hunted to a cliffside, her thoughts minced to and fro, and each step threatened to topple her into darkness. Only a studied detachment allowed her to keep moving. If she thought only of placing one foot ahead of the other, all was well.

The warning pricked her again. Resist! Will you go meekly to destruction? An outside complacency rushed in, soothing her. If you care for nothing, it whispered, nothing can be lost. Then they were climbing a long stair that brought them to a wide landing with a single door at its end.

Yilla knocked softly on the huge portal, and it opened at once. The room beyond was bright with candlelight. In the grate of a high-mantled hearth, a fire danced, gleaming from the gold and silver inlay of the furniture. Scarlet satin edged the pale lavender silks that billowed at the windows and draped the bed. The air wafting from the room was warm, heady with the scent of crushed serila.

Noressa knew at once this room belonged to a woman of authority, of power.

It should have been mine.

Now she battled her lassitude and gathered shreds of determination to herself. She would not show fear before this woman. The time for confrontation had come and she would have it done. Her head high, Noressa stepped inside.

Felaya came to greet her, arms outstretched, warmth in her voice. "Noressa! Welcome, dear child!" She faltered, then stopped as Noressa maintained a haughty silence. Felaya sighed and folded her hands against the skirt of her dark purple gown. "How much of my sister I see in your reproach, girl."

"A sister you killed," Noressa said. She heard Yilla gasp. The maid holding the door trembled. Noressa wondered briefly from where her audacity had come, then braced for Felaya's anger. Instead, her aunt turned away, biting at a quivering lip.

"It was not of my choice," Felaya said over her shoulder. "What Breann stole from our family had to be returned at any cost."

"Stole?" Shock tore the exclamation from Noressa.

Felaya nodded, facing Noressa slowly. Unshed tears glistened in her violet eyes. "You didn't know her as I did. As a child, it was the power of the Token of Dragonsblood—the amulet you wear—that she desired above all else. Our grandfather was chosen g'Hain over her. I watched her grow to womanhood nursing that imagined insult to consuming hatred."

Dumbstruck, Noressa could only refuse Felaya's words with a furious shake of her head.

"Forgive me, Noressa," Felaya pleaded. "Such a revelation is difficult to accept. And I am a poor hostess. Come, settle yourself, and I will answer all your questions."

Noressa let herself be led to a couch. Behind it, a row of windows, slightly open, admitted puffs of the cool night air. Noressa sank into the cushions beside her aunt. In tandem with Felaya's own maid, Yilla removed Noressa's slippers and placed her feet on the padded top of an *aakiet*, a low stone box filled with live coals. A lap robe was tucked in at her waist and mulled wine served. Then the two servants withdrew.

Noressa sat a moment, lulled by the warmth seeping up from the *aakiet*, tempted by the wine's promised oblivion from the angry buzz of thoughts in her head. Then she remembered who she was with and why. Idiot! she berated herself. You sit dreaming into your wine when you may die at any moment? She set aside her cup and faced her enemy.

"I do not believe your accusations against my mother."

Felaya nodded, her golden hair whispering across her gown. "Your heart is just and kind, and so you would not believe such things of another. But let me tell you of the power in the Token of Dragonsblood, then you will decide. In the long ago, there was one of my clan called Tremsan. He was a great warrior and mage. It was he who called into this world the Dragons of Starp. It was he who forged the Tokens of Dragonsblood, which give us power over these creatures."

As she spoke, Felaya caressed the tiny medallion at her throat. Noressa watched the bloodstone glow scarlet at its center, as her own had done that first morning in her cottage. The bloodstone in Felaya's amulet softened, then began to glisten, a true welling of blood upon the gold. An unexpected warmth radiated from her own medallion in response. Dizziness struck Noressa, and she was overwhelmed with a yearning for something unknown. She reached for her wine, gulped at it until only dregs bittered her lips.

When Noressa was again composed, Felaya arched a brow and gave her an ironic smile. "You have felt somewhat the power of your token. Can you see now why it would be a thing worth murder to some?"

Noressa blinked. Felaya hadn't moved from her seat, yet with those last words, part of her changed. For the space of a heartbeat, she seemed to tower in the room. A dark heat of desire pulsed from her. It is the wine, Noressa thought, and blinked again. The image was gone, and her aunt was again fragile and pale, beautiful in her sorrow.

Felaya turned away, and Noressa saw her throat work with some unvoiced emotion. Then her words came softly. "Within the tokens are two classes. The L'erit is given to those who will counsel and support. The g'Hain is for those chosen to rule."

"Who makes that choice?" Noressa asked.

"The Companion bound by the amulet being petitioned." Felaya touched her necklet. "I am L'erit. Our grandfather, sire of my mother and Breann's, was g'Hain. Breann was not bonded."

Felaya rose and began pacing before the windows. "In our tradition, when a bonded clansman or woman dies, any other clansmember past the age of twelve summers may petition for joining with the free Companion. So it was when the eldest g'Hain died. Many petitioned. Breann also, as she had attained fourteen summers. But our grandfather was chosen, and Breann's hatred began to grow. Little sister was strong in her sorcery, and she studied well. When she felt herself powerful enough, she stirred rebellion within the clan."

Felaya stopped and looked into the night. Noressa found herself tensed for the woman's next words.

"There was a great battle, during which Breann struck down our grandfather and captured his Companion at the moment of his death. Then she fled here, to Sidra, and engaged the sympathies of King Brydon." Felaya returned to the couch, a terrible pleading in her eyes. "My people had had enough of war, Noressa. Rather than bring our full clan into that horror, I was sent to retrieve the Token of Dragonsblood." She sighed and sat back in her cushions. "You know the outcome of that. You are but one victim of the conflict. I am another."

"You?"

Felaya nodded. "I am foresworn, Noressa. I may never return to my homeland without the token. That is why I have fought to remain here, why I have sought you for so long. Only you may lift this burden from me."

In her shock, Noressa half stood, the movement an instinctive one to distance herself from the madness of those words. But anger rushed close on her surprise, and she sat down, fixing her aunt with a derisive glare.

"You killed my parents, destroyed my land, and have hunted me all my life. Now you say I am the means to fulfill your duty?"

Felaya hung her head. "I have done all this," she whispered. "But it was not of my choosing."

"You have said that," Noressa snapped, "yet I have seen nothing to prove otherwise."

From the corner of her eye, Noressa caught a glimpse of Yilla's white face. The girl was peering around the screen to which she and Felaya's maid had retired to await the further wishes of either lady. Yilla shook her head once, the movement and her look a warning. But Noressa could not be still. Her anger felt good, cleansing. Her head began to clear, and a hundred questions sorted themselves before her. Then Felaya raised her face, and something in her eyes brought up an old anguish in Noressa.

"Do you believe there was pleasure for me in the death of my sister?" Tears spilled down Felaya's cheeks. Her body trembled. She hugged herself tightly and turned her face back to the star-pierced night.

"When Breann fled to Sidra, we thought at last the war was done. Our land was torn, our people divided, and Grandfather was dead. Breann was bonded, and naught could be done for that lest we, also, bow to murder for control of the Companion." Felaya took a white linen cloth from the serving platter beside her and dabbed her tears. She was calm again, though paler than before, and she returned to her couch. "It was not a good end, but it was a conclusion we thought we could accept."

Felaya tucked her feet up under her warming blanket and sat staring at the cloth she twisted in her lap. "We of the clan began to build our lives anew, but after two years came word that Breann was not to be forgotten so quickly. She had won the sympathies of your father, Sidra's king, and with the influence of the token had gathered a great army. This was too much. The elders of Turalain met and determined that Breann must be stripped of her power. Lots were cast to choose one who would come to Sidra and wrest the Token of Dragonsblood from her—at any cost."

"And so you came." Noressa did not want to believe what she was hearing. But her conscience reminded her that this was the first time Felaya had been given a chance to speak her side of things.

Felaya nodded and let go a long breath. "And I may not return to Turalain without the token. Such was the decree of my elders."

Noressa had no words. Her anger was gone, and the distracting jumble of thoughts assailed her again. Where was the truth? Could she believe the pain trembling in Felaya's voice? If so, then what of the things Medwyn had told her? And if Felaya were lying, then why was she, Noressa, still alive and in possession of the amulet?

Too many questions. It was easier to put them aside and lose herself in the wild scenes displayed in the room's carpet weaving. The portion beneath her feet depicted a golden-haired king, crown askew, dying in a mob of black-crested spearmen. Across from it, another scene, wreathed in gray smoke, showed a young queen slumped dead upon her throne. Long black hair shrouded her body and that of an old woman weeping at her side.

Noressa looked up, startled. Felaya was speaking, and Noressa felt foolish, unable to reply.

As if reading her consternation, Felaya smiled. "Do not trouble your mind on what is past. We are together now. We are blood kin, and that speaks for much. There is no enmity between us. Surely we may help one another."

Noressa felt trapped by Felaya's beseeching look, until her aunt turned to stare through the window.

No enmity. Noressa wanted to believe it. She shook her

head. Remember, you spent your life as a lie to hide yourself from this woman.

Felaya turned from the window, where night was purpled with the coming dawn. "It is a new day—a day for beginnings." She stood and beckoned Noressa to follow. Pulling aside the delicate curtain, Felaya led her through the floor-length window onto a small balcony.

From there, they watched the sunrise rout the last dusty shadows from the sky. Out of the darkness below emerged a tiny walled garden that could be reached by a stair leading from the balcony. Noressa noted the brilliant flowerings of azbel pods, lirsa, and miniature riabom, and heard the trickle of an unseen waterflow. But the beauty of the garden seemed distant and pale, and Noressa felt no regret when Felaya led her back into the apartment, saying, "Come, let me walk you to your room."

Passing through the halls, they encountered several women carrying buckets of steaming water. One, an old woman, stared at Noressa with disbelief, until a look from Felaya sent her scurrying.

Felaya leaned close to Noressa. "The old one has seen your mother in you."

An edge in her aunt's voice made Noressa look her way, but Felaya was smiling. Perhaps she had imagined the bitterness in her words. She caught Felaya looking at her medallion, and a thought came to her.

"Tell me, Aunt, what is the way of the token? Perhaps I could petition a joining."

"No! You cannot!"

Felaya's vehemence surprised them both. Felaya blushed and looked away.

"Forgive me, Noressa. I didn't wish to bring you unnecessary pain, so I have said nothing of it, but . . ." She glanced at Noressa, then away again. "You can never petition a joining. That is only for the true-blooded of our clan."

"But my mother—"

Felaya shook her head. "Your father was outlander."

Shame burned in Noressa's cheeks at the unspoken indictment. Pity filled Felaya's eyes.

"It was Breann's deepest cruelty to have bound you with the

burden of a treasure you may never share. Giving up the token is your only hope of easing that pain."

Defiance held Noressa stiff, an anger that clenched every muscle. How could she accept Felaya's proclamation? Had she not touched the power within the amulet? Had she not bent that energy to her will? How was that possible if she were of tainted breeding and unacceptable?

Noressa saw uncertainty flicker in Felaya's eyes, and the woman spoke quickly.

"It is harsh to say that you will never be accepted as petitioner, but mayhaps you can be accepted as a child of the clan. One day you may wish to come to Turalain and claim your place in our family."

They had reached Noressa's apartment. Yilla, who had followed them in silence, rushed ahead to hold open the door.

Felaya smiled, her composure regained, and said, "Rest now, Noressa, and we will speak again later. Soon enough you will be queen. That is a thing I could never be, though I have held the crown these many years."

Noressa watched her aunt depart, her words echoing in her mind. She was to be queen. The thought should have made her joyous, but she found no triumph in it.

Noressa fingered the medallion. The bloodstone was warm beneath her touch. It is too easy, too fast, a part of her warned. She asks too high a price for what is already mine.

CHAPTER 26

oressa staggered and fell to her knees; her hands slammed into the ground. She cried out at the sting of gravel and sand gouging her flesh. Behind her sounded the cry of demon hounds. Above came the wind-stroked rush of wings. Terror pushed her up and forward. She ran blindly through darkness, sucking in great breaths of stifling mist. She had no direction. She ran to escape the beasts, to answer the silent voice of the summoning.

Again came the stroke of wings, closer this time. Noressa stumbled, caught her stride. She must not be taken now; she was too near! Her mountain was ahead, the cliffside only steps away!

Then the screaming fury was upon her. Plummeting down, it materialized through the mist. She heard the keening whistle of its dive, felt taloned claws reaching for her back.

"Nooo!"

Noressa screamed and twisted away—away and down into nothingness.

Her mind couldn't grasp the whirl and flash of sights as the cliffside slipped past. Below—was it the glitter of water on rock crystals rushing up with such breathless speed? Or the gleam of ancient, knowing eyes?

Then unseen hands gripped her, shook her again and again until . . .

Noressa woke to Yilla's shrill cry. "Wake, mistress, wake! We are invaded!"

She was in darkness again, but it was a known darkness, made incomplete by the flare of a single candle. And Noressa heard a familiar voice ordering Yilla to silence.

"Be quiet, child! I do not bring you any harm!"

"Bydawine!" Noressa wrestled herself out of tangled bed

233

linens and sprang down to embrace the shadowed figure at the bedside. She clung to him, sobbing, the dream fear and her relief at having him near flowing out in an incoherent babble. Bydawine patted her shoulder awkwardly with one hand, holding aloft his candle in the other. Then Yilla was draping a dressing gown across her shoulders, and Noressa heard the remonstrance in the girl's voice.

"Oh, my lady, your modesty!"

Remembering her state of undress, she released Bydawine, embarrassment warming her face. He prudently turned away to light a sconce of candles, and Noressa pulled the robe over her thin nightdress, hugging it tight across her breasts.

She rose to sit on the edge of the bed, and the girl hurried to place the embroidered slippers on her feet. Then Yilla put herself between Noressa and Bydawine's approach.

He stopped, hands on hips, and scowled so fiercely that Yilla took a step back, pressing against Noressa's knees. "I have told you, girl, I mean no harm to you or your mistress!"

For an instant, Noressa wanted to laugh. The sight of Bydawine's impatient frown was so dear that it left no room for the terror of the dream. That fear was fading, replaced by an excitement she found hard to contain. At last she understood what the dream had meant to show her. She wanted to shout the discovery aloud, but an inner voice cautioned her, and she felt obliged to ease Yilla's anxiety at Bydawine's intrusion.

She smiled and shook her head in disapproval at the dwarf. "Speak more gently to the child, Bydawine. With a scowl as terrible as that, you might frighten even me."

Bydawine looked taken aback, and his expression became contrite. Yilla spoke to Noressa without taking her gaze from Bydawine.

"How came he here, my lady? There is but one door, and it is guarded by—by— How came he here at this late hour?"

Noressa put a hand to the girl's shoulder, moving her to one side. "He is a magician, Yilla. And friend. He is welcome in my chambers at any hour and by whatever means he can use to bring himself here."

Yilla stared at Bydawine. Noressa rose, trailing a down-filled coverlet from the bed, and handed it to the girl. "Now I would speak with my friend alone. Go and rest yourself in the next chamber."

Yilla's eyes grew wide. Her dark chestnut braids whipped back and forth as she shook her head violently. "Oh, no, mistress! You cannot be alone with—" she leaned toward Noressa and whispered—"with a man!"

Noressa smiled again, took up a candle, and placed an arm around the girl's shoulders. "I promise, Yilla, that nothing shall pass between Bydawine and myself that would not be fitting before all the court."

Yilla crumpled the softness of the coverlet in her fists. "Then why can I not stay? I will serve you wine and sweetmeats. I will build the fire and warm stones for your feet! I ask only to serve you, lady."

Noressa shook her head, leading the girl toward the heavy doors connecting the bedchamber with the lavish dancing chamber. "You will serve me by doing as I ask—now." Over her shoulder, she said, "Bydawine, light every candle. I will have no more gloom!"

Noressa opened the door to the next room and waited as Yilla dragged the coverlet through it. She handed Yilla the candle and shut the door firmly on her pleading.

Noressa paused, watching Bydawine at his task of lighting candles, and caught his worried glances. The excitement of the dream ran through her again, and she hugged the feeling to herself, smiling. Then she was running across the room to kneel before Bydawine, pressing his hands between her own.

"Bydawine! A wonderful thing has happened, and I could dance with the joy of it!"

His brows knit in the beginning of a frown, but she hurried on. "The dream, Bydawine. I understand it now, and where it leads me—to the mountain!"

Noressa sat back on her heels, joyfully tossing her hair behind her. "I can scarcely wait to leave this place. I feel as if I could run the distance and reach the answer before I lost my breath, the thing is so near."

"What are you saying?" The sharpness of Bydawine's words cut through her elation. His frown was terrible. "You speak as though all is well and good in the world. Do you expect that, come the morrow, you will stroll from here as freely as a milkmaid to the cowshed? Felaya will not let you go until she has the amulet, and there is nothing to say that she will let you live even then! Surely all her beauty and soft words have not fooled you into blind trust, Noressa."

For the first time, Noressa felt that Bydawine was truly angry with her. It frightened her so that she could only stare at him in silence. Then his anger was gone and he sighed, looking weary. He took her hand and led her to a couch before the fire. He stood before her as she sat, and his stern words made her feel like a scolded child.

"You must remember that you are queen now. You have accepted fealty from your people. Will you abandon them now?"

The question hung over her. For an instant, his eyes mirrored her own whirlwind of emotions—fear, uncertainty, and unknown desire. She was struck suddenly by how little she really knew of him. At first, her feeling had been pity for his treatment at Pashet's hands. After came the respect for his determination and strength of purpose. He refused the world's view that a small man might accomplish only small things. What wondrous dreams do you hold in the secret place of your heart, Bydawine? Then the moment was past, and his gaze was stern, demanding her answer. Once again Noressa held to the strength of his practicality to step aside from the clamor of her own emotions.

"I will not abandon my people."

He nodded curt approval. "Good. Now we must think how we may escape this place and rejoin Bohsta and the army. That is our only hope to establish you as true queen. As long as Felaya remains, you will be no more than a puppet." He stopped when she shook her head slowly.

"You have shown me that I may not leave my throne unattended even to follow the summoning. How, then, can I leave it to seek protection for myself?" He stiffened, and she rushed on, trying to forestall his displeasure. "I have said I will not leave my people. But neither can I forego this other. I do not take lightly my oaths of sovereignty, Bydawine, but I carry another vow as important. I must complete this task before all others."

"Even to the cost of your throne, possibly your life?" he asked.

"Even so."

Bydawine sighed and seated himself beside her. "What is to be done, then? You cannot leave here to rejoin the army because you will not leave Felaya to rule over your people. Yet you are compelled to pursue this quest to its end."

Noressa hesitated. She had a plan of sorts. But it, too, was another strategy devised in a moment of haste. "There is much I would tell you, Bydawine, and I beg your patience until it is done." He nodded.

She told him quickly of all that had happened since his journey to Dromund. His lips thinned, hearing of Tylek's fiend and her morning conference with Felaya. She spoke of the untried power flowing always out of her mind's reach and of the changes in her dream. Of her almost constant confusion since coming to the keep, she said nothing. Instead, she let herself be taken again by the passion of her dream.

"*I* was in command!" Sitting upright, eyes closed with head thrown back, she savored the memory. "Even plunging over the cliffside was of my choosing, because it led me nearer to the mountain!"

"To what mountain?" Bydawine asked. "From the Taserel Sea to the Wastelands, the entire eastern border of Sidra is mountain range."

Noressa blinked. His question brought her back within the confines of the castle walls. "I cannot name any one peak, Bydawine. But the summoning has directed me thus far; it will not leave me now. I will know the place when I am near enough." She paused. "And that brings us once again to how I will leave here without abandoning my responsibilities."

She thought carefully, then said, "Medwyn and Bohsra are surely on their way here now."

Bydawine nodded and said, "Medwyn may have knowledge of the magic used to bring us here so quickly, but I doubt he will have the power to transport an entire army. They must come at a forced march, and that means we will not see them until evening tomorrow. Will you wait until then to go?"

"Yes. When Bohsra arrives, I will leave him to hold the keep while I travel east." She paused. "And I will ask Felaya to accompany me." She laid a hand on his shoulder to still his objections. "I know you will argue that I must not trust

Felaya—and I do not. But she will not allow me to leave without surrendering the amulet. If she believes she may have it later, she may not oppose the journey. After all, we travel in the same direction.''

Bydawine looked skeptical. Noressa sighed and pressed the heel of one hand against her forehead, trying to clear the haze that overlay every thought.

Seeing her so, Bydawine laid his hand on her arm. Noressa smiled at his concern. Then, against her own misgivings, she asked, ''Could there not be some truth in what she says? You were yet a child, and I not even born. How can children say what was before their time? Felaya says only the amulet will truly end the war.''

''She says!'' Bydawine growled. ''Who is she that we must accept her word? Sister killer, usurper of a throne! I place no more honor in her words than I would give to Jaaben.''

Noressa winced as his grip on her arm became painful. He let loose and strode away. When he turned and stared back at her, she could feel his anger from across the room.

''Then what of Bohsra and Medwyn and all the others? Did they all lie?'' His voice was hard, cold. Noressa shivered as her own questions returned to haunt her.

''Perhaps we are children ignorant of the true chronicles of this war,'' he continued, ''but there are those old enough who will recall the truth. I say, let her face those who carry equal history and knowledge. Yes, we shall await the army. Then let the people of Sidra arbitrate the witch's claim!''

Was it vengeance or logic that fueled the emotion in his words? No matter, she told herself. Once more his strategist's mind had pointed up options she had overlooked. Despite her continued apprehension, a large part of her worry slipped away. She could wait. For a time, there was no need to contemplate giving up the amulet. Noressa embraced that desperate hope and let her thoughts go no further.

CHAPTER 27

Bydawine sat watching Noressa sleep. She was curled beneath a daxet-skin cover on the couch where they had spent the night talking. The gleaming black pile of her hair pillowed her head; one hand dangled over the side. Brow furrowed, she tensed as if in preparation for flight. He touched her mind with a picture of wind-ruffled ydrosh along a mountain rivulet, and she relaxed.

He heard the maidservant creep into the room. She paused in the doorway.

"My lady?"

Bydawine ignored her. He was still exploring the pleasure of finding Noressa's mind so open to him. Crossing her thought barriers had long been an easy thing, but tonight there seemed to be no restraint at all. He wondered how deep he might travel before encountering those secret places each mind kept hidden from itself.

But could this tampering condition her to be so open to anyone? At the thought of Felaya finding such easy entrance, he contented himself with the simple image of ydrosh when some chaotic thought of her own disturbed Noressa's sleep.

Yilla padded across to them, the soft rustle of the coverlet preceding her. Bydawine waited as long as was polite before turning to her.

He saw her taking in the picture they presented—he on the footstool, the dying fire, and the remnants of mulled wine they had shared. Something hard flashed in her eyes. It was a brief moment, then her face was blank. Still clutching the coverlet round her with one hand, she took up a poker in the other and stirred the fire.

Bydawine felt her anger splashing out at him. In serving Noressa wine, he had intruded upon the child's domain. He knew he should make some attempt at reparation. Of all those in the keep, Noressa's personal servant was not one whose enmity he desired. But he was tired, and it was clear that his very presence was a continuing offense. He gestured for quiet as he stood to go and whispered, "Lady Noressa was just now able to sleep."

Yilla's empty face didn't change. She added short sticks to the fire and said, "My lady should have slept in the night. Now it is dawn, and the mistress expects . . ." She hesitated, biting her lower lip, and glanced quickly at Bydawine. "The lady Felaya awaits my mistress. There is much my lady must learn as queen."

Guilt wrapped about him like a too-large cloak, a muffling impediment to quick movement or clear thought. "Damn me! Now she is exhausted and must face that witch!"

Yilla looked surprised, and some of the hardness left her face. "My mistress has much to learn if she will rule."

Bydawine strode angrily up and down the floor. "There is *too* much. She must learn all at once what royals are taught through a lifetime." He pounded a fist into his open hand. "And doubtless the longest lesson will be Felaya's wheedling for the forfeiture of the amulet." He glanced at Noressa, saw the pinch of fatigue in her face even while she slept. "It is my doing that she will have little strength to deal with this. I should go with her."

At that, Yilla looked hopeful but didn't speak. Bydawine's anger drained away, leaving him empty and tired. "Of course, Felaya will have some polite excuse why I should be elsewhere." Feeling useless, he left the room.

* * * * *

In the tiny garden, Felaya's voice was a muted drone in Noressa's ears. Noressa grimaced and set aside her cup, finding the wine flat and tasteless. Perhaps she had indulged too deeply the night before. Her eyes felt gritty with each blink against the speckles of sunshine piercing the canopy of lirsa vines. She closed her eyes to the bothersome light and thought of the cool darkness of her surroundings.

A trailing vine brushed her face and she captured it. Stripping a few of the leaves, she crushed them and held them under her nose. She opened her eyes and stared at the bruised leaves. The astringent smell of the lirsa should have been strong enough to make her eyes water, but there was nothing.

"Noressa!"

Felaya's voice jarred through her fatigue. Her aunt sat amongst the rolls of parchment that detailed size and history of each province.

"You are not listening. How will you govern if you do not know which lord stands before you?"

Felaya's words were stern, and Noressa sensed the impatience behind them. "I'm sorry," Noressa mumbled. "I didn't sleep well last night."

"You didn't sleep at all." Felaya was openly reproachful. "Your midnight visitor left you no time to rest."

Surprised, Noressa looked at Yilla, who sat beside her. The girl protested.

"No, no, mistress! I spoke of it to no one!"

"True." Felaya's words were sharp. Yilla trembled before her glare. "She said nothing, when she should have come to me at once!"

Yilla was silent, but Noressa saw her anguish. Which mistress to serve?

Then Yilla edged slightly nearer to her, and Noressa smiled. Despite a lifetime of service to Felaya, the girl chose loyalty to her. But she saw the clench in Yilla's jaw and promised herself that no subject would ever have reason to serve her out of fear.

"Leave us. I will assign another who is better able to serve." Felaya's command broke into Noressa's musings. More than her aunt's imperious tone, it was Yilla's blanched face that stirred Noressa's irritation. She'd had too many nights of too little sleep, too much indecision. Now she was at a point of exhaustion where protocol quickly gave way to petulance.

"Let her be!" Noressa snapped. "The child did well to keep her own counsel. What goes on in the queen's chamber is the queen's business!"

Yilla shivered. Shock filled Felaya's face. Something told Noressa she should be afraid, but she had been long enough in running. She held the woman's gaze.

Felaya's cheeks colored. A wildness blazed in her eyes, then she inclined her head in a sharp sign of deference.

"Of course you are right in this, Noressa. I only meant that had I been informed of Master Bydawine's presence at so late an hour, I would have been honored to sit as chaperone. My concern was that should such behavior become common knowledge, it might reflect badly upon your character. Not a propitious beginning to your reign."

"Thank you, Aunt, but no chaperone was needed. Bydawine came first as a friend, and second as advisor to me in Medwyn's absence."

Felaya's shoulders tightened. This wasn't the first sign that some tension remained at the memory of her former adversary. Noressa wondered how it would be when Medwyn, at last, arrived. The thought passed quickly, as a familiar antagonism tapped at her mind. Or was it her own anger?

Felaya was making a visible effort to soothe matters. She pressed a wrinkle from the silk of her dark blue gown. "Your choice of friends is certainly a private decision, Noressa. But should you require counsel, Tylek is your court advisor. He has sworn his fealty and stands ready to assist you in any matter."

Tylek. The name curled through Noressa's bravado like a chidd through evening shadows. He of the beautiful form. His dark eyes could hold her with a single look. His presence was a physical command drawing her to him. Noressa remembered the sensual touch of his magic and shivered.

Was this not the same Tylek who had sworn fealty to her father, the king, before leading this golden-haired invader to victory against his own country? Noressa let that anger grow, used it to block the fear. She would let no one see that her fear could be brought back so easily. She kept her voice calm as she stood and gathered the wide skirts of her day frock in both hands.

"Tylek was your counsel, Felaya. I have yet to appoint my own court. There are others who have also pledged service to me, and I will wait until all are present to make such decisions. For now, I am too weary to continue the lessons. We shall take them up after the evening meal."

Perhaps she had risen too quickly, or she was more tired than she knew, but as she turned for the gate leading from the garden to the main courtyard, the groomed perfection of the garden dissolved. An untamed thicket of weeds and bramble vines caught at her skirts. Her vision lurched sideways. She stumbled. Yilla caught her arm, and Noressa clung to her. A gibber of voices crescendoed, a warning lost in the jumble. Straining to catch the elusive words didn't bring them clearer, but her concentration helped to draw the world back from its crazy tilt.

Then Felaya was at her side, murmuring concern. "You are too weary, Noressa. We shall put off all lessons until the morning. Go to your chambers and rest."

Noressa caught her breath but couldn't look at her aunt. An instant before, the world had been about to crack and slip away. Now the sculptured order of the garden had returned, and Felaya took no notice of either occurrence. Was it only she who had seen it? Wine and fatigue could twist the senses beyond reliance. But when her questioning gaze touched Yilla's face, she knew. In the girl's eyes lay a terror that was more than a maid's concern for her mistress.

So. My mind has not betrayed me. If Yilla has seen it, then Felaya's innocent play speaks much of her.

Noressa pressed Yilla's hand, silent acknowledgment of their shared secret. Not looking up, Noressa nodded and started once more toward the gate.

"Yes, Aunt, I will rest now."

As she moved from the bower, the sharp smell of crushed lirsa rose up, nearly choking her.

Bydawine awaited them in the apartment. He flung open the door of the bedchamber and rushed out as they crossed the foliage-crowded antechamber. He snapped questions, and Yilla's quavery voice gave unknown answers. Noressa shut them out and struggled to control her wild thoughts. She wanted to wail in terror and run from the room, from the keep. Instead, she sealed her thoughts within a brittle shell of passivity.

Not until she was set upon her bed with the warmth of more tart, red wine coursing down her throat and the coverlets about her did Noressa allow herself to feel. Then she felt shame that she had let herself become so overwrought she must be cosseted like a child. With a murmured thanks, she pushed away the wine cup and, for the first time, became aware of Bydawine's draggled state.

He stood beside the bed, brown eyes peering at her from a dirt-smudged face. Dusty clumps of web-spinner's silk were caught in his hair and clothes, and he smelled of a dry mustiness. She plucked the husk of a wax beetle from his sleeve.

He took it from her and made a quick attempt to brush away the more obvious bits of grime. "I have been searching in . . ." He paused and looked at Yilla.

Noressa touched the girl's arm when she would have turned away. "Speak freely, Bydawine. The child has proved herself worthy of our trust." She smiled at the pride that flushed Yilla's cheeks. Then she lay back and closed her eyes, submitting to her exhaustion. Bydawine's voice reached her from far off.

"I have been searching the secret ways of this keep for a way out. The passages are old, and many of them are in disrepair and cannot be used. But I have found one that leads toward the river. Unfortunately, it also passes by the soldiers' barracks."

She heard him move nearer, felt his hand touch hers. But she did not open her eyes. She was drifting far from all that troubled her and could scarcely force herself to answer his question.

"Noressa, what has happened? Why did you call me?"

"Call?"

"Yes, the mindspeak. You called to me and I rushed here."

"Truly, Bydawine, I was not aware of it."

She had given up searching for an explanation of the strange tie between them. She accepted that he would always know when she had need of him.

Noressa wished she could reach another man as easily. The memory of Brameth's face wrapped her with a measure of comfort, and she followed the warmth of his golden eyes down into sleep.

CHAPTER 28

Noressa heard the rush of wings above and felt the hatred that pursued her. But this time, she was not afraid.

The mist had cleared from the plain, and she stood on one-half of a broken mountain. The plain was a huge projection of stone formed when it split from the snow-crowned peak that towered on the opposite side of a wide chasm. Her destination was across that chasm, in the cave that was a splash of darkness above the snowline.

"I await."

The whisper came clear, even above the sound of wings and the baying of hounds behind her. Noressa shouted her jubilance, defying those who pursued her, and raced across the plain to the cliff. Without questioning how she knew to do it, Noressa stepped from the precipice. Then she was across the black ravine, grappling at ice-crusted rocks, pulling herself higher.

The sky darkened and snow scudded before the wind of giant wings bearing down on her. The hunter had come. Its pinions of death railed at her as she scaled the rocky mountainside. But she would not stop, would not turn to fight. By sound and instinct, she dodged the talons ripping at her, using every measure of strength to pull herself toward the dark haven of the cave mouth. She understood now that this ravening demon was more than a childhood nightmare. It was an enemy she had met both sleeping and awake. If she could but turn and confront it, she would recognize the specter's true face.

But she could not spare the instant it would take. That was all the creature needed for her capture. And capture, even in a dream, meant her death.

Noressa pushed herself up onto the snow-covered ledge be-

fore the cave and threw herself into the welcoming darkness.

* * * * *

She woke to the fading echo of the Other's rage.

With the mindspeak, Noressa reached out, found Bydawine's uneasy sleep, and touched him awake with her excitement. *Come to me! I have news!*

Noressa kicked her way free of the bedcovers. The light from a single lamp showed her where Yilla slept, curled at the foot of the bed. Noressa shook her awake.

"Light the candles, Yilla. We must dress quickly. Bydawine comes, and I would not have you scandalized by my immodesty twice in as many nights."

She laughed at Yilla's sudden alacrity. The sound was light, pleasant in her ear, and she realized how long it had been since she had laughed so easily. Yilla was just tying up the laces of Noressa's bodice when heavy pounding boomed from the antechamber door. Noressa ran to answer it, while Yilla called a distraught protest and struggled to pull her own brown shift over her head.

Bydawine hurried in the instant the door was open. Barefoot and tousled, his clothes obviously pulled on in great haste, he was scowling furiously. A young boy stood behind him, clutching a pair of sandals.

Noressa seized Bydawine's hand and spun them both like children at a festival. After several attempts, Bydawine disengaged himself and pulled Noressa into the bechamber. He forced her to sit and demanded to know when she had lost her reason.

"I have found it!" she blurted. "I know the end of my quest!" She sprang up and danced across the room. Standing before the hearth, she spoke a word, gestured, and a rush of flame leapt up the chimney.

"Noressa!" Bydawine forced her down onto a stool. The flames died, a scattering of blue sparks among scarlet embers.

Noressa shook her head against his intended scolding. "Forgive me, Bydawine, but you don't know my happiness. I have found the heart of the summoning. You asked me before which peak in all the mountains of Sidra was mine. Now I know. I have seen it! I know the bridge and the only path to climb. The time is come, Bydawine. I must find a way to leave this place!"

Bydawine looked as if he wanted to be angry. Instead, he rubbed a hand across his eyes. "I am pleased that you have found this thing, Noressa, but how can we leave? Bohsra and the army have yet to arrive, and Felaya keeps too tight a reign on us here."

She clucked her tongue. He was ever the practical man! But she wouldn't let his discouragement lower her spirits. "What of your search in the hidden passages? Surely I was not yet dreaming when I heard you speak of a way out."

"There is a way, but you didn't hear all I said. The way leads to the outside, directly behind the armory and the soldiers' barracks. And we have no weapons or supplies. Then there is the matter of Tylek's and Felaya's magic, as well as the question of who will reign should we leave now."

Noressa shook her head and waved away his argument. "The throne is secure. As soon as Felaya knows we have gone, she will follow. Sidra's crown means nothing to her. She wants the token and its power."

She saw that he wasn't convinced and struggled to find the logic that would make him understand her need to go.

"You know the summoning has always compelled me. This is not a childish whim that draws me, but a living power. It is as great as any Felaya wields, and it is mine if I will only grasp it. I mean to do that. Somehow I will leave this place."

At her words, Yilla went to a large chest and pulled out a heavy cloth traveling bag. She began packing, whispering instructions to the boy who had moved to help her.

Bydawine watched the girl, then turned to Noressa. "Do you see what your foolishness leads to, Noressa? This child takes it on faith that you will go, and no doubt that she will go with you. Do you think we can protect her against what Felaya may send after us? Or do you mean to leave her here to receive Felaya's anger when she finds us gone? Can a dream be of such importance?"

Her anger rose hot in her cheeks, taking the pleasure of her dream discovery. "I wouldn't leave the children unprotected! I hope I'm not as cold as that! But I must answer this call. Everything that I hold dear is dependent on that. How can I make you see this?"

She went to stand before the tall iron cage of the ka'ara. The bird ruffled its black crest feathers and gaped its beak at her. The red and gold of its plumage caught the candlelight, and Noressa shook her head at the irony of its empty beauty. As a child, she had heard stories of the ka'ara, the legendary song-bird of the Molevean marshlands. Now she owned such a legend, and the thing was mute.

Then Bydawine came to her side. "Forgive me, Noressa, if I seem harsh. It's just that I don't understand how things can change so much because of a dream. But if you will tell me of it, I will listen."

They seated themselves on a couch, and she told him of the dream. When she was done, Bydawine shook his head. "But what was in the cave? What is this great thing that would take you from those who need you here?"

Noressa shrugged. "I woke before I saw that," she said, fingering her amulet, "but whatever the summoning is, it is tied to the token."

Bydawine sighed. "If Medwyn were here, he might know better what is happening, but all of this is a strangeness to which I have no answers. Only Felaya knows the truth of it all, and I'm sure we will never learn it from her."

Noressa nodded and went to stand before the cold hearth. "Felaya is a strangeness to me. I have meant to question her, to confront her, but just being near her is a confusion. It's as if I see her through a haze. My thoughts scatter and I have no words."

Bydawine frowned and crossed the floor to her, looking worried. "I know this feeling, and I was a fool not to see it earlier. These things you speak of, they are the signs of an enchantment. Have you not felt the magic around us—the force that brought us here and holds us still?"

"Yes. I have felt many things, and none of them pleasant. When I sleep, I can feel how near is the thing that hunts me. When I am angry, it is as if I would lose myself. You cannot understand, Bydawine. You haven't seen how the world shifts and tears itself apart."

Bydawine looked at her sharply. "You mean how the world

splits itself in two, as if it would slough off its life and leave only ruin and decay." Noressa stared at him, and he shot a quick glance toward Yilla. "We have seen this, too, Noressa." He beckoned to Yilla, and she came to them, holding a dark blue gown sewn thick with lace and pearls.

She curtsied and clutched the gown as Bydawine signaled her to speak. "In the garden, mistrees. I saw but could not understand. It was as if all the old ways were returning."

Bydawine touched Noressa's hand. "Yilla told me things while you slept. This splendor didn't exist before we came here. There was never enough food; the children were beaten. Somehow Felaya has wrought all of this only for us."

Noressa looked from one to the other. "Perhaps you are right. But what are we to do about it?"

A flash of red-gold feathers caught her attention; a dark eye held her gaze. The ka'ara's beak opened and its throat worked rapidly. No trilling burst of song accompanied the pantomime. Instead, Medwyn's words came from a faraway memory: *No matter how strong the power projecting it, a shadow magic will always have one flaw. Discover it, and you will take the shadow's power.*

Noressa stared at the creature, and a tapestry of contradictions wove itself before her mind. Flowers with no scent, wine without flavor . . .

". . . And a bird that cannot sing." She finished her thought aloud and stepped toward the cage.

The bird followed her movement with one bright, black eye, its gaze insolent.

She had known eyes like that before. Deep, compelling, they could twist her will with an invitation to sensual abandon and submission. But those eyes belonged to a man.

Noressa could almost hear Tylek's laughter as she fumbled open the cage latch and groped for the bird. Then she was snatching back her hand, shaking away droplets of blood from her wrist where the ka'ara's beak had punctured the skin.

It took a moment for the pain of her wound to overcome her surprise at the attack. The bird sat quietly, displaying not the terror of a frightened animal but the deliberate regard of a knowing adversary. Noressa's pain was flushed away by rage.

She screamed and lunged. She flattened herself against the

cage and grabbed for the bird. The air was suddenly full of feathers, seeds, and debris as the *ka'ara*'s wings buffeted her face. Its beak and talons struck again and again, ripping her sleeve and skin. From behind, Bydawine pulled at her, shouting for her to stop. But Noressa held tight to the bars of the cage and, flailing madly with her free arm, struck the bird a blow that staggered it. She grasped the bird by the neck and pulled it from the cage.

It was large, a half arm's length, and heavy. It continued to beat at her with golden wings. As she had countless times with a bata fowl taken from the pen behind her cottage, Noressa tightened her grip and jerked. With the bata, she had often felt a quick regret that the trusting fowl gave its life to feed her family. Never had she known the rush of heated satisfaction as when the *ka'ara*'s neck snapped and its purposed attack became a mindless fluttering.

Bydawine and Yilla stared at her, but she didn't care that they surely thought her mad. When she had recognized the mind behind the bird's cool gaze, the world had split apart. Elegance and beauty slipped away, leaving her in a chamber hung with dust and web-spinner's silk. She flung away the dead creature and thrust the image of their true surroundings into the minds of those with her.

The young boy crept to Yilla's side, and they all stared at the black-feathered body of the bird.

"An ebrot! Tylek's eyes and ears!" Bydawine kicked at the feathered lump. "Tylek knows all that was said and done in this room."

Yilla made a small sound of dismay and ran to scoop up the gown she had dropped beside the couch. Its blue was faded and grimed with dust. And when the girl tried to smooth the lace collar, it fell away in filthy tatters, the pearls coming unstrung to scatter across the floor. She ran to the bed and began pulling out all that she had packed in the travel bag. Tears streaked her face as she held out to Noressa the bundle of faded rags.

Noressa went to her and put an arm around Yilla's thin shoulders. "It's not important, child. They were never real at all. It was all like this." Noressa waved a hand to encompass the room that now was no more than a dusty store of rubbish.

"It was all illusion, shadow magic . . . pictures of what Felaya wanted us to see."

Bydawine stepped around the ebrot and an almost hairless sirre-skin rug. "How can you be sure it was her magic? The ebrot is Tylek's creature."

Noressa's anger boiled. "I know the smell of this magic. I have fought it before—at the river, and again in Drael. Felaya is my hunter. Since my childhood, it has always been her. I would have known this last night in the dream if I had looked into the face of my attacker."

"But the ebrot is Tylek's," Bydawine insisted.

"Yes, but the magic was hers. All that we saw or felt or desired, she fulfilled with shadows. That is why she couldn't come against me. All her strength went into this, into obtaining the token and the Companion. And with the dream, I see now why she didn't kill me. Only I know where the Companion is hidden."

Noressa raised her arms, hands weighing the air. "Do you not sense the quiet, Bydawine? The chains of magic are gone."

Bydawine nodded. "You have broken her power for now. They will know they are discovered and come for us. We must leave at once." He took Noressa's hand. "Everyone, into the passage!"

"Wait." Noressa ran to the chamber door and spoke an incantation. "I have warded the door. It won't hold long, but it will give us some time. And we can set others along the way."

Bydawine nodded. "Now pull that sconce." When the door swung open, he took a candle and led the way.

CHAPTER 29

When Pashet entered the fetid chamber that was Tylek's workroom, he was surprised to find Tylek and Felaya speaking quietly between themselves. Moments before, the beauty of the entire keep had blinked and snuffed out like a spark in a high wind. Knowing something of the energy the pair had put into the illusion, he wondered at their calm acceptance of its failure.

Pashet signaled Yalst to stay by the door. Wishing he, too, could keep the same distance, Pashet made his way toward the far side of the chamber. He stepped over the sheen of water trickling across the floor into the grill-covered drain beneath the worktable. The room was orderly, but the stench of old magic and bitter incense made Pashet feel unclean. He hated this room, hated the man who conjured here.

Pashet felt his mouth drawn into a grim line. He couldn't hide his distaste for the room; he only hoped his animosity for the couple working here was not so evident.

The two were seated before a small square table. On its top were carved runes inlaid with gold, ebony, and bone. A few of the more common marks Pashet knew—Diml, the moon goddess; Thaeyl, the sun; and a few of the darker gods.

Tylek and Felaya were intent on the polished crystal set into the dark wood at the center of the rune diagram. Nearly round and two handspans wide, the stone was dark and opaque when not in use. Now it flickered with light and movement from within. Shadows cast up from the bright rock hardened the sharp, birdlike features of Tylek's face and brought a hungry, pinched look to Felaya's eyes.

Pashet stepped to the table and took in the scene displayed in the crystal. The setting was familiar—the drill yard behind the soldiers' barracks. The wide aerial view told him that the ebrot supplying the vision was perched atop the armory roof.

The drill yard was empty save for an occasional soldier or servant hurrying across its dry expanse. After a time, Pashet cleared his throat for attention. Tylek glanced up.

"Yes?"

Pashet was surprised by the cool response, but worked hard to keep his face neutral. "Are you aware that the mistress's conjuration has been broken?"

"Yes." Tylek returned his attention to the crystal.

Pashet looked to Felaya. "This means the girl knows of your deception. No doubt she and my dwarf will try to escape. I have posted guards at all exits, and Jaaben has taken a quar of men to bring the girl from her room."

Felaya smiled. "They have already gone. Jaaben must follow them through the hidden passages within the keep walls. But there is only one course they may take." She pointed to the viewstone, then smiled. Seeming content with the situation, she sat, one hand lightly stroking the length of her own neck.

"Then Jaaben will have them very soon." Pashet spoke with confidence, trying to shake a sudden apprehension. Tylek's laughter only sharpened his fear.

"Let us hope not. For once, Pashet, your brother's blunderings will work to our advantage. I feel the girl's magic as she sets wards of misdirection behind herself. Jaaben will lead his men a wild chase in those tunnels before he has the sense to have my Adept show him the way out. That will leave the mistress Noressa ample time to effect her escape."

Pashet could only stare.

Tylek laughed again. "Yes, Pashet, we want them to get away."

Felaya's tinkle of laughter joined that of her consort. With the eager, feline grace of a cle-er poised to strike, she leaned over the crystal window. "The stupid girl does not even know the treasure she seeks to uncover. Breann was clever enough not to give her babe outright knowledge of the Companion's refuge. A child talks too freely. But a riddle, a dream to follow . . ." Felaya stared hard into the crystal. "Very well, sister, I will let your child lead me." Her fingertips caressed one of the many runes. The carving pulsed to life and writhed beneath her hand.

The magic squirming under Felaya's hand gave off its own

scent, a sharp sweetness that soured the wine in Pashet's stomach. He knew that he held some talent for magic. Through the years, Felaya had teased him about it. But the invitations to enter her tutelage he had carefully declined. He never explained that his very talent turned him from her by showing him the darkness in her beauty. The hatred on Tylek's face at those times also told Pashet he would never survive the apprenticeship.

Now that same talent warned him of another old danger. Pashet knew well of Tylek's hatred for Jaaben. It was clear that Tylek hoped Jaaben would fail in this situation. If things were not changed, Jaaben would surely play himself into Tylek's hands.

Pashet tensed. Instinct held him back from contact with the rune-inscribed table, but anger pushed him forward to confront Tylek. "You must send word to my brother at once. Have your Adept warn him against hasty pursuit. I should have been told of this plan. There is no need to send my men unknowing into danger."

Felaya took no notice of him. Tylek answered without looking up. "Had you known of it, you would have made their escape too easy." Tylek glanced up and smiled. "Be easy, Pashet. At the proper time, your brother will be told what to do. If he obeys, all will go well with him. If not—" Tylek shrugged. "As with any search for great things, sacrifices must be made."

It took all Pashet's strength to hold himself in his place. His fury chewed holes in his belly and squeezed hard against his racing heart. But to attack Tylek now would only mean the certain end of Jaaben and himself. He could only wait and hope. He fixed his gaze on the crystal.

After a time, a section of stone opened in the coarse face of the keep wall. Four figures, two children, his dwarf, and a young woman, emerged from the doorway. They hurried across the drill yard, the children leading them toward the gate behind the armory.

The picture moved as the ebrot turned its head, following their progress. The group peered around the corner of the armory, and Pashet saw yet another example of Tylek's hand in this game. Where he had posted a hand's count of foot soldiers, there now waited two mounted pikemen. With but a moment of conference between himself and his companions, the dwarf stepped into full view of the soldiers. He raised his hand and spoke, though Pashet couldn't understand the words. His soldiers were sent flying from their seats by an unseen blow. They lay stunned, and in the space of a few breaths, the gate was flung wide, the group of four mounted double and riding westward down the valley.

At once, disapproval etched Felaya's face. "What is she doing? Where is she going?" She slapped the tabletop and shouted at the crystal. "Stupid girl, that way does not lead to the mountains!"

"She goes to rejoin her army." Pashet couldn't keep a note of satisfaction from his voice. "Now you will be glad to have my brother in pursuit of them." He turned to Yalst. "Send two more quar of men with Jaaben."

Tylek spoke to the crystal, and the vision lurched away as the ebrot launched itself after the mounted figures.

All morning the bird followed close to its quarry. Much of the time, Felaya paced, muttering her anger. Tylek kept vigil over the viewstone. Pashet sat with Yalst, sipping wine and wishing he were with Jaaben. Toward midday, Tylek roused himself.

"They have found the others."

Felaya crowded against the table. "Medwyn's army!" She spat the words.

Pashet was careful to keep himself clear of the table as he peered into the stone. He followed the glide of the ebrot as it banked in a slow turn. It came back and focused on the two kifera laboring westward and the soldiers close behind.

"It is Jaaben!" Pashet watched with renewed interest as his brother and the army riding with him closed the gap between themselves and the fleeing captives.

The dark-haired girl and her companions whipped their tired mounts on toward the rebel army. The rebels fanned out to enclose the two staggering kifera, and the young woman scrambled down to fling herself into the embrace of a long-bearded old man. At the same instant, the two armies met.

Never had Pashet seen a battle from such a view. Looking down on the scene, he saw every surge and flow of combat.

Men threw themselves forward and were pushed back. A few on either side broke through, only to be swallowed by the larger bulk of the army they had invaded.

He watched his brother fight in the wild rage that often took him in battle. Indiscriminate of who fell beneath the deadly blows of his broadsword, Jaaben cut a path toward the circle guarding his quarry. Tylek's Adept stayed close. Though he bore no weapons, he was untouched in the battle.

Within the crush of men near the girl, Pashet recognized Bohsra and the giant, Brameth. Memory fit the name of Norwick to the blond youth standing with his dwarf and the young queen. The elder could only be Medwyn. The five men surrounded Noressa in a small inner circle.

Noressa's arms were around the two children huddling against her. Her eyes were closed, and she raised her head as if listening to a faint, far sound.

The picture blurred as the ebrot glided by, wheeled, and dipped lower on its next pass. Pashet saw the changes in Noressa's face. He saw the sweat of concentration on her brow. Her eyes snapped open, and she looked down.

A whirl of golden light radiated from the ground, licking at her feet. It twined quickly up her body, spreading along her arms to encompass the children. Snaps of the brightness leaped from her, lengthening, suffusing the inner circle of her five defenders. Her figure shone through the haze of light. She was the anchor to a tenuous web binding those nearest her in a net of brilliance.

Felaya's howl of rage snapped Pashet back from the wonder that held him to the scene. "Nooo! No! She is only a child! How can she have such power?" Felaya screamed at the crystal, "You have no right to it! That power is mine!"

Then Pashet saw Jaaben.

His brother had won his way to the outermost ring of soldiers guarding their queen. His sword still flashed a wide arc of death around him. As he leaned forward to strike another blow, a quick parry from a lucky foot soldier sent the sword tumbling from his grasp.

Jaaben roared defiance, and Pashet saw the berserker rage that was in him.

Jaaben's gaze fixed on the dark-haired girl wrapped in the

net of light. He reached for the end of a spear protruding from a dead soldier's back.

Even Pashet couldn't believe his brother's intent as Jaaben brought the spear up and took aim. Pashet clenched his hands on the edge of the table and shouted, "No, Jaaben! No!"

Felaya's words mingled with his. "Stop him, Tylek! She is mine!" Tylek leaned across the table and chanted words that ripped at Pashet's ears.

The hooded Adept, who had stayed near Jaaben throughout the fighting, gazed up into the eyes of the ebrot.

The radiance surrounding the girl intensified until she and her circle of defenders couldn't be seen. The soldiers of both armies ceased fighting and fell back from the light.

The Adept turned to Jaaben and raised his hand. The web of light shimmered.

From the hand of the Adept, a lance of scarlet struck Jaaben between the shoulders, sending him sprawling into the dust.

A scream raged from Pashet.

The golden aurora pulsed once, and was gone.

CHAPTER 30

Noressa drifted in darkness. The air was cold, with a snap of winter in it. She felt the slow pulse of her heart and found the strength to open her eyes.

"My lady wakes!"

Noressa recognized Yilla's voice. Then she was surrounded by people she almost knew and questions she could not answer.

Pain twinged from uncounted tiny wounds. Her right arm throbbed. She remembered the slashing talons of a mute songbird. Stickiness oozed from scraped places in her palm. When had she done that? What caused the tightness in her arms, the dull ache in her knees?

Memories came, of rushing from tunnels into hot sunshine, of guards and a wild flight down the valley. There had been a battle, and another memory too brilliant to grasp. Noressa sat up and moaned as pain tore through her arm.

"Keep still!" Bydawine ordered, wrapping a cloth around her right arm. "Would you have the bleeding start again?"

Noressa tried to be still as she surveyed the suddenly familiar landscape. She sat on a stone ledge. A spine of broken rock shielded their position from the full force of the wind that nipped her cheeks. Three spears' distance from them, a jagged cliff fronted a gorge and a chain of snow-crisped mountains. Yilla came to sit beside her, and Noressa felt the child tremble.

"Are you well, mistress? I feared you dead or—" she shuddered—"or that *she* had taken your soul. Are you truly well?"

Noressa nodded and slipped her left arm around the girl, ignoring muscles that ached in protest. The action brought her a vision of light enfolding them all and a strength that lifted her away.

Bydawine completed his bandaging and looked up at her. "Have you any other hurts?"

Noressa winced as she closed her fingers over a bloodied palm, but she shook her head in response to his question. She tried to stand.

Bydawine made an impatient sound, grasping her hand and turning the wound up for inspection. "Sit down!" he ordered, and accepted a second cloth from Medwyn.

She did as she was told. Curbing her own impatience, Noressa took note of the people around her. For the first time since finding Medwyn and the army, she was able to fit names to the faces of her rescuers.

The boy, Kej, sat close by Yilla's side. Bohsra stood in silence a short distance away. Brameth watched, silent also, but the welcome in his face made her draw a quick breath.

Bydawine eased the pressure of the bandage and grumbled an apology.

Grateful for his misunderstanding, she turned from Brameth and murmured, "It's nothing."

She didn't look at Brameth again, but at the young stranger standing with Medwyn. He returned her curious stare with a smile and bowed.

"I am Norwick, my queen, lately of Wigram Keep. I am the leader of the Warriors of the Chidd, and your servant." He glanced about the stony mountaintop and looked chagrined. "For the moment, however, I have mislaid my army."

" 'Warriors of the Chidd.' " She repeated his words, the prophecy of the Shay echoing in their sound. She looked to Medwyn. "Where are we? How did we come here?"

He shook his head. "We are where you have brought us, child. And I cannot say how it was accomplished."

But she knew. In the midst of battle, she had called for aid and had been answered. On the planes of energy surrounding her, she had touched the current of strength that had flowed so long beyond her reach. It was another mind that she had touched. The golden light had been *his*. His mindspeak had channeled power through her to pluck them from Felaya's grasp and bring them here. She tried to explain this to them.

"But who is this other?" Medwyn asked. "Is he some wizard who has not revealed himself to us?"

"He is a not a wizard. He is not even a man." Noressa held up the amulet. Her thoughts reached out, searching for the smallest awareness of the Other.

"Now I see what a wondrous treasure Felaya sought to wrest from my mother." The winged serpentine relief trembled as if it might spring from the medallion. The bloodstone pulsed with a dark light. "It was the Companion. It was *he* who brought us here. He is the summoning! That is what I have searched for, and now he awaits me—there."

She turned, pointing behind them over the small ridge. Her fatigue gone, pain forgotten, Noressa scrambled to her feet and moved toward the ridge. Cries of protest followed and hands reached to pull her back. But she shook free, gathered her bothersome skirts in one hand, and drove herself upward. She knew what was waiting before she made the top.

As she expected, the curve of her dream plain lay before her. Far to her left, the plateau was edged with boulders and a tumble of broken granite slabs. But to her right, the plain ended in a sheer cliff that fell away into a canyon wider than the Bourne River.

The others clambered up to stand with her. She pointed to the neighboring peak and the cave opening that showed dark against the backdrop of snow.

"You see, Bydawine? Is it not as I told you?"

He stepped forward and searched the distance. He nodded, his expression grim. "It is, Noressa. But we have no way to reach it. No doubt Felaya will soon follow, and she will find us trapped here."

"She will not find us," Noressa said and moved away from him, angling down toward the cliff. At his cry of warning, she looked back. "Follow me. I know the way across!" Then she was racing across the plain.

She slowed only when the chasm yawned wide in front of her. Blackness hid its true depth. She walked quickly along the edge, trying to ignore the painful thrumming that rumbled deep in the rock beneath her.

Norwick was the first to reach her. Only when he took her arm and tried to lead her to a cascade of boulders nearby did she recognize the danger bearing down on them.

Magic snapped in the air. The sharp taste of it made her jaw hurt. Bydawine and the children arrived. Bydawine was shouting angrily through the wind that had become a tempest. He and Norwick urged her away from the cliff, but she held back.

The *knowing* stabbed a warning through her. "It's Felaya!" Noressa shouted. "We cannot stay here!"

"There is no other place!" Bydawine shouted back.

"We must cross over! We will be guarded there!"

But Bydawine wasn't listening. He turned again toward the hill of boulders.

The menace of death pressed close. With the *knowing*, she sensed the approach of dark wings. In death or escape, her dream would end here. And she saw there would be no convincing them that she knew what she was about.

Noressa twisted, surprising both men, and pulled away. She ran along the edge of the canyon.

The ground heaved. She was blinded by wind-whipped dust, but the dream had shown her what to do. The summoning tugged at her. Following its silent whisper, Noressa turned and stepped out into the chasm.

Her skin tingled with the touch of magic as she felt herself press through an unseen barrier. She stumbled on the unexpected support of rock beneath her feet. Quiet wrapped her. Noressa opened her eyes. She hadn't known what to expect when she stepped out into the canyon. Now she smiled, seeing the wide granite bridge that linked the pleateau with its sundered peak.

Behind her, Bydawine and the others were voiceless puppets gesturing in the wind. Noressa beckoned them to follow. Then she hurried toward the cave.

Bydawine staggered with the lurch of the plain under him. Whatever magic was approaching, the overflow of its power was torturing the earth that would receive it. Hot winds played a howling accompaniment to the rumbling cries of the mountain. His eyes teared, squinting against stringing sand, but his gaze never left Noressa.

She hadn't plummeted to a grisly death as he had expected, watching as she threw herself from the cliff. He saw her stumble, then right herself. Her feet seemed to find purchase on the air itself, or she was buoyed up by the sunlight glancing off the rim of the cliff. She waved for them to follow, oblivious to the shadows of the ravine that tangled themselves about her feet. Now she moved farther out across the canyon, toward the distant peak.

Bydawine hesitated at the place where she had stepped off the cliff. The rolling of the earth threatened to pitch him over the precipice. Angry with his indecision, he almost hoped such a thing would happen.

Medwyn arrived, half carried between Brameth and Bohsra. He hurried to the cliffside. Bydawine shrugged and shook his head at the elder's stream of questions.

Reverberations from the ground shuddered into the air. Bydawine sensed how savage would be the arrival of the magic plunging toward them. Truly they had no protection here.

He watched Noressa retreat from him and heard again her last words: *We will be guarded.*

He took up a stone and hurled it after her.

The missile flew several feet, then stopped in midflight and dropped to the ground. With the next shudder of the earth, it rolled close to the edge of the cliff but did not tumble over.

Bydawine shouted at Medwyn, "Noressa wouldn't call us into danger." Before the elder could react, Bydawine stepped over the bluff.

A web of magic brushed at him but didn't hold him back. The air was quiet, clear of the stifling sand. The mountaintops caught the first blaze of sunset. Tinted rose and gray, the pinnacles appeared to float in bays of purple shadow.

Bydawine felt suspended in a dream, but he stood on firm rock. He shook away his astonishment and stepped back into the ferocity of the wind.

"There's a bridge!" He seized Yilla's hand and pulled her after him.

The girl screamed and fell to her knees, but Bydawine knew she was not injured, and the others were following. Like Noressa, he rushed ahead.

Noressa had reached the foot of the distant peak and begun to climb. Bydawine called to her to wait.

She looked back and waved. She continued to climb.

A flare of scarlet and a shiver through the stone bridge caused them all to stop and look back. An army had appeared on the plain. The black ebrot profiled on a red pennant proclaimed Tylek's presence within the assemblage. Remnants of the magic that had transported the army ebbed in a red haze over them.

A few of the soldiers milled uneasily, pressing back from the cliff edge where they had been deposited. The rest stared skyward.

Bydawine followed their lead.

Over the plateau sailed a beast from legend and nightmare. It was the length of a fifty-man cargo ship. Body scales of coppered gold and scarlet threw off spears of shattered sunlight. Like a striking serpent's, the triangular copper head darted forward on a thick neck. The nightmare beast swooped on crimson wings. Mere sheaths of skin stretched over a delicate bone frame, they seemed too frail to carry such a body. By the cloud of golden hair streaming behind, Bydawine recognized Felaya seated between the creature's wings.

The dragon's jaw opened in a silent roar. No sound penetrated the invisible wall, but Bydawine felt the challenge and fury in that action.

The creature thrust itself forward, aiming for the jagged peak and Noressa. Reaching the edge of the plain, it veered off, sliding away to climb again, taloned forefeet shredding the air. A second lunge at the unseen barrier was also fruitless. The beast screamed again, silent in its terrible beauty.

Kej sobbed, shuddering in terror. Yilla embraced him and whispered, "The mistress has come to destroy us!"

Her words angered Bydawine. "No!" He spun the girl around and pointed to where Noressa was again climbing. "There is your mistress, and she leads us to our only safety." He continued across the bridge.

Bydawine was the first to reach the far side of the chasm. Yilla and Kej were close behind. Farther back, Medwyn and the others were hurrying to join them. Bydawine and the children began climbing, following Noressa's trail.

Ice slicks and puddles of water among the open spaces between the rock at first made climbing treacherous. Then came patches of snow, topping boulders and crunching underfoot. The children scrambled ahead, and Bydawine cursed his short legs that would not carry him fast enough. He pushed himself until he could scarcely breathe.

Medwyn, too, was having difficulty. Now it was Brameth and Norwick who supported the elder. Bohsra, panting his own fatigue, came abreast of Bydawine and offered him his hand. Bydawine shook his head and pushed himself on.

After much scrambling over the partially covered rocks, they crossed the snow line, and the mountain disappeared beneath a white coverlet that extended to the summit. A line of churned snow marked the passage of Noressa and the children. After a time, Bohsra called a halt. Bydawine sat down in the snow, bent double by a lancing pain in his side. He was too tired to curse his short legs, too tired to worry about the redness of his toes in the open sandals. When the others reached him, they all rested, panting breathlessly in puffs of whie.

Bydawine looked back to where the copper-gilded dragon still rushed the bridge's invisible barrier. The chill that took him then was more than mountain air through his sweat-dampened clothes. He stood and willed himself in pursuit of Noressa.

At last he stood on the apron of snow leading into the cave. Without waiting to catch his breath, he hurried inside.

CHAPTER 31

**H**atred. It flamed in his belly; his throat was raw with swallowing its heat. His head throbbed in time to its angry pounding.

Pashet didn't think he could hate more than he did at this moment—but he was willing to try.

When the blaze of golden light faded from the midst of the battling armies, the girl was gone.

Pashet pressed himself against the charm-inscribed table, his gaze riveted on the charred lump that moments before had been his brother. His hands burned as though he squeezed live coals, and something wriggled against the table, and he ignored the pain. For that instant, Pashet let loose his hatred of the wizard, his look swearing vengeance beyond bearing. Tylek's answering glare flashed back the challenge. Before either could react, Felaya lunged from her seat, spitting fury.

She fell upon Tylek. Venting such rage that at times she could not be understood, she clawed and pummeled her surprised consort. "She is gone—gone, you fool! Let her go, you said. She will lead us to our treasure! But see what has happened—she is gone!"

Tylek dodged and twisted, using arms and cloak to shield himself from her attack. But when the abuse showed no sign of letting up, he lashed back with a single blow that slapped her to the ground.

Quiet slammed into the chamber. Not silence, Pashet noted, for he heard the rush of blood in his ears and his hissing breath, like that of an angry animal. In the turmoil, Yalst had pulled him from the burning agony of the table.

Pashet cradled his spasming hands to his chest. The last three fingers of the left hand were seared together. In the palm of his right hand was branded the sign of Maeluun, god of betrayal. Clearly he would not soon hold a weapon. Bits of crisped flesh were dislodged by his trembling, but the pain was fading, draining all feeling from him. Pashet looked up, watching Tylek through a growing numbness.

The horror of his action was engraved on Tylek's face. "Felaya! Mistress! Regent of my soul, forgive me!"

He reached down for her, but she snarled and scuttled away. She stood, one hand touching a reddened cheek, and Tylek paled before her unspent rage.

"You would strike *me?* I, who am all that you possesss—all that you are?" She advanced on him, and Tylek sank to his knees. "But that is what this has all been about, is it not? I see your intentions now. Your power, your youth, even your life, come from me. From my Companion. But it isn't enough that you are greater than any save me. It was in your mind to take this second Companion for yourself. Fool! Did you think that even a g'Hain bonding would make you greater than I?"

Tylek shook his head. Tears of naked terror streaked his face. "Not greater, Felaya! Never that! But I thought if we both held such power, we could rule together, unopposed. We—"

"Rule together!" Felaya laughed and shook her head. "You have always thought yourself greater than you are, Tylek. You dream greater than you should." She looked down at him, touching a fingertip to his tears, and smiled. "But then, you have always been greater than any other, eh, my beloved?"

Hope smoothed over Tylek's face. He took Felaya's hand and filled her palm with kisses. "None can match my feelings for you, Felaya."

"I thought as much." She smiled again, a mirthless stretch of her lips. "That is why yours must be the greater punishment."

Her free hand grasped him by the hair and snapped his head back. She pulled her other hand from his and reached for his throat. Her fingers shimmered, passed through the fabric of his robe, and fumbled against his chest. Tylek grappled at her arm and touched only air. Felaya withdrew her hand, clutching a broken gold chain. The bulge of some unseen talisman filled her grasp.

"No! No!"

Tylek wailed and would have torn the thing back, but the

hands he raised were suddenly gnarled claws. Blue-veined arms stretched from his sleeves. Strange sounds gurgled in his throat. Dry lips puckered into a near toothless maw accented by sunken cheeks. His eyes bulged in their sockets. Wisps of white hair hung in clumps across the mottled scalp. Tylek's body shrank beneath the sudden weight of unnatural years. He collapsed to the floor, one palsied hand still spasming toward Felaya.

She stepped out of reach, twitching the hem of her gown away from his groping fingers. "You would have done well to remember the humility of your true position, Tylek. Now you must accept your punishment gracefully." Felaya leaned down and dangled the broken chain before him. "Do not thrash about so, beloved. You will tire yourself. And that is not wise, for if you can live long enough in this state, it may convince me to restore your precious beauty."

Even hating him as he did, Pashet had to look away from the pleading in Tylek's half-blind eyes. Then Felaya raked him with her angry gaze.

"Gather your men and supplies in the courtyard, Pashet. We leave at once!"

She strode past him, and he hid his ruined hands in a deep bow.

Yalst assisted him to the courtyard, and for Pashet, every move was an agony. His pain had returned threefold. The magic in the rune table held a vicious protection against any touch by the uninitiated. The memory of its silent attack screamed along his spine and throbbed in the ruined flesh of his wounds. While Yalst gave the men their orders, Pashet sat in the shadow of the keep wall and stared at his hands.

Yalst brought wrappings and ointment for the wounds. He frowned on seeing the extent of the mutilations. "The physician should see to this."

Pashet shook his head. "Bind them and speak of it to no one. The mistress must not think me unfit. I will not be left behind."

Nearly ten score of men and their supplies crowded the area when Felaya stepped into the courtyard. She was followed by a small retinue staggering under the weight of her own quickly assembled goods. Behind them shuffled four Adepts with a makeshift sling bed bearing the wizened Tylek. Without pre-amble, Felaya stood among the men and invoked a web of scarlet light not unlike that which had carried away the girl.

There was a jolt that sent more pain across Pashet's back and a sensation of being whirled at the end of a long tether, then Pashet stood upon the crown of a decapitated mountain. His army filled the plain. Tylek lay among them, a mewling, shriveled thing writhing in the dust. Across a jagged ravine, a single figure scrambled up the face of a second peak; suspend-ed over the chasm, a group of seven others followed.

Pashet heard his men shouting. Some prayed, most cursed, all looked to the sky. Pashet tortured himself further, enough to look up.

On a hill of shattered boulders bordering the far side of the plain, Felaya stood unmoving. A vision of her soared the skies on a winged scarlet beast. Pashet watched her vain assault on the air at the edge of the cliff.

Pashet was jostled as many of the soldiers rallied near, their terror coming hard at him. He nearly shouted with rage at their ignorance. Did they expect him to soothe their fear?

But the idea pierced him deep, and a part of him closed against the anger—against all emotion. Of course they turned to him; he commanded them. Numb to all sensation, Pashet began issuing orders.

CHAPTER 32

**B**lind after the sunlight on the snow, Bydawine fumbled his way down the black tunnel. The way became easier when Medwyn entered and the light from the staff allowed Bydawine to avoid most hazards. The others weren't so fortunate. Steel rang on stone and someone cursed. The shuffling of boots on sand and rubble grated on Bydawine's nerves. He was imagining a horde of monsters awaiting them at the tunnel end, and some terrible fate for Noressa.

Then Norwick pointed and whispered, "There's a light!"

Bydawine looked to Medwyn in a moment of panic before he saw that his cousin was groping his way ahead, not looking at the staff. Content to stay near the staff's light, Bydawine had missed the softer glow emanating from a second tunnel to their left.

Cautiously they followed the narrow passage. It curved inward, then opened to the entrance of a long, deep cavern.

Without torch or flame of any kind, the light that had guided them washed down from the jagged ceiling. Noressa and the children stood together in the center of the cave. Beyond them, the chamber was nearly dark. In place of stone, a curtain of smoke formed the far wall. From the tunnel, a cold wind cut across Bydawine's legs. He stepped into the room and was enveloped by warmth.

"Noressa!" He ran to where she stood with the children before a pile of stones. His fear subsided only when she smiled and spoke his name, then turned and greeted the others.

"Bydawine! Medwyn! Come, see what my mother has left to me!"

A low granite pillar stood within a V-shaped space formed by two slabs of black rock. Atop the pillar rested a bowl of transparent dark blue glass filled with water. The glow of a small white stone floating in the water illuminated the chain of runes around the bowl. Bydawine could distinguish the signs warning of time, heat, and death. The others were a jumble that blurred away when he tried to decipher them. If Medwyn could make sense of them, Bydawine did not know, for the magician was staring at his staff.

Always bright, now the wand pulsed with light. From the bowl, the white stone gleamed an answering cadence. Noressa looked suprised by the stone's activity; Bohsra and the others shifted uneasily. None gave any notice to Medwyn.

The magician looked between the two lights, sadness in his face. "More and more, I am surprised by the power my mistress held." He stepped away from the altar, and both staff and stone dimmed.

Kej sighed and looked up at Noressa. "It is truly a wonderful shrine, mistress, but which god does it serve?"

"One not of this world," she answered.

Bydawine's gaze moved to the wall of smoke. It hadn't advanced into the chamber; it hadn't changed its shape or size. Motion eddied across its surface, but clearly it was restrained. He stepped past the altar.

His first sensation was of cold, a burning cold that drained his strength. Next was pain, as Noressa cried a warning and jerked him back. The sudden warmth from the shrine seared his skin.

Noressa addressed them all, her face stern. "No one is to touch the shrine or pass beyond it. All that we require is here." She pointed to an opening in the left-hand cave wall, another on the right.

Only when each person had nodded his assent did she relax. Then she smiled. "We are all hungry and in need of rest. Let us make use of the things provided." She started for a chamber in the right-hand cavern wall.

Bydawine felt a touch on his shoulder and paused as Norwick bent to speak to him. "I think it best that someone keep watch outside. Tell Bohsra that I have returned to the entrance."

Bydawine nodded, then hurried to catch up with the others. Inside the new chamber, he found it lacked the warmth of the main cavern, but it was lit with the same soft light. And it was filled with foodstuffs.

Large packets of cured meat were stacked against the stone walls. Sacks of grain and flour alternated with wheels of cheese across the room's center. Suspended from the ceiling swung ropes of dried fruits. A small spring welled from a knob of rock near the entrance, sending a tiny waterfall down a crevice in the floor. A second doorway opened to a further chamber.

Bohsra sifted a handful of grain and tested the freshness of the fruit. "The grain is clean," he pronounced, looking surprised. "And there is no rot among the fruit."

Bohsra's battleknife cut deep into the skin of a cheese wheel. The smoky aroma of the buttery white cheese filled Bydawine's mouth with juices.

When Bohsra offered the thick slice to Noressa, she broke it in two and gave half to each of the children.

"Enough for all, if you please, Bohsra."

He bowed. "An honor, my lady."

Soon each was chewing contentedly. While Bohsra cleaned his knife, Bydawine carefully packed the wax peels against the exposed interior of the wheel. He quickly tied up the coarse cloth around the cheese and hurried to join the others as Noressa led them into the second cave.

That chamber led to another and yet another—eight in all, each lit with the soft light that burned without flame, and each revealing a wealth of supplies. Some held blankets and men's clothing and the tools for the repair of weaponry. Others contained wood and tinder.

In the last chamber, Brameth pulled a fur robe from a pile of clothing and draped it around Noressa's shoulders.

Bydawine saw their hands touch, linger, as she drew the robe tighter. Then she was leading them back to the main cave. Bydawine followed last, grinding unspoken anger in the dust beneath his sandals.

Without hesitation, Noressa made for the last passage across the cavern. A short corridor and a right turn led them into a small antechamber.

A single cot crowded one wall. There was room enough to pass by it, and through the heavy drape screening a final room.

A cot, similar to the first, sat across from a camp table and two stools. A leather traveling bag stood at the foot of the bed. On a broad shelf of stone were gathered a lady's grooming articles and a small wooden chest.

Noressa touched a silver hairbrush, caressing the top of the chest. She whispered, "It was my mother's room."

In unspoken accord, the men withdrew.

They set up camp inside the entrance of the main cavern. The smaller rooms provided all they needed to be comfortable. Norwick was supplied with warm clothing, food, and arms to continue his vigil at the cave mouth.

Soon a cookpot held a bubbling soup of meat and rice. Kej surprised them by turning out three golden loaves of coal bread.

After they had eaten, Bydawine took Medwyn aside and told him what had occurred in his few moments beyond the altar. As they passed near the shrine, the staff brightened and dimmed.

Medwyn sighed, his wonder evident. "This place is a mystery to me." He nodded toward Noressa's chamber. "She is a mystery. The power she displays is not of her own making, of that I am certain."

"A legacy from her mother, perhaps, awakened by Noressa's presence," Bydawine offered. He looked at the staff, then quickly away, battling the desire to snatch the wood from his mentor.

"There is truth in what you say," Medwyn answered. "It is clear now what Mistress Breann was about when she left Ac-'talzea. But there is something more—someone more." He looked back at the shrine. "This smacks of the power of gods. It is a thing that could lay to waste our world or raise up countless others. Who can say how it came here?"

"Noressa's amulet? The Companion?" Bydawine whispered. "It is the thing for which your war was fought. And Noressa has spoken of a great magic that is always with her but cannot be touched."

Medwyn frowned. "She has not told me of this."

Bydawine looked from the shrine to Noressa's doorway. "What could it be to hold such power?"

"A curse!" Medwyn's anger snapped in his words. He kept his voice low, but his finger stabbed a warning at Bydawine.

"My mistress had the strength to destroy Felaya in one stroke. She died rather than unleash it and destroy a single child!" He shook the staff at Bydawine. "I know your love of wizardry, Bydawine, but remember that power seduces without mercy. Consider the devastation Felaya has brought in desiring this token. Beware that you do not follow her example!"

Anger crackled between them. The moment seemed endless as Bydawine glared his defiance, but he was the first to look away. He turned to go. Medwyn blocked him with the staff.

"Do not push so hard for rank, Bydawine." Medwyn's voice was soft, the anger gone. "Enjoy your time as a pupil. The weight of master will come too soon."

Bydawine could make no civil response, and so he strode away in silence.

CHAPTER 33

Well into his third cup of wine, Pashet watched the evening activity in the camp.

Only a few men were out. The winged horror had disappeared from the sky hours ago, but Pashet knew the feelings of his men. They preferred the imagined safety of their tents rather than risk being caught in the open should the beast return.

Pashet had no such fears, but his mind was as dark as that of his men. The vision of Jaaben's death played itself through his mind constantly, and the pain in his hands alternated from throbbing lances of agony to periods of complete numbness. For now, the pain was quiet, and the wine carried him comfortably from moment to moment. Only a single regret marred his drunken serenity.

Since their arrival, Pashet had watched the four Adepts guarding the sling bed and its occupant. When Tylek's pavilion was set up, they had carried their master inside, leaving one Adept as sentry at the tent entrance.

If it were not for those four . . . Pashet sighed and signaled for more wine. He had missed his chance. Not long after Felaya's and Tylek's shelters were put up, a maid had crossed from Felaya's tent and spoke to the hooded figure at Tylek's door. Immediately the sorcerer was carried into Felaya's pavilion. Pashet had slipped into line behind the Adepts and settled quietly near the door.

When the sling bed was deposited at Felaya's feet, Pashet could scarcely believe the thing upon it lived. Tylek could have been one of the countless unburied corpses from the desert caves of Drinlar. Toughened skin stretched over a skeleton framework. Tendons stood in hard shadow against bone. The skull sheath of skin pulled his jaw agape. His robe had been removed and a light woven cloth drawn up to his waist. The anguish in his clouded eyes was the only sign that Tylek still lived.

Felaya frowned at him as a mother might when confronted with a vexing child. His talisman lay in her lap, the chain whole again.

"Ah, beloved," she cooed. "Arrogance and ambition are powerful tools when used against any other save your queen. I trust you have learned this thing?"

In answer, a single tremor coursed over Tylek's body.

With unexpected gentleness, Felaya bent and placed the medallion in his clawed hand. His fingers twitched over it. Tender new skin plumped the hand, spreading in a pink flush up the arm and down his entire body. Sinew flexed. As quickly as he had withered, Tylek revived. When he was whole, he sat up. An Adept came forward carrying the mage's silver-shot robe and wrapped his master in the garment. Silent, Tylek knelt and trembled before his queen.

Pashet saw the satisfaction in Felaya's smile as she accepted Tylek's homage. Then, with a wave, she dismissed him and the gathered company.

Now, hours later, from the door of his own tent, Pashet still watched the mage's tent. He strained his eyes trying to focus on the Adept at the door. The man seemed to be fading within a dull red haze. Wind kicked up swirls of dust that further obscured the tent.

It was then that Pashet saw the scarlet cloud growing over Felaya's tent. It seethed with a lambent brilliance, a flush of dark color against a darker sky. Flames from torches and cookfires leapt up, straining toward the cloud. Pashet was drawn from his tent by a high, wild keening that filled his skull. A furious wind scorched across the plain, scouring the strength from him. Soldiers rushed from their tents, and Pashet heard the terror in their shouts.

Above, the hovering redness drew itself into a shimmering glazed ball. A crimson lightning bolt crackled, splitting the cloud. Thunder rolled. The winds died, and an oily rain fell.

Hands bleeding afresh, Pashet staggered back into his tent, too exhausted to do more than endure the pain.

CHAPTER 34

he rain continued through the night. It fell in dark sheets, quickly eroding the snow until the rocky skin of the mountain was exposed.

Bydawine doubted that even Tylek would attempt to lead his men over the bridge in such a downpour, but Bohsra ordered the watch to continue. Each man took his turn, though each was careful to remain inside the cave mouth. They were all men accustomed to the rigors of camp life, including the discomfort of rain, but this deluge was something new. Despite the cold wind that flung the rain against the mountain, the water itself was warm. The great oily drops left a faint coating on the skin and brought an irritability to any it touched.

After his watch, Bydawine spent a fitful time trying to sleep. He dozed, racing through unremembered nightmares, and woke often, starting up at the sound of imagined voices. Finally he abandoned his efforts at rest and left his tent to stir up the cookfire.

Toward morning, Yilla padded from her chamber, scrubbing the sleep from her eyes. She filled a bowl with some of the stew and took the last of the coal bread. Bydawine returned with her as far as the outer opening to the women's chambers. When he asked after Noressa, Yilla sighed, her young face pinched with worry.

"The mistress has not slept this night. She sits hour after hour, reading missives left by her mother." Yilla looked down at the tray she carried. "Perhaps if she will take some food, she may also rest."

Bydawine watched her disappear around the corner to her room and returned to his place beside the fire. When the others began to emerge from their own restless sleeps, he went to stand with Norwick at the cave entrance. Together they watched morning manifest itself as a fading of the night's blackness to a pale gray. But there came no sunlight nor any slackening of the rain.

After a time, they heard the pound of running feet, and Kej rushed toward them. "The mistress commands that all attend her," he said breathlessly.

Bydawine reached the inner cave before Norwick or Kej. Noressa stood before the black-walled altar. She looked pale and vulnerable in the soft gray gown she had substituted for the tattered homespun. Her hair had been brushed to a glossy black and hung loose, almost to her knees. Its color accentuated the dark circles of fatigue under her eyes, yet her eyes blazed with intensity.

Her look frightened Bydawine. Was this the same girl who, just the night before, was giddy with joy on discovering her greatest desire? He reached out to her with the mindspeak.

Part of her greeted him, then sped past. Her thoughts were a chaotic race of puzzles and enigmas, chasing round and up toward a distant conclusion that was ever out of reach. He tasted her emotion, a wavering of sweet delight, bitter sorrow, and the rancid cloying of new fears mixed with old. From somewhere, she had received an inpouring of knowledge, an exposition of magic and strength that all but smothered him with its potency. Though he tried, Bydawine couldn't hold to even one of those magical secrets. The force of her greeting and passage hurled him back into himself.

When they were all gathered, she addressed them in a quiet voice. "I have learned much since coming to this place, but there is more that awaits me. Soon I will leave you to complete this task." She quickly silenced their objections. "This is a thing I must do alone, and there is little time left to me. From this moment on, I must depend upon you and the others to guard for me this small margin of time."

"What others?" It was a chorus of voices, Bydawine's the loudest.

In answer, Noressa turned and walked past the altar toward the swirling haze at the back of the cave.

They all followed, but even knowing what to expect, Bydawine wasn't prepared for the seizing cold that fell upon him. The others gasped and shivered, but Noressa proceeded, giving no sign that the cold had touched her.

She stepped into the mist. It retreated, rushing back as though sucked into the lungs of some great god and taking the cold with it.

Revealed was an army of stone.

Soldiers fashioned of glittering black stone were mustered at attention. Each stood with weapon in hand, looking into some unseeable distance. They were chiseled perfection. Each was a master's crafting; each detail was complete. Men of war who had seen battle, they stood shoulder to shoulder, nine across, in rows that led far back into the mountain.

Bydawine heard Bohsra's exclamation of surprise. The rebel rushed forward to touch the giant stone officer standing apart in front of his men.

"Sarel! It cannot be!"

Medwyn and Brameth flanked Bohsra, each with his own expression of disbelief. Bydawine and Norwick moved to stand with Noressa.

"What is this?" Norwick asked.

Noressa smiled at him. "My army."

Brameth ran trembling fingers over the hard jawline of the sculpture that stood as tall as he. "It is my father," he said softly.

Norwick stepped forward to inspect the figure. "How can you be certain?"

Brameth let his hands fall away from the stone but continued to search the immobile face. "I was so young when he left, I thought I had forgotten. But I know him."

Noressa went to Brameth. Taking one of his hands in both of her own, she leaned close, murmuring words of comfort.

Bydawine watched them and felt jealousy twist inside him. The emotion came out in his words as hauteur. "This cannot be a true man. It must be only a monument to the memory of a brave soldier."

Bohsra stared up into the unseeing eyes of the man Brameth had called Father. "Sarel was my brother in all but blood. We traveled together from Drael to join the king's service. We trained together, fought together. It was I who accompanied King Brydon into the land of the sorcerers. And when we returned with our queen, Sarel became her captain. It is fitting that he should stand as testament to the loyalty of our people."

Medwyn shook his head. "I believe we have found the lost warriors of the queen, the same ten score of men who left with Breann but never returned from her journey. I knew many of these young men." Moving to the first row, he touched the petrified dressing on the thigh of one man. "Maen took an arrow as they departed Ac'talzea, but he would not be left behind."

Noressa stepped beside Bohsra. She smiled as she gazed up into the chiseled face of the soldier, Sarel. "He is not lost to you, Bohsra. He lives. He is part of my legacy."

White-faced with fury, Bohsra glared at his queen. He jerked away when she tried to touch him.

"I do not speak out of disrespect for your sorrow, Bohsra. I mean only to say that it is misplaced."

Medwyn's face was hard as he came near her. "Cruelty does not become you, Noressa. Are you now so jaded by your power that you will take pleasure in another's grief?"

Noressa looked from Medwyn to Bohsra, then back at Brameth. "Your comrades are not dead. They only sleep, and at my command, they will come forth to stand with you again." She took in all the cave with a gesture. "You wondered why your queen would leave her people in their most needful time. This place is why. She came here to prepare a last stronghold. In this fortress—and here—" she touched her forehead—"my mother left all that was important for her country and her child."

Bydawine felt a tightening in his chest. Again Noressa was changed. She had grown. Her independence was like a crest emblazoned on a pennant. She was in control, and the danger outside the cave held no terror for her. Her future held only greatness. She smiled at Brameth, and Bydawine felt his own future hurtling away in darkness.

Noressa put out a hand to Brameth.

"Your father will soon be restored to you." She looked to Bohsra. "Many of your friends will breathe again. For you, it will be as a revival of the dead; for them, it will be as awakening after a single night. But their world is no more. Children will be grown. Wives and lovers will be dead or mated with others. They will have gone to sleep in war and will awaken to war, having lost all their lives between. There will be little time to accommodate their loss, for they must wake ready to do battle. They, and you, are my vanguard. We must be ready at any moment to engage the final contest."

The ground tremored against their feet. The air grew heavy, as though holding against an inward pressure. Noressa looked to the cave entrance. "Felaya grows impatient and my time grows short."

She faced Sarel, again looking into his blank stone eyes, but Bydawine saw that her vision had already turned inward. He sent a touch into her mind, determined to be with her in whatever journey she was beginning.

But Noressa slipped away, not rejecting his contact so much as she was pulled from it. With hands out before her, palms up, she moved further into herself. Bydawine felt her go, felt the tingle along his spine that signaled the approach of magic. Startled looks from the others told him they felt it also.

The floor trembled again, and Noressa swayed. Brameth and Norwick started forward, but Bydawine called them back. "Leave her! Whatever happens now, we cannot interfere."

The floor vibrations ceased. Noressa continued to sway, matching the rhythm of an unheard beat. The chamber brightened, filling with a soft yellow light that quickly deepened to warm gold. Around her, cracklings of light flickered down into a shimmering diffusion. Bydawine shrugged hard against the itch crawling over his skin. The gathering magic lifted the hair along his arms, and the metallic taste of it was sharp under his tongue. Yet the only sounds were the mingled breathing of those around him, coming harsh in the cool, damp air.

In moments, Noressa was enmeshed in the same radiance that had transported them from battlefield to mountaintop. Surrounded by a lacework of power, she was buoyed by a silent wind. Her skirts billowed, tendrils of hair lifted to merge black with gold. The light entered her body and flowed out from her hands.

The others had withdrawn at the first brightening. Bydawine remained near her and was hard put to hold his place. He was buffeted by silence. The influence of her magic drew him;

the essence of it refused him approach. He threw up his arms against the deepening brilliance. At its core, Noressa was only a dark shadow. When it seemed the terrible pressuring would fling him away, Bydawine heard the snap and roar of a gods-whipped thunderstorm.

The web of light distilled itself into a molten column. Brilliance shafted from Noressa's hands into the body of Sarel and thence into the row of soldiers behind him. It cracked and writhed its way back through the rows from man to man, encircling each in a web of blue-edged gold. Definition of features and form wavered as light masked the stone figures. There came a surge of wind, accompanied by sounds that were almost voices. Sarel's face softened, then took on shadow and the ruddy blush of life. On a whirling of wind, the light rushed up out of each man and away into the mountain. A collective sigh wafted upward, and the lost warriors of Sidra stood as flesh and blood.

Noressa reeled with true exhaustion, and Brameth hurried to her and gathered her into his arms. Bydawine could only endure the pain that gripped him as she rested herself against Brameth. Then everyone turned his attention to the soldier advancing on stiff legs.

Sarel came forward, dark yellow eyes darting from one to another of the group before him. Bohsra stepped forward to embrace his old friend.

"Sarel, my brother! The years have taken nothing from you!"

Surprise took Sarel's expression at the weight of time in his comrade's face. "Years?" he whispered, and his gaze swept the circle of companions again. He hesitated when he saw Brameth, then stepped before Noressa. Sorrow and bitter understanding flowed across his face, and he whispered again, "Years."

Then, with sword half drawn, hilt proffered to Noressa, he cried, "My queen!"

In his words, Bydawine heard both agony and acclaim as Sarel bent to one knee.

* * * * *

The rumbling of the voices of over two hundred men was only a faint noise from the outer cave. Bydawine squeezed past Brameth into a narrow space at the end of Noressa's bed and watched her. She was pale, sitting up against a pile of dark furs.

After Sarel's vow of allegiance, the entire army had come forward to give homage. The men wept for their old queen and cheered the new. All rejoiced in their awakening. Father and son cried openly as Sarel embraced Brameth. Medwyn and Bohsra passed through the army, greeting old friends. Noressa had remained among them, all morning, seated in a camp-stool lined with furs. She smiled and spoke with any soldier who came to swear his allegiance. But her face had thinned, and Bydawine saw her shiver often, despite the furs and the warmth of the altar. After a time, exhaustion overcame her, and Brameth carried her to her chamber.

Now she sat clutching a handful of parchments taken from the chest beside her and sipping wine stirred with one of Medwyn's herbs. Medwyn and Yilla attended her; Brameth towered at the doorway.

After a low-pitched conference with his queen, Medwyn rose to leave. Brameth preceded him out, and Bydawine eased from his place to follow. Noressa put out her hand to him.

"Stay but a moment, Bydawine."

Yilla looked from him to Noressa but said nothing. With only slight disapproval on her face, she stepped into her own room.

"Come sit with me." Noressa's voice was little more than a whisper.

Bydawine hurried to bring a stool from the small table to the bedside. Even so, by the time he settled himself, Noressa lay with eyes closed, her breathing long and slow. He waited, thinking her asleep, and not wanting to wake her by leaving too soon. He was glad of the chance to be near her, with no others clamoring for her attention. It was his chance to take in the look of her.

Her hair was pulled over her right shoulder. It spilled in a dark swath across the blanket, the ends a curly mass in her lap. In her face, he saw shadows cast by the single candle and was haunted by images of the child-soft Noressa he had met in early spring. That had been the Noressa of the easy laugh, of the trust given to everyone, and the innocent confidence that all must work well if one were in the right. That Noressa sparkled like an emberstone cut raw from its matrix. Now she wasn't so innocent to the ways in which the world could be cruel. Laughter didn't come as easily; trust was tempered with caution. Like the skilled hand of a jewel master bringing out the treasured glow of the emberstone, experience had honed and polished her.

It hurt Bydawine to see the cost of that experience. Her gaunt look was more than a trick of candlelight; she was thinner since their arrival at the mountain. Her face was sharply defined with fatigue. Determination put a firmness to her lips even in sleep. He wondered what power she had wakened to bring them all here and raise to life an army of stone. It was obviously one that required sacrifice of self from the user, as well as desire and spellbinding. He could only hope that her inner strength was enough to see her through this siege. If she survived, she would be well fitted to take the throne.

If?

Bydawine drew a sharp breath at the unintended doubt in his thoughts. Noressa opened her eyes.

Her arm tightened around the scrolls, and she glanced down, as if to assure herself of their presence. Looking relieved, she lay back and closed her eyes again. As if from her sleep, she spoke suddenly, catching him by surprise.

"You must keep the army within the wall of protection as long as possible. Let no soldier spend his skill without need. Soon enough Felaya will penetrate our defenses."

He struggled to understand her. She spoke as if these future actions would happen without her. Did she foresee herself absent in the final battle? Fear twisted his insides. Noressa was the strongest among them. If she could not withstand Felaya's might, what chance had the rest of them against the witch? As so often happened, his fear became anger.

Why does she speak of this to me? he questioned himself. Why not Bohsra? He is commander of the army. Or Brameth. He is—

Noressa was watching him. Her gray eyes had darkened to the color of storm clouds.

"Bydawine, you are my oldest friend in this war of blood kin. We share a bond even Medwyn cannot explain. I trust you with all that I am; Bohsra will trust you also. One final test awaits me before I may confront Felaya. I cannot say how long its completion will delay my return. To maintain my sovereignty, Bydawine, I need your strength."

Her voice faded, and she seemed to sleep again. Bydawine stared, dumbfounded. Had he spoken aloud without realizing it? Or could she read him without his knowledge? Had she looked into those sheltered places inside him where even he did not enter? He remembered that morning in the keep when her mind lay so open to him. Now he saw how vulnerable he, too, could be. He stared hard at her. Perhaps she had only anticipated his question and . . .

The substance of her words penetrated.

"Return? From where? You cannot mean to leave us. How can we fight without you?"

When she did not answer, he shook her arm and whispered sharply, "Noressa!"

She started up, recognized him, and sank back with a sigh. "Forgive me, Bydawine. I must gather myself from time to time."

Ashamed at his panic, Bydawine remained silent. Noressa realigned the scattered scrolls into the crook of her arm. A tenderness came into her face, and she touched the crinkled edge of a scroll.

"I now know better this legend who was my mother. In these letters, she left a study of her magic, her craft, to be used as a weapon against Felaya. But she tells also of how she came to a new land and made it her home. I know the dreams she had for her people and her love for my father." Tears brimmed as her hand went to the medallion at her throat. "She was a strong woman, Bydawine. From the beginning, she held the power to destroy her sister. Oh, but Felaya was wickedly clever. She waited until a time that use of such a power would have exacted too high a price."

The flash of something ugly came into her face. Bydawine shivered to see again the toll Noressa's new magic had taken on her. He understood what such power would have taken from a woman ripe with child.

"You," he murmured.

Noressa nodded.

The ugliness was gone, washed away by tears flooding down her cheeks. "She could have given my father a keepful of princelings. Our people would have lived peacefully in a prosperous land. The alliance of our two kingdoms would have stood unbreached. Is that not a worthy goal for any queen? Why would she sacrifice all that might have been for the life of a single child—even her own?"

Bydawine couldn't say where his answering words came from, but they slipped quietly from his lips. "Perhaps the lady Breann knew the child would be much like herself, a soul who cherished life."

Great sobs shook Noressa. Parchment rolls scattered to the floor as she sat up, arms raised to him. Bydawine sprang to his feet and pulled her close.

He drew into himself her rage at Felaya. He didn't shy at her anger with others, like Medwyn and himself, whom she blamed for having shown her where her duty lay. He took in the fears that stalked her—death, and failure in the eyes of those who trusted her. They struggled together in her sorrow for the loss of those she had loved, and with her self-censure for the offense of being alive.

He clung hard against the savagery of her emotions, doing no more than keeping them afloat in the storm of her pain. When the tempest was spent, he filled her emptiness with images of life—water singing over stones, the cradled weight of an infant, hot embers on a cold, white morning. The small contentments of being he threaded into her mind. He coaxed from her the dreams of what could be, until she no longer clutched at him, only lay against his shoulder, drawing shuddery breaths.

She didn't wake as he laid her down and smoothed the damp hair from her face. He stood a moment, flexing fingers and arms to lose the stiffness in his shoulders.

The old loneliness rushed at him. An ache of futility brought up the shielding anger to battle the heat of disavowed desires. He watched Noressa sleep and fought himself. Familiar arguments beat down the yearning to have still more than was now his. I am sufficient to myself. Had he not pursued and won his place in life? Magician, advisor, confidant, spokesman, and now regent. What need had he for recognition from this girl beyond that of queen to counsel? She had come to him in her weakest moment, and he had served her well. Her faith was in him above all others. Was that not recognition enough?

It must be enough. Nothing more was required; nothing more would be allowed. The unacceptable fervor was again thrust into an oblivion of denial. He was a nobleman of intellect, with no need for the passions of common men.

He bent and retrieved the scattered parchments. He hefted them slowly. On these rolls were charms and magic spells that could give him power above all he had dreamed. He stood a long while considering it, then carefully placed the scrolls in the chest and closed the lid. They were not meant for him.

Noressa stirred. She mumbled in her sleep and turned to one side. Bydawine pulled the coverlet over her shoulders. He touched her cheek. So many things were not for him.

He stumbled from the room, past Yilla curled on her own bed, and out into the midst of the army to find the day gone.

Through the night, his pain would not let him rest. It drove him out to the cave entrance to stare, unseeing, through the endless rain.

He was there still when Yilla's cries raised the alarm of Noressa's disappearance.

CHAPTER 35

Sorcerer and sorceress remained in their tents for two days, gathering strength. Pashet, too, remained in his quarters, nursing his hands and his hate.

On the evening of the second day, Felaya again demanded Tylek's presence, and the two retreated to their sorceries. Felaya was intent on breaching the invisible barrier that kept her from the far peak.

Pashet and his men could only wait as the pressure of gathering magic grew over the encampment, and the ground shuddered more often than not.

During that night, Pashet watched a procession of torches wind its way down from the cave. The procession did not stop at the canyon edge but continued out over the chasm to form a ring of flames suspended in the darkness.

At dawn, the press of Felaya's magic surged. The air at the edge of the cliff shimmered red against blue. Pashet felt the sizzle of competing magic, then the barrier shattered in a spray of sparks. Pashet had his orders, and when the wall fell, he stood at the cliff edge with his troops.

What they saw was a wide stone causeway bridging the two peaks. Across the bridge waited an army. Before a row of tents, armed soldiers stood in formal ranks. Pashet recognized the figure of his dwarf standing among them. Beside him was an old man in the robes of an elder. A brightness streamed upward from a staff in the magician's left hand. The light thinned and spread over the gathered soldiers as a blue-edged canopy against the rain.

Muttering swept through Pashet's men. He heard their displeasure at this latest surprise. Under Felaya's magic, they had expected an easy end to this venture and a quick return to the comforts of their lowland base. Already disoriented by the manner and suddenness of their arrival at the mountain, now their frustration and the rain brought out a strange defiance. But before their rebellion could take hold, Pashet sent them into battle.

CHAPTER 36

Noressa kept a steady pace through the unlit tunnel. She was barefoot, but she felt no discomfort from the cold stone. Were she seeing only through her eyes, she would have been blind. But *he* guided her.

His mindtouch had sought her out between the warm layers of sleep. *Your journey is not complete*, his voice thrummed. *Come, come to me.* And still responding to his summons, she pulled herself up through dreams of tears, and past the memory of a healing embrace to harsh wakefulness in her tiny room.

Yilla had not wakened as she passed. Neither Medwyn nor Brameth nor any soldier saw as she walked among them; she was a phantom outside their awareness. She moved past the altar and, without thought, past the farthest rock wall. Had the wall opened to receive her? Or did she move within the mountain, unchallenged by its substance? Even now, her double vision didn't tell her if she moved in spaces between stones or through the stones themselves. She observed from two vantages. As herself, she saw the rock walls loom and fade. But another self watched her approach, a self that flickered between the here and not-here.

He was a detached darkness at the edge of her sight, a quick-silvered sheen centering his own vision. Memories skirled at her feet.

Then she was in his place.

Welcome, petitioner. You are long awaited. Anticipation flared from him, snapping in green-black sparks. *I have not slept this passage of time for fear that your life would play itself out before my waking. Now again I may sleep with purpose.*

His words were a warmth around her. His voice was not

sound, but a soft thrumming that touched into her mind. *His* vision faded, leaving her alone with her own. The sense of him was overwhelming yet intimate. She wanted to touch him but found her body in so small a space that her arms were pinned to her side. Her back and breasts touched rock with each breath, and empty air supported her feet. She was buried at the heart of the mountain! Noressa thrashed against her rock prison.

Tiny pulses shivered along her body, distracting her mind from the terror sweeping down.

Rest awhile, sister-child. Recall a time when you were here only as a spark of being in another, and you will lose your fear of this place.

She laid hold of the depth that was him and tried to obey his prompting. The memories dancing in the rock slowed, wafting across her thoughts. Was there a time when she had been held in this darkness? In a pressuring, cushioned strait that bespoke only peace? Noressa shook her head. She couldn't remember such a time. But her fear slipped away, allowing more of him to envelop her. More than anything, she felt the greatness of time in him.

"So old!" Her words tasted musty, whispered against the crowding rocks. She felt his mirthful agreement.

Yes, I am thought to be well aged in my place and ancient beyond counting in yours. But I am strong and have many passages yet to share with future Companions before I go to meet the High Ones.

"High Ones?" Noressa couldn't mistake the respect in his reference.

Those who create; those who will judge. In your understanding, the gods.

"But are you not a god?"

Warm laughter brushed her. *I have been worshiped as such, but never demanded it be so. The difference of our worlds makes my kind great within your sphere. And only because our power cannot be wrested from us, your kind offers reverence to mine in exchange for its use.* He paused. *It is easy for your kind to build glory from our strength, yet it was not always so.* Sorrow colored his patience. *In the First Bonding, we were joined from love. Though we had often touched into your world, it was Tremsan, first brother, who made us know your kind. He called us to a new knowledge, a new perception. Now we crave our bondings with the same fervor as your kind.*

Noressa shivered beneath the yearning that caressed her. He drew back, remorse filling the space between them. His thoughts whispered entreaty through the rocks. *With a joining, our long sleeps are rewarded. Your passions become our dreams. Your lives are a measuring of our own. In you, we are made aware of self-time, and its passage is compensated. In the bonding, we build our glory upon your strength.*

Noressa was startled. He spoke of men's passions as though they were an elixir he must consume. His welcoming joy of moments before was gone. She couldn't touch him bodily, but she was Shay, sister to all that dwelt within the earth. She sent herself out into the mountain to meet and set aside his distress.

"We build upon each other, then. There is no shame in that."

Had he possessed body or breath, Noressa knew she would have felt him sigh. Instead, he slipped into her mind, using the channel she had opened to reach him. His hunger palpated, a need akin to pain.

Come join with me, sister-child, and let me sleep. I would ride the currents of my dreams touching unnumbered worlds. I would see beauty and pain and, through your eyes, know their worth. And these things I would share with you.

Noressa recoiled from the touch. She had felt such hunger before, on a distant riverbank and in a forest cottage. She fought to close herself, to push him from her mind, but he held fast. Still, he did not force himself further, and after a long struggle, Noressa lay spent, cursing herself for having been captured so easily, and waited for what was to come.

He moved closer and wrapped her with his own comfort. *Rest easy, treasured one. I am not this other you fear.* Unspoken behind his words lay the promise to withdraw if that were her true desire. She saw the pain in that oath and hesitated.

"Who are you?"

He became a stir of memory, a thread of pleasure. *My life-mothers called me*—Noressa held an instant's view of flame-bordered seas and black skies that melted to blue and an

emptiness scrubbed by a sweet-scented wind until a patina of
gold glimmered at the edges. The sights reeled past, a thousand images shattered through crystal. Senseless pictures, horrific in her eyes but understood and cherished in him. She
caught her breath, dizzy with the whirl of his alien language.
Then the vistas snapped away, leaving her in the dark.

*In your speaking, I am Kortmath. And I am wearied by this
long passage of waking.*

His weariness lapped around the stones. His eagerness to be
gone crowded at her, and she sensed again his reluctant promise to sever the hold on her mind he had established. She remembered why she had come and reached out with a thought,
suddenly fearing he would really leave her.

"But you cannot sleep! Felaya waits to destroy me, and all
who stand against her, to hold you as the prize. Unchecked,
her crimes would herald the end of my people. I will confront
her, and I need your strength to defeat her!"

*Then send me to my sleep. Only in my slumbers can you
take my power. In times ago, we destroyed your kind, unaware. But to Tremsan we gave oath, never again, and took in
exchange the delights in our bondings. Now Sister Felaya
holds to ransom the fulfillment I have come to crave. Yet I
cannot judge the right or wrong of her action. That must be
left to her own kind and the High Ones.*

"Then how may you offer your power against her in the face
of such an oath?"

*You might use my strength against her, sister-child. Or you
may not, as was the choice of your own life-mother. But that
judgment will be your own. And in my sleep, I cannot be held
to account for the actions of a dream.*

Noressa juggled thoughts crowding close, some hers, some
not. The presence of this unworldly being within her was a
frightening intrusion pointing up how truly solitary was the
mind of each man and woman. So often she had complained
of loneliness, yet now she saw how valuable was the isolation
of her mind. Still, she had come seeking to be joined. And
what was a joining but the bringing together of things that
were apart? Fatigue tilted her into a sense of displacement,
and she struggled back to the solid weight of her body. She still
hung within the mountain, the cold a brittle encasement.

Panic fluttered at her. How long? she wondered. What was happening outside?

She has not yet penetrated the wall, but soon. Our sister's anger is strong.

"Sister!" Noressa lashed out with her anger. "How can you call her such, knowing what is in her heart?"

Her fury was sent back. *She is bonded! There is naught else I may call her!* Noressa flinched before the heat of his response, and the fear beneath it. Then Kormath was repentant, drawing himself around her, soothing. *Forgive me, sister-child. I forget you do not know our danger. And in her search for power, Felaya has forgotten the lessons of Tremsan, the first brother. She remembers only that he was many-bonded with power beyond any before him, and she would recapture such a time for herself to the last Companion. But the full gathering of ourselves to one outlet would tumble both worlds. Even Tremsan could not abide the weight of all our joinings. He wisely set us each upon our own bridge of passage and sent us among his children.*

Kormath's voice warmed the amulet against her skin.

You are his child. Will you come to me?

Noressa shifted, not certain whether it was mind or body that wriggled in unease. Why was she never given time to think, to examine?

It was a petulant thought, an errant question to which she expected no answer. Yet Kormath drew away at once.

She remembered the excitement that had carried her to this moment. She came expecting to find a god, some all-knowing one who would show her the answers she sought. Instead, here was a being, certainly with powers far greater than hers, but who was so constrained he couldn't employ his strengths even in his own defense.

Or was it a ruse to test her faith?

Without her panic, she found his presence unaccustomed, but not uncomfortable. She touched at the place where he entered her mind. He quivered with desire, but said nothing. Silent, she turned from him, surprised that he didn't follow through the sequestered paths of her thoughts. He waited, tangled in the weariness that dragged at them both. She hid herself, gathering shreds of composure during the respite.

Once he pleaded, not in words but, through a flash of that double vision, showing herself through his eyes. She was a lambent star, veiled by a denial of silence. In time, the first eddies of resignation swirled from him. His hunger loomed, sharpened by desperation, but was forced aside. It was a hunger steeped in fear. His hopes in her faded. She felt him turn away, prepared to embrace a dreamless sleep if only for the sake of that sleep. Now she saw that, for him, to sleep was to live. And she knew at last that he was no god, for he had missed her greatest failing.

She felt the loosening of his hold and fought the pain of that letting go.

"I would gladly join with you," she whispered, the part of her he touched rising up to embrace him. "But it cannot be."

Kormath hesitated, new hope mingled with puzzlement. *You bear the talisman. You are the spark of being I touched within your life-mother, the one for whom I have waited.*

"But I am outbreed to the Clan of Dragonsblood."

Understanding swept him, and his laughter resonated through the mountain. His joy squeezed tight about her. *Foolish child! What matter is lineage? Even Tremsan was not of the clan until he set its name upon his children.*

"Then a joining has naught to do with blood? Why, then, has it only been with those of the clan and no others?"

She felt him smile, like a child with a secret. *Because no others have tried.*

Noressa blinked at the sheen that was the only part of him visible in her world. "Do you say that any may be joined if they will but try?"

She sensed his happy shrug, heard the drowsy slur already creeping into his thoughts. He nestled himself deeper into the part of her that still embraced him. *It is easier for those who are trained in the ways of the craft. And none but those of the clan have ever petitioned. But we have never denied bonding to any of your kind.*

"Then Medwyn was right. The token has no power of its own. But if it means nothing, why is Felaya so desirous of it?"

It means much. Kormath's voice rumbled, vibrating the stone. He sank deeper toward sleep, contentment radiating from him. *It is the bridge by which we are petitioned. Within*

*it, our two worlds become one and we are bound to any who
possess the token and can abide the joining.*

"I possess a token." The old happiness rose up, then was
checked as the meaning of his last words devoured her elation.
"Any who can abide the joining? Is there the chance I may
not? What further test must I face to prove my worthiness?"

His slide to the sweet darkness of repose slackened. She felt
his flash of dread, a moment of denial, then resignation,
coupled with that untouchable sense of sighing. *If test there
is, sister-child, it is within you, for I have none. That each ac-
knowledges the other is right enough to join. Some petitioners
before you had not the tempering to be joined and have gone
to meet the High One. But I believe you are strong enough
that we will be entwined. If not—his* thoughts fell to a
whisper—*then you will be no more, and I must wait another
space of time to be petitioned again.*

Noressa was silent. Doubt gnawed her determination. She
trembled in the cold but couldn't even cross her arms, pinned
as she was inside the mountain. She was suspended over a bot-
tomless shaft, enveloped by a being so alien that it had no true
form in her world. Nor did he share the risk of death as did she
who was being asked to surrender herself.

He waited, balanced on the lip of oblivion. Soon, she knew,
he would abandon himself to the pull of that darkness. What
would become of her then?

And what of Kormath? She already knew. Felaya would destroy the mountain down to the bottom of the world to retrieve the Token of Dragonsblood. Then Kormath would be,
not Companion, but slave. And her people even less.

Her people. She thought of all those who waited, their faith
strong enough that they would risk all to follow her.

*Should I not have as much faith in myself? And am I not
meant to protect my Companion as well?*

She reached back to the place where Kormath touched her.
But she was still afraid. She longed for someone to guide her,
someone who always knew her questions and how to answer
them. Brooding, ascerbic Bydawine could tell her what to do.

Yet she did not send out her mindspeak. This was her decision; she would find her own answers. She pulled back to Kormath.

He was gone.

He had slipped over the precipice into slumber. Noressa found herself rushing through stone, speeding toward light and air. She was being sent back to her own world. Kormath had read her fear and made his decision.

Noressa decided as well.

Groping blindly, she caught fast to those tendrils of him that carried her out. Racing along the slim channel, she sought him. She touched back to the primal energies of the earth. Dipping into the molten river that was the blood of her world, she used its impetus to slough away fear and anger. All that might hold her back was seared from her. She was a gleaming naked spark of being.

Noressa found Kormath, focused, and poured herself into him.

Together they soared. Two lives in one mind, they plumbed golden depths. Riding a maelstrom of possibilities, they tilted on azure tangents to climb a breathless void.

* * * * *

In Felaya's tent, Pashet watched Tylek huddle in the confines of his high-backed chair. Felaya sulked on her couch. Pashet stood behind Tylek occasionally, observing the battle in the viewstone and sensing the hard emotion in the air.

Two days before, Felaya had erupted into fury. Raging across the confines of the tent, her frenzied screams were a counterpoint to the clash of fighting from outside.

"She joins! She bonds this very moment! The filthy outbreed child takes my power!"

Even Pashet had felt something at that instant. Untrained though he was, he had felt the sudden rise and release of energies nearby. Now, two days later, his ruined hands still ached in response to the memory.

He looked over Tylek's shoulder and caught the man's covert gesture. Tylek caressed the soft skin on the back of his hand. He chanced a darting touch of his cheek.

Pashet smiled. Four days, and Tylek wasn't over his terror. Felaya's punishment had broken something in the magician.

Pashet's attention returned to the viewstone, a useless gesture, since the scene had changed little in two days. His army was still held at the edge of the precipice. They had gained no advantage. Worse, they were losing their zeal.

Rain and lack of maneuvering room meant that only a small group of his men could engage an equally small band of rebels. Each group fought under a canopy provided by its magic-users. Each group was replaced often by fresh troops. But the rain wasn't all that unnerved his men. Several times it seemed the rebels held the upper hand and could have gained a foothold on the plateau. But each time, the rebels drew back, using the time to rest or change men. They seemed content with their position. To Pashet, it appeared they would all remain in this dismal place, forever battling an opponent who showed no interest in ending the fight.

He glared at the tiny figures in the stone. One figure, smaller than all the rest, held his attention. His dwarf stood with Tylek's old enemy, Medwyn, dispensing magic that held at bay the best of Tylek's Adepts.

His anger mounted at the newly exposed talents of his dwarf. Had he known from the beginning that the little creature possessed such power, things might have gone very differently. Jaaben might yet live, and he himself might not feel the pressure of time so keenly. More than once these last two days, he had caught Tylek watching him and had seen the promise of death in those black eyes. Pashet was certain the sorcerer would do nothing until Felaya's conquest was complete. But when it was—

Both Pashet and Tylek jumped as Felaya sat up with a tiny gasp. She stared in the direction of the bridge as though seeing across its length through the tent wall. She was listening, every fiber of her straining. Felaya rose slowly.

"She is coming."

Tylek pressed hard against the back of his chair as Felaya took two steps and stopped beside him. Pashet held his breath. In a voice as cold as the glint in her violet eyes, Felaya gave her orders. "I will brook no mistakes this time, Tylek, so attend my words carefully. The girl is joined and comes forth from her bonding-flight. She is weak and will require some while to regain her strength and fully return her thoughts to this world. I will not give her that time. I go to send challenge, and she will not refuse me."

Felaya paused to stare at Tylek's throat. His hand flew to the top of his gown and he clutched his medallion. Felaya nodded. "Remember well what your talisman means to you, Tylek. And know that the Token of Dragonsblood means as much to Noressa. That token is what I want. When she answers my challenge and our battle is joined aloft, her body will stand helpless on the ground. Take the Token of Dragonsblood from her throat and place it upon mine." She smiled, anticipation lighting her eyes. "I will bond her Companion before she breathes her last agony."

Tylek quickly nodded his understanding. Pashet nodded also, though not because he shared Tylek's fear. Pashet's long-trained caution barely restrained a wild hope.

Then Felaya stepped away, shimmered in a crimson haze, and was gone.

CHAPTER 37

The return was more painful than the joining. They had lived a thousand lives, touched twice that many worlds. In the ecstasy of their flight, Noressa lived only through Kormath. With him, there was no other life than dreaming. Buoyed in a wash of colors that could not exist, she enfolded the depth of Time and felt its heartbeat.

Now she was being sent back, and there was only dread. Kormath herded her along dark channels, never allowing her to reach out for those flashes of brilliance that signaled other worlds. She pleaded, but he would not listen.

You must return. You must live or there will be no dreaming.

Noressa remembered a distant part of her that was fading for want of care. She was thrust into that cold, clay self hidden within the mountain.

She wasn't completely settled into that self before she was speeding outward again. Now it was her body that moved, pressed between the rush of stone and the weight of darkness. Great energies pulsed nearby, and she was drawn there. She emerged into pale light, and the open air threatened to crush her. Then she was down, collapsing among incoherent babblings.

Her mind slowed its whirling, and she recognized random touches as hands, noise as voices. She looked up into faces. Soldiers. Men of war armored against a death they called down upon themselves. They crowded close, and Kormath withdrew. He didn't leave her, but his presence pulled away from her conscious thought and she ached around that emptiness.

Someone gave her wine. She drank, demanded more. Food was brought and she ate without restraint. She stuffed herself, and flashes of memory built a shaky foundation of life. Images came of an old woman in the hands of fiends, a struggle for life upon a cold riverbank, and the haunting summons of a thing unknown.

Then familiar faces were before her—real faces of bone and flesh—and she smiled at Bydawine and Medwyn. Noressa would have reached to touch them, but she couldn't spare the effort from her feasting. Instead, she flicked into their minds with a hurried greeting and saw their horrified image of her: hair knotted and wild, gown a tattered sack hanging on her, a dust-blackened face so thin it might have been a death mask if not for the fevered eyes. "Where have you been? What has happened? How did you leave us?" Questions that she could not answer blatted against her. Recognitions of her world were coming too quickly to be spoken. She was wet, seated upon a pallet of furs and cushions. Within a tent. The food still had no taste, but her stomach now acknowledged its substance. And her ears were battered by the hollow thudding of some driving force upon the roof and walls of the tent. Part of her still searched for a path back to the glories of Kormath's mind. After her dreamtime, how could she console herself with this mundane wakefulness? What was here worth living for?

The answer blasted into her mind. A challenge. From riverbank and forest, from the hounding terrors of old sleep, Noressa recognized that call.

"Felaya."

She looked in the direction from which the challenge came, aware that no others had heard it. She was aware of many things, including the hunger still gnawing her belly and the thrill of Kormath stirring deep in his hidden place.

With regret, she swallowed the last bite in her mouth and pushed away the platter. The throng of men who crowded round pressed closer when she tried to stand. Medwyn laid firm hands on her shoulders and sat her back onto the furs. His face was gray with fatigue. Strain etched hard lines around his mouth, but his voice was still gentle.

"Don't worry yourself with Felaya. She hasn't yet shown herself, and we have the battle well in hand. Now the knowledge of your return will give our men greater courage. They are prepared to rally and take this band of traitors."

Noressa was tempted to stay. Here was food and comfort

and the chance to sleep, perhaps dream. But sensitized by her wild flight, she was still tender to the life pulses around her. Something of the struggle that had gone on in her absence played upon her new senses. She was surrounded by a tent full of reasons to live. She took hold of Medwyn's hands, kissed them, and lightly touched his mind, and Bydawine's, with the challenge still ringing in the air. Understanding filled their eyes, and with Medwyn's assistance, Noressa rose and left the tent.

An insolent rain slapped her as she emerged. Without thinking, she gestured, spoke, and the rain ceased. A cheer went up, but she scarcely noticed it. Noressa stood upon the stone bridge, staring across the distance to the jumble of boulders on the plateau ahead. She yearned toward the golden-haired figure waiting there. "Let it be finished here." She whispered the prayer to whatever gods were listening and felt her *self* follow her yearning.

Then she was high above the ground. Up on a flat black speckled rock, she faced her enemy. Felaya smiled, calm in the wind that howled around them, the expression of her eyes almost jovial. Her pale beauty was stark against the backdrop of storm clouds.

"You have learned quickly the use of your Companion's power, sister. It is sad you will not have time to grow accustomed to its stolen pleasures. That power should have been mine after Breann's death, and I intend to have it." The gentleness of her look set a razor edge to the menace in her words. Any other time, Noressa might have withered before it. Instead, she smiled as well.

"And if I give you this Companion freely, Aunt, will that be enough? Will it satisfy your hunger?"

Surprise took away Felaya's smile; wariness narrowed her eyes. Then the friendliness returned. "Of course, child. With a Companion of both L'erit and g'Hain, I would have the great and the small. My circle of power would be complete."

"But would that be enough for you?" Noressa pressed. "Would you be content with one circle of power? You would not desire a second, or a third? Perhaps a circle of circles?"

Felaya's eyes were cold. Noressa took a hard satisfaction in the anger clipping her aunt's words.

"Give me what I seek, child, and I will spare your people."

"And will you spare me as well, Aunt?"

Felaya spread her hands in a helpless gesture. "Alas, child, that is not in my power. I must snare the fleeing Companion at the moment of your death."

Noressa felt her restraint crumbling. The heat of her anger flared, but she kept her words as cool as the stone on which she stood. "You lie, Felaya. Even heavy with child, my mother endured the agonies of unbonding and lived. Why must *I* die?"

Silence. Then Felaya's eyes were black with hatred. Her face contorted in her scream of rage. "Because I wish it!"

A scarlet wave of malevolence soared out at Noressa. It would have toppled her had she been unprepared, but she held forth with her own fury, and Felaya was forced to call upon the Other within her.

Noressa pulled the essence that was Kormath around her, and together they unfolded into the sky.

CHAPTER 38

Dragons!

Pashet stared at the spectacle above him.

Two beasts sailed the black clouds. Wheeling in wide arcs, dipping and rising, each sought the underbelly of the other. They blasted the air, roaring challenge and defiance. Felaya's mount made a tight bank, turning sharply to come up beneath and behind the other. Copper-edged gold scales shone in the glare of flame that spewed from its mouth, and the thing was like a molten sunset splashed against the clouds. The fire leapt from its gullet, farther than any flame could fly, and gouged across the throat of its opponent. The other dragon bellowed and fell. It was a glittering liquid blackness plummeting across the valley between two mountains. Taloned wings beat heavily, cupped the wind, and slowly turned the creature's fall to a long glide. Pashet caught a flash of gold flushing the underside of those dark wings spread against the sky. Then the black dragon was lifting itself, spitting its own volley of flame.

Pashet was awed. He saw the two great beings strike out across the heavens, guided by riders so small they were hidden with each upward stroke of a wing. To control such strength would be an accomplishment worth any price. He understood now Tylek's desire to capture the Token of Dragonsblood for himself.

With that thought came the realization of where he was and what he should be doing. He still stood beside the great pavilion, but Tylek was gone. He and Tylek had raced outside following Felaya's departure. They were in time to view the blinding appearance of the girl, Noressa, on the crown of the rockfall where Felaya also stood. Pashet had watched the explosion of Felaya's anger and the comingled fountains of blue and scarlet thrown to the skies that resolved themselves into the scaled nightmare warriors. Now Pashet remembered his own peril. Searching for his adversary, he saw Tylek making his way to the base of the rockfall.

Tylek began to climb, his attention on the two women who waited, unmoving, above him. Pashet raced after him.

The magician was already high into the rocks when Pashet began his ascent. A roar to rival any issued by the dragons went up from the men below. Pashet looked down to see that the entire plain had become a battlefield. The rebel army had poured into the midst of their enemies. Tylek's Adepts were hard put to counter the new sorceries being thrown by his dwarf and the elder magician. Pashet put all he had into the climb.

It wasn't difficult at first. Boulders at the bottom of the slide were broken and tumbled. Long slabs of raw stone gave ample purchase for foot and handholds. Even with his burned hands wrapped in dressings, Pashet was gaining on Tylek.

Part of the reason for this, he saw, was that Tylek had reached an impasse. The sorcerer stood on the last of the broken stones; above was a layer of solid boulders. Large, round, and smooth, their surfaces offered no safe grip. Another reason was Pashet's anger, which propelled him upward faster than he expected. In his mind, he held the image of Jaaben, dead. He had watched his brother's body slump forward on the ground, one leg doubled beneath him. His neck was twisted, his head canted at a terrible angle over his shoulder. The memory of it made Pashet shudder, and he lost his concentration. His boot scraped along a sandy spot, slipped from under him, and he grappled at a projection of stone. He cursed, feeling the sharp-edged rock gouging his tender palm. When he regained his balance, Pashet slipped his long knife from its sheath and cut away the bandages. He would miss the protection to his burns, but now the dressings were a hindrance that bound his fingers and made grasping clumsy.

Blood oozed from his palm. Pashet stared at the sign of Maeluun crisped into his skin and prayed to invoke that god's assistance. If nothing else, the stench of betrayals should have drawn him long ago. Pashet needed some potency as great as Tylek's to turn the odds in his favor. He remembered his own latent power and, for the first time, regretted that he had never been bold enough to put himself under Felaya's tutelage. He saw, too late, that it was not talent that separated him and Tylek, but control. Tylek had been wise enough to see it and had contrived well to keep him from developing those abilities. Now the magician was about to use his one advantage to escape Pashet's vengeance.

Pashet saw Tylek's hands move in a hidden pantomime, his lips form unheard sounds. The sorcerer left the rock, levitating gently toward the summit. Pashet watched his final chance for justice fade until a sizzling green ball flashed by him, slamming into the rocks beside Tylek. A shower of rubble covered Pashet, and he choked on the sudden metallic taste at the back of his throat. One of the rebel magicians had broken through!

The shock of the explosion knocked Tylek against the side of a boulder. Now the magician was sliding toward him on a wave of rock debris and dust. Pashet watched Tylek twist and bump over the jumble of rocks, scrabbling for a handhold to slow his skimming descent. At last he caught a grip on a rock that didn't slip away from him, and he jerked to a stop.

Pashet blinked in disbelief. Tylek lay scarcely two arm lengths above him. He heard the magician's groans and smiled. Perhaps Maeluun had heard him after all!

He started to climb, stopped, and hid his face as a winged scarlet form swooped upon the plain, belching fire. Its black twin followed, thundering by in a rush of wind that almost tore him from the rockslide. Then Pashet was climbing. When he looked up, Tylek was scrambling away. The sorcerer looked back for a single instant, and Pashet saw the terror in his eyes.

Tylek again invoked his spell of levitation and lifted away. But this time, some force also rose in Pashet. All the rage he had held in abeyance came seething out of him. The frustration, capped by grief, engulfed him, and something that had slept too long within his heart awakened. The whole of his being expanded with that awakening. He had come into his own power and he *wanted* Tylek. Pashet's vision darkened to a sea of red, narrowing to that single black figure.

Pashet's hands ached, the right more so than the left. They burned at the touch of the cold stone, and something writhed in his palm. But Pashet wouldn't stop to deal with it. For some reason, Tylek's rise had slowed, stopped. He still hovered alongside the rockfall, but that was all. Pashet swarmed upward, his strength fed by the terror in Tylek's face. Then his fingers were tugging at the hem of Tylek's robe; he grasped a handful of the garment, pulling himself up. Tylek swung at him, missed, and swung again. Pashet caught Tylek's wrist and, using the strength of his rage, brought the magician sliding down onto the rocks. He felt the force of magic in the words Tylek screamed at him. He drew up his right hand, still aware of that cold-hot thing writhing in his palm, and smashed his fist into Tylek's mouth.

Tylek groaned through bloodied lips. Reeling from the force of the blow, he still managed to capture Pashet's hand in his. They struggled, hand to hand, on a narrow ledge, each hating the other with his eyes. Then Pashet felt a subtle shift in the strength that supported him. He saw Tylek begin to smile. The raw energy of his newly awakened magic had run its course, and Tylek's control of ritual and form was asserting itself.

Pashet closed his eyes, drawing in all the hatred that touched him, drawing strength from that, and in his last moment of domination, jerked free his right hand. He pulled his long knife and raised it high over Tylek's shoulder. Tylek brought up both hands to ward off the intended blow. His hands were up for only a moment before he realized his mistake, but it was a moment too long.

Pashet slid his free hand up along Tylek's chest until his fingers closed over the hardness of the amulet beneath the gown. He stripped away the talisman, the sound of ripping cloth masked by Tylek's high wail. Then he shoved the dark-haired magician from him.

Pashet recognized nothing of Tylek, the wizard, in the shrunken, silent body that crashed to the plain below.

But by then he recognized little save the angry slice of pain in his belly as a sizzle of green light cut him in two.

CHAPTER 39

She was free! A gossamer wish on winds of emptiness. She drifted up, and light passed through her, too heavy to be held. Merging into Kormath, Noressa was caught in the anodyne of other-place dreaming.

Those other worlds for which she yearned spun before her. Ebbings of song and color, sparks of white heat in a cauldron of black, they beckoned. She looked to Kormath, eager for whatever new pleasure he would show her, but Kormath lay placid around her. He did not direct or command. He channeled into her mind and pooled, a great silent reservoir. The choice of worlds was hers. Noressa teetered on the familiar edge of her own place, eager to launch into the new. If only she could free herself of this single tie. Something was left undone.

She looked back into the place she was leaving and found a nightmare bearing down on her. She remembered all that had passed before and knew what was yet to be done. And she saw then why Kormath had fought so hard for his dreaming. Long ago, his kind had made alliance with hers, relinquishing strength and sovereignty in exchange for the narcotic of dreams. And he kept silent now, for as a sleeper holds no responsibility for the actions of his dream, so, too, he is barred from any control of those actions. Noressa knew her place in the balance of that alliance. In exchange for his power, she had freed him from all reproach. Now she would share the joys of two hearts, but she would bear the liability of two lives. Below spread her armies of Sidra. Loyalist and traitor alike, they were her own. And she would not let them be destroyed by the reckless hunger of one who drew her pleasure and strength from all life but refused accountability for that drawing.

The realization struck even as she moved to avoid the charge of the scarlet beast above her. She slid away on a flow of air, astride a dragon form like that which pursued her. But the body beneath her was black, scales glittering like the surface of a hidden lake on a moonless night. She leaned far forward, clinging to the broad long neck stretched into the sky. This was Kormath in her world. Bringer of fiery death, demon of legend, a creature long since banished to the nebulous trust of nightmares and fireside tales. But now he was real, as real as the body she had left on the rocks below.

The screech of her scarlet predator cut the air, drawing an answering cry from her. Noressa's mind reached out, and she put herself into the double vision that was Kormath. Her sight shattered into the prismatic wonders of unhuman perception. She was Noressa-Kormath and felt a touch of recognition spark between the two scaled other-place dreamers. Then Felaya took reign over her scarlet Companion and sent her into a twisting dive. That other turned, climbed, and Noressa caught the agony of flame that scathed across the tender part of Kormath's neck. Their pain trumpeted from his throat as they fell.

Rough mountainside tilted up to meet her. Noressa angled away, lunged into a warm wind current, and began to climb. Wild energies danced around her, pulled from the nether planes by the conjurations of those below. But they were of little matter to Noressa; she had another interest. Felaya sped upward, spiraling into the sodden darkness of the clouds. Noressa gave chase, her anger spewing from Kormath as blue flame to steam away the blinding moisture.

She caught a flutter of surprise from Felaya as the other turned and found Noressa too close. Noressa sent a blast of fire to that tender place beneath the wing, and it was Felaya who screamed in pain. Felaya dropped, wings laboring to slow her descent. She had begun to rise again when she veered away, dropping once more. Her shriek of rage was directed, not at Noressa, but at those who fought upon the ground. Noressa saw the object of her dive—the men of Sarel's guard! Medwyn! She plunged in a thundering fall close behind Felaya.

Felaya swerved slightly to avoid the blast of flames Noressa sent over them. Noressa followed, and her opponent swerved again, returning to her original path, though she was now beyond the plateau. The second maneuver was too quick for Noressa to turn and follow, but it brought the scarlet other close beneath her. Noressa-Kormath stretched, and one powerful foreclaw caught a grip as Felaya's Companion slid by. Tough flesh ripped beneath her talons, and Noressa watched the other writhe in its anguish. She gave quick pursuit. Dropping low, Noressa matched her flight to the erratic struggles of the other, buffeting them with strong surgings of her wings. Her long hindquarters scrabbled, trying to pluck away the golden rider.

But Felaya guided her Companion down into the gorge, circling the plateau, and drove hard by the sheer walls. At the same time, she flung behind her a lightning web of magic. Noressa was forced to give way, and Felaya urged her mount higher.

Then despair struck. It was a shrilling of dark energy, warped and held too long, finally released. It was death. Kormath shivered beneath her. Noressa gasped as the passing soul raked through her. It was a soul strong in Talent and Knowledge.

Felaya, too, was affected by the passing. Noressa heard the pain her aunt raged at the heavens. Felaya's Companion reared, clawing the air.

Noressa knew from whence that terror had come—the battle below. She searched frantically among the active magic there, fearing that either Medwyn or Bydawine had been lost. But their energies were strong, easily read among the scattered pulses of other, less developed magic. Still, the sense of something different remained, and she searched again. When she found the answer, a joyous Noressa-Kormath leapt high into the clouds. The dark wizard was no more. Tylek, whose arrogant sensuality had so dominated her will, was gone.

Now there was nothing that could hold her back. And nothing that could stand against her! She spread herself on the sky and bellowed a final challenge.

Noressa was oblivious to the din of the armies below. Her body stood on the escarpment, but *she* soared the black-clouded skies. She filled with power, throbbed with might. Through Kormath's green-yellow eyes, she saw the world as a clear, crystalline dream. And through those eyes, she saw her instant of triumph.

Below, Felaya's Companion rose toward them. Copper-gilded wings scooped great drafts of air. But Kormath already had the ascendance, and the other bled from a score of psychic wounds. Kormath's gaze fixed on the other, on the vulnerable place where wing joined body. Noressa trembled with expectancy, and it was she who roared their victory as Kormath spat blue flame.

The scarlet dragon shrieked its agony, spiraling away and down. And Felaya's scream of anguish rang sharp through its pained trumpeting.

Hurtling into the maw of the crevasses, the dragon was nearly out of sight before it was able to achieve level flight. With slow, strained sweeps of its battered wings, the defeated Companion lifted itself to the lip of the fissure, then collapsed in a heap behind the battling armies. There was a ripple, a shimmer of magic across the ground, and then the scarlet beast was rising again. It flew low, angling away toward the east, a still figure draped before the lone rider astride its back.

Noressa-Kormath hung suspended and thundered their conquest. In that instant, they were rulers of all that existed. Kormath spewed a geyser of flame that burned away the clouds to leave them soaring beneath a brilliant blue dome of sky sparked by golden sunlight.

CHAPTER 40

They fled the mountain soon after the battle, for winter came early at such heights. As it was, the first storms were threatening before they were four days gone from the Stone Fortress, and Bydawine feared that Noressa wouldn't survive the rigors of the first snow. They were almost a halfcycle in returning to Ac'talzea, and that long again before Noressa did more than sleep and cry for food.

When she was strong enough to hold court, the Council of Lords was reestablished and the Table of Judges appointed. That day, Bydawine watched Noressa search the crowds, her excitement becoming disappointment, then worry. At last she voiced the question they all feared.

"Where is Brameth? Why does he not appear and accept for himself the lands and title I confer on him?"

"We should speak of this in a more private moment," Medwyn whispered as he continued to smile and nod at the passing dignitaries.

But Noressa wouldn't be put off. And as Bydawine knew she would, she turned to him with her questions. He couldn't answer. How could he tell her of that swath of magic that had swept across the plateau, paralyzing all in its path? He had been helpless to react, numbed by that magic, seared by the hatred that propelled it. He felt Felaya's cabalistic touch cut into their ranks, saw Brameth lifted out and away, to be flung across the back of the copper-scarlet beast.

In the end, it was Sarel himself who stepped forward to reveal the fate of his son. Before her astonished guests, Noressa fled the great hall. She was found in her chambers, rushing to and fro, giving orders for the raising of an expedition.

"I should have been told of this long ago! You had no right to keep it from me! Now much time has been lost, and I must use all my magic to follow them!" Her anger was terrible to see, and only Medwyn was brave enough to gainsay her leaving.

"You cannot—will not—go, Noressa. You are queen, and there are too many who need your leadership now. There is a country to be put to right!"

She whirled on the elder, and Bydawine hoped never again to see such a look. "Then put it to right yourself! Or give it to Bohsra, or even Kej. I care not! I have sacrificed too much for this land. Now I will have something back. I love Brameth, and I will not endure without him!"

It was then that Sarel, Captain of the Queen's Guard, committed the greatest crime. He laid hands on his queen.

Stepping between Medwyn and Noressa, he grasped her arms and shook her. He stared hard into her eyes. "Do you love him more than I? He is my son, and I have lost him twice in this war—both as a child and as a man. Can you love him so much and care so little for that which he gave his life to protect? Prove to me you love him more, and I will follow you to any of the six hells!"

Then they wept together, not as soldier and queen, but as man and woman who loved one who was lost to them.

Noressa lay abed another quartercycle. When she left her sickbed, she resumed her throne with a dedication and fervor Bydawine hadn't seen in any noble or king.

Noressa planned carefully for the arrival of the ambassador of Molevea. She worried over land disputes and taxation. She smiled, sometimes, and entertained the castle children with minor magic. She often paced the halls of the keep, speaking low with Sarel. Occasionally she walked with Bydawine in the snow-muffled garden. It was in the garden that she told him of her plans for vengeance.

The day was cold and windy, and she spoke without looking at him.

"One day, Bydawine, I will go after him. And *her*. I shall destroy her and then beg forgiveness of Brameth that I didn't follow sooner."

"Then you believe he still lives?"

"Oh, yes." Her smile was bitter. "His death would have been too quick a misery for me. That he lives and she holds him is her continued challenge to me."

Before he could think, Bydawine blurted, "I wish it had been me!" Then his mind regained control of his tongue and he stilled the rush of emotion that would have spilled from him.

Noressa, misinterpreting his pain, knelt before him in the snow and took his hand. "Do not blame yourself, Bydawine. I should have felt him leave me. Sarel explained all to me. There was nothing you could have done."

Her words were meant to comfort, but the kindness stung him with the return of his self-doubt. Had he really been so helpless? When he saw who was taken, did he hesitate—just for a moment? Could he have warned Noressa, had he pressed a little harder with the mindspeak?

Perhaps. And for his punishment, he must love her silently while he assisted in her search for Brameth.

* * * * *

It was seven cycles since the battle of the dragons. Snowmelt was just past. Spring planting was the main concern of most folk.

Bydawine stood in the protection of the tower's lee side and waited. He was certain Noressa knew he was there, but clearly she wished to be alone.

He pulled his cloak tighter. The late spring wind was cold this high above ground. Its sharp breath riffled the white fur of Noressa's robe and whipped her hair into a cloud of black silken ribbons that streamed out over the tower wall. But she was oblivious to the chill. She nestled deep in her furs, attention fixed to the eastern horizon, and Bydawine tried to guess which memory haunted her now.

Likely it was Felaya's treachery. But she was entitled to a moment's respite from her duties. She had presented herself well at this morning's signing of the new treaty with Dromund. Now there were only the feasts and court celebrations. No official judgments were left to be made, but her appearance was expected from time to time. So he had come to escort her back to the festivities, but a few moments more would mean nothing to the revelers below.

Bydawine waited in the bitter company of his memories as long as he was able. When he couldn't bear to be even these few steps from her, he moved to her side.

"It is time, Noressa. Your guests await."

Noressa stared over the battlements. She let her gaze sweep eastward to the distant snow-covered spine of mountains. She was at peace here. White snow and silence made no demands.

She couldn't say that she was unhappy with the duties of reigning; she loved her people. But there were moments when even the patient company of friends was too much burden. Here she could watch the mountains and wait for the pain to fade. And she could plan.

She hadn't probed Kormath's sleeping presence since the battle, but she knew his strength was there and she knew that Brameth still lived. He would live until she could search him out, for his captivity was Felaya's promise that they would meet again.

Noressa sighed and nodded when Bydawine spoke beside her. She looked a last time at the far mountains. To those who waited beyond the white peaks, her heart chanted the familiar promise.

Soon.

■ THE HARPERS ■

A Force for Good in the Realms!

This open-ended series of stand-alone novels chronicles the Harpers' heroic battles against forces of evil, all for the peace of the Realms.

The Parched Sea
Troy Denning

The Zhentarim have sent an army to enslave the fierce nomads of the Great Desert. Only one woman, the outcast witch Ruha, sees the true danger—and only the Harpers can counter the evil plot. Available July 1991.

Elfshadow
Elaine Cunningham

Harpers are being murdered, and the trail leads to Arilyn Moonblade. Is she guilty or is she the next target? Arilyn must uncover the ancient secret of her sword's power in order to find and face the assassin.
Available October 1991.

Red Magic
Jean Rabe

One of the powerful and evil Red Wizards wants to control more than his share of Thay. While the mage builds a net of treachery, the Harpers put their own agents into action to foil his plans for conquest.
Available November 1991.

B·O·O·K·S

Web of Futures   Jefferson P. Swycaffer

Maddock O'Shaughnessy—born liar, tavern goer, and idle fisherman—is inexplicably chosen by a strange alien to save men's lives, collect their souls, and roam the future. His unusual mission takes him along the strands of time in the house of webs.

Sorcerer's Stone   L. Dean James

For a thousand years the Red Kings guarded the magical sword Kingslayer. Now a young prince is the only one who can hope to master the blue light of the Sorcerer's Stone and control the mystical blade in time to save his kingdom and his life.

The Falcon Rises   Michael C. Staudinger

An overworked college professor is struck by lightning, and his energy pulse propels him to another plane. In this medieval fantasy world, he enlists the help of a falcon and some good dragons to fight the evil powers of the warlord Mordeth.

B·O·O·K·S

The Cloud People   Robert B. Kelly
When a "flying machine" crashes in the mountains, the prince of Fief Karcan goes to investigate. The missing pilot may well be the savior whose coming had been prophesied, the only man who can open a powerful medallion and save both the prince's father and his world from the evil Lord Thyden. October 1991.

Lightning's Daughter   Mary H. Herbert
In this sequel to *Dark Horse*, young Gabria comes to terms with her magical ability and her role as a strong woman leader in a male-dominated world. The magic-blessed outcasts from the horse clans make Gabria their mentor, but before she can become their teacher, she must lead them against a magical creature bent on destroying the Dark Horse Plains. December 1991.

SPELLJAMMER™ novels

✧ The Cloakmaster Cycle ✧

Follow one unlucky farmer as he enters fantasy space for the first time and gets caught up in a race for his life, from the DRAGONLANCE® Saga setting to the FORGOTTEN REALMS® world and beyond.

Book One
Beyond the Moons
David Cook

Little did Teldin Moore know there was life beyond Krynn's moons until a spelljamming ship crashed into his home and changed his life. Teldin suddenly discovers himself the target of killers and cutthroats. Armed with a dying alien's magical cloak and cryptic words, he races off to Astinus of Palanthas and the gnomes of Mt. Nevermind to try to discover why . . . before the monstrous neogi can find him. On sale in July, 1991.

Book Two
Into the Void
Nigel Findley

Plunged into a sea of alien faces, Teldin Moore isn't sure whom to trust. His gnomish sidewheeler ship is attacked by space pirates, and Teldin is saved by a hideous mind flayer who offers to help the human use his magical cloak—but for whose gain? Teldin learns the basics of spelljamming on his way to Toril, where he seeks an ancient arcane, one who might tell him more. But even information has a high price. On sale in October, 1991.

Ravenloft ™

novels

One step into the mists, and a world of horror engulfs you. Welcome to Ravenloft, a dark domain of fantasy-horror populated by bloodthirsty vampires and other unspeakable creatures of the undead.

Vampire of the Mists
Christie Golden

Jander Sunstar, an elven vampire from the Forgotten Realms, is pulled into the newly formed dark domain of Barovia and forges an alliance with the land's most powerful inhabitant, Count Strahd Von Zarovich, himself a newly risen vampire. But as Jander teaches the count the finer points of being undead, he learns that his student may also be his greatest enemy. On sale in September, 1991.

Knight of the Black Rose
James Lowder

The fate of the villainous Lord Soth was left untold at the conclusion of the popular DRAGONLANCE® Legends Trilogy. Now it can be revealed that the cruel death knight found his way into the dark domain and discovered that it is far easier to get into Ravenloft than to get out—even with the aid of the powerful vampire lord, Strahd Von Zarovich. On sale in December, 1991.

Prism Pentad

BOOK ONE

The Verdant Passage

Troy Denning

KALAK: AN IMMORTAL SORCERER-KING WHOSE EVIL MAGIC HAS REDUCED THE MAJESTIC CITY OF TYR TO A DESOLATE PLACE OF BLOOD AND FEAR. HIS THOUSAND-YEAR REIGN OF DEATH IS ABOUT TO END.

BANDING TOGETHER TO SPARK A REVOLUTION ARE A MAVERICK STATESMAN, A WINSOME HALF-ELF SLAVE GIRL, AND A MAN-DWARF GLADIATOR BRED FOR THE ARENAS. BUT IF THE PEOPLE ARE TO BE FREE, THE MISMATCHED TRIO OF STEADFAST REBELS MUST LOOK INTO THE FACE OF TERROR, AND CHOOSE BETWEEN LOVE AND LIFE.